CHILDREN OF ABRAHAM

Books by Sholem Asch

Children of
Abraham

THE SHORT STORIES OF

Sholem Asch

TRANSLATED BY MAURICE SAMUEL

NEW YORK

G. P. PUTNAM'S SONS

Designed by Robert Josephy

CONTENTS

Contents

CHILDREN OF ABRAHAM

The Boy Saint

IN his earliest childhood Joel had already learned to think of this world as a brief preparation for the world to come and upon this life as a prelude to the true and eternal life beyond the grave. His father taught him that our earthly existence is nothing but the vestibule to the palace of reality, and Joel looked upon his being born as a dying away from eternity, just as the day of his death would be a rebirth into eternity.

And truly he saw little about him worth being born for. His father considered the business of life so unimportant that he turned it over to Joel's mother, who supported the family on the meager earnings of her drygoods stall in the marketplace. In the heat of summer and in the cold of winter she stood there and sold the poor peasant women lengths of cotton and calico for shirts and dresses. When she came home at night she cooked a pot of potatoes or dumplings, and this one dish was their daily sustenance. Joel's father sat from morning till night over the holy books and amassed great wealth for the life to come.

While Joel was still a baby he stayed with his mother in the marketplace and shared her worldly, too worldly, life. But almost as soon as he could walk his father took him to himself and gave him his first lessons in the holy books; ever since then Joel was no longer of this world.

The true world, for which he was preparing, was incomparably richer and lovelier than the world around him. The heavens opened for him, and he saw the Divine Presence in all its glory; he saw the angels and the blazing seraphim; he saw the souls of the righteous in Paradise. They sat on golden stools against a background of blue-white cloud; light streamed on them while they studied Torah under the direction of God Himself. Joel heard a sound of singing, the quiet music of perfected souls divested of all needs and all weaknesses. Whichever way he turned his eyes he beheld only saints. He saw the patriarchs, the fathers of Israel, exactly as they were depicted in the Pentateuch. He saw Moses, our Teacher, leading the hosts of Israel and teaching them from the graven tablets. He saw David passing his fingers across the fiery strings of his harp, and around him were grouped the Levites, who sang verses from the Psalms. He saw the great Rabbi conducting the academies of the Tanaim and Amoraim, all the illustrious scholars he had heard tell of, and among them many saints whose presence had remained unrecognized on earth but whose places were reserved for them in Paradise. How could one compare with this shining multitude his mother's pitiful cottage, with its potatoes and dumplings in the evening, or even the market days and fairs, with their drunken peasants?

He pitied his mother, of course; pitied her that it was her bitter destiny to carry the burden of this world. It was no easy thing for her to earn the wherewithal for the nightly meal of potatoes or dumplings. In the winter nights he would be awakened by her groaning. In the summer her skin peeled with the heat, and when she smeared it with salve she screamed with the pain. If Joel prayed for anything connected with this world, it was to have the strength to help his mother by carrying the bolts of cloth from the house into the marketplace. Every morning there was a dispute between him and his mother; she said that he was not strong enough to carry the heavy bolts, and Joel wanted to prove that he was strong enough to carry these and even the planks for the stall. God answered his prayer and gave him strength in the morning and again in the evening when the time came to bring the stall and the goods home. Joel's mother knew that she had her share in the sacred studies of husband and son and that her portion in the world to come was assured. Joel knew this too; but he pitied his mother because she knew nothing of the joy of prayer and because she could not, like him, pass her years in spiritual exercise, but must spend them arguing about stupid matters with peasants and peasant women. And while he was still young enough not to be ashamed of spending time with his mother, he would sit by her on summer evenings and tell her of the things he studied in the holy books. Then his mother's heart would fill to overflowing. She was not at all ashamed of the gross earthly life she had to lead, and did not feel humiliated by it; on the contrary, she was as proud of her labor and of her making of a livelihood as her husband was of his learning; and Joel knew that his father regarded it in the same light.

More than once, during the hot summer days, when Joel was sunk deep in a holy book, his father would break in on him and say:

"Go to your mother and see if she needs something—perhaps a drink of water, perhaps another errand."

And sometimes, when the two of them were coming home from evening prayer, he would hear his father, who was a man of few words, murmur something into his sparse beard:

"Her labors and her suffering in the marketplace are as acceptable to God as our studies of His sacred books. She is a saint."

Joel knew that these words were spoken of his mother; but he did not quite understand them until once, coming into the marketplace, he saw his mother standing up to a drunken lout of a peasant. The peasant had paid for a piece of cloth and, after Joel's mother had cut it from the bolt, had changed his mind and demanded his money back; and his friends who were with him joined in insulting and bullying the Jew-woman. But Joel's mother would not yield and would not be intimidated; she was defending the bread of her husband and son. It was then that Joel understood his father's words.

Once a week Joel saw the link between this world in which he lived and the eternal world to come; and in that hour his mother was lifted up in his eyes till she stood on a level with his father. That was on Friday evening, when the sun went down mournfully in the west and his mother lit the Sabbath candles. Night came, quietly, modestly, and laid its grace on the darkening world.

Children of Abraham

Then Joel felt that this world was part of the eternal world and, like the other, part of the eternal purpose. It was no longer a vestibule or corridor which would some day be abandoned and destroyed. He felt the soul of this world, and knew it to be everlasting; the Sabbath would remain for ever, and for its sake this world would endure. His mother, standing before the candles with the Sabbath kerchief on her head, was no longer the woman who sat in the marketplace, chaffering and quarreling with the peasants, fighting for a customer; no, his mother was herself now, a sacred presence. Even the lines on her face, graven deep by the years of struggle, the marks of her self-immolation, became beautiful. Her big eyes shone purely, and the softness and innocence of her womanhood triumphed over the bitterness of her daily slavery. Such was the transformation wrought by the Sabbath candles, and in their light Joel felt a boundless reverence for her.

The weekdays were not lived; they were merely passed through. But on Friday evening the table was covered with a white cloth, and on it stood meat, fish, white bread, and wine. The candles filled the house with light; the beds were freshly made. All this, the food, the warmth, the light, the tastiness of the evening, was not for the comfort of the body, but for the honor of the Sabbath. The pleasures of the flesh were transformed into the delights of the soul; the boundaries of the two worlds, the illusory and the real, were dissolved for a moment; the body became one with the soul and was able to anticipate the loveliness of the eternal world to be.

But all this lasted only for one day in the week. When the Sabbath ended the meanness of the world closed in once more upon Joel; and the taste of the Sabbath filled him with a sharper longing for the world to be, the Sabbath without end.

The older Joel became the more definitely he was linked with the world to be; the more intimate he became with the wisdom of the holy books, with the sayings and parables of the saintly sages of the past, the more he longed to be with them; he longed to see Moses in the heavenly academy, teaching the secrets of the Torah to the chosen scholars; he longed to hear David interpret his own Psalms on his harp, accompanied by the choirs of the angels; he longed to listen to the converse of the sages who had filled with undying glory the schools of Yabneh and Pumpedhita and Sura, to feel and understand the ineffable mysteries of the Zohar, which is the Book of Splendor, to hear, even from the distance, the words of a Simeon ben Yochai or a Reb Meir, to linger in the company of the later scholars and pietists, to look upon the mild radiance of the Master of the Good Name. But all this, he knew, would not and could not be granted to him in this world; it was withdrawn for ever into the glory of the world to be, where all reality was made eternal. It was a wearisome thing, this sojourn among the ugly shadows of the mundane world; and were it not that it was God's command that he should linger here and make his preparations, he could not have found the patience to wait for the end.

But since it had been so decreed, he would at least seek to make all experience subservient to the great and ultimate purpose. The body, to begin with, had to be made subservient to the soul. He knew from self-observation, and this knowledge was confirmed by what he read in the holy books, that body and soul are for ever at war. The body tugs man to the earth in which it is rooted, and the soul is homesick for its source, which is God. The lusts of this world spring from the body, the pull to the heavens is of the soul. The soul is imprisoned in the body, and the body seeks to bend it to its will, so as to enlist its service in its own gross purposes. But the imprisoned soul is not helpless; it can withhold its co-operation from the body and can in turn make the body the vessel and instrument of the soul. This it does by denying will to the longings of the body and starving its lusts into impotence. So Joel did with his body. He denied it any food beyond what was essential to its mere existence. As a boy he already acquired the practice of fasting two days in the week, Mondays and Thursdays. Returning from evening prayer in the synagogue, he accustomed himself to the thought that the only joy in eating consisted in the occasion it offered for the pronouncing of the benediction. And as he progressed in the discipline he found it always easier. The resistance of the body diminished steadily. The flesh became so light and so obedient that whenever the soul made an ascension into the other world the body

seemed to come along, or to oppose no inertia. The body was out-
witted and, seeking to become the master, had become the slave.

When he had established his will over his body as a whole, he
proceeded to establish his will over the separate parts of the body.
The tongue, the one bodily advantage which God had granted man
over the animals, had been created for the service of the soul.
Joel therefore used his tongue almost exclusively for prayer and
study; he limited to a minimum his talk of profane things, as if he
had only a small store of words for this purpose and would use it
up before he died if he were not very careful. After the tongue, he
went on to the discipline of the eyes. These existed only to guide his
soul along the printed lines of the prayer book, the Talmud, and
the other sacred books and draw out from the close, four-cornered
letters the wisdom of God; for the purified eye the light of sun,
moon, and stars, the colors and the shadows of earth, did not exist.
And when he was not bent over his books, when he walked along
the synagogue alley to and from prayers, his eyes were fixed on the
ground, seeing only as much of it as was needed to guide him to his
destination. For the rest, he taught his eyes to dwell on inward per-
ceptions and to accustom themselves to the sevenfold brightness of
the world which had been purged of matter. Thus, even when they
looked on sky and earth and trees, they saw the pure soul of these
things, the emanations of the soul.

The body did not yield at once but protested and fought back. It
did not want to serve the soul; and when it was denied its desires,
it set up a great clamor by falling sick; it broke out in rashes, it
withheld its service, it put up a thousand ingenious objections. But
Joel would not let himself be taken in. He treated these pitiful de-
vices of the body with contempt. And as the body, knowing itself
defeated, gave up its mean struggle, Joel realized more and more
clearly how unworthy of consideration it was. Indeed he had been
right to have as little as possible to do with this wretched thing
which was destined for corruption in a few years.

His parents were distressed by the rigor of his discipline. His
mother wept; she could not bear to see him fading from the world.
Even his father sought to restrain him. "The body too is part of

God," he said. "Though it is not an end in itself, it is the instrument of the soul. Without it the soul could not stay on this earth; if the pitcher is broken the wine is spilled."

But Joel was moved neither by the tears of his mother nor the admonitions of his father; he was determined to establish complete mastery over his body. He, and not it, would determine what it needed in the way of sustenance; he and not it would determine that it could bear the touch of icy water on winter days. He and not his eyes would determine what they were to see. His tongue would follow not its own impulses, but the dictation of the soul.

People were a hindrance to his discipline; they intruded on him with foolish thoughts, dragging him down into the lower world. He learned to avoid people. He would disappear for days into the woods outside the village; he found a hiding place among the tall rushes in a bend of the river. For miles around no human being was to be seen. Thither Joel went while the earth was still dark, and at the rising of the sun he would immerse his body in the icy water. There he recited his morning prayers, and there he could devote himself completely to meditation. There he could make his ascensions into the higher world, taking his body with him as if it were a featherweight. All the senses, touch, smell, taste, hearing, sight, became instruments of the soul. The forest was transformed; the dumb trees, which grew only that they might be cut down, ceased to be trees; they were revealed in their meaning and purpose; their tree-souls unfolded and uttered their destiny. The rushing of the wind in their branches became their plaint over the meaninglessness and purposelessness of the physical world to which they were fastened; and they too longed to be united with the spark of the eternal world.

Among them Joel stood and, addressing himself to God, was their spokesman, their prayer leader, while they in their silence accompanied him in prayer. But soon the silence was broken; the whispering of the branches, taking on another tone, became audible to the spirit, grew louder, and swelled into a song of adoration. Boundless joy spread among the trees as they felt themselves becoming one with the eternal world and as their own meaning and

9

destiny was made manifest to them. The rushing of the water likewise became a voice, and the waves fulfilled God's command cheerfully and unquestioningly, and God, hearing them, took pity on their condition, and lifted them out of their dumb and unperceiving simplicity into the understanding which filled His world. Everything in the forest, the bushes, the mosses, the undergrowth, the creeping things, every grain of sand, felt the power of God's command and will. They became the equals and partners of man, and knew themselves created with him. The world was flushed through and through with this perception, so that its inmost core knew the power of God. The boundaries which held all things apart began to dissolve, and unity wrapped round earth and heaven. There was no more death, no more transitoriness; there was only one universe, one will, one being.

. . .

Joel was sixteen years old when he first heard this song of the one world and began to feel that the earth was something other than matter and something more than a garment which would pass away. He learned to hear the song elsewhere than in the forest. It came to him nights as he lay on his bed. In the silent house the darkness expanded and became an all-enveloping ocean, and the waters of the ocean gave forth the music he had heard in the forest.

Once he watched a sunset, and saw the clouds being drawn down into a fiery cavern; it seemed to him that he heard a loud crying and that this crying was the lament of the world's soul, which wanted the world's body to be coeternal with itself. He understood then why, in the moment of parting between man's body and soul, the soul, the daughter of God, weeps, though it is returning to its home; it weeps because it has come to love the body, the garment of its earthly sojourn.

Once, during the benediction, he looked into the moon and heard her keen voice ringing through all space from end to end of the universe. He asked himself whether it was not possible that moon and stars alike were not material things, but pure spirit and apparition. How else was he to explain the purity which streamed out of them into his spirit? But if moon and stars were not material things, might it not be that all living things were pure spirit too and that, if he learned to see them always and everywhere under this aspect, they too would fill him with purity? He strove thenceforward to hear always more clearly the essential voice of things, of grasses and beasts, uttering ceaseless praise to God.

But he passed beyond this stage. He learned that even the inner voice and cry of things were a seeming and that the ultimate utterance of their spirit was silence. It was the night that taught him this. Of all the manifestations of God none revealed him more completely than the night. The night was endless; and it was not without, like the sun, the moon and stars; it was within, in its endlessness. In the night all things reverted to their true shape, for they threw off the limitations of their seeming. The green faded from the forest, the blue from the river; man's bodily outline faded from him, too. Forest and river and man became their true selves, not divided from each other, but interpenetrating. There was no longer tree or beast or man, there was neither heaven nor earth, there was oneness, and the oneness was silent. It poured, this oneness, from end to end of space, and was silent. It spoke with its being only, its being was its voice, and this was the greatest song of all. And when Joel had achieved the stage of silence, he apprehended the infinite.

. . .

Once, when Joel's mother stood in the marketplace on a fair day, selling cloth, a peasant from a neighboring village approached her and said, in the presence of others:

"Your son is a secret Rabbi; he is a very holy man."

Joel's mother ignored the words, but others who were about, workmen, peddlers, and shopkeepers, heard the peasant too. They asked him:

"How do you know he is a holy man?"

"How do I know it? Ask the birds in the forest, and they'll tell you. He stands day-long in the forest and converses with God.

And when he prays a little flame descends and waits in front of him, like a candle."

The peasant's report spread swiftly through the village; it was repeated that same afternoon in the synagogue. The Talmud students, who studied there all day long, were angered by it. For a long time Joel's bearing, his fasts, his absences, his silences, had displeased them. But so far they had found no handle to their displeasure, and they had left him alone. Now the report of the peasant proved to them that Joel harbored foolish and arrogant delusions: that he was a spirit apart from all, a great Rabbi, an adept in the mysteries; that he was above them and their like; that he needed silence and loneliness, so that they might not intrude on him. They therefore waited for an opportunity to ensnare Joel in the Study House of the synagogue, to make their reckoning with him.

The pietists of the little prayer-house to which Joel's father belonged, all of them followers and disciplines of a certain Chassidic Rabbi, were also angered by the report; they accused Joel of spiritual pride and, like the Talmud students, waited for an opportunity to call him to account. Only among the simple people, unlettered workers and peddlers, there were some who were half inclined to believe; that is to say, they believed and did not believe. They remembered the old stories of secret saints, of the Thirty-Six Hidden Ones who, in every generation, sustain the world. In their hearts a hope awakened that Joel was one of the Thirty-Six. But they heard that the pietists of the little prayer-house, and the Talmud students of the town, were against Joel, and they were silent out of respect.

.   .   .

It was a summer evening, a few days before the Fast of the Ninth of Ab, the Black Fast of the destruction of the Temples. The community was depressed, as though a dead man lay in its midst. Reb Aaron Meir, Joel's father, had made it a practice to observe mourning rites for twenty-one days before the Black Fast. Early every morning he went to the prayer-house, took off his shoes, and sat in his stockinged feet, like a mourner, studying and lamenting. Every day he fasted until evening. Chaya Leah, his wife, prepared the evening meal of dumplings and milk. One half of the table was left bare, in sign of mourning; but the other half was covered with a folded tablecloth, because the table at which man eats has been likened to the altar of God, and it may not be treated with disrespect.

At the hour when his father returned from the prayer-house, Joel returned from the forest. He was a strange sight as he walked through the village. His frail body was like a withered rush, which barely manages to stay erect and seems on the point of breaking every moment. His big head, supported by a slender, childlike neck, swayed as he walked. But his forehead was broad and luminous. The temples on either side were shrunken and taut, exposing the thin network of veins. His eyes were gray, stern, and unfriendly; the nose was bold; only about the lips and chin hovered the suggestion of a helpless smile.

Joel came in silently. Absorbed in his own thoughts, he sat down by his father. They did not speak to each other. Then Reb Aaron Meir muttered, as though to himself:

"Desires like these are born of self-delusion. The Evil One, too, sends such beliefs into the heart of man. God save us from him."

Joel made no reply to this reproach. He had heard it once before from his father, and he had passed it over in silence then, too.

Chaya Leah sat apart from them, in a corner. She watched her son and her husband. She knew of the rising feeling against Joel in the village, and she did not know her own mind. Love and hope moved her to belief; fear held her back. She had nothing to say here, when the great mysteries were being spoken of.

"What then?" asked Reb Aaron Meir. "Have you passed beyond the stage of honor to your father, that you do not answer? Are you perhaps engaged in the forbidden learning which denies the commandments?"

"Father!" exclaimed Joel, starting back in fear from the suggestion. "I am not studying the Kaballah."

"If not that," continued his father, "why this strange behavior?

Why the forest? Why the secrecy? Prayer and study may be pursued in the Synagogue, too."

Joel could not speak; he could not tell his father what he had learned in the forest, of the stillness which is beyond the voice of things, and of the oneness which proceeds from it. It seemed to him that the secret had been entrusted to him, and to him alone. Moreover, though he dreaded the sin which he seemed to be committing, of lack of honor toward his father, he did not know with what words he could make his visions intelligible. Joel understood the way of his father: it was the way of a merchant, except that Reb Aaron Meir dealt not in worldly but in divine things. Reb Aaron Meir looked upon the world as a marketplace, where a Jew of understanding bought up all the merit, all the good deeds, he could lay his hand on, because these were the only things that had currency in the world to come. Well for him who came to the heavenly gates with a large supply of good deeds; alas for him whose provision for eternity was slight. Joel could not accept this view of man's destiny on earth. He had learned in the Book of the Ethics of the Fathers that man shall not serve God like a slave who expects a reward. Therefore he sought to fashion his human labors in the mold of God's labors in the upper worlds and to impart to all things the realization of their oneness with eternity. But how could he say this? And how could he—God forbid it!—imply that his father's understanding of man's duty was inferior to his own?

The room was quiet. Father and son sat at table, by the light of the kerosene lamp. The mother sat on the edge of the family chest, her plate in her hand. The three shadows lay on the wall and reached up to the ceiling, imitating there the silence of the living.

. . .

The next morning, when Joel entered the synagogue and went up to the bookcase for a volume of the Talmud, he felt a hand on his shoulder, and turning round he was flung back by a violent slap across his mouth. It was Leibel Bear, the chief officer of the

Study House, who thus displayed his zeal and who, with eyes flaming and black beard bristling, called out at the top of his voice:

"Heathen! Blasphemer! Outside!"

Joel stared at him out of his great eyes. His face was expressionless; the lips trembled slightly. After waiting a moment he turned back to the bookcase; but this time many hands laid on him, and he was lifted up and carried toward the big table.

"Clear the way, there! The saint is coming, the secret man of God!"

There were lads among the students with faces as pale as Joel's, with bodies as frail and tormented as his. Some were with earlocks, some without. In a tangle of hands and feet, the struggling mass, with Joel at its center, made its way to the table. There they flung him down, crying:

"Great and learned Rabbi, will you deign to conduct the feast for us?"

A rain of blows descended on Joel's body.

"Wait now! Give me a chance, too!" shouted Leibel Bear, pushing his way through. "I want to be in on the feast." Leibel Bear, the oldest of the students, was already a married man. But he had not outgrown his student days, and whenever he could he came back to his cronies in the Study House. He considered himself the leader in this place, and he was proud that he had been the first to strike Joel.

When they stepped back from Joel he lay motionless for several minutes. Then they helped him to sit up. His face was as expressionless as before, except for the same hesitant smile trembling on his lips. He showed neither anger nor shame. It was as though he had said: I shall go on doing what I have done till now; and all of them read those words in his face.

He sat thus a long time, the Talmud students grouped around him. No hand was raised against him now. Some of them pitied him. But Joel saw no one; his eyes were fixed on something far away.

Meanwhile, with the speed of lightning, the message had been

15

carried to the marketplace: the "young saint" was being beaten in the Study House of the synagogue. The faces of the butcher boys flamed with anger.

"But why?" shouted one of them. "Why should he be beaten? Isn't he a saint?"

"Fool!" shouted back his neighbor. "They're jealous because they're not saints like him."

Aaron the capmaker left his stall and came running toward the butchers.

"Berel! Let's go down there! They'll never let go of him!"

Aaron the capmaker was known for his credulity in all things; he was known of late, too, as a great believer in the mission of Joel the saint. His excitement infected the others, and in a moment a group of working men had abandoned the marketplace and rushed down the street of the synagogue.

Two butcher boys and Aaron the capmaker were the first to break into the synagogue. Behind them came Notte the fisher, who was a great believer in magic, and some other workers. They found Joel sitting on a bench; his clothes were ripped; his face was paler than usual, but his eyes were calm. A gust of anger passed through the simple people from the marketplace.

"Who hit him?" roared Chaim the butcher. "Who dared to lay a hand on him? You lazy dogs, you useless eaters, I'll split your heads open!"

"They can't stand him because he knows how to be a saint and they don't; so they take it out on him with their fists!" said another, between his teeth.

The Talmud students trembled. The ringleaders in the beating of Joel, with Leib Bear at their head, shuffled uneasily, sneaked into the background, and then made themselves scarce.

"Reb Joel!" voices said, solicitously. "Are you hurt? Who was it hit you? Do you want a glass of water?"

"Give him a glass of water. Don't you see what the louts did to him? They've nearly knocked the life out of him," cried Aaron the capmaker.

Joel did not answer, made no comment. He looked at Aaron

the capmaker with the same tranquil, lustrous eyes which he had turned on his tormentors; and when Aaron took his hand gently, and spoke to him softly, he withdrew his hand and made a gesture of indifference.

"I'll kill them, the murderers," raged Aaron and relieved his feelings by slapping one of the students, an innocent bystander throughout the whole affair. "He is a holy man, a Rabbi. Even the ignorant peasants know it. They said he was a holy man. But you!"

These words, uttered by Aaron the capmaker, cast a spirit of dread and awe upon the other folk of the marketplace. The butcher boys suddenly stepped back from the proximity of Joel and looked at him timidly out of great round eyes. It seemed to them that they had perceived something, just at this moment, which they had not perceived before; it was on his face, all the glory and power of a saint, which ordinary people should not see too closely. Soon he would open his mouth and they would hear from him words they had never heard before.

But suddenly Joel rose, walked over to the barrel of water, washed his hands, put on his phylacteries and, turning his face to the corner, began to say his prayers.

The prayers lasted a long time, but no one interrupted him. Others came into the synagogue, from street and marketplace; all stood and watched. There were householders who had never paid any attention before to Joel and to the rumors of his spiritual pretensions. They stood with the butcher boys, the workers, and Aaron the capmaker, and were drawn into the spirit which reigned in the synagogue. There was complete silence. All eyes were fixed on the tall, swaying figure, crowned with prayer-shawl phylacteries, absorbed in devotion. They saw Joel bury his face in his hands, in the intensity of prayer. At intervals a twitch passed through the body, the head trembled, the hands were withdrawn for an instant from the face, and they saw a mask, from which all life had been withdrawn; the eyes were closed, the lips drawn convulsively tight. Then the face sank again into the long, bony hands, the body became motionless and sank into a sort of sleep.

The more sensitive among the beholders, and especially those who had begun to accept Joel as a saint, were overwhelmed by the sight. The evidences of a supernatural devotion, an adeptness in prayer and ascension, were manifest to them in Joel's behavior. They remembered famous saints who had held congregations in thrall by their manner of praying. They thought again of the Thirty-Six who sustain the world.

"Did you see? Did you see?" whispered Aaron the capmaker in awe, when Joel momentarily uncovered his face.

"Look how he twitches in prayer!" whispered another.

"Foolish one," murmured a third. "*He* twitches? He is not here at all. He's far away somewhere, in other worlds, where we can't follow him."

The words were spoken by a little Jew, a shoemaker who peddled his handiwork in the villages. The others looked at him in astonishment, for he was known as a simpleton, and no one would have credited him with the perception he now displayed.

Those plain words, "He is not here at all," sent a shudder of awe through the listeners. Something marvelous was happening in their presence; they had been singled out, it seemed to them, for a great revelation.

But suddenly Joel's body relaxed its rigidity and began to sway like a reed in the wind, first to the right, then to the left. And before they could reach him he had fallen and had struck the floor with his head, so that the blood began to flow from a bruise which had been inflicted on him in the beating. A thin, white foam showed at the edges of his lips.

"Water!" shouted Aaron the capmaker.

They brought a ladle of water, but they could not make Joel drink it. They parted his lips, but could not pry open his teeth, between which the white bubbles forced their way out. At last the seizure passed, the rigidity passed out of the muscles of his body, he lay breathing heavily, with wide open eyes which saw nothing of what was before them.

"They've half killed him!" muttered the capmaker, wrathfully.

"Why, man, do you think that's from the beating? It's from his praying."

"It's from the long journey he's made," put in the shoemaker. "He's been in worlds other than ours." The shoemaker's voice was full of mystery. "Who knows through what spaces he's traveled!"

When Joel came to, he struggled to his feet and, still swaying, walked toward the door. The capmaker and the shoemaker ranged themselves to right and left of him and accompanied him.

"Do you see that!" gasped someone. "He's walked out into the street with the phylacteries still on his head."

"The phylacteries are on his head! Look!"

"And where were they when he fell down?"

"They were on his head!"

"And they didn't fall off?"

"No! They didn't fall off!"

And this was the miracle of that first manifestation. Joel had fallen to the ground, the phylacteries on his forehead, and the phylacteries had stayed where they were! The story spread through the village as the procession made its way from the synagogue toward Joel's house, and wherever the story was repeated it moved people to awe and wonder.

At the door of his house they left him, by common consent. Joel went in and saw his mother seated, weeping, in a corner. She had heard of the shame of his beating but not of what had happened later. When Joel entered she wiped her eyes and prepared a cup of coffee and a roll for him. Joel drank the coffee, but did not eat the roll.

He was being watched all the time, through the window, at which faces were clustered, and through a crack in the door. Voices carried back to a waiting crowd every action of his, while on the outskirts of the crowd the marvelous story of the phylacteries which could not be dislodged from the forehead of the saint was being repeated again and again.

That night Joel disappeared from the village.

• • •

He stole from the house and set out on the road to the nearest village. He walked very slowly. When he could walk no more he sat down on a stone and remained there until the morning came. The children of the peasants saw and threw stones at him, shouting: "Jew! Jew!"

He looked at the peasant children exactly as he had looked on his tormentors the day before. He got up, turned off the road, and went across the open fields toward the woods. There he fell down and lay in the sunlight for several hours. When he woke he felt weak and hungry. His body called for food, and this insistence of the flesh hurt more than the hunger itself. He tried to suppress the call of the flesh, as he had so often done before, concentrating only on the needs of the soul. But because he was weak he could not conquer himself, and therefore he began to weep like a child. He addressed himself to God, saying: "Father, Father, free me from these human needs."

He wept so long that he fell asleep again, and dreamed. Someone was caressing his head, and with each soft stroke a burden was taken from him. His body became light, his limbs free. He was rising without effort, he was floating between heaven and earth, he was bathing in silvery clouds, he was weaving a path from cloud to cloud, in and out of blue and silver. He heard quiet music and was himself a song. No, he was a cloud, he was both a cloud and a song. He was mingling with the other clouds, mingling with them, separating himself from them, floating off alone in space.

He lay thus until people found him. He opened his eyes. Strange figures were standing over him. They were peasants, woodchoppers, with axes in their hands, but he did not recognize them; he did not know what species of living thing they belonged to. Somewhere he had seen such creatures, but he could not remember where. They spoke to him, and he understood, and tried to answer, but could not find words. They lifted him up, they set him on his feet, and, half-carrying him, they conducted him to a house, the Jewish village inn. Joel then felt the taste of milk on his lips and the tang of apples in his nostrils.

• • •

The Boy Saint

Joel's disappearance broke like a thunderclap on his native village. Early in the morning the synagogue was filled with an agitated crowd. There was little doubt now that something quite marvelous was coming to pass. The story of the phylacteries which could not fall off the saint's head had already become a commonplace. Other wonderful things were being remembered; the little mannerisms of the saint, which had been ignored till then, incidents which this or that man had witnessed but which he had been ashamed to speak of, lest he be ridiculed. The Talmud students who, only the day before, had beaten him, now recalled that they had entertained secret suspicions of his importance. One said that, entering the synagogue late at night, he had seen Joel seated over a volume of the Talmud; and next to Joel sat a very old man, a stranger with a long white beard, and taught Joel mysteries which no earthly teacher could unveil. But, as this Talmud student drew near, the old stranger suddenly dissolved, and Joel was sitting alone.

When one student had spoken, others came forward with similar stories. They said they had seen Joel walking at nightfall toward the cemetery, and the old man with the long white beard was with him. That old man could be none other than Elijah the Prophet, unless, perhaps, he were the holy Ari, the unforgettable master of the Kaballah. Other students told that they had seen Joel standing at his prayers in the synagogue, and suddenly the candles before the Ark had lit themselves.

Prayers were said hurriedly, and without eating, several of the market people, with Aaron the capmaker at their head, set out in a wagon in search of Joel. They sought all day and found no trace of him. They only encountered the peasant who had first come to Joel's mother with the news of the sanctity of her son. This peasant told them that on the spot where Joel had done his praying, a gigantic tree had suddenly sprung up. And he insisted on taking them to see it.

"Look at it," he said. "A hundred years are needed for an oak to grow to this size; this one grew up overnight. There was no tree here before; I know this forest as I know my own hand."

The searchers returned to the village with this new testimony of Joel's great destiny but without news of his whereabouts. Joel's mother wept. She could not have told whether she wept for the sufferings of her son or out of maternal pride. Sometimes she accompanied Aaron the capmaker on the search for Joel. Her husband would not interrupt his lamentations for the destruction of the Temple; he sat without food from morning till night in the little prayer-house of the pietists and wept for the glory that was gone. And of the saint there was not a sign.

During those days Joel stayed with the innkeeper of the other village, some fifteen or twenty miles from his home. The innkeeper said to him: "Twenty-four hours or so you can stay with me just so. Thereafter, I will give you food and drink and a place to sleep, if you will teach my children. But if you will not teach them, you must go."

Joel elected to remain. The children of the innkeeper were very young; they had learned nothing, not even their Hebrew alphabet. Most of the day Joel spent in the woods. He had no books with him, and he needed none. Every day he found himself a new hiding place and gave himself to the duty of uniting the world with the eternal spark.

Once, on a beautiful, sunlit afternoon, several carts arrived at the inn, bringing Aaron the capmaker, the little shoemaker, some householders, a few butcher boys, and a wheat merchant. They had heard that the innkeeper had recently acquired a young man as teacher for his children, and they suspected that this was Joel. They asked the innkeeper for a description, and as this tallied with Joel's appearance, they asked the innkeeper further whether he had observed anything strange about the young man who was, they told him, a hidden saint.

When he heard these words, "a hidden saint," the innkeeper became frightened and confused; and it seemed to him that he had indeed observed many strange and wonderful things about the young man, but that he had as it were refused to pay attention to them, not knowing their significance. He pointed out to them the wood toward which he had last seen Joel going, and they all proceeded in search of him. They found him at prayers, his face and body illumined with the same ecstasy as on that first day of the revelation in the synagogue. They stood respectfully at a distance, till they saw him sway and then fall down; then they ran up to him and lifted him to his feet.

When Joel opened his eyes and beheld the group of Jews, a look of fear came into his eyes, and he made as if to leave them.

"Rabbi," said the wheat merchant, "we have come to ask you to return with us as the Rabbi of our congregation; we know now that you are a secret saint."

Joel stood rooted to the spot.

"Rabbi," pleaded the wheat merchant again, "come with us. We will give you a fine house to live in."

Joel kept his eyes fixed on the ground, and spoke.

"Man, God's chosen creature," he said, "is less apt than all other creations of the divinity to receive and absorb the true reason for his being, to harbor the spark of the infinite; for he is hampered by the freedom of his will. The arrogance of his free will cripples his understanding and empties him of force, for he believes that he can achieve everything with his own hands and through his own resolution. And thus man sinks lower and lower into the death which is this world. The silent, simple things, like the plant, and even the animal, with its weaker sense of will power, are purer than man. And if they have not the strength to achieve unity with the source of all being, because the spark of their soul is weak, they at least offer no resistance when another lifts them to this unity. Therefore a man should spend his time only among the voiceless, simple things, the plants and beasts of the forest. He will then find it easier to negate his will, and to attain to unity with the infinite."

They did not understand him at all and were therefore the more impressed; and when he walked away from them they stood still awhile and followed only at a distance.

"What did he say? What was it?" asked the capmaker excitedly of the shoemaker.

"Do not ask. It is beyond understanding. Sanctity! Whatever he utters is sanctity," answered the shoemaker, breathlessly.

Joel returned to the inn, and from that time on there was an abyss between him and the others. The saint sat in his own room, the congregation in another. The capmaker mounted guard at the door between the two rooms and permitted no one to approach the "Rabbi." The "Rabbi" stood at the window and longed for the silence and loneliness of the forest.

After a time the wheat merchant was admitted, and he sat watching the Rabbi, afraid that the latter might try to escape through the window. Great thoughts were passing through the merchant's mind. He was a rich man. He had an only daughter, a beautiful girl. The Rabbi was unmarried.

The next day the merchant sent his cart back to the village to bring Joel's father and also Reb Itzikel the Chassid. Joel's father would not come, but the cart returned with Reb Itzikel. The latter was an agent of the wheat merchant. He was also known as a pietist who for the time being was not attached to any Rabbi. Since the death of his own Rabbi, the old saint of Razamin, Reb Itzikel frequented no Rabbinic court, saying that there was no Rabbi worth the following now. When he heard, that day, of the wheat merchant's acceptance of the new young Rabbi, Reb Itzikel was filled with astonishment and incredulity. He came at the wheat merchant's bidding, intending to cry down the pretensions of Joel; but on the way he thought the matter over, and said to himself that if the rich wheat merchant had been so impressed, it might be well to reserve judgment. Arriving, he was shown into the presence of the new Rabbi. The less Joel talked, the more Reb Itzikel thought of him. Finally, when Reb Itzikel put the question to him bluntly and asked whether he would become the Rabbi of the community, Joel repeated what he had said in the wood: he did not know whether he had the power to lift up the souls of men, for he did not know whether he could overcome the arrogance of their will. He had succeeded with plants, because of their simplicity; but he could not speak for man.

"But you can try," suggested Reb Itzikel.

When the wheat merchant asked what all this talk was, Reb Itzikel answered: "These are high matters." And at once all the others, the workingmen and the householders, were thrown into agitation. "You hear?" they whispered to each other. "Reb Itzikel the pietist himself says that these are high matters."

There was great happiness in the inn. The innkeeper put on his Sabbath gaberdine in honor of the occasion; his wife put on her Sabbath kerchief. Food was prepared, and candles were lit in all the rooms, all at the wheat merchant's expense. When the time came for late afternoon prayers, there were present more than the requisite number of a congregational quorum. Joel prayed with the others, and in the midst of the Prayer of the Eighteen Benedictions he forgot himself again and remained standing a long, long time, and no one dared to finish the prayer before he came to. Afterwards, when the company sat down to the feast, he would not eat with the others. They interpreted this as meaning that they had offended him; and again there was much whispering, and much speculation. The wheat merchant exchanged secrets with Reb Itzikel in a corner of the room. He was talking about his daughter and about his wealth, and he was promising Reb Itzikel a good commission if he could arrange the match.

And during all this Joel stood at the window and looked out into the night; his heart was drawn to the woods, and he longed for the music of the silent and simple things which were his natural companions.

•   •   •

He made one more attempt to escape. He left the inn before sunrise and walked in the opposite direction to his home. He came to a village and entered the synagogue. At once a crowd collected, and a whispering and murmuring spread behind his back. Respectable householders came up to him and greeted him humbly. Before long all the village was there, eager to look on the hidden, wonder-working saint. Here too a rich merchant (who also had a beautiful daughter) invited Joel to his home. Without the strength to fight them off, Joel yielded and was soon isolated in the best room in the house, while a special guard was assigned to him, so that his meditations would not be interrupted.

25

Children of Abraham

In this village, where no one had known Joel before, where no one could speak familiarly of his father and mother, his reputation was higher than in the place of his birth. But that same afternoon the searchers caught up with him again, and a procession of carts brought into the village the rich wheat merchant, Itzikel the pietist, the capmaker, the shoemaker, and the others. The moment they heard that Joel was isolated in the house of the richest local Jew, they suspected a plot to steal their Rabbi, and they were ready to foil the attempt by force if necessary. For now it was clear that a matter of great communal importance was involved. This new Rabbi might very well become one of the great world figures of his kind. The village in which he settled would then become one of the world centers of Chassidic Judaism. Hundreds, thousands, perhaps ten of thousands of men and women would seek the advice and intercession of such a Rabbi. Villages had become towns, towns cities, under similar circumstances. They saw a great future before the forlorn village: honor, fame, wealth.

They had a just claim to Joel, they argued with the local Jews. He had been born in their midst, in their village. But the local Jews replied that Joel had been driven out of his native village; he had been beaten and humiliated there. The place of his birth had therefore forfeited all claim to him.

By the next day it looked as though war would break out between the two villages. Messages were sent back to Joel's native place to report on the negotiations; reinforcements were sent forward to take the Rabbi home at any cost. But by the evening of the second day a compromise was reached. The village which had given shelter to Joel received an indemnity and relinquished its claim. Joel was conducted home by a great procession of carts illumined by torches.

Whoever was still left in the village, the young, the old, the sick, came out to meet the procession. The window of every Jewish house was adorned with lighted candles, and had this not been the three-week period of mourning before the Black Fast, a band of musicians would have waited at the entrance to the village.

Naturally the procession did not end up before Joel's poor cottage, but before the stone house of the wheat merchant. There, in fact,

Joel's parents had already been installed, to await his homecoming. Henceforth this was to be known as the Rabbi's house. One room was set aside for prayer; it contained an Ark and Scrolls of the Law. Other rooms were set aside for the exclusive use of the Rabbi. They contained bookcases, rich furniture, heavy armchairs, thick carpets. Here the Rabbi was to live, and his parents with him. His mother would not be permitted to work any more. It was unbecoming that the great Rabbi's mother should sit at a stall in the marketplace, exposed to the insults of peasants.

All doubt as to the authenticity of Joel's ministry had vanished; or if any existed, it was no longer vocal. This was a matter affecting the prosperity of the entire community; and who would dare to risk the opportunity which now beckoned so miraculously? The Talmud students who had taken part in the beating of Joel came to him in stockinged feet, and at the door of his room begged his forgiveness. Reb Itzikel the pietest became Joel's chief officer, the capmaker his beadle, the wheat merchant his nearest friend and right hand man; all the Jews of the village became followers of the new Rabbi.

During the first period a guard was set before the Rabbi's room, ostensibly to prevent intrusion, actually to forestall flight. On the eve of the next Sabbath, which was the Sabbath of Consolation, there was a great gathering from the surrounding villages. Some came because they had been caught in the spirit of the rising faith, others out of curiosity, still others simply because the merchant and Rabbi Itzikel had sent for them. There were doubters, there were mockers, there were ready-made believers. When evening drew on and the assembled congregation, in silk and satin gaberdines, was ready to usher in the Sabbath, with the appropriate prayers, it was suddenly learned that the Rabbi refused to be present with his followers. He would not leave his room. He had locked his door. Reb Itzikel and the merchant stood outside; they pleaded, they argued, they grew angry. Joel neither answered nor opened the door. Meanwhile the congregation waited; the hour of prayer was passing, a calamity impended.

It was averted by Joel's parents, who persuaded him to open the door. Joel's father, who had been reluctant to accept the new order of things, had not been able to withstand the pressure of public opinion. Without quite believing, he had thought it unseemly to hold out against the unanimous declaration of the community. He went now for the first time to speak with his son in his new role and capacity. Joel's mother, who had believed in him before anyone else, was radiant with joy. She had put on a costly dress, a string of pearls, and a silken Sabbath kerchief, all the gifts of the merchant's wife. Father and mother came in respectfully, almost humbly.

"My son," pleaded the mother, "do not shame me before all these people."

Joel wrinkled his forehead, bit his lip in anguish, and answered, almost in tears:

"Mother! I don't know whether I can do it. These are not simple creatures, but men of flesh and blood chained to their own will."

His father intervened. "If you have begun, no doubt there is a way for you to continue."

"My way is for green plants and for dumb animals," said Joel.

His father could not understand that. "But if God has given His spirit to plants and dumb animals, He has surely given more of it to that which He made in His image. Are you lacking in faith?"

Joel had no way of making himself clear to his father. Meanwhile the congregation waited in the prayer-room, and the hum of its impatience became louder and more insistent, like a gathering storm at sea. Reb Itzikel now ran in. The perspiration was streaming down his face, his Sabbath skull cap was on awry. "They won't wait any longer," he cried, despairingly. "They threaten to start prayers without you, to induct the Sabbath without you. I shall be shamed for ever; all those who have believed in you will be shamed for ever."

And still Joel did not answer. He stood at the window and looked out longingly at the trees.

His mother began to weep; great tears, more luminous than the pearls at her throat, rolled down her cheeks.

"Child," she sobbed. "Is your mother's pain nothing to you? How shall *I* survive this humiliation?"

The Boy Saint

Joel looked round at the sound of her voice. His heart contracted with pity. This should have been the moment of his mother's greatest happiness, the first happiness in her life. He saw the sweetness of the Sabbath yielding on her furrowed cheeks to the gray sorrow of the weekday. What should become of her? Would he force her to return to her stall in the marketplace?

It was beyond him to refuse. Without saying a word he walked into the prayer-room.

The place was packed. A shimmer of silken gaberdines and fur headgear passed back and forth in waves. Innumerable candles dazzled the eyes. Silently, without looking into anyone's face, Joel walked through the crowd, which made a lane for him, and stopped at the eastern wall. He buried his face in his hands and heard the cantor begin the service with a gay melody—"Come, let us sing!" And all at once he felt the weight of his body diminish, the grossness of his limbs rarefy. His soul took the ascendant over his flesh, the world swam away from under him, and he was in the midst of light, pure light, which deepened and spread, issuing always from within him and filling wider and wider spheres of space. A song came to his inward ear; the light itself was singing; and within the brightness shafts of an intenser brightness came through to his soul; the shafts, slender at first, broadened until the new intensity filled all space; then, within that new, uniform intensity, still brighter shafts broke through to him. And all this was repeated again and again, so that an ever-increasing radiance grew all round him. Then he became aware of his followers; but they were not individual souls; they were a single soul interfused with his in the brightness. He carried them, or the unity carried him and them, deeper and deeper into blazing space.

Then he found himself, he did not know how, at the Sabbath feast. White tablecloths, a long table with dozens of bright candles, the luster of wines, pale and crimson, the two rows of his followers, in flashing gaberdines and furry hats. His father and his mother were at his side—so Reb Itzikel had ruled; the woman, the mother, was to sit with her son. The room was filled with the delicious aroma of food. Joel closed his eyes. He barely touched the food

29

with his fingers. The dishes which he touched were—after the Chassidic custom—passed down the table and eagerly snatched up by his followers. The candlelight shone through his eyelids, and he began to talk to himself; short, half-heard sentences, as if he were communing with a spirit rather than uttering wisdom for his followers.

"Be like the simple things of the earth, caught in the prison of earth, but not chained by the chains of wilfulness. Let your minds be with your souls, for they alone will bring you back to the source of being, and in that reunion they carry the world with them. For then you, and the world, and all separate things are resolved into the oneness of the one universal purpose."

Those that had understanding for such matters understood his words; those that had no understanding accepted his words in faith. The followers of Rabbi Joel scattered the next day from the village and began to spread his name to the four corners of the world.

.   .   .

The more Joel preached to his followers of the denial of the flesh, the more he found himself entangled in the temptations of the physical world. He neither observed nor felt when this began; but at a certain moment he perceived that the pleasures of the world had made a silent conspiracy against him, and had drawn him into partnership. The room which had been assigned to him, the Rabbi's room, with its beautiful tables, its bookcases, its finely embroidered tablecloths, had become his own in a treacherous sense which he did not find unpleasant. The people who surrounded him were for ever thinking of strengthening his body. They prepared the most delicate and tempting dishes. At first he would not eat. But they sent his mother to him. To her pleas were added those of Reb Itzikel and the wheat merchant. He must not endanger his health; he owed it to them, and to his ever-increasing following, to take care of himself.

But it was not only the physical temptations of this world which were leagued against him. There were spiritual temptations, too, more subtle, and therefore more successful. The celebration of the

The Boy Saint

Sabbath, the lights, the throngs of followers who came for the weekend, the silken gaberdines, the ascensions which he made for all of them, carrying them into the upper worlds—these were sources of pride, of spiritual infection, which were all the more potent because they were insidious mixtures of the worldly and the other-worldly; and no man could say which of the worlds predominated.

It came to such a pass that even his moments of unification with the eternal principle became suspect. The act of dissolving the power of the physical body seemed to have in it an assertion of the physical; his fasting ceased to be physically painful; or, at any rate, it was a preparation for pleasures of this and not of the other world. The honor accorded him was not an other-worldly experience. There came many hundreds from ever-remoter towns: men and women, the learned and the simple, the hale and the sick. They sought his counsel, they sought his good offices in the upper spheres. And he needed to sit alone, in order not to lose his contact with the upper spheres; otherwise he would lose faith in himself, and his followers, in turn, would lose faith in him. The pure joy which he had touched in the loneliness of his first experiences was withdrawing from him.

He would try to recapture it. He stole out of his house late in the night, found his way to the forest, and, wrapped in the ancient silence, would look once more for the ecstasy which had been his. But he was never alone. He knew that, at a respectful distance, his beadle followed to keep watch over him. Sometimes others were permitted to observe the spectacle of the great Rabbi communing with the spheres. And because he knew this Joel felt himself impotent to recapture the spirit. He was even aware of his pleasure in the gratitude of his followers; and this was assuredly worldliness in a most unacceptable form.

Yielding gradually, he even tried to find justification for the new course of his life. The Torah, the wisdom of God, he argued, had been given to the sons of man for their enjoyment on this earth. He would therefore increase the spiritual pleasures of this world. He sought to multiply his good deeds, to distribute charity, to pray

31

much. Prayer was no longer his instrument for ascension into the higher world; it was a thing of this world, it was an end in itself. He even consented to eat often, because as often as he ate he naturally uttered the appropriate benediction; and the uttering of a benediction was the fulfillment of a divine commandment. He also gave himself much to formal study, in order that, like his father, he might ensure for himself a larger portion in the world to come.

In the beginning, when the wheat merchant first raised the subject of his daughter and sent his father to him to discuss marriage, Joel would neither listen nor reply. It did not enter his mind to yield. His father pointed out that the commandment, the law, the tradition, made marriage compulsory. But Joel would not reply. Reb Itzikel was appalled, the rich merchant alternately incredulous and infuriated. Even among his followers at large there was discontent at the impropriety of it. Joel was beyond the age of marriage; why did he withhold himself from the fulfillment of the commandment? Some tried to defend him: "He is holy; he has his own way; and it is not for us to seek to understand." But for the most part it was considered a shocking thing. Then, suddenly, Joel accepted. It was not that—as they thought—their arguments had won him over; it was rather that the general decline into worldliness entailed this particular change too. To marry was a good deed in the eyes of the world and of God. He would do it in order to acquire this additional measure of merit. There was joy everywhere: among the Chassidim, the followers of the Rabbi; in the village; in the two families—Joel's and the bride's; and above all in the heart of Joel's mother.

It was the most brilliant marriage that had ever been celebrated in these parts. Famous Rabbis were invited from distant cities; musicians were hired; vast preparations were made. For eight days in succession the village, expanding now into a town as it accommodated the hosts who streamed in, ate and drank and sang. The followers of Rabbi Joel interpreted his marriage, the marriage of the Sacred Boy, as a portent. Rabbi Joel had obviously destroyed a decree against his own marriage. Did not this signify that great forces of evil had been overcome? Was not this perhaps the marriage from which would spring the long-awaited Messiah?

At first it was Joel's intention to deny himself any joy in the fulfillment of the commandment of marriage; he would, he thought, transform the moment into one of spiritual significance. But here he suffered his greatest defeat. It was as though his body, long tormented and frustrated, had been waiting only for a little rehabilitation in order to renew the assault upon him. It asserted itself with an arrogance of which he never believed it capable. The blood clamored for its rights and swept his denial aside; and in the moment of its triumph it drove the soul out of him and he knew nothing but earthly bliss.

The day after his marriage Joel went about like a broken man. No one could understand the reason for it. But no one could have understood either the horror and alarm which filled him. It was not only that he had been signally defeated. He had discovered something unknown to him before: that in the delight of the flesh, in the gross joys of the body, there were ranges and colorings of experience which matched, for variety and intensity, almost everything that the spirit could offer. In the confusion of the moment he lost his sense of the reality of that which he always believed to be real; he could not have told whether the path led upward or downward.

From that night on Joel felt that he was delivered for ever into the bondage of the body.

．　．　．

The young Rabbi sat in the deep armchair, pulling gently at the long, curiously wrought pipe which a wealthy follower had brought him as a gift. The fine spirals of smoke went up from the delicious Havana tobacco and made a bluish canopy over his head. His fingers toyed with the curls of his earlocks and with the thin strands of his beard. On the other side of the door a host of suppliants waited for a glimpse of him, men, women and children, some of them sick of body, others sick of soul. But the beadle was on guard at the door. The Rabbi was not receiving. He had to be alone. It was the time of his meditation. . . . Such at least was the excuse. But Joel was not in a reverie. It was his flesh which was meditating and brooding pleasurably on itself. For the flesh had become strong and had established a sweet ascendancy. It was pleasantly lulled in silk and satin; it reposed luxuriously in the softness of the huge armchair. Joel's eyes rested with half-conscious sensuousness on the fine bookcase and on the huge tomes with their white parchment and red leather bindings. The loops of pearls on the silken curtains of his Ark seemed to touch his flesh; from a distance he seemed to be caressing with his fingers the delicious texture of the curtains. Through the window came in the odors of the meadow, the savor of ripening apples, the sharp aroma of hidden jasmine and violets. He heard, through the wall, the sweet treble of his young wife's voice, and his spirit stirred in response. She was in conversation with Reb Itzikel, who was now part of the household.

"Let us take something in to the Rabbi," said Reb Itzikel. "It is a long time since he has eaten. He must be famished."

A few moments later the capmaker, now also permanently of the Rabbi's suite, came in. He was dressed in a long gaberdine. In one hand he carried a tray of assorted cakes, in the other a dish of rich fruit jelly. He smiled as he advanced toward Joel and placed the food on a corner of the table near-by. Joel did not stir. The capmaker watched timidly, then withdrew. Soon Joel heard his plaintive voice raised on the other side of the door.

"The Rabbi is refusing his food again! Won't you please go in to him?"

The door opened again. It was the young wife of the Rabbi. She looked like a little girl who had been dressed up to look like an adult. Her cheeks had the smoothness of babyhood; the tiny mouth was like a closed bud. She wore a white silken kerchief on her head, which imparted a sweet incongruousness to her appearance. Standing at a respectful distance from her husband, she pouted:

"Joel, didn't you promise me that you'd never let yourself get famished again? And you know the doctor said you have to build yourself up; you have to eat something every hour or two."

Rebellion, or pretence at rebellion, stirred in Joel.

"What do you want of me?" he said, bitterly. "I've been stuffing my body, I've been yielding to the flesh till there's nothing else left of me. I've become the servant of my body and my fleshiness. Aren't you satisfied yet?"

The young wife started back in fear. She would have left the room had she not felt, standing behind her, Reb Itzikel, who would have barred her way. She turned again to her husband, and added timidly:

"Joel, I don't know whether I'm doing right or not. But the doctor said you forget to eat, and we have to remind you. Your body is precious to all of us."

Joel was silent. He could not fight them any more. At that moment the capmaker, slipping in behind Itzikel, dared to approach the table and to push the two trays nearer to Joel. Joel's young wife exclaimed:

"Do it for me, Joel."

He yielded to her, as he always did. He tried to think again of the good deed represented by the saying of the benediction over the food—that would be his excuse. He repeated the benediction, and his wife responded with a pious "Amen!"

They left him alone after that, but not for long. There was a knock at the door, and his mother appeared, pulling after her a poor, frightened woman, who hung on to the door, and had to be dragged in. Clinging to the terrified woman was a little boy, but though he pretended to be frightened, too, his black eyes gleamed with self-possession and mischief. The Rabbi's mother, in her velvet dress, her silk kerchief, her ribbons, stopped two paces from her son, and said:

"Rabbi, help this woman! It is a pitiful case."

The woman at the door tried to push the boy forward. Her eyes were red with weeping, but she was restraining her tears; it was unbecoming to weep in the presence of a great Rabbi. But she averted her gaze, and only tried to make the boy go nearer the Rabbi.

Joel looked at the woman, and the expression on his face changed. The color withdrew from his cheeks, his lips tightened.

"Mother!" he said. "Do you think I am God in heaven? Are these things in my hand? Is there not the Father of all, above us? Let her pray to Him, and He will help."

"My son," his mother pleaded. "This woman was for many years our kindest neighbor. When you were a baby, and I had nowhere to leave you when I was pressed for time, she used to look after you. She took you among her children and was a second mother to you."

The woman at the door gathered courage and came forward a step. Her face lit up; she seemed suddenly to realize that she had her portion in the great Rabbi who sat before her.

"But what can I do for her? What power have I?" asked Joel, his impatience yielding to pity.

"She wants nothing for herself, Rabbi. She brought her son to you that you might intercede for him. She wants him to grow up God-fearing, to study the holy books, to serve the Almighty—nothing more."

The little boy, hearing himself spoken of, was seized with shyness. He buried his face in his mother's apron and resisted. Very gently Joel's mother brought him forward to the Rabbi, who put his hands on the child's head for a moment, in benediction. Then Joel turned his face toward the wall, and his mother led the child back to the woman in the doorway.

"All things are possible with God," said Joel. "Let her weep to him, pour out her heart. God loves the hearts of the simple, and most of all He loves the hearts of mothers."

The woman in the doorway was afraid to touch her son, as though the sanctity imparted to him by the Rabbi's hands were too much for her. She was speechless with joy. She made a deep obeisance, not to the Rabbi, who was too high for her, but to the Rabbi's mother; and the Rabbi's mother, following her one-time neighbor, had on her face the look of a woman who realizes she has given birth to a king.

The hour had come for the general audience. Reb Itzikel, the

Rabbi's chief officer, admitted the people one by one, in a never-ending stream. There came workers, peddlers, merchants, ignorant villagers, men of learning, men of high standing in their respective communities. Most of the time Joel kept his eyes closed, or else turned toward the wall; for he was ashamed to look these people in the face. There came men who had no request to make; they only wanted to look on the Rabbi and perhaps be permitted to touch his hand. Others were sick, and hoped for a cure—were certain of it if the Rabbi would only exert himself for them. All of them had notes in their hands, on which they had written down, in the regular formula of the occasion, their requests; but some would not rely on the written words, and they began to describe in great detail, and with passionate emphasis, the nature of their diseases, their case histories, their futile search for a cure. Others poured out intimate confessions and begged the Rabbi to instruct them in the ways of penitence; and among these were some who, having confessed and received such instruction, left with shining faces, like manumitted slaves. To some the Rabbi spoke; on others he bestowed only a look. Always he kept repeating weakly that he could do nothing, that they were to address themselves to the Almighty One. But the more he disclaimed power, the more power they attributed to him.

Always, at the end of an audience, Joel felt unhappy and unclean. It was then that the memory of early days, of the purity of first spiritual experiences, came most strongly over him. He would then lock the door, and answer no call. He would say the afternoon and evening prayers alone. The remaining hours of the day they did not always let him keep for himself. Very often Reb Itzikel, his chief officer, or Reb Ozer, his father-in-law, would bring to him a distinguished visitor, a rich man who was looking for a Rabbi to follow, or the follower of another Rabbi whose allegiance they hoped to win for Joel.

Bad as Joel felt after his general audience with the common people, he preferred those contacts a thousand times over to those which his father-in-law thrust on him in the search for rich followers. The first were people in need, believers, unhappy men and women who turned to him as a last resort; but these had need of nothing, they were not suppliants. They were not takers but givers, and they had to be wooed for their gifts, for their possible allegiance. Often he was so wretched in their presence that they felt his distaste for them and never returned. But many were greatly impressed by his silence and indifference.

For the evening after this general audience Reb Ozer had an extremely important "prospect," a rich man who, for some reason, was prepared to change Rabbis.

"We can't take any chances," said Reb Ozer to Reb Itzikel. "This is a fortress we have to capture. He must be received with all honor."

So there was a preliminary audience with Joel, who was in a blacker mood than was usual with him even after the general audience. His afternoon prayers had been a failure. He felt definitely that he had not been admitted to heaven; and this extrusion poisoned for him all his pleasures in the mundane world. But he had seen it coming. This reversion to gross, carnal happiness, which had taken place again and again since the time of his marriage, was producing its inevitable consequence. He heard his chief officer and his father-in-law saying something about an important visitor, a rich and learned man who would have to be treated with special skill and courtesy; and all the time his mind was with his misfortune, the irreparable loss of his contact with infinity. Finally he burst out:

"What kind of contract do you think you have with me? Am I a cart on which you load souls, which I must drag up into the sky, because you feed my body? Give me food for my soul, and I will lift souls and carry them. You tie me down to the earth, and you want me to take others to heaven."

The deputation withdrew, and sent in his young wife. Quietly, guiltily, the young woman stood at the open door; she did not dare to speak.

"What do you want? Has your father sent you to me?" asked Joel.

"I only came to ask you to eat something," she stammered. "It is

38

now after evening prayer, and you haven't had anything to eat since early afternoon. And that long audience."

So it began again. The capmaker came with his tray, which he put down on the table. Then he brought a pitcher of water and a towel so that the Rabbi might wash his hands and say the benediction. And all the time the young wife, her eyes troubled, stood near the door. Joel looked at her, saw the rounding figure which told of approaching motherhood, and felt he would never break the coils which had been thrown about him. He was tied to the earth now, would remain so for ever. He would have liked to hear his wife say something; and when he could not bear the silence any more, he said:

"Very well, let it be so. Tell your father to bring the man in, and I'll receive him with all honor. With all honor."

. . .

The Rabbi had fallen into a melancholia. He would sit at table with his followers, the hours would pass, and he would not utter a single word to delight them. His silence was not the silence of perception and joy; it was the silence of that melancholia which is sinful and contrary to the law of gladness which is the ultimate law of the Chassidic approach to God. The first one to observe this condition in the Rabbi was not a scholar and not one of the prominent followers of the Rabbi; it was the shoemaker, who had been among the first to proclaim the sanctity of the Rabbi.

The summer had come round again and with it the Pentecost and the Day of the Rejoicing for the Law—that day in the year when God had given Israel His eternal heritage. Thousands of followers had assembled from distant places, to be present at the Rejoicing. The new prayer-house was filled to overflowing that Friday evening; and hundreds of worshipers could find no admittance and gathered in the courtyard of the synagogue. The sun sent upward its last beams from below the horizon, gilding the clouds which floated high up in the west. The candles shone in the windows of Jewish homes. The day was dying, not in torment, but in bliss, in sweetness and in beauty. The cantor began the song, "Come, my friend, to greet the Sabbath," and Joel stood in his corner. To all outward appearance he was the same as on every other Friday evening; and only he knew how different it was with him. He was desolate. Not the slightest intimation of a spiritual gift was in him. The beams of light, which had used to shine on him from the source of all light, were extinguished. Where was the spark with which he had fused in earlier days? Where was the brightness which had once enveloped him? Instead of brightness, there was a gross, animal envelope of bodies; he stood in the midst of them; the sweat of their decay entered his nostrils; and he repeated mechanically the words of the prayer. He understood the meaning of the words, but they were dead things, dead and old and dry, words that were repeated every Sabbath eve: *"L'chu n'ranenoh"*—come, let us sing. But what did this song mean? For one it meant his daily bread, for another a good piece of business, for a third an entry on the credit side of his heavenly account, an act of piety stored up for him, like a deposit in a bank: it meant a thousand things for the perishable body, nothing for the eternal soul. Mendicants, they stood with outstretched hands before God, exposing their wretched little needs. And here he was, standing among them. What did *he* want? What supplication had he to address to God? Was he not, indeed, the king of these mendicants? Was he not their leader and spokesman, entrusted with the task of obtaining satisfaction for them? And was he able to serve them in their miserable demands? No. Such service he could not render; he was a mass of deception.

These thoughts were in his mind when he turned from the wall at the end of the prayers and faced the congregation. And when the little shoemaker saw the expression on the Rabbi's face, he knew everything.

"Did you? Did you see?" he said excitedly, to his neighbors.

"See what?"

"The Rabbi! He is in the grip of the evil black mood! On the Sabbath! Before the great Rejoicing for the Law!"

The Rabbi's followers started back in rage. Had they not been in the synagogue they would have beaten the shoemaker for his blasphemy.

Then came the feast, with the most distinguished of the Rabbi's followers seated at the long table. They waited for him to speak. They would not partake of the food until the Rabbi had sanctified the occasion with glowing words, with the wisdom he drew from the higher spheres. But the Rabbi was silent for a long time. At last he began to speak, but he had scarcely uttered the first word, when he caught sight of the little shoemaker standing behind a seated guest, watching him intently. Then the Rabbi remembered suddenly that it was this face which had been fixed on him most intently when he had come out of his first ascension in the synagogue. His lips closed tightly, and he spoke no more.

His followers looked at each other; a wind of disappointment and bewilderment passed along the length of the table; and they ate that evening without edifying words from the Rabbi. The next evening, at the ending of the Sabbath, the little shoemaker was standing outside the synagogue, and he was heard to say:

"Something has gone wrong! Something has been spoiled! I don't know what it is, but something in the Rabbi is not as it should be."

A devoted follower of the Rabbi, a leader among the followers, a man of wealth, standing, piety, and learning, heard these words, turned round, and slapped the little shoemaker resoundingly—once on each cheek.

"Heathen!" he thundered. "Blasphemer! Ignoramus! Keep your nose out of things you don't understand!"

The little shoemaker took the slaps without protest; and a few moments later he was heard humming a psalm under his breath.

. . .

The forest was silent all about him: thick, massive trunks, branches breaking heavily from the trunks, thick twigs starting out of the branches, a vast growth of green leaves, and all of it sent forth by the earth. And not only the forest: he too had come forth from the earth. To what end? He was like a sick growth, like the mushrooms and toadstools which the rain brought out and which would be uprooted and burned. These things lived; they were either burned or else they decayed and re-entered the earth. So it went, generation after generation, till the great end would come and the earth would be dissolved in heat, would be carried off, and another power would take its place. In vain had he tried to rise above the cycle and remember the source of his being. In his failure an awful thought had come to him: that the power which had created him was itself evanescent.

It was morning. The grasses were steeped in dew, the trees were awakening from sleep. The autumn sun came up, pale, reluctant, like a prisoner making the last journey, to the place of execution. Far off a woodpecker awakened echoes; there arose a humming of insects. In the distance faint voices called: "Rabbi! Rabbi!"

Joel rose from the damp earth. His legs were stiff, his body filled with weariness and the need for sleep. What folly had driven him out of the house in the night, to look for the old secrets in the wood? Had he not forgotten their meaning? Had he not forgotten the approach to them? Was it not time for him to resign himself to defeat?

He came out of the thicket where he had been hiding. The cap-maker saw him and came running toward him, with a warm gaberdine. A second beadle also came, with a thick muffler for his throat. And having wrapped him round they followed him timidly at a distance as he returned toward the village.

Halfway to the village, the Rabbi saw coming toward him the little shoemaker, who had a pack slung over his shoulder; these were his tools, and he was going out into the villages to sell his services. As he came along, the little shoemaker sang a psalm, with a Sabbath melody.

The Rabbi waited for the little shoemaker; but the latter did not seem to notice the Rabbi; for he passed on, still singing his psalm; and Joel stood there, thinking, and trying to remember something; he stood there as long as he could hear the shoemaker's voice, and then he resumed his way, slowly.

. . .

Again there was a gathering of the Rabbi's followers. There was great rejoicing in his house. His young wife had given birth to a son; the ceremony of the circumcision, the entrance into the Abrahamitic covenant, was to be celebrated with the pomp and luxury befitting the occasion. None other than Reb Chaim of Gastinin had been brought to the village to act as the circumcising Rabbi. Great stores of food had been assembled, and preparations were made as for a wedding. And in the between days of the Festival of Booths, the village was filled to overflowing with visitors; the streets were impassable.

Friday afternoon came, warm and sunlit, but windy. The ritual baths were crowded with visitors preparing for the Sabbath; and from the ritual baths the crowds streamed toward the Rabbi's house, wet earlocks, white collars, black satin gaberdines, white stockings. They were gathering there for the lighting of the Sabbath candles. The prayer-house walls were cracking with the strain; it was impossible to get through the yard. In the Rabbi's garden groups of young Chassidim sat under the apple trees, singing the Song of Songs. Some climbed the trees, tore off the fruit, and made a benediction over it. There was a coming and going of important people, massive heads, broad shoulders, impressive beards, white, black, silvery, brown. Each of them was known by name; each of them was mentioned in awed tones: "There goes Reb Berel of Zamasch, who's half a Rabbi himself." "Look, there's the Rabbi of Plotsk, who used to be called the young genius of Plotsk." Or else it was: "See that one? He's one of the richest men in Warsaw; he came all the way in his own carriage, drawn by relays of three horses." But not all the important people were either impressive in appearance or reputed to be rich. There were some who looked like beggars; their faces were hollow, their bodies frail, their clothes in tatters; and yet their fame was established over the whole world.

But in spite of this coming and going, the Rabbi had refused to receive anyone. Reb Itzikel flew anxiously from house to courtyard, from courtyard to house, explaining, mollifying, pleading. Something mysterious and portentous was in the air. "The Rabbi is not receiving! He is making preparations for something."

Before long the nature of the preparations was revealed. The Rabbi had decided to lead in the sanctification of the Sabbath; no cantor or singer would act for the congregation, he himself would be cantor and singer. And the sanctification would not take place in the synagogue, but in the open, where no walls and no ceiling stood between man and God. In the fields, between heaven and earth, he would sanctify the Sabbath.

A tremor passed through the assembled followers. Here was something new! Friday night, the Sabbath eve, not in the synagogue, but under the heavens! And not the cantor to lead them, but the Rabbi himself. A mood of unwonted solemnity settled on the village, the premonition of a Sabbath such as they had never known before.

The wide fields stretched from the back of the Rabbi's house to the edge of the forest. As the sun set that day a strange light flushed the green-gold levels and was thrown back from the countless black satin gaberdines of the men and the white silk headcoverings of the women. Singly, in pairs, in groups, they waited for the Rabbi to come out, and when he appeared on the steps of the house, a pious murmur went up from the crowd and died into prayerful silence. Quietly, looking neither to right nor left, the Rabbi followed the setting sun, and the assembly followed him, with short, rustling footsteps. Hundreds held their breath, as though a miracle were impending, as though a revelation were about to be made. The skies grew darker, the shadows deepened on the earth. And suddenly there was heard the sound of a flute. "Do you hear?" they whispered. "The Rabbi is playing on a flute! He is receiving the Sabbath to the music of the flute! No words, but the prayer of music!"

They went on, till the fields ended and the forest began. The birds took up the music of the flute, and responded; the trees responded too, with a joyous rustling. It was as if they were awakening from a deep sleep. The birds lifted their voices higher; the trees swelled the chorus; the grasses underfoot seemed to join in the adoration.

The Boy Saint

It seemed to those hundreds, who were advancing into the forest, that in another moment they would understand everything that the Rabbi had ever preached, the simplicity of growing things, the denial of the gross materiality of the world, the unification of life with its eternal and infinite source. And on the brink of understanding they were thrown back by a sudden, harsh cry:

"Sinner! Blasphemer! The stars are out, the Sabbath is here, and you dare to play the flute!"

The congregants came to with a gasp. Dark forest, the Sabbath, the starlight—and their Rabbi playing the flute. The little shoemaker confronted the Rabbi, shook his fist, and yelled:

"Blasphemer! Desecrator of the Sabbath!"

Silently, by ones and twos, the congregants crept back to the village, avoiding each other's eyes. The Rabbi was forgotten. He had disappeared into the forest. Prayers that Sabbath eve were not said in the synagogue, but each one prayed for himself in his own house or lodgings. And when the Sabbath was over, twenty-four hours later, the assembly scattered to the four corners of the world, as if from a frightful infection. The Rabbi had not yet returned.

After the prayer of farewell to the Sabbath, twenty-four hours later, the young wife of the Rabbi and her father hired carts and set out in search of him. They did not find him that night, nor the next day, nor the day after. Weeks passed, months, a whole year. Only then rumors flowed back of a strange man, a devotee, who was wandering about the land. He avoided cities and villages and the homes of men and stayed in the fields, nourishing himself on roots and wild fruits. Peasants had caught glimpses of him, and tried to catch him; but he had eluded them. They said that this was the hidden saint who had once been the great Rabbi and who was now doing penance for an indescribable sin.

Yoshke the Beadle

IN the ancient and sacred city of Worms there lived once, generations and generations ago, a Jew who went by the name of Yoshke the beadle. His real name was Joseph, and he had been named after Joseph the righteous one, of the Bible, whom he grew up to resemble; and he became the beadle in the old and hallowed synagogue of Worms, concerning which there is a tradition that it was founded as far back as the days of the Second Temple. But the little children of the town called him, out of their love for him, Yoshke the beadle, for he spoiled them greatly. Every morning he would make the rounds of the Jewish houses and gather the children; and singing a Psalm to a beautiful melody, he would lead the children to Hebrew school. Evenings he would come for the children and lead them home, again singing a beautiful Psalm.

In the venerable synagogue of Worms there were two charity boxes, fastened into the marble pillars near the entrance; of these boxes it was said that in olden days, when the Temple was still standing in Jerusalem, they had been brought to Worms by Jews of the Holy Land, so that the community of Worms might throw into them their contributions for the upkeep of the Temple. Every day, between afternoon and evening prayers, Yoshke the beadle used to gather the children in the shadow of the two pillars and tell them marvelous stories and legends out of the records of the community of Worms: how, in every generation, wicked rulers had risen in the land and sought the extermination of the Jews, and how in every generation a miracle had been performed and the community saved. He told them of the shepherd boys who had set out for Jerusalem in the days of the Crusades, and had taken two geese with them, because the two geese had been trained by a magician to fly over roofs and fields and to come down in any place where Jews were hiding from murderous Crusaders; and he told them how, when the Crusaders came to the city of Mayence, the geese had alighted on the steeple of the church, because the bishop of Mayence, having received a huge bribe, had hidden the local Jews in the cellar of his church. He told them also the marvelous story of the saintly Jew, Mar Amron, whose body, after his death, came floating down the river Rhine to the city of Cologne. The Christians of the city tried to lift the coffin out of the water, but they could not, for the more they tugged at it the heavier it became. Then Jews came, and they lifted the coffin easily out of the water. Mar Amron had been born in Cologne, and he had gone away to another city on the Rhine to teach the word of God in a Jewish community; and when he died he told his pupils that he wanted to be buried in the Jewish cemetery of the city of his birth. They had asked him: "Rabbi, how shall we bring your holy body to the city of Cologne? The roads are infested with robbers, and the robbers spare neither the living nor the dead." Thereupon he had told them to put his body in a coffin, and the coffin in a little boat, and to let the boat float on the river; and the waves would carry the boat to the city of Cologne and bring it to the bank. And that was what came to pass.

Or else Yoshke the beadle told the children about the Jewish Pope who had been visited in a dream by his father; and about the great and holy scholar Rashi who, when he was still in his mother's womb, wrought a miracle. For it happened that one day Rashi's mother, in the days of her pregnancy, was walking down a narrow lane between two walls, and a horseman came bearing down on her and would have trampled on her, but that she shrank to the wall, and the wall yielded at that point into a curved hollow, so that Rashi's mother was sheltered from the furious horseman: and the hollow in that wall has remained even until this day.

All these stories Yoshke the beadle told them, and others too,

47

which are to be found in his "Book of Miracles," which he wrote afterwards and which is still extant.

The children became so accustomed to hearing marvelous stories from Yoshke, that they looked on them as their due, and asked for them whenever they saw him. They would run after him in the street, shouting, "Yoshke, Yoshke, a story!" And they would not leave him alone until he promised them that that evening, between afternoon and evening prayers, he would tell them a new story. And sure enough, when twilight came and the children gathered for him at the base of the two pillars where the charity boxes were, Yoshke would appear and would tell them a new story. For this was Yoshke's nature: as soon as he saw the children gathered around him, with open mouths and eager eyes, he would immediately remember a story which had been told him in his childhood out of the legends of the ancient Jewish community of Worms. For much had happened to this community in the course of the generations, much that was good and much that was evil, and it was a sorely tried community. His way of telling stories was such that the events he described seemed to be unrolling in the presence of the listeners; he forgot who he was and where he was, and so did they. Therefore it would often happen that the grown-ups, who had assembled for prayers, would be shouting, "Yoshke! Yoshke! Where are the candles!" and Yoshke would be living through a miracle of the long ago; Yoshke would be in prison with the illustrious saint, Reb Meir of Rothenburg; or he would be one of the two strangers who came to the city of Worms, and who let themselves be burned alive so that by their sacrifice they might take the burden of sin off the city and save it from a great calamity; or he would be walking the streets of the holy city of Jerusalem; or he would be on the road to Rome, to interview the Pope. In vain would the head of the synagogue shout, with growing anger: "Yoshke! Yoshke! We cannot pray in the dark!" As long as those children's eyes, black and flashing, were fixed on him, Yoshke had to finish his story. Only then would he remember that he was the beadle of the synagogue and that he had certain duties to perform.

Yoshke the Beadle

But of course Yoshke did not by any means pass all his time telling stories to children. When prayers were over and darkness had settled on the city, Yoshke locked and double-locked the two huge doors of the synagogue and went into his poor room, where he lived alone. There a pot of porridge hung from a tripod, over the fire. Yoshke would pour hot porridge into pitchers and carry the pitchers down dark cellars and up narrow stairs. Yoshke always knew where to find the poor strangers who had stolen into the ghetto and were hiding from the officials of the community. Sometimes he himself would hide such a stranger in the attic of the synagogue; or else it might be a sick inhabitant of the city, who had to be hidden and kept apart, lest it be known that there was a disease in the ghetto and the sick man be hunted out into the fields to die there.

Now it happened once that a frightful, choking smell invaded the air of the ghetto of Worms. No one knew where it came from. There was not even one sick man who had been concealed from the authorities. But the smell suddenly invaded the ghetto, and on that day many people who had been walking about hale and hearty in the morning, were found in the evening lying in their beds with swollen limbs and purple faces. A great dread descended on the community. People were afraid to encounter each other. The masters of the city locked the doors of the ghetto and set guards about the walls and gates, with instructions to send an arrow through the heart of anyone who tried to escape. They even forbade the Jews to come near the ghetto gates, and trumpeters were stationed on towers to blow their trumpets when Jews came within a certain distance of their own gates. It was as if an enemy were besieging the city from within.

Within the ghetto walls death reaped a fat harvest. Because of the danger the Rabbis closed the synagogue in order that Jews might not congregate and infect each other. But the prohibition was superfluous, for the Jews stayed indoors. They laid up provisions and locked themselves in; and there they stayed, week after week, waiting for the frightful pestilence to subside. When someone died in a house, the members of the family removed the body at night, secretly, and brought it to the cemetery, where the burial brotherhood, without performing the proper rites for the departed one, flung him into a common grave.

Now the only one who ventured about the streets of the ghetto was Yoshke the beadle. Indeed, he was busier than ever, and the smoke hung thicker than ever in his room, as the fire burned under the tripod and the porridge cooked in the pot. For now there were more to be looked after; there were sick ones, the last of their families, to whom no one would minister; and they were exposed to death from hunger as well as from the pestilence. Yoshke did not fear the pestilence. He crawled down cellars and up stairways, in houses where the disease lay heaviest; to some he brought a little food, to others a healing herb; here he bound up an open sore, there he washed a feverish face; he closed the eyes of the dead and comforted the hearts of the living.

One night, while Yoshke was hurrying with a pot of porridge down a narrow lane, he heard a frightful groaning and recognized the voice of a woman. He thought, of course, that this was another case like the hundreds he had attended; and since this was a woman, he decided to let the others wait and see what might be done here. He went into the dark house, and, guided by the moans of pain which came down the stairway, found the room in which the woman lay. He saw her by the moonlight which came in through the tiny window; she was calling, as in a delirium, for her mother, but there was no one about to help her.

"Good woman," said Yoshke, "what ails you? Is there any way I can help you?"

The woman, hearing his voice, covered her face with the bedsheet and answered:

"How can you help me, seeing you are a man? I need a woman, because my time has come, and I must give birth."

"Good woman," said Yoshke, "do not despair. I will bring you a midwife at once."

Yoshke ran from house to house, knocked at one door after another, but no midwife would venture out. And since the midwives refused to do their office, Yoshke pleaded with other women to come to the rescue of the poor soul in labor. But everyone was terrified of bringing the pestilence home, and neither man nor woman would venture forth. Then Yoshke, bethinking himself that these were desperate times, and this a desperate case, resolved on desperate measures, and called down God's help on his resolution.

He went home to his poor hovel. Behind a sheet hung a woman's clothes, his wife's. She was dead this many a year, and he had never disposed of her clothes. Now he was glad that he had kept them; for in a trice he had drawn a woman's dress over his men's clothes and put a woman's shawl over his head and a woman's veil over his face, so as to hide his man's beard. Then he said:

"God, thou wilt forgive me this blasphemy, for thou knowest I do it to save two lives."

He prepared also whatever was needed in such cases, for he knew of such things from his departed wife, took with him the big cauldron in which to warm water and bathe the newborn child, and the scissors with which to cut the cord. Thus accoutred, he returned to the house where the woman lay in labor pain, and standing in the door, he said, in a changed voice:

"Good woman, good woman, do not despair; I am here to help you bring forth your son."

The woman in the bed was astonished by these words.

"Who sent you here?" she asked, "and how did you know that my time has come."

Thereupon the "midwife" answered: "Yoshke the beadle passed my way and told me that your time had come and sent me to you."

Thus the woman in childbirth knew that the stranger in the doorway was not the evil Lilith, and not a witch or another snatcher of young souls; and she cried out with mingled joy and pain:

"Dear midwife, hasten, for the child is almost lost."

Eight days Yoshke, in the guise of a woman, spent in that room. He helped bring forth the child, a lusty boy, and cared for the mother, who was greatly weakened by the birth pangs. He washed the child and fed the mother. He cooked, and he made the bed and kept the room clean. He bound the child in diapers, and did everything with skill and love. And when the eight days had passed, the time had come to bring the child into the Jewish fold according to the commandment of circumcision.

Then Yoshke went home, and changed back into his men's clothes, and took with him the circumcision knife and the ritual book, and returned to the woman's house, and stood in the doorway, saying:

"Good woman, good woman, be happy, for I have come to bring your son into the fold of Israel."

Thereupon the woman asked, in astonishment:

"But how did you know that there is a newborn child here to be brought into the fold of Israel?"

"The midwife who attended you came to my window," said Yoshke the beadle, "and she knocked and told me that a boy is waiting to be brought into the fold."

Thereupon the woman knew again that it was not Lucifer or another of the demons who prowl about the world in search of young souls, and she rejoiced that her son would be brought into the Jewish fold according to the law.

And thus Yoshke the beadle was at once both midwife and circumcision Rabbi, and saved two lives, and brought a man into the fold of Israel, fulfilling the commandment in a time of peril.

The Song of Hunger

ALL day long the village slept in the warm sunlight. The inhabitants hid themselves in their dilapidated little houses, closed the shutters on the broken windows, and took refuge from the light. For the most part they kept to their beds, and in a half coma they dreamed of food. The sun poured its wasted brilliance on the marketplace and on the roofs; no one wanted it. The streets were like the streets of the dead. Here and there a skeleton of a dog would come to a semblance of life, drag itself over to the gutter, muzzle the earth hopelessly, and collapse once more into immobility. More rarely, a door would open, and a skeleton of a man would issue forth carrying a jug, totter to the nearest pump, fill himself with water, and totter back with a jugful of water to his house. But at one end of the village a handful of boys in ragged shirts and trousers lay on the withered grass in the yard of the ritual bathhouse. Trees grew there, yielding late autumn pears; but it was long since anyone had espied something eatable on the plucked branches. The children rooted in the grass, hoping to find a rotted pear which had fallen of itself and escaped their hands or a few leaves of sorrel which could be eaten raw or boiled into an imitation soup.

Toward sunset the doors of the houses open and the population, men and women in rags, barefoot youngsters, a procession of tatterdemalions, wends its way to the synagogue to render God his due. They walk slowly and uncertainly, like the sick. Reb Isaac Aaron, the furrier, who has established himself in the privilege of leading the afternoon prayers, raises his thin, womanish voice. It does not take long to get through the *Minchah* and *Maariv,* but when it is over the congregation does not disperse. What is there to draw them home? Neither food nor the need for rest. Have they not slept through most of the day? The beadle snuffs the candles and replaces the butts in the Ark, to be used again on the morrow. No candles are needed, for the moon sends in its strange, milky beams through the broken windows; and moonlight is better, too, for dreaming and remembering. So the men sit and tell stories of happier times. The merchants tell of great market days and lucky purchases and sales. The fishers tell of mighty hauls which filled their nets for a festival, the butchers of the hefty cattle they once slaughtered, the tailors of the marvelous stuffs they once made into suits of clothes. Only Reb Meyer the scholar takes no part in the wistful recitals. He sits close to the perpetual light before the ark, and though he knows of the prohibition, he makes use of this light for study and murmurs the words of the Ethics of the Fathers to himself.

The youngsters in the synagogue imitate their elders. A group of them clusters in the corner about the chest which holds the remnants of sacred books, and they talk of food. The big ones remember very clearly the meals their mothers used to cook when food was an ordinary thing. Isaac, the haberdasher's son, cannot get out of his mind the yellow cookies and the golden sponge cake his mother always baked for the Pentecost; he speaks of them now with feverish affection and puts into the recital the remnants of his childish energy. From the cookies and sponge cake he goes on to other delicacies and passes his tongue over his lips as he talks:

"And do you remember the cheese patties mother used to make for Pentecost? I'll tell you how it's done. You take white Sabbath meal, and you bake it with oil, and with raisins, and you take cottage cheese, and cream, and butter, and you mix them, and you fill the white bread with them, and bake it all together," and as he speaks a thin dribble of saliva comes into his mouth, and he swallows hard.

"And what about blackberry tarts?" another youngster cries, eagerly. "Remember how you make those? You cook the blackberries first with lots of sugar, then you bake them into the white cake, and you put on sugar and ginger."

"And my mother," a third one broke in, "used to make a marvelous noodle pudding, with chicken fat and cracklings."

The little ones among the youngsters, whose days or memories did not reach back to the time of miracles, but who had heard of them, listened openmouthed to the detailed descriptions. At bottom they could not really believe it all, still less could they believe that their own brothers, who were only boys like themselves, should have been the witness of such a time and, what was more, the actual beneficiaries, the tasters, the eaters of those incredible productions of pot and oven. For that matter, they could not conceive of a world, anywhere, at any time, in which ordinary people, not kings, not rulers, should have such foods prepared for them. But it was not necessary to believe; one could listen and enjoy and pretend. A tiny urchin, the younger brother of Isaac, put his bony hand caressingly on Isaac's gaberdine, tugged it eagerly, looked up out of enormous eyes and a prematurely old face, and piped:

"And was it good?"

"Was it good!" repeated Isaac, pityingly. "Was it good! You felt nothing but milk and sugar in your mouth. It just melted away with sweetness."

"And you mean they had white bread whenever they wanted?"

"Every Sabbath," answered Isaac, pompously. "With poppyseeds and raisins."

"And do you remember the onion rolls?"

"Onion roll! What's that?"

"It's made with oil; cakes made in oil, with onion chopped in; every boy gets a roll for himself, a whole roll, with a little flag stuck in it. M-m: it was so fresh, and it had such a lovely smell."

"Tell us! Tell us!" came from the little ones.

But the conversation took another turn. Another Isaac—the slaughterer's son—put in, apropos of nothing: "Do you know I can fast all day long now; just one drink of water in the middle, and I can fast from morning to night."

"Pooh! That's nothing!" flung back Chaim, the son of Leibel. "I can fast every day."

"Every day?" several asked, incredulously.

"Sure I can," insisted Chaim. "My daddy taught us how to do it. He found a new system and taught all of us."

"Oh, tell, tell!" the children urged.

"This is how you do it. First you go to sleep at night. Then, when the morning comes, my daddy gets out of bed and puts the hands of the clock back to midnight. The shutters are kept closed, so we go on sleeping far into the day. Then we get afraid that we'll be late for the morning prayer, but when we take a look at the clock it's only six in the morning. My father takes his shawl and phylacteries and goes to the synagogue. And mama says to us, 'When daddy'll come home from the synagogue we'll all eat.' But daddy goes on praying until it's late afternoon, so he waits for the *Minchah-Maariv* prayers and finishes those, too. And then he comes home, and all of us eat a piece of bread which mama got somewhere, and we drink as much water as we want, and we go back to bed again. That's how we can fast every day. At first it was very hard. But now we can all fast; even my little sister fasts every day. And the fasting goes so nice and so easy."

"Oh, my mama has another system for not eating," put in Shabsi, the son of the village pietist. "I tell you, it's a marvelous system. It's wonderful. You don't eat, and yet you have the taste of every kind of food in your mouth, just as if you were eating."

"How? Tell us! Tell us!" chorused the youngsters.

"I'll show you how in a minute. But first you've got to have some water. Notte, go out into the yard and bring in a ladle of water."

"No! Tell first."

"Well, this is how it's done," yielded Shabsi. "You take a mouthful of water, and you hold it, you hold it and hold it, and you close your eyes, and you make up your mind you're eating something, let's say, fish. And you chew with your mouth the way you would if you had a piece of fish in it. You can do it that way with any kind of food, because you chew different for each food. If you want, you say to yourself that you're eating meat, roast duck, or white Sabbath bread. All you have to do is close your eyes and say you're eating it. And you can even say how many eggs and how much oil you want in the Sabbath bread you're eating, and how much ginger and how much poppyseed sprinkled on top."

"Oh, that's wonderful!" they cried. And at once there was a demand for white Sabbath bread; that was what took their fancy; and when Notte came in with the ladle of water, they surrounded him impatiently.

"Give me a piece of white Sabbath bread."

"No, give me first."

The ladle was passed round, the youngsters took a gulp of water each, they held it in their mouths, according to Shabsi's prescription, they closed their eyes, and they concentrated on the white Sabbath bread.

In a few minutes faces lit up, and a pleasurable gurgling was heard from some of the children.

One of them swallowed, chewed on his saliva, and whispered blissfully:

"Oh, that was a good, thick one."

Another, less successful, looked at him enviously.

"What did you get, Joel?"

"A hunk of white Sabbath bread, with big, fat raisins."

"Silly!" cried another. "I had a better idea. I changed to a slice of sponge cake with honey on it, with sugar icing—like you get on Passover."

"I got a plate of noodle soup," said Zelig, who was known to be grown up and practical. "Not right away, I mean. First I had a piece of roll, and made the benediction, and after that I got the noodle soup. I was just to have a piece of chicken, too, when you interrupted me."

Those who had failed to "get" their food asked for another try.

"Notte! Please get some more water. I want some noodle soup and carrot stew."

"I want roast chicken, the white meat, please."

"Oh, Shabsi, this is the best system of all!"

"We've been doing it a long time," said Shabsi, carelessly. "We don't wait for the Sabbath, either, to have white Sabbath bread. Every day when we come home from synagogue we sit down for a regular feast. Daddy washes his hands first, for the benediction. Mama fills the big soup tureen with water, and each one gets a bit in his plate and she says: 'Here, children, I've made a nice, thick potato soup today.' We do that every evening, and every noon. Mother cooks something different every day. Sometimes cutlets and sometimes soup meat; but of course on the Sabbath it's always roast."

"I'm going to tell my mama, too," exclaimed one of the youngsters. "Then we'll eat what we want every day, too."

There was one boy, standing at a little distance from the group, who had not taken part either in the transformation of water into food or in the talk which had preceded it. Joey, whose eyes were larger and shinier than those of the other children, only stood and smiled. He too had something to tell, but shyness held him silent until one of the children offered him the ladle, saying:

"Joey, don't you want some nice noodle soup?"

Joey put the ladle by, saying, "No, I don't want any noodle soup." He closed his eyes, which seemed to shine through the eyelids, showing up the thin network of blue veins, and shook his head, so that his earlocks danced.

"Look at him!" cried Zelig. "He doesn't want a plate of noodle soup."

"Maybe he wants sponge cake with raisins."

Again Joey made his earlocks dance.

"And what about ginger snaps and almond cookies and soda water? And what about raspberry juice? And what about pickles with lots of pickle sauce?"

Joey kept his eyes closed, and shook his head to each question.

"Oh, what a big fool!" And in a last assault on the dissenter a boy offered breathlessly: "Bread with chicken fat and cracklings, and after that strawberries on the stalk and a white plum and a soft yellow pear!"

The others swallowed repeatedly at these words; Joey alone was unmoved.

"Well, what *do* you want?"

"I don't want anything."

"You don't want to eat?"

"No!" Still he shook his head. "Eating isn't good."

"Eating isn't good?" They were baffled. "He's crazy."

"Not to eat," said Joey, "not to eat for a long time, that's good. It's so good, and sweet, and easy." The haggard face softened with recollection, the big eyes swam.

"And suppose you're hungry?"

"You aren't hungry."

"Not even a bit hungry?"

"No, I'm not hungry."

"Never, never, never?"

"Never."

"Why?"

"If you don't eat you can fly."

"Can you fly?"

"Yes, I can fly; like a bird. Like a dove. I fly wherever I want to."

"And what are you doing now?"

"I'm flying," he murmured, closing his eyes. "I'm flying round the pulpit, I'm flying above the cherubim on the Ark, I'm flying as high as the eagles, and all of you look so tiny."

"Can you fly up to the sky?"

"Yes, I can. If you come outside with me I'll show you."

The children went out into the synagogue yard, Joey at their head. The moon was sailing through rifts of blue, cutting her way out of one nest of clouds and into another. Then she came forth for good into a long stretch of pure blue, and only at great distances from her wandered little fleeces of cloud, like strayed sheep.

Joey remained standing on the wooden steps of the synagogue. He closed his eyes again and lifted his pallid face to the moon. In a moment it seemed that the milky light on his face shone outward from within. He spoke softly, ecstatically:

"I'm flying, oh, I'm flying."

"No, you're not, you're standing," objected Isaac, the haberdasher's son.

"No, no, no, I'm already up in the sky," answered Joey, his face radiant. "It's beautiful up here, blue curtains waving, as if water was passing through them, or a wind. I'm flying between the curtains, in and out between them. I'm trying to catch up the moon. The curtains are in the way; but I'll catch up with her. Oh, Father, it's so beautiful up here!" He became silent.

"What's beautiful, Joey? What do you see? Tell us."

He would not answer. With eyes closed he smiled joyously at the moon.

"Joey, Joey, tell us what you see."

"Hush-sh!" He gestured at them with his hand. *"I've reached her!* Waters like silk, and a synagogue floating on the waters. No, not a synagogue, a booth filled with light. Blue tapestries inside. And light, so much light! And more booths, and someone singing in them. I see a lot of people praying, old people, with white beards and blue prayer-shawls. And mothers in Sabbath dresses, with diamonds and pearls, and Sabbath candles, and girls standing with their mothers"—his voice dropped shyly. "Their hair is washed and braided, they're helping in the benediction of the candles. The boys stand with the fathers in booths, as on the Feast of Booths. It's a festival! It's a festival in the moon. Guests are coming, visitors, friends."

His voice died away, and the children watched him breathlessly. Then Leib caught the mood and began to imitate him. He closed his eyes like Joey, lifted up his face and cried: "I see! I see, too. There's a big ship on the moon, and musicians on the ship. It's a wedding. No, a great Rabbi is traveling, and his congregation with him. Oh, mothers in lovely dresses, and precious stones that sparkle and blind you, and big tables set, with white Sabbath bread, good, white Sabbath bread, sweet-smelling."

A third child took up the theme. "Me too, me too! I can see the tables. They're handing up fish, they're cutting big pieces of sponge cake. I want some, I want some."

"No, no bread, and no cake, only booths and singing," responded Joey. "There's no eating and no hunger; there's only singing."

"Where? Where?" asked Isaac, desperately. "I see no tables, no booths, no bread, no cake."

"But I do! I see a great big baked fish, it's so big it's everywhere! Nothing but fish!"

"Go beyond!" whispered Joey. "Beyond that! Till you reach the singing on the blue water." Then he became silent, and his rapt face, with closed eyes, was fixed on the moon.

The Mother's Reward

THE four sides of the square-shaped marketplace consisted of little white-washed houses. The one opposite the well was the bakery; a thick cloud of smoke issued from its chimney and spread a veil between the marketplace and the blue sky. White pigeons flew through the veil, and at the door of the bakery stood a tall youth and whistled to the pigeons.

On the other side of the well the women had their "stands," doors laid on trestles, and on the stands were displayed fruits and vegetables. The women wore shawls and kerchiefs even on the hottest days; and their faces were tired with years of waiting.

At this moment two of the women were quarreling.

"I don't know why I take the trouble to talk to a piece of dirt like you! You low-down washerwoman, you! You haven't a kopeck to your name!"

Yente, a hardfaced woman of some forty-odd years, uttered the words venomously, flapped her dirty apron with both hands, as if she were shaking off an unclean thing.

"And you?" called back Toibe, to whom the words were addressed. "Do you think you've got hold of God Almighty's beard? You'll get yours, don't you worry." And Toibe the widow shoved her kerchief up over her head, as if preparing for battle.

A customer approached Yente's stand, and Toibe, who stood idle, continued to curse.

"What's the good of all your dirty money? When you die there won't even be a dog to say a prayer over you."

The Mother's Reward

There was a bitter implication in these words, as both women knew. Toibe was referring to her own son Isaac and reminding the other of her childlessness. Realizing that she had gone too far, and that to boast of her children was to invite the evil eye, Toibe became silent.

"Oh, yes!" cried Yente, measuring out a quart of pears for her customer, but keeping her eyes fixed on Toibe. "And if you hadn't been the kind of thing you are, your husband wouldn't be dead, and your son wouldn't be ashamed of you. Because everybody knows he's ashamed of you."

Toibe crimsoned with rage.

"Liar!" she screamed. "My son isn't ashamed of me. And how dare you mention him? Your lips are too dirty to utter his name!"

She was on the verge of tears, and it was only by an extreme effort of will that she kept them back, lest the other should have the satisfaction of seeing her weep. But she said no more, and the other, knowing that the shaft had gone home, also held her tongue.

Evening drew on. Jews hastened across the marketplace toward the synagogue alley. Boys returning from the Hebrew school gathered about the well.

Toibe picked up her baskets of fruit and vegetables. She left the stand where it was—no one would bother to steal it—and muttering a last curse under her breath she turned homeward.

She could not get Yente's poisonous words out of her mind—those about her son. What Yente had said concerning her husband, that he had died because of her, had not touched her at all. The whole village knew how she had tended him, slaved for him and over him. But that remark about her son being ashamed of his own mother rankled deep. Because, more than once, she had brooded over the fact that when her Isaac came home nights he seldom touched the food she had prepared for him.

"Father in heaven," she panted, as she struggled along under her burden, "choke her with that lie."

It seemed to her at this moment that it would never have occurred to her that her son was ashamed of his mother if Yente had not put the idea in her head.

63

"My son, my Isaac!" she went on. "What business has she to mention his name?" And she raised her voice in a wail: "Father in heaven! They call you the help of widows, the guardian of orphans. Remember me, remember my son. And remember that woman and punish her as she deserves!"

"Toibe! Toibe! Whom are you cursing so?"

Neche, the rich merchant's wife, was standing at the door of her shop; it was she who called out the question to Toibe.

"Whom should I be cursing, dear lady, if not that loud-mouth, that Yente?" answered Toibe, without even lifting her head.

Trudging on, Toibe remembered how that same morning she had entered Neche's house by the back door and had delivered a hen to the kitchen. For on this day of the week her Isaac took his meals with Neche's children; every day of the week he ate with another householder, according to the custom. And Toibe had brought them a hen, so that her Isaac would have chicken soup. He was so weak, he needed a good, nourishing, strengthening soup. And standing in the kitchen, the slaughtered hen still in her hand, she had heard her son's voice on the other side of the wall. Her Isaac was arguing with the children of Neche, the rich merchant's wife; he was arguing with them about a point in a holy book, and very clearly he was having the better of the argument. She knew that at once. And why shouldn't he have the better of the argument? Who was there among the children of Neche, or for that matter in the whole village, to compare with her Isaac? Standing thus in the kitchen, her heart full, she had said to herself: "I'd better go away, lest they come in here and see me. A fine picture for my Isaac! His mother, the market-woman, standing in the kitchen with a hen!" And then again she had thought, in a surge of pride: "I've never been able to spend a kopeck on him, and he outshines them all! How much money hasn't Neche spent on her children! If I had what my Isaac's learning should have cost, I'd be a rich woman!" So she remained standing, listening ecstatically to her Isaac's dominating voice. "If only *he* were here, and heard that voice! He would get up from his bed a strong man!"

She stood there so long that at last the door opened, and the children saw her—Neche's children, and her own Isaac. Isaac's cheeks flamed.

"Good morning!" he said to his mother, in a weak voice, before the door closed again.

She knew she had done wrong. She should not have embarrassed her boy like that. But how could she help it? It was her son, her Isaac; he had fed at her breast. Who were Neche's children, to come between her and her son?

All this Toibe remembered as she neared her home, and she poured out the bitterness that was in her on the absent Yente's head, because Yente had dared to say that Isaac was ashamed of his mother.

"God!" she said aloud, "take up my quarrel with her, and punish her as she deserves, this very night, before morning comes!"

It was dark by the time Toibe reached her house. She dragged herself up the steps and opened the door. An outburst of children's voices greeted her out of the darkness. "Mama! Mama! It's mama! Mama, where have you been so long?"

The single room that was home to Toibe and her children was filled with smoke and dust. Toibe put down her burden at the door, and cried:

"Quiet! Let me catch my breath."

For a minute or two she stood still, and panted, while the children clustered about her, some laughing, some crying. When she had come to, she lit the lamp on the mantelpiece, and the darkness retreated a little distance toward the corners of the room. Now one could see the dust-covered sewing machine (all that her husband, the tailor, had left her) and one half of the bed. The bed was covered with straw, on which lay various fruits and vegetables, part of Toibe's stock. The remainder of the room lay in darkness, beyond the reach of the feeble rays of the lamp.

Less than two years had passed since the death of Lazar the tailor; but it was much more than two years since Toibe had been the sole support of the family. What had she not done? In whose home had she not worked? Month after month she had watched her husband's decline, hearing his cough become dryer and harder, seeing his eyes sink deeper into his head, before the light died out of them for ever.

In those closing days, when the last illusion of hope was gone—whether they admitted it or not—Lazar the tailor had one consolation, his oldest son, Isaac. Isaac had a good head; he was cut out to be a scholar. Some day he might achieve fame. Lazar the tailor could feel that he had not lived in vain. The son that would say the *Kaddish* for him would plead the cause of the dead father in the courts of heaven.

When Lazar died at last, the leading householders of the village met and took council as to what should be done. They collected a little money to set up the widow in business; and they honored Lazar's dying wish in regard to his gifted son. Isaac was taken into the school of the synagogue, and his days were portioned out among the well-to-do householders, according to the ancient custom. Every day he ate with another family, so that he could give his time to his studies.

It did Toibe's heart good to know that her son ate daily at the tables of the rich, where the best was served. He was a weak child; he needed something more than she could offer. But she suffered, too. Her son was everywhere a stranger. And she did not know whether, in the long run, it was a good thing or a bad.

Sitting one morning at her stand in the marketplace, she saw her Isaac go into the house of Sundel the wheat merchant, for his breakfast. The sight of it stabbed her, and she turned to Yente, with whom she was then on good terms, for it was soon after Lazar's death, and everyone was kind to her, and said:

"Yente, believe me, I just don't know what to think. Why should I have anything in my heart against those rich people? They've done nothing but good to me and to my Isaac. They've given him a place at their tables, they treat him like one of their own children, and not a bit as if he were the son of an ordinary marketwoman. And yet every time I give my children supper, I set a plate for Isaac, and when I remember that he doesn't eat in my house, I cry like a child."

"Silly woman!" answered Yente, scolding her in a friendly way.

66

"Would you really prefer to have him eat with you? Much good that would do him! What can we offer our children, God help us?"

"Yes, yes, Yente, I know you're right. But every time I cut bread for the children, and not for Isaac, it's as if I were cutting my heart."

And it was still the same, though she had had two years of it. She still had to hold back her tears this evening as she served the other children, and she still could not help feeling that the rich people, with their goodness and kindness, were robbing her of her child.

When she had put the children to bed she seated herself near the lamp and by its feeble light mended a shirt for Isaac.

Before long the door opened, and her son came in. Isaac was a tall, thin boy of fourteen. His white, serious, almost stern face stood out against his black gaberdine and his black cap.

"Good evening," he said, quietly.

His mother moved away from the table, to make room for him. She felt that her son was entitled to respect, though she could not have said why. More clearly, however, she felt that she, with her poverty and her low occupation, was a calamity for her son.

Isaac sat down at the table, opened a book, and read. His mother turned up the wick of the lamp and wiped the glass with her apron.

"Will you have a cup of tea, son?" she asked in a low voice.

"Thank you. I've just had one."

"Or perhaps an apple."

He did not answer. Toibe wiped a plate, put on it two apples and a knife, and pushed it over toward her son. Very slow, very deliberately, just like a grown-up man absorbed by his thoughts, Isaac peeled the fruit, made the benediction, and ate. Toibe, seeing him eat something she had prepared for him, felt nearer to him, more as if she were really his mother. She moved her chair closer to the table.

As he peeled the second apple Isaac spoke in a low, grave voice.

"I had a talk today with the Rabbi about my going away. Here in our synagogue study house there is nothing to do. We haven't the teachers. The Rabbi himself says as much. He advised me to try the Talmudical college at Mokeve. He said he would give me a letter to Reb Chaim, the head of the college, who's a good friend of his, and Reb Chaim would befriend me."

This was the first time that Isaac had ever mentioned the subject of his departure for another town, and a shock of fear passed through Toibe. But his grave way of talking, and the expressions he used—"the Talmudical college"—"the head of the college"—"befriend me," expressions which in the Yiddish retain their original Hebrew form, and have about them a ring of culture and piety— impressed her, and filled her with a vague fear. But as he went on talking she found a little reassurance. So far, after all, they had only been talking about it.

"Well, if that's the Rabbi's opinion," she said hesitantly, a pious look coming into her face.

"Yes," continued Isaac. "Over there, in the Mokeve academy, they have regular formal hours and lessons, with all the best commentaries. Reb Chaim, the head, is the author of 'The Glory of the Torah' and a celebrated scholar. At Mokeve a man can hope to become something."

The high words fell like a soothing balm on Toibe's heart. A sweet exaltation brought a new light into her eyes. This was her son, she was the mother of such a son, and were it not for her there would not be this Isaac in the world. But behind the exaltation something frightening stirred, a premonition of loss.

She remembered her husband, and tears began to flow down her cheeks.

"If he were only alive," she sobbed. "If he were only here to taste this joy."

Isaac kept his eyes steadily on the book.

．　．　．

It was only in the night, when she tried to compose herself for sleep, that the reality of Isaac's impending departure came home to her. A dreadful emptiness opened in her heart. Toward morning, between sleeping and waking, she had visions of processions of great Rabbis, with vast fur hats on their heads and long earlocks dangling down their cheeks, leading her Isaac away to a remote place. Her Isaac, too, wore a vast fur hat and had long earlocks like the Rabbis; he carried a thick, leather-bound book. She stood at a distance and watched him go away with the Rabbis, and she did not know whether she ought to be happy or whether she ought to weep.

She woke up later than usual the next morning. Isaac was gone. She gave the children their breakfast and hurried off to her stand in the marketplace. But because she had not slept well she was pursued into the day by a dreaminess which she could not shake off. She kept thinking of Isaac. She saw herself sitting, not at a wretched stand in a marketplace, but in the house of her son Isaac. He was a Rabbi in a great city. There he was, seated in his big leather chair; he had on good stockings and a stout pair of shoes. His head was covered by a rich fur hat. He held an open book in his hand, and read in it silently. She sat at his right hand and knitted a stocking. The door opened, and Yente the market-woman came in carrying a fowl; she was afraid there was a defect in the dead bird; she wanted the Rabbi to tell her whether the fowl was *kosher* or not.

A customer tore Toibe out of her day-dreams.

Night after night Toibe sat at the table in her one-room home and by the light of the smoking lamp mended and patched the linen which her Isaac would need in the new town. With every stroke of the needle she reflected that she was doing this for her Isaac; her Isaac was going away to study in a Talmudical college; there he would begin a great career; and every Friday he would put on a fresh shirt, which his mother had prepared for him.

Isaac himself sat on the other side of the table, his eyes glued on a book. His mother would have liked to say something to him, but she did not know what.

. . .

On the morning of the departure Toibe and Isaac rose before dawn. Isaac kissed his sleeping brothers; and to his sleeping sisters he only said, in a low voice, "Good-by, little sisters." One of them, Goldie, woke up suddenly, perceived at once that her brother was setting out on a journey, and began to cry. She wanted to come along. Toibe soothed her, lulled her to sleep, and then stole out of the house with Isaac.

The street still slept as they came out, Toibe carrying her son's heavy box. All the windows were shuttered. The brilliant morning star glittered above the steeple of the church and shimmered in the dew which lay on the roofs of the houses. Silence rested on the street and on the village. It was only when they came to the market-place that they saw the first signs of life. A peasant's cart had already arrived with the first load of fruit and vegetables. The market-women were gathered round the cart, and from a distance Toibe and Isaac heard Yente's shrill voice: "Five gulden and ten groschen for the whole load." And Toibe, carrying Isaac's box across the marketplace, straightened up, and as she passed Yente looked at her proudly and defiantly.

They went out of the village and took the road to Lentchitz; there Isaac would get a lift as far as Kutno. The sky began to grow gray above them. A cold, hard light filtered down through the low-hanging clouds, and a dewy mist went up from the fields to meet it halfway. The wide, curving road stretched away in front of them between silent fields. On the crossroads near Lentchitz they set down the box and waited for the diligence. Toibe took out a little bundle of coins from the pocket of her apron, and tied it around Isaac's neck. When the diligence arrived she bargained for a place on it for Isaac—forty kopecks as far as Kutno. She lifted the box on to the diligence.

"Good-by, my son. Don't forget your mother," she said, weeping. Isaac could not answer.

She would have liked to kiss her child, but she knew that it was not proper for a grown boy to be kissed in public, so she restrained herself. Isaac climbed on to the diligence and the passengers made room for him.

"Good-by, mother," he said at last, as the vehicle began to move.

"Good-by, son. Study hard and don't forget your mother," shouted Toibe.

She stood there, watching the diligence grow smaller and smaller.

Slowly it climbed up the little slope and disappeared on the other side. She kept on looking at the spot where the vehicle had disappeared. Only when several minutes had passed did she tear herself away and return to the village. But she did not go straight to the marketplace. She made a long detour, skirting the village till she came to the enclosure of the Jewish cemetery. A row of wooden palings separated the cemetery from the open field. The gate was locked, and Toibe could not force her way in. She managed, however, to thrust her head in between two palings, and her anxious eyes sought out the familiar little tombstone.

"Lazar! Lazar! Your son Isaac has gone away to the *Yeshivah* to study *Torah!*"

She waited till she was certain that the message had gone home, and only then did she bethink herself of the marketplace and the day's business. It was late. No doubt Yente had already supplied all of her, Toibe's, morning customers; but no matter. She had been busy with matters of high importance, and her spirit was at peace.

.   .   .

Two weeks later the first letter arrived from Isaac. Since she was unable to read, Toibe took the letter to Reb Jochanan, the Hebrew teacher, and asked him to read it out to her. Reb Jochanan put on his glasses, coughed impressively, and began:

"*L'imi ahuvati ha-tzenua—*"

"What is that, what is that?" asked Toibe, eagerly.

"It's Hebrew, of course. A title of respect for a mother."

Toibe's face was irradiated with joy. She put her apron to her eyes and wept. Reb Jochanan paid no attention, but went on reading in Hebrew.

"What's that? What is it?" sobbed Toibe.

"It's still Hebrew."

"But what does he say?"

"You wouldn't understand if I told you. It's a very neat little piece of Talmudic argument."

How wonderful! Toibe wept afresh, controlling her sobs so as not to lose a single syllable of the marvelous Hebrew words. Then,

71

toward the end of the letter, in plain, intelligible Yiddish, was added:

"I send my greetings to my beloved mother, to my sisters Sarah and Goldie, to my brothers Joseph and Jacob, and I bid my brothers to be attentive to their books and to study diligently."

Ah, that was good! Something she understood. Toibe took back the letter, folded it reverently, put it in her apron pocket, and went back to her stand. "Tonight," she said to herself, "I'll go to the Rabbi, and ask him to read the Hebrew part and explain it to me."

That evening after feeding the youngsters and putting them to bed, she rushed to the Rabbi's house. They admitted her to the study, where she saw long rows of books on shelves that reached to the ceiling, and the Rabbi himself, grave, white-bearded, seated in his arm chair.

"What is it?" asked the Rabbi. "A ritual question?"

"No."

"What is it, then?"

"A letter from my son, Isaac."

The Rabbi rose from his chair, came over slowly, took the letter, began to read it to himself.

"Excellent! Excellent!" he murmured, with a pleased look. "The boy will go far!"

The tears poured again down Toibe's cheeks. "If only *he* were alive!" she whispered.

"According to Maimonides, however . . ." the Rabbi murmured, reading from the letter, "while on the other hand the Tosaphists say—" He pulled down his brows. "Extraordinary!" he exclaimed.

"That's my Isaac," thought Toibe, "Isaac, the son of the ordinary market-woman, Toibe."

"Well, well," said the Rabbi at last. "Here's your letter. I've read it through."

"Yes—but—" stammered Toibe.

"But what?"

"What's in the letter?" she asked, in a low voice.

"Bless my soul!" said the Rabbi astonished. "These things are not for you." He smiled. "You would not understand them."

The Mother's Reward

• • •

Isaac's letters arrived regularly every fortnight. From one letter to the next the Yiddish section became shorter, the Hebrew section longer and weightier. Invariably Toibe took the letters to Reb Jochanan the teacher, and the same scene was re-enacted. Reb Jochanan read aloud the few Yiddish words of greeting, keeping the Hebrew for himself.

One day she brought a letter to Reb Jochanan, who read it with great absorption, and said nothing.

"Nothing for you," he said at last.

"How can that be?"

"That's how it is. There's nothing for you."

"Please, read me whatever there is."

"It's all in Hebrew. You wouldn't understand."

"So I won't understand."

"Good woman," said Reb Jochanan, patiently, "I haven't time for that nonsense."

That evening she went to the Rabbi.

"Rabbi, won't you please translate this letter for me?"

The Rabbi read the letter through to himself and shook his head.

"It isn't for you," he said.

"Rabbi," pleaded Toibe, timidly, "just translate the Hebrew words for me."

"It's Talmud, difficult Talmud. You wouldn't understand."

"Then please read the Hebrew words for me, in Hebrew, so I can hear what he writes."

"You won't understand a word," said the Rabbi, smiling.

"So I won't understand," answered Toibe.

The Rabbi thought a moment, shrugged, and began to read. The strange haunting syllables sent a thrill through Toibe. She strained her ears, as if by greater attentiveness she could penetrate to the meaning of the words.

The Rabbi looked up and was startled. He stopped reading and handed her the letter.

"There now, that's enough," he said, compassionately.

73

Toibe went out, thinking: "It's my Isaac's letter, it's my Isaac's learning in it. Why shouldn't I hear what he writes, even if I don't understand?"

When she came home she took down the lamp from its hook and set it on the table. She sat down, took out the letter, and looked at it long and earnestly. Then she lifted it to her lips and kissed it, but immediately she regretted the act, as a desecration. A letter filled with such holy learning ought not to be touched by the lips of an ordinary, sinful woman.

She went over to the bookcase and took out the prayer book of her dead husband. She opened it, added this letter to the others which were already there, closed the prayer book and replaced it. Then she sat down at the table and looked at the bookcase.

The Lucky Touch

HE was a quiet, unobtrusive man; when he spoke you hardly heard him, and when he passed you hardly noticed him, though he was tall and broad-built. His face was lightskinned and covered with freckles; the big yellow beard ended up in two points, like a fish's tail. He reminded you of a fish in other ways, too; the pallor of his skin, for instance, which suggested perpetual immersion in water.

He was one of the most goodnatured men that ever lived, incapable of saying "No." You only had to ask a favor of him, and, if it was possible, he granted it.

Such was Reb Nachman Weinberg, on whom God had conferred "the lucky touch."

Here is how it all began.

Year after year the people in the village played the state lottery. Every one bought a ticket, elderly respectable Jews with shops on the main street, women who kept stalls in the marketplace, young men ready for military service, girls preparing for marriage. If a young man or a girl could not buy a whole ticket, two of them—sometimes three or four—clubbed together to buy part of a ticket. The well-to-do gambled on the "Big Winner," the 75,000 rouble stakes; others were content with "Eighths," or fragments of eighths. As far as the village knew, only one person had ever won anything and that a minor prize; but the playing of the lottery went on earnestly and undiscourageably.

And then, one night in the early summer, round Pentecost time, when everyone was fast asleep, there came a sound of running feet and of a great panting. Boruch Shpiliter, the lottery dealer and collector, waving a telegram and trying to shout something, stopped at the door of Reb Nachman Weinberg.

"Reb Nachman! Reb Nachman!" he gasped, and with a last supreme effort, he added: "It's the Seventy-fiver!" And with that he fell in a dead faint.

They brought him round in a few minutes. But they had a harder job with Reb Nachman Weinberg, who lay in a coma for three days and nights after getting the good news. It was touch and go with him.

The news spread the same night; and on the following morning, after prayers, half of the village collected in Reb Nachman Weinberg's house. Men, women, and children came; relatives of Reb Nachman, friends, acquaintances and even enemies. Sponge cake and drinks were passed round, the benediction was made, toasts were drunk, good wishes exchanged. Only the lucky man himself lay moaning; the village healer was sent for; he recommended cold compresses, smelling salts, rest and quiet.

On the fourth day Reb Nachman rose from his bed and accompanied the collector to Warsaw.

At the bank it was made clear to Reb Nachman and the collector that the number in question did not represent a "Seventy-fiver" but an "Eighth" of a "Seventy-fiver." Moreover, as Reb Nachman suddenly recalled, he had sold a half interest in his "Eighth" to some visiting Jew; and that just one day before the drawing of the lottery. What remained with Reb Nachman was therefore a sixteenth part of a "Seventy-fiver"—enough, of course, to make him the richest Jew in the village, but not something to lie in a coma about for three days and three nights.

So it was easy enough to calculate exactly how much Reb Nachman was bringing home from Warsaw, even if the local Jews had not been the brilliant mathematicians they were: one half of one eighth, which made one sixteenth. They sat down with pencil and paper and had the answer in two minutes. For all that, everyone had the feeling that Reb Nachman was bringing home from Warsaw the wealth of the Indies and the Czar's crown to boot; nor was the impression diminished when it was learned that Lazar the smith was putting iron bars on Reb Nachman's doors and windows.

"Easy come, easy go." This ancient piece of folk wisdom must have been garnered through the ages from the lives and destinies of the Reb Nachmans. I do not know how other Reb Nachmans got rid of their unexpected wealth; this one, I can relate, was the center of a conspiracy of benevolence. There was not a Jew in the village who did not lie awake of nights thinking how he could double Reb Nachman's money for him. It was a sin, a shame, a scandal, an unthinkable and unpermissible state of affairs, that Reb Nachman, having brought back the big prize from Warsaw, should do nothing with it, when there was so much to be done. For instance, what was the matter with a chicory factory, asked one Jew of Reb Nachman. There was a great demand for chicory. Reb Nachman would provide the capital, the Jew would provide the brains and the initiative, and the money would come rolling in. Another, without denying the possibilities of a chicory factory, pointed to the need for a yeast factory. A third pooh-poohed these laborious enterprises and told Reb Nachman that there was a good forest to be bought up and resold—quick action, quick profits. A fourth suggested a general loan and banking business. Reb Nachman's door was open from morning till night; and Reb Nachman combed his forked yellow beard with his fingers, rubbed his brow, and listened. And since he was incapable of saying "No," but at worst returned a "Maybe," or "I'll think that over," he found himself, at the end of a year or two, without the slightest justification for the iron bars on doors and windows. The big prize was gone. Some of it was sunk in the chicory factory, some in the yeast factory; but the greatest part was lost in the forest, quite literally. For it appeared, after the Polish nobleman had sold his forest, and run off with the money, that the forest did not belong to him, but to his creditors. Reb Nachman Weinberg emerged from the series of transactions the same pauper as before the winning of the big prize, squeezing a wretched living out of his little drygoods store; actually it was a matter for some astonishment that Reb Nachman had not sold the store, or given it away, in the exciting days of his great transactions. But whether through oversight, or sheer habit, Reb Nachman retained the store. All there was left to show for the visitation of glory was the condition of Reb Nachman's heart, which had suffered irreparable injury from the shock of the good news.

That, and one thing more: Reb Nachman's reputation as the child of good fortune.

For ever since that unforgettable night the village looked upon Reb Nachman as "the man with the lucky touch." Reb Nachman had only to take a hand in an affair, and it would prosper. Even the "hand" was unnecessary. Reb Nachman had only to look at an affair, nod his approval, and it was giltedged. How could it be otherwise with the winner of "the big prize," the fabulous one-in-a-million?

Sometimes Reb Nachman, walking thoughtfully from the marketplace toward the synagogue, as evening was falling, would feel a slight tug at his gaberdine; and turning round he would catch a woman, who had apparently slipped toward him from a side alley, furtively rubbing the tail of the gaberdine between forefinger and thumb. Hiding her face in her shawl, the woman would say, timidly:

"Excuse me, Reb Nachman. You're the man with the lucky touch, you know."

Then Reb Nachman would feel just as ashamed as the woman. He had nothing to say. He only hurried off lest he should recognize the woman.

When someone in the village fell sick and hope was given up, when the Rabbi had said "the good word" in vain, when Psalms had been recited, and the graves of the pious visited, measured and invoked in the local cemetery, without the sick man getting any better, when the village healer had tried unguents, medicines, and leeches without results, they sent for "the man with the lucky touch." Whenever a marriage was celebrated, Reb Nachman had to be there; his presence would ensure the permanence and happiness of the union. No plates were broken to the cry of "good luck" at a betrothal, without Reb Nachman to look on and approve and drink a toast. Once it happened that a sceptic neglected to ensure the presence of Reb Nachman at his daughter's betrothal (Reb Nachman was at a sickbed and the sceptic would not wait); and sure enough, at the end of a month, the young couple quarreled and the match came to nothing.

But Reb Nachman's reputation was highest for one kind of service: the easing of labor pains. They said of him, everywhere, that he had only to show himself near the bedside of a woman who was having a hard time of it, and the child would come out into the world of its own accord.

At what point in his career Reb Nachman was discovered to be the specific for childbirth, and why it was in this—or any other—field that he sustained his reputation, let no one ask. It is only certain that after the discovery the hope of a peaceful life deserted Reb Nachman for ever.

Reb Nachman would be sitting in his store, biting his beard and looking for ways and means of obtaining fresh credits, when a woman would burst in, all tears and supplication.

"Reb Nachman, good, dear, kind Reb Nachman, my daughter-in-law has been struggling and suffering these last two days. It won't budge. Good Reb Nachman, won't you please, please come over?"

"But what can I do?" Reb Nachman pleaded. "Am I a midwife?"

"Look at him!" the woman cried, turning instantaneously from supplication to denunciation. "God gave him the lucky touch, and he grudges it to a sufferer! Will it cost you anything to walk over to my house?"

What could Reb Nachman, being the man he was, do about it? He would put on his coat, pick up his walking stick, and accompany the woman.

On one such occasion Reb Nachman held out in a manner quite alien to him and yielded at last to the pressure of half the village. The woman had been lying in torment for three days; Reb Nachman had almost to be dragged from his shop. Arriving at the house of the expectant mother, he was conducted into the room adjoining hers; they gave him a chair, put cake and whisky on the table before him, withdrew, and locked the door.

An hour went by, a second and a third. Evening was drawing on. Reb Nachman thought of his shop, thought of the synagogue, and of his family. He went to the door and knocked.

"Well? Anything happening?" he shouted.

"A little while longer, good Reb Nachman. Just a little while, God bless you," they answered through the door.

The little while expanded into the night. They brought Reb Nachman's supper from his home, carried it into the room, retreated, and locked the door again. There was no help for it; the man with the lucky touch had to stay where he was. When half the night was gone Reb Nachman, exhausted with the burden of his responsibility, knocked weakly at the door.

"Chaya Sarah, how about it?"

"Dear Reb Nachman, what can we do? We daren't let you go. God will help soon, for your sake." But they did not open the door, lest Reb Nachman make a dash for freedom.

Toward morning, while he was dozing in his chair, they opened the door, threw in a cushion and a quilt, and closed the door hastily again. Reb Nachman woke, picked up cushion and quilt, and tried to make himself comfortable for the remainder of the night.

Late in the day the great moment came. The child emerged successfully into the world of man, and Reb Nachman emerged tottering from his prison.

"See?" the woman crowed, triumphantly. "What would we have done without your lucky touch?"

Reb Nachman flew into a rage, or, rather, he came as near it as his nature permitted.

"Leave me alone!" he wept. "There's no more lucky touch about me. I'm the same pauper as I used to be, the same miserable, hopeless, useless pauper. No more lucky touch! No more lucky touch!"

And he crawled out of the house, clutching at his weak heart, the one thing left to him of "the big prize."

God's Bread

THERE once lived in a certain town two bakers, one rich and one poor. The rich one was of course a distinguished householder, one of the notables of the town, a man of learning, the follower of a great Rabbi. The poor one was simple, obscure, and unlettered. The rich one baked for his own kind, that is, for the other rich people—great, white twisted loaves, tasty rolls shining with oil, and the special bread of the Sabbath and the holy days. The poor one baked for his kind, too, for penniless laborers, for peddlers who carried their packs into the villages, and for peasants. So it fell out that the rich baker never had occasion to use his trade for the performance of good deeds. He forgot that there were such as needed bread and could not buy it or could buy it only by the sweat of their brows. The wealthy householders whom he supplied with his produce always paid him on time; no one ever owed him anything, and never was he asked for a favor. But the poor baker was the daily witness of the want and poverty of his customers. A woman from a neighboring street, or a peasant from the village, would come into his bakery and look long and earnestly at the loaves of bread, would think long and earnestly before digging down for the last few coppers. Sometimes his customers were short of a groschen or two to make the purchase, and the baker, knowing what their life was like, would give them the bread nevertheless.

When a rich family arranged a marriage, or celebrated a circumcision, it was of course *their* baker who supplied the cakes, rolls, loaves, pastries, cookies, and other baked delicacies, for he knew how to prepare the bread of the rich. He used only the finest white flour, with the best fresh eggs; and he besprinkled the loaves with the sweetest poppyseed. His loaves shone like the sun. The poor baker had no occasion to bake a costly loaf of delicate white flour. His bread was thick, coarse, and black, compounded of corn-meal and rye, and heavy, like the lot and food of the poor every-where; and what he had learned in his apprenticeship of the finer kind of baking he gradually forgot, from lack of practice.

A famous Rabbi, a wonder worker and a descendant of a dynasty of wonder workers, whose name was uttered with awe wherever Jews congregated and whose followers were legion, came to settle in this town. He made his home, as was to be expected, in the house of the richest Jew, one of the customers of the rich baker; and when Sabbath was approaching the proud and happy house-holder told the rich baker to prepare him twelve pairs of Sabbath loaves, such as the town had never seen before.

The whole town spoke of the twelve loaves over which the great Rabbi would utter the benediction on the forthcoming Sabbath and which would be served at the Sabbath meal. The rich baker sought out the finest meal and put into the labor all the skill at his command; and before the loaves were delivered he dis-played them in the window of his bakery, and Jews came from every corner of the town to admire his handiwork.

The poor baker heard of all this, and his heart bled in him, because he too wanted to be represented at the table of the great Rabbi. But he had never baked for the rich, and his bread was the bread of the poor. Nevertheless, he made up his mind that he would bring half a dozen loaves to the table of the Rabbi, in order that the benediction might be said over them and that they might be eaten at the feast while the Rabbi edified the assembly with words of learning and piety. He chose, from his poor store, the best flour he had, and he put into the baking whatever he remembered out of the days of his apprenticeship. What was lack-ing in the quality of the ingredients and in the skill of his labor, he sought to make up in devotion. He kneaded the dough lovingly, put the loaves in the oven, and watched tremblingly that they should be neither raw nor overdone; he smeared the tops of the loaves with the white of egg and sprinkled poppyseed on them, and when everything was ready he carried his offering to the house in which the Rabbi would celebrate the Sabbath.

There was laughter in the kitchen of the rich man when the poor baker came with his half dozen loaves. "What? He too brings bread for the Rabbi?" they asked. And they turned him away, saying that his loaves were unfit for the feast, and that an un-lettered man such as he did not merit the attention of the Rabbi.

The man went home broken-hearted, carrying with him his re-jected gift, and, being indeed unlettered, he bethought himself that if the Rabbi would not take his bread for the Sabbath feast, per-haps God would. For he believed that God too needed loaves on His table for the Sabbath feast. Late that night, then, he stole into the street of the synagogue and, having looked round carefully to make certain he was not observed, he broke into the synagogue, went up to the Ark, and opened the doors, saying:

"God, O God, I have baked six loaves for You, for Your Sabbath table. Take them and use them, and do not shame me."

And with that he closed the Ark and went home.

There lived in this same town an old tailor, a man of great piety and no possessions. All his life he had earned his daily bread with the ten fingers of his hands. But he had not eaten his daily bread; he and his wife had made it a practice to all but fast from week end to week end and to save his earnings for the celebra-tion of the Sabbath. From Sunday to Friday they went short of food; but on Friday morning the tailor's wife went out into the marketplace and bought the best piece of meat in the butcher's shop, the handsomest loaf on the baker's stall. She also bought many candles, so that on the eve of the Sabbath her poor home shone like the home of a prince. There were many who, not know-ing how the hunger of a week went into the preparation of the Sabbath, were amazed and angry at the wife of the tailor and behind her back spoke sneeringly of her extravagance, especially when she outbid a rich buyer for the best-looking morsel on the butcher's block. But the tailor had made up his mind that, being too poor to observe all the commandments of God, he would concentrate on the observance of one of them, and he picked out the commandment to keep the Sabbath day holy and to make it a day of rest and rejoicing. He said; "On this day, which is God's day, I will forget all poverty, all pain and all humiliation; I will rejoice, even as the Law enjoins, in the beauty and peace of the Sabbath, and no memory of the week's want shall disturb my repose."

As the tailor grew older he found it harder and harder to observe the one commandment which he had singled out for his special devotion, for his hands began to tremble and he worked slowly; his eyes were dimmed, and he could no longer undertake the tasks which brought better pay. Therefore he could not prepare for the Sabbath as he had always been wont to do, except by selling, one after the other, the few things that stood in his home. But he sold them, one after the other. For, besides his determination to make the Sabbath his province, he had also taken a vow not to make his Sabbath an object of charity. He would ask help of no man of flesh and blood but would depend on God, and on God alone, for the means to carry out his resolve.

The time came when the last of his household things were gone and his earnings of the week, which he and his wife had saved, did not suffice even for the purchase of the Sabbath bread. Late on Thursday night, when he had been wont to give his wife the week's money to make her purchases for the Sabbath, he left the house and stole into the street of the synagogue. Having looked round carefully to make certain he was not observed, he broke into the synagogue and went up to the Ark, and laying hold of the doors of the Ark he said:

"God, O God, You know that as long as I could work and earn something, I saved whatever I made for the proper celebration of Your Sabbath. Now I am old, and my eyes are darkened, and my fingers tremble, and I can earn no more. And I have put my trust in You and have not turned to man of flesh and blood for succor. So I implore You, send me at least the loaves for the celebration of the Sabbath. For the rest of the week we will live, my wife and I, on crusts and water; but help us to observe Your commandment to keep the Sabbath day holy."

With that he opened the doors of the Ark, and there, at the foot of the Scrolls, lay half a dozen loaves of Sabbath bread, fresh, crisp, and warm, as if they had just been sent down from the heavenly bakery. They were shiny with divine oil and fragrant with divine poppyseeds.

The tailor knew at once that the loaves had been delivered from above in answer to his prayer. He gathered them up, stole out of the synagogue, and ran home with the gift to his wife.

Ever since then the custom continued in town. Every Thursday night the poor baker brought God's bread into the synagogue and deposited it in the Ark, and shortly thereafter the tailor would come and would pick up the Sabbath bread which God had sent down for him and his wife.

Before the tailor died he entrusted his secret to another Jew, as poor and as pious as he; and the baker continued to deliver, and God continued to take from him. As long as the baker lived and delivered his bread, there was peace and plenty in the town. No pestilence came near it; childbirths were easy; no fires broke out; and little children grew up strong and went gladly to school to learn the word of God.

They said everywhere that this was due to the loaves which the rich baker prepared for the Rabbi and over which the Rabbi made the Sabbath benediction before he sat down with his disciples to edify them with words of learning and piety.

The Carnival Legend

I

REB SAMUEL HORDES accompanied his daughter to the door. There was something he still wanted to say, but her look choked the words back. The girl had lowered her head, and her lips were tightened. The old Jew stood there, stroking his gray beard, then he turned back into the room, his last admonition unuttered. Only when his daughter had passed into the night, accompanied by her brother, who carried the lantern, Reb Samuel muttered: "Lord God of the universe: suffer this too to come before Thee, the shame which Thy young children bear without complaint for the glory of Thy Name."

The girl, carrying a bundle of silk, needles, hooks, and silver thread, walked quietly by the side of her brother through the narrow streets of the Roman ghetto. A bright moon shone overhead, and the lantern which her brother carried was intended rather to proclaim her status than to light her steps; for it was not considered proper for a bride to walk alone at night and without an honorable escort, who, with his lamp, was also a herald: "Behold, a bride walks!" Without a word to each other, they traversed the Octavia Alley, where, according to the tradition, Titus was received by the Romans on his triumphant return from Jerusalem, and where a cross was now reared, with these proud words inscribed on it, in Hebrew: "O thou stiff-necked people, which hast turned thy back upon God's word."

This was not the first time that they had glanced at these words, on the cross above the church: indeed, they could no longer have counted the Sabbath afternoons on which they had been driven by the guardians of the ghetto into this same church, to hear, under compulsion, the sermons of the friars. But on this night, for some reason they could not have named, the inscription on the church cross smote on their hearts with unaccustomed force so that they held their breath until the church was far behind them. Silently they walked side by side till they came to the house of Reb Joseph. The brother would not enter. He knew that his own bride was inside, and he was disinclined to face her at such a moment. He knocked, and when footsteps were heard he said good night and withdrew as silently as he had come.

In the large main room of Reb Joseph's house were assembled the daughters of the most distinguished Jewish families in Rome. By the light of innumerable little oil lamps they worked with gold and silver and purple thread on costly tapestries of red silk.

There was no cry of greeting at the entrance of Reb Samuel's daughter such as would have been heard on another occasion. There was no exchange of friendly words. The girl nodded lightly at her brother's bride, who had lifted her dark Spanish-Jewish face from her embroidery frame, glided to her chair, and, sitting down by an oil lamp, began to work on the head of a lion, the feet of which were being embroidered by one of her friends. The labor proceeded in silence, not as when young girls, filled with the laughter and joy of the bridal years, sit together and compete in the preparation of love gifts for their grooms, but as when old crones sit together in a night of pestilence sewing the shrouds which will be needed before sunrise.

For this was a labor of slavery and shame. The Jewish brides of Rome were beautifying the tapestries which were to adorn, on the morrow, the Arch of Titus, the arch which was erected in ancient days when the Roman returned from the conquest of Jerusalem. Through this arch the Procession of the Holy Father would pass on the first day of the Carnival; and the Holy Father would put his foot on the head of the elder of the Jewish community of Rome, who would come to him bearing the Holy Scroll. And the candelabrum and the shew-bread table, hewn out in the walls of the arch, would look down from among the tapestries woven by the Jewish daughters of Rome, and would endure with the dignity proper to their age and origin the insults of the gentile.

So they worked, permitting no word to intrude on the protest of their silence.

But before the night was far gone there was an interruption. The overseer of the Carnival was announced. Addressing himself to no one, he strode into the room, went from table to table, lifted the draperies in his hand, assayed the weight and workmanship. The fathers of the girls stood in the doorway, in order that their daughters might not be left alone with the gentile, which the law forbade, but not daring to enter lest they give occasion for anger.

The overseer threw down one piece after another. His face clouded over, but he lacked the arrogance to vent his savagery on the young women, who, in their black silken robes adorned with pearls, looked like captive princesses. He therefore turned to the men in the doorway and burst out: "Jewish thieves! What swindle is this you would perpetrate on us, with such material and such thread?"

Giving them no time to answer, he strode to the door. "If you will not get me better draperies for the Arch of Titus, I shall tear down the curtains of the Arks in your synagogues and strip the Scrolls of their mantles, and use them for the celebration."

"But see, these are the best obtainable—" they began.

"You have time until the first bell of St. Peter's!" he snarled, and was gone.

The girls sat motionless, needle in hand. Some of them looked down, others at the men, still others at the window; but they did not dare to look at each other. The fathers in the doorway were also silent. There was one thought in all of them.

At last the oldest of the fathers, Reb Joseph, the master of the house, found speech:

"Daughters! The honor of our prayer houses and our Scrolls is in your hands. Do what you think best."

The Carnival Legend

The daughter of the house, the bride of Leah's brother, rose from her stool and went to her room. She opened the chest which held her bridal trousseau and took from it a black velvet cover. On the velvet was embroidered a design, the Wailing Wall of the Holy City and four cedar trees. The outlines of the Wailing Wall were done in golden thread, the leaves of the trees in clouded silver, and the whole was enclosed in a wreath of vine leaves in silver and purple. Three years she had worked on this cover, in which the prayer shawl of her husband to be would be handed to him on the wedding day. Her bridal dreams were in the cunningly woven lines; her tears had darkened the colors; her laughter had brightened them. Uttering no word of complaint, she brought this gift, this gift of gifts, the symbol of her dedication, into the room, and laid it on the table.

So it was that evening. Every girl in the room went home and brought back with her the most precious of her possessions, the container of her bridegroom's prayer shawl, or the matzoh cover which was prepared for her new home, and laid it on the table side by side with the others, in order that they might all be made into a tapestry to adorn the arch of the conqueror of Jerusalem.

II

In the same night the heavy gates of St. Peter's swung open, and the Jew of the city of Nazareth, which is in Galilee, climbed down from his cross on the eastern wall and went out of the church. The wound in his side was covered by the sheet of Joseph of Arimathea. So clad, he wandered through the streets of Rome. He did not wear on his back the yellow badge, the sign of his people, and therefore the watchmen of the city did not molest him, though the gates of the ghetto had long been closed and he, a Jew, had no right to be outside the gates after the ringing of the bell. Nor were there many to mark his passing, for those Romans who were awake were busy putting the last touches on the masks and costumes which they would wear at the Carnival. They were not aware of the presence of the Man-God in their midst; they did not know he had left his accustomed place on the eastern

wall of the church. His sheet glimmered palely as he slipped
through the great columns of the Square of St. Peter. Unnoticed
he passed by the ancient synagogue over against the Colosseum
and heard the lamentations from within. He caught the words of
their prayer, in which they supplicated the Almighty to be with
them on the next day, the first Carnival Sunday, so that their
humiliations might be fewer; and above all they implored their
Father in heaven that the Holy Father might be gracious to them,
and, when he put his foot on the head of the elder of the Jews,
might not kick the Scrolls of the Law to the ground. The moon
hung over the vast, ancient ruin, as if it could not find the way
out. It seemed to the Jew of Nazareth that here, under the shat-
tered walls of the Colosseum, he could still catch the last cries
of those who, long ago, dying in the jaws of the wild beasts, had
called upon him.

The Man-God crossed the city and reached the Augustus Gate
which led into the country. On the other side of the gate, cur-
tained by the night, he came upon the figure of the Messiah,
seated on a stone, and chained with both feet to the wall of the
city. He held a trumpet in one hand; the cruse of oil was at his
side; and, so sitting, he waited for the word of God to sound the
call to the liberation. His eyes were fixed on the ground and the
high, steely forehead glimmered down the length of the Via
Appia. To him the Man-God said:

"I have come to thee, O Messiah. Forgive me for that which
they do in my name."

The eyes of the Messiah remained fixed on the earth.

"Did I not come to you? Would I not have gathered you under
my wings as a hen gathereth her brood? Did I not shed my blood
for you in the presence of my Father? To whom else did I go?
Was I not always to be found in your prayer houses, and did I
not spread my word in your courts? And when you turned from
me strangers came; they tore the sheet from my body and made
themselves banners. They dipped the banners in my blood, and
with these before them, and my name on their lips, they spread
desolation among my brothers. My word of peace they have dis-

90

torted into a war cry; the forgiveness I proclaimed they have turned into vengeance. The young men of my people have been harnessed to the chariot and their brides, my sisters, shamed unto death."

The eyes of the Messiah remained fixed on the earth.

"They have seated themselves upon my chair, to gorge and swill and rule over the earth. See, they utter in my name words which I did not speak; they have not comforted the lowly; they have not wiped away the tears of those that suffer. They add their oppression to those that are oppressed, and they crawl at the feet of the mighty. O ye strangers, who has given you the right to enter into judgment between brother and brother? You knew not and know not my pain, you understood not and understand not now my sorrow."

Still the eyes of the Messiah remained fixed on the earth.

"Here, by thy side, I will take my place upon a stone. Let my limbs, like thine, be chained to the wall of the city. Let my eyes, too, be fixed on the earth. With my brothers and sisters I will bear all suffering and humiliation, for my soul is weary of their songs of praise. For they bow down to my image, and have forgotten my word. Here I will sit with thee and wait for the day which God has appointed, and thou wilt blow thy trumpet to assemble the peoples under the hill of God. Then, like the shepherd who brings water to his sheep in the heat of the day, I will bring together my flock, I will warm those that are frozen, and I will make whole those whom the lions have rent and the dogs bitten. I will wipe away the tears of the unhappy, and lift up the broken of spirit, for then I will be with them and my words will live in them."

III

The moment of the "races" had come. The narrow Corso, lined from of old with the dignified houses of the patricians, was a sea of Persian hats and Turkish bonnets. The balconies were crowded with the noblest *signori* and *signore* of Rome, clad in wild and dissolute robes and masks. From the Arcade at one end to the San

Marco church at the other fluttered innumerable, multicolored
tapestries, bannerets, and gonfalons. The heads of the watchers on
the balconies and of the rabble in the street were adorned with
wreaths of flowers. The Carnival police, barefoot, but wearing
crimson uniforms and particolored hats, labored to make a path
for the runners. Along this Corso, in pre-Christian days, the young
men of the noblest families of Rome ran naked, in the wildness
of their spirits, from meta to meta, and the loveliest daughters
of Rome flung themselves in their path to distract them; along
this same Corso, under the eyes of the multitude and of the Holy
Father, who sat in the window of the meta, now ran eight gray-
bearded old Jews, whipped on by Carnival police on horseback.
The Jews were naked, except for light shirts; their bare, crooked
legs and their sagging stomachs—they had been forced to eat
heavily before the "course"—evoked the wild laughter of the
watching Romans; and the laughter became a madness when,
in a gesture of helpless shame, the old men tried to cover up their
nakedness and, being whipped and prodded from behind, fell
down and rolled over on the ground. The men and women on
the balconies cheered the competitors on, the crowd closed behind
the last runner and urged him to catch up with the others. They
ran, deafened by the clamor, stung by the whips of the riders,
ran blindly, in confusion, sometimes in the wrong direction, ran
with the froth gathering on their lips, seeing neither houses nor
people, ran as in a dream, aware only of demons pursuing them,
ran till they came somehow to the meta of the San Marco church.
And then, as the race was closing, as the insane and uncontrollable
laughter of the spectators rose to a climax, an invisible hand
seemed to pass in a swift gesture across the multitude. Silence,
sudden and terrifying, blanketed the Corso. Hats were removed,
and the spectators swarming about the San Marco church flung
themselves to the ground, while on the balconies the noble *signori*
and *signore* fled to their rooms and slammed the windows to, or
dropped in terror to their knees. From end to end of the Corso,
bared heads and kneeling or prostrate figures.

He, the Man-God, had been among the runners, under the lash of the pursuers. At the very wall of the San Marco he turned his pale face to the multitude, and drew about his body the white sheet given him by Joseph of Arimathea. With cross uplifted he passed down the length of the Corso and disappeared.

From the Beyond

THE queer story of Boruch Mordecai happened quite a number
of years ago, exactly how many I could not say. He fell sick—
nobody seems to remember with what—and declined so rapidly
that they had to send for Solomon, the head of the burial brotherhood. Solomon entered the room, looked once at Boruch Mordecai,
and ordered the company to light candles and say Psalms. Boruch
Mordecai's wife let out a scream and began to tear her hair; the
children sent up a heartrending wail; half the village heard and
came crowding into the street—none of which did any good. For
when Solomon the burial man held a goose feather to Boruch
Mordecai's nose there was no sign of breath. It was all over—at
any rate, that is what everyone believed.

Solomon and an assistant lifted poor Boruch Mordecai from
the bed and placed him on the pile of straw on the floor. But no
sooner was Boruch Mordecai stretched out with the candles at
his feet, than he suddenly sneezed. In less time than you can count
ten, that house was empty, except for Boruch Mordecai; for everyone fled in terror, even Boruch Mordecai's wife; even Solomon
the burial man, who was used to dead people, more used to
them, in fact, than to the living. But he was not used to people
who were both dead and alive, and no such case had ever been
heard of in the village. When they crept back into the house, they
found Boruch Mordecai sitting up on the straw and looking round
him vaguely. He was repeating, in a weak voice:

"Sarah! Make me a bowl of grits."

94

Boruch Mordecai did not realize what had happened. It was only later, when he had become well, that they told him of the candles and the Psalms and the preparations for the burial. And then he actually remembered, not what had taken place about him, but his visit to the other world. He had been in heaven and had seen the Dark Angel, who consigns people to the other place. Yes, the Dark Angel had come up to him, up to Boruch Mordecai, and had asked him, "Well, what's your name?" as though he— the Dark Angel, that is—was already sure of his man. Indeed, he got hold of Boruch Mordecai by the lapel of his coat, as much as to say, "You come along ·with me." But at this point another angel, with white wings and a kind face, interfered. Boruch Mordecai was of the opinion that this was the archangel Gabriel but could not be sure. At any rate, Gabriel, or whoever else it was, called out: "Take it easy, there! No grabbing, if you don't mind. Because first of all we have to find out where this man belongs; which means that we have to hold a trial." And at a distance Boruch Mordecai saw people standing in cerements, with prayer-shawls over them; and all the people nodded approvingly at the archangel Gabriel.

"I guess," added Boruch Mordecai, reflectively, "those must have been my forefathers, pleading for me with their good deeds. I also saw my father, God's peace be with him, and my grandfather, Reb Chanan, who, as you know, was a great saint. My father, peace be upon him, even stretched out his hand to me in welcome. At least, I think he did. I can't remember it too clearly," went on Boruch Mordecai. "Because at this point someone, maybe the angel Gabriel, flicked me with his finger on my nose, and said: 'Boruch Mordecai, you're not wanted here yet.' And that's when I opened my eyes."

And having finished this recital Boruch Mordecai suddenly realized something, for he murmured, in another tone of voice:

"Bless us all! Doesn't that mean that I've already been in the beyond? I've been in the world after this!"

From that day on the Jews of the village began to treat Boruch Mordecai with a certain respect and even to fear him a little. A man who had been in the beyond! To some extent they even avoided him. If they saw him coming toward them on the same side of the street they crossed over; that is, if he had not seen them first, because it would not have done to offend him. And if they had to stop and speak to him, they said "Good morning" hurriedly and timidly, as if he was liable to fly into a rage, and they cut the conversation short and slipped away as quickly as they could.

Boruch Mordecai soon became aware of the respect, mingled with fear, which he inspired; and this filled him with a pride and self-confidence which he had never known before. He began to display a certain touchiness. If he wasn't called up to the reading of the Law in the synagogue to the point which he thought his due, if someone got in his way accidentally at the ritual baths, if someone fell foul of him in the marketplace, and offered a peasant a better price for a sack of grain or a bushel of potatoes, Boruch Mordecai would pull his belt tighter, and say, significantly:

"I don't stand for that sort of thing. I'm a man who's already been in the beyond, in the world after this."

Hearing the words "the beyond," and "the world after this," the offenders shrank back, muttering apologetically: "Why, Boruch Mordecai, I meant no harm; there's nothing to get angry about."

As time went on, Boruch Mordecai developed a possessive attitude toward "the beyond," as though his visit had given him prescriptive rights. He remembered the incident with increasing clarity; and when he heard that someone had died, had "gone to the other world," he would say with a shrug: "Oh, I've been there," and make a rather contemptuous gesture, as though he could not understand why people made such a fuss about it or even talked about it at all.

So, whether people wanted to listen or not, whether they tried to avoid him or not, Boruch Mordecai would insist on recounting the details of his visit. He would come upon a group sitting on the bench before the ritual baths in the cool of the evening or before the stove in the synagogue some winter afternoon, and he would begin to talk. The topography of "the other world" became clearer and clearer, his relations with the Dark Angel and with Gabriel more and more intimate. Also his own role increased and took on character.

"I wasn't a bit afraid of them," he said. "Take my word for it, a man who knows how to use his tongue doesn't have to be afraid of anybody. The main thing in life is to be able to stand up for your rights, and to speak up."

Thereupon he shifted his hat to the back of his head, poked his fingers into his dusty beard, scratched himself vigorously, and went into details.

"Lying there on the straw, after Solomon the burial man put me down, I kept saying to myself, 'Well, now, let's see what's going to happen.' And all of a sudden who do you think turns up, if not *he*—you know, the Dark One, the Dark Angel, the soul-snatcher—grabs me by the lapel, and asks me: 'Name, please.' Just like that, as if he already had me! I didn't answer him right away. So he tugs me, and says, 'Come along.' I suppose you think I was frightened. Not a bit of it. 'Listen, you,' I say to him, 'I don't doubt for a minute you're a very important sort of person, the Dark Angel himself and all that, and I guess it's your business to try to grab everybody who turns up in these parts and cart them off to the other place. Oh, yes,' I say, 'I know all about that, don't you worry. I know your profession. All the same, take it easy. Do you think we're still in that miserable, sinful world which I've just left? With its police, and officials, and magistrates, and what not, where anybody can come into your store and drag you off to the police station, without a reason, without a by-your-leave? Oh, no. This is the world beyond, the world of truth and judgment. They don't do things that way here. They have a system here, they have justice, they have law and order. I know that, because I've read the good books. So take it easy, because you can't frighten Boruch Mordecai. And if you start anything crooked or irregular, I know exactly what to do and where to lodge a complaint. I'll report you right away to the Throne. I may have been a nobody down there, in the world I've left, but I'm a somebody here. I'm one of the grandsons of Abraham, I am, a child of the

Covenant. And Moses himself taught me the Torah and the word
of God at the foot of Sinai. I have a friend at court, if you
know what I mean. If you've got anything against me, a complaint, or accusation, you know where to lodge it. You're not judge
and executioner all rolled in one,' I say to him. Because what did I
have to be afraid of? My record's clean. I've never eaten meat and
butter together, I haven't spent my money in the beer saloons, or
gone dancing with strange women. I tell you, if you know your
life's been kosher, and there's nothing on your conscience, you take
a very different tone. And all around me stood my saintly forefathers, in cerements and prayer-shawls, and they nodded and
said: 'Good for you, Boruch Mordecai! Speak up for your rights!
Don't let him try any of his games on you.'

"Well, I didn't. It's not in my nature. And you should have
seen him; yes, I mean the Dark Angel himself. The moment I
spoke up he softened, used a different tone of voice. 'Why, Boruch
Mordecai,' he said, 'I'm not dragging you. I'm taking it easy. I'm
only telling you that you've got to be put on trial like anybody
else. You've got to appear before the heavenly court.'

" 'Sure,' I say. 'Everybody has to do that, and I'm ready for it,
too. I'm kosher through and through, not a mark against me. I'll
stand up before the Judge of the Universe, and I'll speak up. What
do you think I did, in that world I've just come from? You can
be sure I didn't sleep in a feather bed and drink wine in the
morning—or at any other time. No,' I say, 'it was a life of labor,
morning until night and through half the night. Summer and
winter, heat and cold, and never a bellyful of potatoes. I brought
up my children decently, made them go to school and learn the
holy books. I'll stand up before the Judge of the Universe, and
I'll show him the bruises on my shoulders, from the sacks I carried
to the villages and farmhouses. I'll show him the welts on my
sides, where the police lashed me because I couldn't afford to pay
for my peddler's license. So what are they going to do here, in
this world of justice? Lash me again? I had enough of that in
the other world, down there; I had enough of it to make up for
all the sins I committed and didn't commit. I'll speak right out to

the Judge of the Universe. What have I got to be afraid of? I've brought with me a wagonful of prayers and Psalms—all the prayers and Psalms I said in the world below. Here—I've got them with me.'

"Well," continued Boruch Mordecai, "you should have seen him open his eyes! And you should have seen all of them open their eyes, I mean the members of the heavenly court, the angels and archangels, the whole divine council. Not a word was uttered against me. I tell you that's the main thing, to be able to open your mouth, and speak up for yourself. Even in the life beyond, in the world after death.

"They listened without interrupting me once. And when I was finished the archangel Gabriel came up to me, flicked me under the nose, and said, in a laughing way, 'Reb Boruch Mordecai, you can go back to your wife and children. You're not wanted up here yet.' So I took off my hat to him—because there's no sense in being a boor, is there?—and took myself off."

Years later, when Boruch Mordecai really died, he lay three days and three nights on his bed. They were afraid to go near him. Who could tell? Perhaps Boruch Mordecai was having it out a second time with the divine council, and perhaps it would end up the same way as before. After all, he was a man who knew how to stand up for his rights.

My Father's Greatcoat

WHEN I used to wake up in the middle of the night I would see, with eyes accustomed to the darkness, my father's sheepskin greatcoat, lying on the bench or hanging on its nail, and it would seem to me that it was a living thing and that it was trying to frighten me. There was a time when I used to draw the quilt over my head and tell myself repeatedly that after all it was only father's old sheepskin greatcoat pretending to be a monster; and having convinced myself that this was the case, I would say to myself: "Now you can stick your head out from under the quilt." But I didn't do anything of the sort. Conviction was one thing, courage another.

Actually that greatcoat gave me the feeling that it was a living thing, not only when father was wearing it, but when he had put it off for the night and hung it up on its nail. It was like father's shadow, or father's essence, detached from him, but not lifeless in detachment. There was something in the folds and shadows of the greatcoat which repeated all the gestures that father used to make; and when the greatcoat was hanging on the wall, long after father had gone to sleep, I—who had gone to sleep before father came home—could tell whether father had been sad or in good humor that evening, whether he had been harassed by an unpaid bill or delighted by an unexpected payment, whether he had been able to make the loan he needed or had been turned down ignominiously.

At certain times I would be aware that the greatcoat was growing older and grayer, like my father; the years were overtaking it, as they were overtaking him; and I would recall the days when the greatcoat was dark and glossy, just as my father had been. That was, of course, in the days of my early childhood, when my father was tall and erect, and had a black beard. I remembered, in particular, one evening. It was the last hour of the Sabbath, when the ceremony of the leavetaking from the Sabbath queen was about to be performed. We were expecting guests; for it was the season of Chanukkah, the festival of the Maccabees, and we used to entertain then. But neither father nor the guests were there yet. There was an important meeting being held in the Rabbi's house. I refused to go to bed; I was excited by the festive atmosphere, by the expectation of guests. I sat on the floor spinning one of the tops which children are given for the festival of Chanukkah. Then at last father came, a whole host of Jews with him. Father was tall, erect, gay; his face shone; his beard was a glossy black; he was smoking a cigar. He had his greatcoat on, and the greatcoat was tall, erect, glossy; the collar flashed with newness, the hair of it bristled, as on a young, living animal; I was afraid of the hairs on the collar; I thought they would fly out at me. And when my father came near me, I shrank from the collar, and father laughed, and the greatcoat laughed with him. Then father took the greatcoat off and handed it to mother; and mother looked at it lovingly, and caressed it, and hung it on its nail. It was a very different greatcoat in those days.

It aged gradually; it accumulated the burden of the years. I remember a certain gray, dim morning; a milky light seeped in through the windows, which were covered with frost ferns. I was lying in mother's bed, and father was sitting at the table. He was studying by lamplight, or he was praying—his voice rose and fell in a pious chant. The light coming through the windows whitened, the frost ferns on the panes began to melt. Then father got up from the table and turned down the lamp, so that the room was steeped in half darkness. He went over to the wall, took down the greatcoat and sighed deeply. It was time to go out and earn his daily bread; and the earning of one's daily bread was a bitter and difficult task. And mother echoed father's sigh.

I looked at the greatcoat which father put on. It seemed to be depressed and worried, like father; it wasn't as young and gay as it had been in years past; the collar didn't flash, as of old, and the hairs didn't stand up stiffly and aggressively, threatening to fly out like arrows. They were lying wearily, as if they had had a bad night and looked forward to a bad day.

That must have been a weekday, because it was only on weekdays that father let the burden of the world oppress him. When Friday came, the eve of the Sabbath, the coat perked up, found its youth and gaiety again. When the Sabbath candles were shining on the table, next to the rich, white Sabbath loaves, and the wine flashed in the cut-glass decanter; when the house was warm, and the floor was strewn with fresh yellow sand, father would return from synagogue services; he would enter, wrapped in his greatcoat; and the greatcoat was refreshed and renewed, young and vigorous; the hairs stood up on the collar, they bristled aggressively, they threw back the gay candlelight, they radiated life and assurance. The coat was erect again; it confronted the world like a conqueror.

That was the way the greatcoat behaved all Friday evening and throughout the Sabbath. But as the Sabbath drew to a close, and the shadows gathered, and the time for evening prayer came; as mother chanted mournfully the woman's valedictory to the Sabbath Queen, "God of Abraham and Isaac and Jacob," and father, entering, gave the traditional greeting to his household, "Good week," while the candles were being lit, the greatcoat collapsed again; it wilted and surrendered; its age was back upon it; and it could not stand up, what with weariness and despondency.

I looked at the greatcoat as it hung on its nail; it was a sad, defeated and lonely greatcoat; it was no longer smooth, but all wrinkled, especially round the left arm, because father used to put his left arm to his brow whenever he was worried and did not know what to do next in the struggle for a livelihood; the greatcoat stooped, it almost had a hump; the collar was bedraggled, the great lapels were shapeless. Then I was not frightened at all; I was only filled with sadness and pity; and with remorse, too, because it seemed to me that the greatcoat was growing old and weary and hopeless on my account. It hung there on the wall worrying, calculating, wondering what it would do on the morrow and during the week to come, to provide me with bread. I was the cause of its wretchedness, I who had to eat every day. And it wasn't only my nourishment it worried about. There were other things. I was not a good boy. I did not take to my books as a good Jewish boy should; I hadn't the reverence one ought to have for the sacred lore of my people; I didn't behave with the piety that was expected of me. And what was going to "become" of me? That question, "What's going to become of him?" which I heard father and mother repeat so often, was eating into the greatcoat, too. It was for my sake that the greatcoat had to go out in all sorts of weather, in wind and rain and snow and frost; for my sake it had to stand for hours in the marketplace, waiting for the peasants to bring their loads of wheat. I was so sorry for the greatcoat then that, when nobody was looking, I would go up to it, and caress its folds, which were like the folds on my father's face. I would pick up the sleeve, all wrinkled and weary, and pull it out from behind the coat—because it was always behind the coat, just like my father's arm, lying on his back as he walked up and down—and I would put it to my face and kiss it and console it.

.   .   .

The coat was something more than a coat; it served as a bedcover. That was true even in the years of its first glory. When winter came, when the nights had a burning frost in them and the ferns on the windowpanes never melted, father would take the coat off its nail and put it gently on mother's bed; that is, on *our* bed, because we little ones slept in mother's bed. That would happen only when mother was fast asleep, and didn't know what father was doing. But in the morning, when she woke up, mother would reproach father for humiliating the greatcoat like that, for reducing it to the status of a bedcover; all the more so because father, who used to get up before everybody else, would not go to the synagogue, where he could pursue his studies more comfortably, because all the books were there, but would sit at home, and study by lamp-light, so as to leave the greatcoat on mother's bed as long as possible. And I, sleeping next to mother, would wake before her; and I would feel the cosy heaviness of the greatcoat; and then it didn't matter how sharp the frost was outside, I knew it couldn't get at me. I would put my hand out into the cold, and caress the great-coat furtively; it was as though I were caressing my father's beard. Then I would fall asleep again, in the protection of the greatcoat, until father made a fire in the stove and the house warmed up.

As the years went by, the greatcoat became less greatcoat and more bedcover. It was heartbreaking to see the steady decline, the gradual loss of dignity. Once upon a time the greatcoat had been the glory of the family, our most distinguished possession. Now it was being relegated to the status of "an old coat"; its place was among ordinary, outlived things, which could be put to any use. It had once stood alone, in unapproachable dignity; now its com-panions were cushions and quilts and ragged gaberdines. We were no longer proud of it. Father no longer put it on to show himself in the synagogue and Study House or among the peasants in the marketplace. It no longer saw the light of day but was hidden among the bedclothes. It was mother herself who hastened the decline. She wouldn't let father put it on any more; she said she couldn't bear to think of him being laughed at by the people in the village. "What will they think?" she said. Yes, she said it right in the presence of the greatcoat, and I saw the greatcoat shrink and almost blush, but it said nothing; it swallowed the insult in silence. It was hard to grow old.

And of course father had to get himself a new coat. It took a long time to persuade him to abandon the greatcoat; mother pleaded with him for years; and secretly she put away, coin by coin, a store from her house money, to get father a new coat. Till at last the tailor came, and measured father for a new coat, and the old great-coat was definitely and permanently degraded to the rank of a bedcover, and it went to sleep its long sleep, by night on the bed, by day in the bedclothes closet.

It accepted its fate with silence and dignity, like an old, faithful house dog; it was glad that at least it could serve some purpose, that it did not eat the bread of charity, that there was enough fur left on it to make it useful as a cover; and if it could not serve the master of the house any more, it would serve his children.

. . .

And then a wonderful thing happened. The greatcoat which had died to this world as a greatcoat, was vouchsafed a resurrection! It was reborn, and entered into a second youth. And that happened when I reached my thirteenth year and was ready for induction into my duties and responsibilities as a son of Israel.

For a long time before the great day my mother had been worrying about a decent coat for me, in which I could present myself for the ceremony of my bar mitzvah. The time was again the festival of Chanukkah, when the winter covers the land. My mother worried, reckoned, counted the coins in her store, and could not reach a decision. And then, one day, when she was taking the bed-clothes out of the closet, she saw light. For as she held the great-coat in her hands her face brightened and she called out to my father:

"Don't you think we could cut this down and make a new coat for our Solomon?"

I could have sworn that the coat understood; for he seemed to hunch himself up, to hide the tattered and furless places; he tried ever so hard to put a new stiffness into the few hairs on the collar; all to prove that he could indeed be used, even in reduced and amputated form, for his original purpose. And my father answered:

"Perhaps we could."

The next morning my mother took me by the hand, and with the rolled up greatcoat under her other arm, she went to see Mordecai the tailor.

I remember Mordecai the tailor clearly. He was a little man, with a little black beard in which were always tangled the white threads of his profession. He wore spectacles, not in order to see—for they were always either on the tip of his nose or at the top of his fore-head—but for some mysterious reason which nobody understood.

When we entered, and mother explained the reason for her visit, he shoved the spectacles from the tip of his nose to the top of his forehead, picked up the greatcoat and scrutinized it with great intentness, like a professor examining a patient. He turned it upside down, he looked at the collar, he fingered the chest, and now and again he frowned, and shook his head, as though the case were practically hopeless. Then he spread it out in front of him, and there the aged greatcoat lay, suppliant, as if pleading for its life. And all this time my heart was beating painfully, and I looked miserably at Mordecai and wanted to put in a kind word for the greatcoat. Mordecai scratched his head in perplexity, detached a couple of white threads from his beard, gazed on the greatcoat, and at last consented to perform the operation.

"We'll see what we can do," was all he said, just like any cautious physician. And the old greatcoat almost started up with joy.

"Come here, you young rascal," said Mordecai, and began to go through the ritual. He passed his tape round my chest, he tickled me under the armpits, so that I burst out laughing, and he took the measure of my length.

Every day for eight days I had to go to Mordecai the tailor, to have my measurements retaken and the new coat tried on. Every day I saw a new stage in the transformation and watched the greatcoat descending into the pit of death in order that it might be drawn up again into the world of the living.

On the ninth day, when I was to be inducted into manhood, I went to synagogue in the new coat; and my father's old greatcoat, in the fullness of resurrection, entered on its second life.

The Rebel

THE mother came stormily out of the bride's room and fixed her blazing eyes on her husband, who was seated at the dinner table rolling breadcrumbs and waiting to say grace.

"You go talk to her! I haven't an ounce of strength left."

"Rachel Leah the mother, Rachel Leah the educator of children!" muttered the husband, speaking of his wife instead of to her. "The whole world's going to laugh at you! The whole world will point at you."

"At me!" shrieked the mother. "Oh, no, not at me. At *you*. Why didn't *you* stay home and bring the children up? Where were *you* all the time? It's you they'll laugh at."

"Quiet, woman!" said the husband, sternly. "Is this a time to stand there quarreling with me? The bridegroom and his parents will be here any moment, and you have nothing better to do than quarrel with me?"

"What shall we do, Menasseh, what shall we do?" wailed the mother.

"Bethink yourself, woman! There is a God in heaven! We will go in once more to our daughter and plead with her not to disgrace us before the whole world."

The father rose from the table and went into his daughter's room, his wife following him. On the little sofa near the window sat a girl of eighteen. Her hands clutched wildly at her thick, black hair in which she was hiding her face. The girl must have been weeping, for her breast rose and fell; but no sound came from her.

On the bed opposite her were laid out the white silk wedding dress, the black silk dress for the visit to the synagogue, and the black woollen dress for everyday wear—all three delivered that morning by the trousseau-tailor. Near the bed stood a woman, with a pair of scissors in her hand, and at her feet lay several open boxes with wigs in them.

"Hannah, daughter, how will we live down the shame of it?" began the father. "How shall we show our faces among people?"

No reply came from the girl. The father changed his tone.

"Look at her!" he said. "Menassah Gross's daughter! Genendel Freindel's daughter wasn't too high and mighty to cut her hair off for her marriage and wear a wig. But Menassah Gross's daughter thinks it beneath her. Why?"

And as the girl did not answer, the mother took up the theme.

"Yes, indeed! Genendel Freindel's daughter is more educated than you, her parents gave her a larger dowry, she has every reason in the world to be stuck up. But *she* didn't refuse to cut her hair off."

Still there was no answer.

The father went back to his first tone.

"See, daughter," he implored, "what you are doing to us. How much labor and worry and love it cost us to bring you up, and to reach this day, which should be a day of fulfillment and rejoicing for us, your parents. And now you would turn our rejoicing into mourning, and our fulfillment into disaster. Is there no fear of God in your heart? We shall be put under the ban! Decent folk won't talk to us! And your husband-to-be will leave you! He will scurry away from this town as fast as his legs will carry him."

"That's enough foolishness, daughter," the mother seconded her husband, half in command, half in entreaty. She picked out a wig from one of the open boxes and approached her daughter. "Try this wig on, child! The color is exactly the color of your hair"—and she laid the wig awry on her daughter's head.

The eighteen-year-old girl felt the weight of the wig on her head. She unclenched one hand, felt the top of her head with it, and shuddered. Among her own, soft, smooth, living hair was the stiff, cold hair of the wig. One thought kept hammering in her young brain. "Whose hair were those? Where now is the head from which they were shorn?" She was filled with horror, as if she had touched an unclean thing. Suddenly she grabbed at the wig, flung it to the floor, and ran out of the room.

The parents stared at each other dumbly.

.   .   .

The morning after the wedding the bridegroom's mother rose early and unpacked the wig and the hat which she had brought with her from her home as a present for her new daughter-in-law. With these in one hand, and a pair of scissors in the other, she made her way to the bride's room, to prepare her for breakfast.

But she remained standing outside; for the bride had locked the door and would let no one in.

The bridegroom's mother, scandalized and terrified, ran off to find her husband, who was still asleep, along with ten or fifteen others—cousins, uncles, brothers, and in-laws of all degrees—after the exhausting festivities of the previous day. She banged on the door where these were all asleep, until her husband sorted himself out and answered he was coming. She went in search of the bridegroom, who had left the bridal chamber early. He was of the same age as the bride, a timid youth, his lips still wet with his mother's milk. Knowing of the scandal that was brewing, and unable to face it, he had hidden himself in the kitchen. But his mother found him, cowering in his silk gaberdine behind the stove. Then she went off screaming for the bride's mother, and the two women besieged the bride's door.

"Daughter dear," began the bride's mother, "why do you lock us out? You don't have to be ashamed before us."

"Assuredly not," chimed in the bridegroom's mother. "It happens in all Jewish homes."

There was no answer from the other side.

"Your mother-in-law has brought you two lovely presents, a wig and a hat, in which to go to synagogue," pleaded the bride's mother.

From the other room, where the guests were re-assembling, was heard the sound of the orchestra tuning up.

"Now, bride, sweet, darling bride," cooed the bridegroom's mother. "Let us come in. The guests are ready to go to synagogue."

At this point the door yielded, and the two mothers almost fell in. But as the bridegroom's mother approached the young wife, shears in hand, the bride flung herself on her mother's bosom with a great cry:

"Mother, mother darling, I can't do it. My heart won't let me." And as her mother tried to disengage herself, the young wife covered her head protectively with her hands.

"Daughter, daughter!" said the mother. "Have you forgotten there is a God in heaven?"

The mother-in-law was losing patience. "What?" she said. "Keep your own hair after your marriage? Do you know what punishment is reserved in the world to come for such sinners? Demons tear the locks from your head with fiery tongs."

"Mama, mama, darling," sobbed the young wife, and held on convulsively to her hair. Her hair! It had grown together with her, it was part of her. And if she let them cut it off, it would never, never grow again like this. She would be wearing, for the rest of her life, someone else's hair, hair that had grown on some unknown woman's head. Who knew if that woman was alive? And suppose the dead woman, long since rotting in the grave, would rise out of it, and come to haunt her, demanding her hair. She could almost hear the dead voice: "Give me back my hair! Give me back my hair!" An icy wave passed down her spine.

Then suddenly she heard the click of the shears above her head. With a scream, she grabbed the shears from her mother-in-law's hand, flung them to the floor, and cowered back in a corner.

"No, no!" she screamed in an inhuman voice. "My own hair! I'm going to keep my own hair, and let God punish me if He wants!"

There was nothing they could do. That same morning the outraged mother-in-law packed up and departed, taking with her the roast geese, the spongecake and the other good things she had brought along for the marriage breakfast. She also wanted to take along her son, but here the bride's mother had something to say:

"Oh, no, not my son-in-law! It's too late. He belongs to me now."
And on the Sabbath Menassah Gross's daughter was conducted
to the synagogue as unshorn as any heathen woman. The whole
village knew that the lovely black coils under the big new hat
were her own; and one-tenth of the curses that were hurled at the
wicked woman would have sufficed to obliterate the village, if the
powers that be had paid any attention to them.

.   .   .

Late one summer evening, four weeks after the wedding, the
young man came home from the Chassidic meeting house, and
went into his and his wife's room. Hannah was already asleep.
The pale lamplight fell on her upturned face, which was partly
hidden by her coal-black hair. Even in sleep she had her hands
on her hair, so deep was her terror of losing it.

The young husband had come home perturbed and unhappy. In
the four weeks since his marriage he had not once been called up,
during Sabbath services, to a reading of the Scrolls of the Law. This
was the punishment for the wickedness of his wife. And this evening Chaim Moishe, one of the zealots, had shamed him in public.

"Do you call yourself a man?" Chaim Moishe had asked, when
the meeting house had been crowded. "You're not a man! You're
a worm, a chicken-livered image of a man! What sort of excuse is
it that your wife won't let you cut her hair? Is it not written,
specifically: 'And he shall rule over her'?"

The young husband had returned home determined to have it
out with his rebellious wife. He was going to say to her: "Woman!
This is the law of Israel! You are married and must not wear your
own hair. And if you insist on wearing your own hair, you are
divorced without a bill of divorcement! It is the law." Having said
which, he was going to fling from the room, pack his things, and
depart. But when he saw her asleep under the dim lamplight, the
black hair awash over her pale face, his heart was filled with pity.
He approached the bed softly, looked down at his wife a long time,
and called in a whisper:

"Hannah! Hannah! Little one!"

She opened her eyes sleepily and, only half awake, she murmured: "Nathan, were you calling me? What is it?"

"Nothing," he replied. "Only your night-cap's fallen off." And he bent down, picked up the white lace night cap from the floor, and gave it to her.

"Hannah! Little one," he said. "There's something I have to tell you."

The soft, pleading words went straight to her heart. In the four weeks of their marriage he had hardly ever spoken with her. In the daytime he was away, either in the synagogue, or in the Chassidic meeting house. When he came home to supper, he sat down wordlessly. If he needed something he would address, not her, but some invisible person. And if he did address her, he would do it with downcast eyes, as if afraid to look her in the face. This was the first time that he had really spoken to her, and his voice was tender and persuasive in the intimacy of their own room.

"What is it that you have to tell me?" she asked, in low tones.

"Hannah, my sweet, I beg you, don't put me to shame before the whole world; and don't put yourself to shame, too. God Himself brought the two of us together; you are my wife, I am your husband. It isn't fitting, it isn't proper, it isn't seemly, that a married woman should wear her own hair."

Her body was only half asleep, but her mind, her energies, her will, were wholly asleep. She was weak, she longed to yield, and when he sat down by her side and lifted her head on to his breast, she let it lie there.

"Child," he said, still more tenderly, "I know you aren't as wild as they make you out to be, you aren't bad and spoiled. I know you are a sweet, loving daughter of your people. And God will be good to us, and send us children, decent, God-fearing children. Leave these follies, my sweet one. Why should we have the whole world against us? Are we not husband and wife, and isn't your shame my shame?"

It seemed to her that somebody new, somebody at once remote and yet indescribably intimate, had approached her and was speaking to her. No one had ever spoken to her so gently, with such endearing, homely words. And he was hers, her only one, her husband, and she would live with him for so many years to come, so many years, and they would have children, and she would be the mistress of a household.

"I know," he went on, "how it hurts you to lose your hair, the crown of your beauty. I saw you for the first time when they brought me to your house, when they told me you were to be my bride. And I understand. I know that God has given you beauty and grace. It will cut into my heart just as much as into yours. But what can we do? This is the Jewish law, and there is no escape from it. We are Jews, are we not, and who knows how we will pay in our children for the breaking of the law, God help us and save us and keep us!"

She did not speak. She only lay lightly in his arms, and the perfume of her hair ascended to him and bathed his face. There was a soul in his wife's hair; he knew it and felt it. He looked at her long and earnestly; there was an entreaty in his eyes, and the entreaty was for her happiness, and his, and those to come.

"Let me," said his eyes, and she did not answer, saying neither yes nor no.

He went quickly to the dresser, opened the top drawer, took out the shears, and returned to her. She put her head in his lap, as if she were bringing an offering and a sacrifice, a redemption, for her, and for him, and for those that were to come. The shears flashed palely above her head, the black tresses fell one by one. She did not dare to move. She lay thus, her shorn head in his lap, dreaming through the night.

In the morning she awoke and cast a glance at herself in the mirror which hung opposite her bed. A dreadful fear rose in her heart. She thought for a moment that she was in a hospital. On the little table at her side lay the black tresses, dead. The soul which had been in them only the night before, when they had still been part of her, was gone from them, and the shadow of death was in the room.

She buried her face suddenly in her hands, and the sound of her weeping filled the little room.

Young Years

WHEN you came out of the dense, lightless Dombrov forest, the first thing you glimpsed—like the far-off suggestion of a dream—was the twinkle of the windmill lights. And when the wagoners caught sight of those lights on the hill, which seemed to battle with the waves of darkness and to cry out for help, they breathed a heavy sigh of relief at having left behind them the ominous haunt of the Dombrov robbers.

Many years have passed since those lights twinkled their last; and no wagoners drive now through the Dombrov forest. Today a railroad line connects the villages Z and G, and it never occurs to the passengers to keep their eyes open for the little twinkling lights which once spelled safety. But there is one person who still sees them, and that is Rachel, the miller's granddaughter. Far from the little hill in a great city, among alien faces, Rachel still glimpses the twinkling lights which struggle against the waves of darkness and implore help. She sees the hill and the windmill on the hill—sees them distinctly though they have long ago disappeared, their place taken by a gigantic barracks: she sees from out of the midst of an alien world the place which was her first home and the setting of her remote childhood.

I

Rachel was a baby when her mother died, so that Rachel had no recollection of her; her father went away to another town, married there, and founded a new family. She grew up with her grandfather and the windmill—in the place where her mother had died. She still recalls, as across the spaces of a dream, how her grandfather used to complain about the pain in his legs, and yet would always have her on his lap at mealtimes, so that they would eat together, one spoonful for her and one for him. And grand-mother, who was jealous because the child would rather be with grandfather, used to scold grandfather all through the meal: "You're spoiling the little one!" she kept on saying. "Don't you see she can't eat properly because of your beard prickling her?" And she scolded so long that grandfather had to let little Rachel down from his lap and lift her on to her high chair. But she hadn't been on the high chair for more than a minute when her grandmother snatched her up and put her on *her* lap, and made her eat out of *her* plate. Only Rachel wanted to eat with grandfather, and she began to cry, so that grandmother had to set her down angrily. Thereupon grand-father would laugh gleefully.

"See, Yente," he crowed, "she'd rather have me with a beard than you without a beard."

Then grandmother would be still angrier, and she would cry out: "Just like her mother she is. Our Sarah was always a capricious thing, so what can you expect of her daughter?"

And suddenly there was silence at the table. Grandfather and grandmother looked at each other dumbly, remembering their only daughter, whom they had married off to the son of the Rabbi of Schachlin and whose young body now lay rotting underground. And grandmother's eyes filled with tears; she lifted her apron to her eyes, pushed away the plate, and ate no more.

Then grandfather left his chair, went over to her, patted her on the shoulder, and said:

"There, there! Our daughter is happy in Paradise, and she has left us her little one to look after."

At such moments Rachel would think she saw her mother. She saw her, young, beautiful, draped in lustrous silks, adorned with bracelets and gleaming earrings and dazzling pearl necklaces, walk-ing to and fro in great halls filled with marvelous light. In every hall there was a huge table covered with a white cloth, on which stood the gigantic silver candelabra of the Feast of Lights: this was Paradise. And her mother, young and beautiful, paced from hall to hall and in each hall paused to say the benediction over the candles. Not a soul was to be seen in the halls besides her. Mother was alone; she had been led in and bidden to stay; and she was waiting there, waiting, waiting, for grandmother and grandfather, and for Rachel, too. She had been waiting for ever so long, and nobody came; and she was feeling lonely and forlorn in that Paradise of lights, so that Rachel couldn't help crying out:

"Grandmother, when will we go to mama in Paradise?"

"Child, when a hundred and twenty years have passed, we'll all go to mama in Paradise."

"A hundred and twenty years! Why, grandmother, a year is such a long time, one Passover to the next; and a hundred years is so much to wait, and mother's all alone!" And Rachel wept for her mother's loneliness.

She had always been fonder of grandfather than of grandmother. Grandfather was tall and pale and had a thin face. His big white beard hid his lean cheeks. He always wore a long white cloak too. The peasants used to call him "the white Jew." They all respected him—they even feared him a little. And it was true that when he went out of the house and walked across to the mill, his white face, his long white beard, and his white cloak spread a kind of fear about them. The people who met him stepped out of his way. And, as soon as he came into the mill, the great wings began to rotate and you heard the rushing of the wind in them. The wings chased each other round and round, and there was a kind of quiet wind-talk among them. Shadows began to race over the green meadow on the hill, wild shadows with the strangest shapes: men and animals without heads, without limbs. One shadow would run after another, and catch up with it, and swallow it; and it really frightened you to watch the shadows chasing each other under the wings.

But Rachel loved the sound of the wind in the wings of the windmill. As soon as evening fell, grandfather would walk over to the mill, and at once the wings would begin to turn. The lights

flickered out from the windows, and you heard the lamenting of
the wind, caught in the wings of the mill. Sometimes Rachel
thought that somebody was crying there, a little girl, perhaps, whose
dress was caught in the wings, so that she had to go round and
round with them. And perhaps the shadows were the shadows of
dead women, wailing from among the wings; and it was her grandfather who was driving them, to make them turn the wings.

At such times she was afraid of her grandfather when he returned from the mill. Perhaps her own mother had been among
the shadow-women who made the wings go round, the women who
had to obey grandfather and turn the wings to grind the flour
for him.

But she was much more afraid of her uncle, her grandfather's
only son, who lived in the city. Her uncle was a *shochet,* a cattle
slaughterer, and was reputed to be a learned man; but he was sick.
He had a weak chest, and every summer he used to come out and
stay with his father, the miller. Uncle Boruch was a silent man;
you would have thought that he was really dumb. And whenever
he answered a question—which he did briefly, and reluctantly—
you were astonished, as if a dumb man had suddenly found his
speech. Uncle used to go out for lonely walks, way out across the
fields, and always he came back with a sorrowing face. Sometimes
he would close himself in his room and stay there for hours, or
else he would sit dumbly just looking straight in front of him.
Even grandfather and grandmother were afraid of him, and always
spoke to him very gently. The people in the city considered uncle
a holy man; it was as if they all knew that he was going to die soon.

And indeed he did die young, when Rachel was still a child.
He went away and never came back. And Rachel used to think
that he had gone away to her mother in the bright-lit halls of Paradise, and now mother would not be as lonely as she used to be.

And after that her father came for her. She remembers it clearly;
it was a summer day, and she was playing in the meadow in front
of the mill, pulling out daisies, when grandmother suddenly called
her into the house. And there was a man, a stranger, seated at the
table, a man with a velvet hat, wearing a scarf round his neck.

And grandmother took her by the hand, led her up to the strange man, and said:

"Rachel, darling, this is your father. He's come to take you home."

The stranger wanted to take her in his arms, but Rachel burst into tears, hid herself behind her grandmother's apron, and sobbed: "I don't want to go with that strange man!"

And so the strange man went away and never returned. Since that day Rachel never saw her father again. Ah, how she would love to see him now! How she longed to know at least the whereabouts of this man who had the same dark eyes as herself, who had once known her mother, and was now with her family—this strange man who was her father! Why had she refused to go with him? Perhaps, if she had gone with him, her life would be a very different one now.

Vain regret! She never saw her father after that one visit of his. She remained with her grandfather and her grandmother and grew up in the shadow of the windmill. In the winter, when the snow fell, the wings stood still; and then she and grandfather and grandmother stayed in the house. When spring came, and spring winds began to blow, her grandfather went across to the mill, and then Rachel listened again to the sound of the wind in the revolving wings. So, between the mill, and her grandfather, and her grandmother, the years of her childhood passed. Now and again grandfather and grandmother would have a squabble and would not talk to each other; and when they sat down to eat Rachel would be the intermediary and peacemaker.

"Rachel, tell your grandmother that your grandfather wants to know whether she's cooked beans for supper."

"Grandmother, grandfather wants to know whether grandmother cooked beans for supper," repeated Rachel, as if grandfather and grandmother could not hear each other just because they had had a squabble.

"Rachel, tell your grandfather that your grandfather will eat whatever he gets," answered her grandmother.

"Grandfather, grandmother says that grandfather will eat whatever he gets."

And the old people stayed on the outs until Rachel managed to pull them together and get them to speak to each other.

But now, when Rachel sits in her little room on an upper floor, and looks out at the great city in which she has been cast away with so many thousands of others, it seems to her that all these things are incredibly and impossibly remote, as if they had been in another world and another life.

II

That was a long, long winter; you thought it would never end. The snow never disappeared from the fields, and whichever way you looked there was snow. The river was frozen over. The wings of the windmill stood motionless, and no peasant's wagon was seen. The festival of Purim came, the Passover was close at hand, and still the snow was there, covering all the world. Then, before you really knew how it had happened, there was no more snow; a little wind blew, a wind familiar and loved, bringing with it a far-off recollection of childhood days; and the snow yielded to its caress. It softened, melted, ran off, and suddenly great big patches of black earth showed through; and when you saw those black patches you were filled with laughter and happiness, as though you had come across an old friend, a dear, beloved friend, who had been dead and had come to life again. The ice was just as suddenly gone from the river, and the water flowed fresher and freer than it had ever been before, as if it were a new kind of water, created for this occasion.

And the peasants' wagons returned to the mill, bringing the last stores of grain, to grind the last bit of bread which was to sustain them till the next harvest. Grandfather was terribly busy with the mill, and the wings turned day and night. And the faster the wings turned the freer became the world and the brighter the light of day.

In those early spring days Rachel wandered over the awakening fields and listened to the rushing of the winds which chased each other from horizon to horizon. In their passage they shook the last snow off the branches of the trees, they awakened the black trees by tugging at their limbs, they brought new strength to the rushes and bushes which had survived from last year; and at the same time they poured through Rachel's body, blowing her hair wildly about her neck and shoulders. She wandered over the fields as in a dream, her great dark eyes distended with fear, so that her face was nothing but eyes, and she wept. The wind drove at the big tears which welled from her eyes and made them tremble on her cheeks.

What was it she wept for? She wept for everything. She wept because she was already fifteen years old and did not know what was going to become of her, and because the wind which blew across the fields and through the trees heralded the spring, and she was not ready for the spring. She wept because her mother was alone in Paradise and because her grandfather was becoming frailer from day to day, so that before long the wind would be able to lift him as it lifted the wings of the mill and carry him off. Standing in the middle of the field she wept as she watched the snow melt and run down the banks of the river, to be drawn into its waves and hurried away to strange places.

Often she wept without knowing why, till she became aware of a hopeless longing for wings, so that she might lift herself up over the world; and then her weeping was filled with envy of every bird that passed over her head.

Then a time came when she wanted to know who "he" would be, the one who was destined for her. Unable to repress her impatience, she took a basket, stole into the hencoop, laid a fat young chicken and some new-laid eggs in the basket, and paid a visit to Antoshya the witch, who lived at the other end of the village.

Antoshya took the chicken and the new-laid eggs and told Rachel to look into a mirror; there she would see "him," her destined one. But in the mirror she saw nothing save her own big, frightened eyes: and yet she did see her destined one. For that matter, however, she was always seeing him, though she was not sure what he was like. Sometimes he was young and strong, striding through the world in search of her. Sometimes he was weak and sick, with wasting lungs, and he always coughed; but somehow all this was put on, so that no one might know how beautiful he was. Only she, Rachel, knew; she knew likewise that he wandered through the world in search of something which mankind had lost, and when he would find it he would restore it to mankind; and having done that he would throw off the mask of sickness, reveal himself in his strength and beauty, and come to claim her as his bride.

And thinking of her destined one she hid herself in a corner of the house, or she went out alone into the field, far from the house, and waited for him; and there were moments when she was certain that he was at hand, she heard his footsteps on the soft, moist earth, and her heart trembled as she waited.

In whichever form he was to come to her, with beauty hidden or disclosed, she thought about him most when the spring winds began to blow. And it was with the spring winds that he came to her at last.

He came one Passover—the Passover of that long, long winter. Grandmother was dead by that time. Very quietly she had withdrawn from the world, and no one was surprised at her going. Rachel was alone with her grandfather, who grew thinner and thinner, and frailer and frailer; his body shrank in on itself, the hands became bonier, the throat stringier. Only his eyes grew larger. And as he became increasingly silent he became more and more like Rachel's uncle who had died young. All day long grandfather remained closed up in the mill, although there was no wind and the wings stood still because the snow had covered everything. Evenings he came home, sat down at the window, and looked out; and Rachel sat in a corner of the room and was silent with him. So they passed the winter in silence until the first signs of spring appeared and the peasants came with their last sacks of grain; then grandfather sat day and night in the mill and drove the wings like witches. Meanwhile spring moved on toward summer. The black earth began to sprout green; the branches of the trees were clear at first, as if they had been washed and combed, and then they too began to sprout. The wind shook up the rushes and cleansed them of their winter dirt. The ploughed fields still lay black, waiting for the hand of the sower. By the time Passover arrived the whole world was ready—only they, Rachel and her grandfather, were not ready. They had made no preparations for the Passover; so for this festival grandfather closed the mill and left the fields and the rushes to celebrate the spring without him. He was going with Rachel to the city for the eight days of Passover. There they stayed with Aunt Hinde Leah, grandfather's sister, the "wealthy woman" of the little town. And it was there, in the midst of the Passover, that Rachel met "him," her destined one, and he came in the likeness of the "concealed" lover, who was going to give back to the world that which it had lost.

III

Aunt Hinde Leah still lived in the old house in which grandfather had been born and had passed his earliest years. It was the house of the Lentchintzkis, for this was the town of Lentchitz. The furniture, it was said, had once belonged to King Sobieski—the big-bellied sofa covered with heavy green brocade, the high armchair, and the huge dresser with the bronze handles, on which were ranged the family "treasures": the Dresden porcelain, the round coffee trays with deep blue centerpieces and wrought golden edges, and the golden horseshoe which a far off grandfather picked up somewhere on a road—it had fallen, the legend told, from the hoof of one of the king's horses; there was also a big jar of cut glass, in which Aunt Hinde Leah kept a decoction of herbs, a sovereign remedy for any kind of stomach-ache, and a bundle of dried poppyseeds suspended over the dresser. Right in the midst of all these treasures lay, under a glass cover, aunt's myrtle-wreath, the long-surviving witness of the innocence which had been hers when she stood under the bridal canopy. This was the center and focus of all the family treasures, and side by side with it stood the photograph of the bridal couple, uncle wearing a short, smart overcoat and a German hat, and auntie a vast crinoline dress with a delicate lace collar, and a Breslau silken shawl. There was a third picture, of their son Saul, who had gone away to America and had sent this picture with a letter, whereafter he had disappeared, as if the earth had swallowed him up. In the house they spoke of him as of one dead. From the center of the ceiling hung the cande-labrum, its brilliant, swinging crystals scattering patches of light throughout the room. So the "salon" stood guarding its "treasures," with locked door, from one year's end to the other; nobody went into it, nobody even thought of it.

Auntie and uncle spent their lives in the little shop, where they sold French cloth. A little room was attached to the shop, and in this room, which was filled with cardboard boxes of all sizes, there was a tiny oil stove. It was an extremely capricious kind of stove. Whenever it felt so inclined it burned very nicely, heated the room and the shop, brought the big brass tea-kettle to a boil in a matter of minutes, and cooked a pot of soup just as readily. In brief, when its humor was good, the stove did everything that was asked of it; and when the humor was not on it, you could use up a whole box of matches: it just would not burn, and there was no power on earth and no law in heaven to make it change its will.

On this capricious stove auntie did all her cooking, and round it also gathered at all hours of the day the Jewish intelligentsia of the town. Here, in the perpetual twilight of the living room, close by the stove, the most interesting games of chess were played. Here too the entire political activity of the town was reviewed, revised, and remodeled, this Rabbi dismissed, another inducted, this teacher demoted, another engaged. Here a cantor was conceded to have a voice, or a voice was denied him. Nor was it local Jewish politics alone which engaged the attention of the assembled. Far-ranging decisions of national and international import were made here. Kings trembled and thrones tottered in the old room of Uncle Joel, in the circle about the stove which burned so beautifully when it wanted to, and which could not be coaxed, bribed or bullied into action when it was not so inclined.

For the *Seder* ritual of the Passover auntie opened the doors of her salon. Here the ceremony was performed, and the couch of the chief celebrant was none other than the green-brocaded sofa. As through a dream Rachel still remembers that particular *Seder,* and her uncle, in his fringed, four-cornered satin skull cap, half-seated, half-reclining on the ceremonial couch, reciting the *Hagaddah.*

Uncle passed for a *Maskil,* one of the enlightened, modernized Jews, a man of reading and scholarship; he was in a perpetual huff with the rest of the family, and chiefly with grandfather, who had married into a family of ignorant village Jews. This huff of his came to high expression at the recitation of the *Hagaddah.* Uncle conducted the service loudly, pedantically, giving the right stress to each syllable, so as to indicate his grasp of grammatical rules, and at the same time to remind his wife's family, and particularly his brother-in-law, the miller, of the excellent match Auntie Hinde Leah had made.

Rachel's grandfather sat at the *Seder* table like a stranger. He wanted to get through with the recital of the *Hagaddah,* and so he read rapidly, and ran ahead of Uncle Joel. But Uncle Joel always pulled him back by correcting his reading of the Hebrew words, and especially his accentuation of the syllables. So when grandfather started off, in a great hurry, with *"There*fore shall we praise the Lord," Uncle Joel said, loudly and sternly, "There*for* shall we praise the Lord." On this particular point, however, grandfather was obstinate, because *his* Rabbi had taught him to say *"There-*fore." And when Joel corrected him, by saying, loudly and sternly, "There*for,"* grandfather repeated, just as loudly and sternly, *"There-*fore." It was *"There*fore" and "There*for"* for the next two or three minutes, till they both gave up without having come to open agreement or, for that matter, disagreement. Throughout the remainder of the *Hagaddah* Uncle Joel kept the brakes on, chanting the words distinctly, and adding roulades of his own to the traditional melody. By the time the service was over uncle and grandfather were at daggers drawn—still without an open quarrel—and it was not until auntie served the hardboiled eggs and the salt water, which are part of the traditional *Seder* meal, that they became more or less reconciled; it was a fortunate thing that both of them were extremely fond of hardboiled eggs dipped in salt water.

It was there, in the house of her uncle, that Rachel made the acquaintance of Meyerovitch, the teacher from Lithuania, who led a lonely life in the little Polish town, and who, when his boredom with the place became too much for him, used to drop in on the old cloth merchant, Reb Joel Vidovsky, for a game of chess or for a learned talk on Bible texts.

On the festival Passover days the salon was thrown open, and the visitors were permitted to sit on the big-bellied sofa and the lofty armchairs, while grandfather treated them to a glass of specially prepared Passover brandy. Thither were transferred the literary and political discussions which throughout the rest of the year were conducted about the stove: concerning this or that interpretation of a verse, the latest article or story by Smolenskin and Mapu, the Hebrew writers who dominated that generation, the merits and inadequacies of the Rabbi and the cantor, the future of Franz Joseph, Emperor of Austria, and of Queen Victoria of England, the secret plans of Bismarck and Disraeli. And these same conversations, which had become commonplace in the little room attached to the shop, took on, amid the furniture which had once belonged to King Sobieski, and by virtue of a glass of uncle's special brandy, an unwonted significance, solemnity, and brilliance. You could not compare the moods, any more than you could compare the ordinary glass of tea, which the stove furnished whenever it was in the humor, with the delectable, laboriously prepared brandy which was the pride of Uncle Joel.

Among the guests who were invited that Passover to the salon and the brandy was Meyerovitch, the Lithuanian teacher: a very young man, twenty or perhaps twenty-one years of age, pale and sickly looking, and poorly dressed. His ill-fitting hat was always dusty; he wore a rubber collar, the kind that did not have to be sent to the laundry but could be cleaned by passing a damp sponge over it; his ancient Prince Albert coat fell in stiff folds on his flat chest, and his trousers were frayed and flabby from the frequent— and imperfect—removal of mud. In this queer and pitiful garb Meyerovitch wandered about the town, a forlorn and disconsolate stranger. He was regarded with universal suspicion not unmixed with fear, though everyone knew that this Lithuanian, this Litvak, was a better scholar than the Rabbi, wrote a better hand than the magistrate's clerk, knew more Hebrew than the official Hebrew teacher, and spoke a better Russian than the city Governor. They were afraid of him; the Hebrew teacher trembled lest the young Litvak take it into his mind to examine a pupil of his, and the Rabbi trembled lest he be drawn into a learned dispute with him; and they disliked him because he was a stranger and had not a kopeck to bless himself with and despised his own abilities. They laughed at the Litvak who, with all his learning and education, did not eat a square meal from one week's end to the other; there was a perpetual whispering behind his back; some went so far as to say that the young man was an apostate, secretly wore a cross next to his skin, and had come to the city with the sole purpose of putting wicked ideas into the heads of the Jewish girls and of ensnaring the young Talmud students into his own apostate beliefs.

I remember them well, these young Lithuanian students, who came out into our remote Polish villages and townlets, bringing with them the savor of a new world. They had a word for this young man, a book for the other, for a third lessons in Russian, for a fourth a translation of a chapter of Job. They asked for very little in exchange, and lived on dry bread with an occasional piece of cheese. They bore with patience the contumely and loneliness which was their lot, and carried out, with the utmost honesty and fidelity, their mission of enlightenment to Polish Jewry.

Meyerovitch was among the first of these apparitions in the Polish villages. No one knew where he had come from, this young Litvak with the sunken cheeks and the hollow cough. Had he a father, a home? Weekdays, Sabbaths, and holy days he wore the same clothes. He never appeared anywhere without a bundle of books under his arm. When he first turned up in the town he took up his lodgings in the synagogue house and slept on a hard bench. Then he gave lessons in exchange for a bed or a meal; but no one invited him as a guest. They laughed at him, at his unchanged yellow collar and his dusty, crumpled hat; and soon they had a name for him: "the king of the Lithuanian ragpickers." And Meyerovitch heard the venomous whispering behind his back, suffered without rancor the looks of contempt cast at him, and went on with his work. In time one house was opened to him, and he was free to drop in occasionally on Uncle Joel and play a game of chess or discuss a point of Hebrew grammar over a glass of tea.

What was it that drew Rachel so powerfully to him the first moment she saw him? She saw in him the image of the alternative form of her "destined one": the young man unlike all other young men, the sick wanderer, despised by all, who carried with him the secret treasure destined for the world which despised him. Everything about him conspired to heighten the instantaneous impression: the poverty, the modesty of the lonely Litvak, the big, peaceful eyes, which seemed to be illumined by unshed tears, the gentle, earnest smile on his lips. In the seriousness of his demeanor Rachel saw something mysterious, the answer to the riddle of the world. Externally wretched, this strange young man, knowing everything, was filled with inward bliss. Hence the contempt of the world could not harm him, could not even reach him. And Rachel wanted to know the mystery of his tranquil strength. She wanted to be part of it. It seemed to her that he, the lonely one, could tell her what it was she had to do, the path she had to tread. He had to become her teacher.

IV

Meyerovitch passed that summer in the shadow of the windmill. Rachel asked her grandfather to invite him to the village, and her grandfather did it gladly. He was anxious to provide Rachel with a teacher; and he, unlike the townsmen, was well disposed to Meyerovitch from the first. It was the loveliest summer in Rachel's young years. It seemed to her that Meyerovitch was a great Rabbi; every word he uttered was sacred and true and charged with a meaning which was as yet beyond her.

She needed a teacher. She had begun to understand that the world was big, very big, endless almost; and everywhere were people who looked for something and desired something and did not know what they were to do in order that life might be good. But there were also men like Meyerovitch, who did know what was to be done; and the world had to listen to them and obey them.

They took long walks together in the summer afternoons,

through the standing corn or the shadowy wood, and Meyerovitch told her of the great cities, like Warsaw and Vilna and Kiev and Odessa, and of the people who lived in them, young people who were born to happiness, but who surrendered their happiness for the sake of their "ideals."

She did not quite understand all the words that Meyerovitch used in speaking to her. She did not know what an "ideal" was. But she was filled with deepest reverence for those who sacrificed themselves for an ideal and began to love the young men and women of the big cities who could have been happy and who were not permitted to be happy, because of an ideal. She envied those young people; she saw them in her fantasy, creatures more of heaven than of this earth, carrying about with them the great secret, and knowing therefore what had to be done in order that this might be a good world.

She asked Meyerovitch to describe these young people to her. Did he know them personally? And when Meyerovitch answered, Yes, he knew quite a number of them, her reverence for him increased, became more deeply religious. He was more beautiful, and holier, and greater, because he knew intimately the people who had an ideal.

The hot summer days passed over the land like a procession of brides. The sun rose with sudden strength and poured out its heat on the broad meadows, the golden, ripening bread, the running water of the river and the shadowed forest. Rachel did not know what to do with herself those hot summer days. Half naked, with loosened hair, she ran about over the hot meadows. The wings of the mill stood motionless, as if consciously waiting for the grain to ripen.

And grandfather, too, waited, just like the mill, for the corn to ripen. He went out often into the fields of the peasants, to look at the standing ears and to speak to the bearded grain as one might speak to a friend: "Get ready, get ready," he said, "little ears, my millstones are waiting for you." Sometimes he would stretch himself out in the sun and read aloud from a moralistic book, chanting the text piously with the melody of the New Year prayer.

On top of the mill were the dovecotes, and every afternoon Rachel used to climb up there and poke a stick into the cotes to make the lazy pigeons come out and take the air. She loved to see the golden light shining through their frail wings. Afterwards she would run down to the cold river, undress hastily, slip into the water, and, only half-dried, put on her clothes again, and run through the heated fields and into the warm forest.

On one such summer day she broke in on Meyerovitch's studies and dragged him out of his room, away from his books, to walk with her in the forest.

On the way to the forest she was silent, and her heart hammered. Meyerovitch told her about the books he was reading, but she scarcely heard him. Suddenly, seeing a broad stone, she sat down on it and drew Meyerovitch down to her side. He turned to her to say something, but she put her hand on his mouth. Then she took off his hat and played with his hair. Meyerovitch did not know what to do with himself. He went red and pale by turns; he smiled, and his lips quivered as though he were about to weep. And because he made such a queer grimace, which made him look ugly, she drew him to her and kissed him on the lips.

He smiled again, in his odd way, then became very serious, and his face was overcast, so that Rachel became frightened, and she began to cry out of her fear and out of shame for what she had done. Then they rose, and walked on, and kept on walking until the evening shadows began to fall. At first he was silent, and his silence hurt her more than if he had reproached or even insulted her. Then he took up once more the subject of those young men and young women who had an ideal. Such people, he said, had to be pure, so that they might be able to surrender their personal happiness for the sake of the ideal. The ideal, which had the power to ennoble and unite human beings, was their happiness. Without quite understanding all this, Rachel felt she herself was not pure, she was a sinner; she would never be able to compare herself to those young men and women; she carried around nothing but impure thoughts. She saw herself as a lost soul, and that night she was the unhappiest creature in all of God's world.

The next morning Meyerovitch packed his few belongings in his
tattered valise, which was tied round with string, and returned to
the city. Neither grandfather's plea, nor Rachel's tightened lips
could move him from his resolve. The Litvak smiled patiently at
the old man's words, and kept on repeating:

"What can I do if the city pulls me like that?"

But Rachel knew that he was leaving because of her, the impure
one. And this only made her think with more reverence of the
young men and young women who guarded their ideal in the big
cities. She was overcome by an unbearable longing to be among
them, perhaps even be one of them.

V

It became impossible for her to stay on in the village. Everything,
the field, the river, the forest, the mill itself, had become tiny and
ignoble in her eyes by contrast with the wonder of the ideal which
could be found only in a great city. The life to which she had been
accustomed became intolerably dull. Whenever she had the chance
she would make a trip to the city and visit her uncle, in the hope of
finding Meyerovitch there. But when they met he hardly spoke to
her. He only smiled. He also lent her books to read, and she did
read them, though there was much in them that she did not understand. But like a pious Jew reading the Psalms, she did not omit a
single word. Then the books too became wearisome. She wanted
some activity which she could understand.

When she began to look for something in her life, she perceived
things which had escaped her attention till then; she stopped to
consider the life of the peasants in the village and to compare it
with her own life.

The village where grandfather's mill stood was a very poor one.
It had no more than eighty families, two or three hundred souls in
all—a small colony wedged in between the estates of two great and
wealthy families. On either side of the colony there was abundance,
rich fields in which the grain grew thick, fat meadows for the
cattle of the noble families, well-timbered woods. But the village
peasants hungered together with their beasts; all year round they

lacked food, and in the winter they lacked wood for heating. Their children ran about barefoot and in rags, fought with each other for a crust of bread, and rolled about in the mud like animals. Two morgans of earth, less than nine acres, was alloted to each villager; there was not earth enough for a potato crop to feed him the year through. In the spring, the loveliest time of the year, when the village peasants were sowing their potatoes, their children went hungry. And because of this perpetual hunger, because of the watery food which failed to satisfy them, many of the children grew up cripples; they were undergrown, undeveloped; some of them were idiots, others had big heads and thin, rickety legs, so that they did not walk naturally, but crawled about on all fours.

Rachel had never paid attention to this picture before. It had seemed to her that this was the way of the world—some were poor, others were rich. The village peasants lived one way, the noble families another way. And not only the noble families, but she and her grandfather, too. It was natural for the girls in the village to fight tooth and nail over a pair of shoes or an old dress which she threw out; it was natural for them to wear on Sundays what she found too tattered for weekdays. She and grandfather ate good white bread and lived in a strong stone house, while the peasants ate potatoes and lived, together with their beasts, in ruined hovels. It seemed natural, too, that Anton and Stepan should work in grandfather's mill, that their wives should wash the floors and the laundry in grandfather's house, and that their children should cast envious glances at the clothes which were made for her in the city; all this had to be because it had always been.

But since she began to think about the young people who sacrificed themselves for their ideal, she realized that this did not have to be. It was wrong that the world should be so. No one was to blame, but somehow rich and poor had been placed under a curse, and someone had to come now and liberate them from it. Everyone, it seemed to her, rich and poor alike, longed for a better world. Nor was it just the human beings who were filled with this longing. The earth itself longed for another life. The fields lay stretched out in the dewy nights and wept that they had been condemned to feed only the rich, leaving the poor to starve. The forest wrapped itself in dark shadows and lamented. The lean cattle of the village peasants turned an imploring gaze on the fat meadows of the rich, fenced off from their watering mouths. Even the stars looked down in the night like eyes filled with pity for the earth which had sunk so low. Everything, Rachel believed, had to be liberated from the curse, and who knew the path to this liberation if not "they," the young people with an "ideal"? They were all working for the salvation of the world, they sacrificed their lives to this end, and she, Rachel, could not compare herself with them, she could not be of them because she was a sinner, she was an "egoist," who went around filled with base and wicked thoughts which made the blood rush into her face whenever she became aware of them even though she was alone.

She wanted to transform herself into one of the young people with an ideal and engage in their activities. And she began by carrying things out of the house, her personal possessions, dresses, shoes, underwear, and distributing them among the peasant girls in the village. Finally, when she had not a good dress left, she felt contented. And when grandfather pleaded with her to have a new dress made, she refused and wore the same clothes on Sabbath as on the weekdays. When she had nothing of her own left to give away, she carried other things out of the house—food, crockery, dishes, and even linens. Then the idea came to her that she might teach reading and writing to the village children. She gathered some of the little ones in her home, and gave them rich white Jewish bread, which they ate greedily; but they did not want to learn anything. Rachel struggled with them for some time, then gave it up.

As autumn drew on her restlessness became a fever, and the tugging at her heart toward the great unknown city where Meyerovitch's young men and women lived became a torment. She decided finally to see Meyerovitch again, but to see him alone this time, and to beg him to send her to the people with an ideal, the people in the big city.

Swallowing her pride and her modesty, she clambered with beating heart up the steps which led to Meyerovitch's garret, above the shop of a Polish cobbler. It was evening, and the room was filled with the acrid fumes of a lamp. Meyerovitch had not heard her knock, had not heard her enter; he sat hunched over his books, and she slipped into a corner and watched him as if he were a holy man, and waited till he would notice her. When he learned what it was she wanted, the names and addresses of some of the people with an ideal, he smiled, and the smile was followed by an unhappy grimace. He answered:

"I can't give you names and addresses. If you look for those people, you'll find them."

As she was leaving, he rose abruptly, and tried to dissuade her from her resolve.

"Don't go to the big city," he blurted out.

"Why?"

"You are so young—it's pitiful—" he answered, and got no further, stopped by a fit of coughing.

The compassion which Meyerovitch had displayed only strengthened her will, for now she was determined to show him that she was not afraid; she too could sacrifice herself for an ideal.

When her grandfather heard from Rachel that she had made up her mind to go to the great city, he made no answer, did not try to dissuade her. He only became more silent than ever and absented himself more and more from the house. He passed all his days and half the nights in the mill, set the wheels to turning, whether or not there was something for the stones to grind. Sometimes in the dead of night Rachel, half asleep, was aware of a frail old figure stealing into her room, felt rather than saw it approach her and sit down on the edge of the bed; long and silently her grandfather's face was bent over hers. She would not open her eyes, lest she disturb him.

But once, when they were both sitting down to the evening meal at the end of a mournful autumn day, her grandfather suddenly drew her to him and made her sit on his lap, as she had been wont to do in her childhood. And he played with her again, feeding her, one spoonful for her and one for him, and he rubbed his beard against her face, and called her by the old baby-names. Then suddenly he took her hand, and fixed upon her two big, strange eyes.

"Little one," he said, "how can you leave me like this in my old age? Wait a little while, I'm going to die soon."

"Grandpa," she answered, hiding her face in discomfort and shame, "I must, one *has* to."

"I've no one left. All have died. All, all. And you are going away. Wait, wait a while, little one, I too will soon be dead."

She wiped the tears from his eyes, and began to laugh, as if he were talking nonsense. Soon he too forgot everything, forgot that she was going away, and laughed with her out of his tear-filled eyes.

The Festival of Booths came and went; the leaves fell in a drift from the trees, and the wind carried away the withered fir twigs from the tattered roof of the booth. Then grandfather began to prepare her for the journey. He took her to the town, ordered dresses for her, shoes, linen, and a new suitcase. He himself packed the things, and while he did so he spoke long and earnestly to the suitcase: "If my little one wants to go to the city, am I the one to hold her back? Let my child go where her heart desires." Before he finished the packing he clambered up to the attic and brought down two cheeses which had been dried in the sun. "That goes along, too." Then he took out a little bag which he had sewn himself, put some paper money into it, and hung it round Rachel's neck. He also had a letter for her, addressed to a cousin of his, in Warsaw.

"I wrote him quite a time ago," he said, "and told him that you were coming to live with him. They're expecting you."

Astonished, Rachel asked, "But how did you know that I was going to Warsaw?"

"I knew it, my child. I've known it a long time."

The next morning grandfather harnessed the white gelding to the wicker-work cart. Then he went into the house, washed himself, combed his beard, and put on his Sabbath clothes; and Rachel saw him carry out to the cart his own valise, covered with the rep sheath which grandmother had made for it years and years ago.

There was a long, secret conference between grandfather and Anton, the mill caretaker, after which grandfather carefully locked the doors, put the keys into his pocket, and ordered Anton to drive to the railroad station.

Throughout the long drive grandfather was silent, communing with himself. When they came to the station he left her to buy the ticket, and when the train arrived he got on with her, to find her a comfortable place. But instead of getting off, he sat down next to her, and when Rachel, frightened, told him that the train stayed only a minute and was about to pull out, he broke into a sudden smile, and turned two, big pleading eyes on her.

"Where my little one will be, I will be too."

And he accompanied her on the journey.

VI

It was in Warsaw that I became acquainted with Rachel.

She had already been in the big city several weeks. She lived with her grandfather in two little rooms under the roof of a house in the Soletz Street, near the Vistula. I became a visitor to this modest home. But let me tell of these incidents in their proper order.

I, in my youth, traveled the same road as Rachel; I too had come to Warsaw driven by the longing for an ideal, for something which would give content to my life. For the content which had been instilled into me by my upbringing in the faith of my fathers seemed then, as it seemed for thousands of my contemporaries, to lack meaning. The daily prayers, the daily studies in the synagogue house, had become like an empty melody with which I sought to beguile my desire for that which would restore, in its original strength, my faith in God, in the sacred books, in the Messiah. I thought that in Warsaw I would find this ideal, and thither I came like Rachel, and like hundreds of other Jewish boys and girls out of remote and scattered villages in Poland. I knocked at the doors of all the Jewish writers who lived in Warsaw, the men whom I, the village boy, had long regarded as gods. I visited all the editorial offices, I met many well-known persons, many obscure ones, and I had got no further. I did not know what I was looking for; I drifted about the city without an aim or purpose, in utter loneliness. I did not want to take up a trade. There was no special kind of work I wanted to do. I thought that something big was in store for me, but what this big something was, and how I would chance across it, I had not the slightest notion. Until at last I fell into a despairing mood, became a "pessimist" and turned teacher; which is to say that I gave private lessons and taught others what I did not know myself. I was a piece of flotsam in the great city, convinced that there was no future either for humanity or myself.

There was an acquaintance whose house I frequented, an elderly man, likewise a teacher, to whom the majority of newcomers like myself turned for help. He was widely known as a friend of the desperate young Polish Jews who came to Warsaw in search of light. He found lessons for them and loaned them a little money now and again—in effect shared with them his last piece of bread. One day, coming into his room, I saw, seated at his table, a young girl; and the first impression she made on me was of eyes—nothing but eyes. It was as if the spirit which dwells in the eyes had poured itself over her whole face. She sat with arms folded; the delicate hands might have been made of the finest porcelain; and as she spoke the hair trembled on her high forehead. In a naïve, childish voice she asked him, the teacher, to tell her what to do. She had come to Warsaw as she was, and all that she was she would gladly sacrifice for the sake of the ideal which brought happiness to human beings. She had come to him believing that he could give her the content of the ideal, in order that she might know its bliss.

She spoke so simply, with such infinite faith, such childlike purity, that it would have been the meanest sort of crime to shatter her illusions; and though my friend was only too well acquainted with these naïve provincial spirits, he took her question with the utmost seriousness. He had, besides his fineness of spirit, not a little of that naïveté which was so characteristic of our *Maskilim* of that day, those devoted men whose desire it was to bring enlightenment to the Jewish people. He sat with her a long time and told her what an earnest thing life was. He promised her that he would have her meet his friends, asked her to visit him frequently, gave her some books to read, and introduced me to her as one of the young people who was seeking the same thing as she. She listened to him as a pious Jew might listen to a great Rabbi, and at once she transferred to me the feeling of awe and respect which my friend had awakened in her. She gave me a look of frank, smiling happiness, as though she was quite certain that having found a fellow-searcher, she had practically found the ideal itself. Her trustfulness sent a wave of shame through me, and I was suddenly aware of the emptiness that was in me. It was as if at that moment I was filled with a real longing for a great faith, not for the sake of my own crippled life, but that I might endow with it this innocent child who turned to me with such infinite trustfulness.

My friend left, to attend to a lesson, and the girl and I went down. I saw neither the street nor the people on it. All my attention was given to the girl. I cannot remember now what either of us said, or whether we said anything at all. The impression remains of someone who walked at my side, singing in pure joy; an impression of childlike laughter, though she did not laugh. We walked along together, really as if we had had an appointment for this purpose; we walked a long, long time, and whether in conversation or in silence, the realization grew in me that I had achieved a great purpose, I had found that which I had come to seek in Warsaw, and of which I had despaired.

We found ourselves at last on the Soletz Street. She took my hand suddenly and said:

"Come up and visit us now. I live here with my grandfather."

I went with her, of course. I came into a tiny, double-room apartment, furnished in the old Warsaw style. The rooms were dark. Near the window a frail old man was seated, holding a book in his hand and chanting the Psalms mournfully. Rachel ran ahead of me, threw herself into the old man's arms, kissed him, caressed him, and laughed out loud in her joy. I stood awkwardly on the threshold, not knowing what to do with myself. Then Rachel remembered me, brought me into the room, and introduced me to her grandfather as one of the young people she had been looking for in Warsaw.

The old man took off his glasses, looked at me searchingly, passed his hand several times down his beard, and became very earnest. He asked me to sit down, then began plying me with questions, just to make conversation. Rachel went down with a pitcher to buy milk and rolls for supper, and she was absent for several minutes. Before her return the old man suddenly came over to me and took my hand. His was as cold as ice. The gaze which he fixed on me again sent a shiver through me. He said, without preamble:

"Young man, I do not know who you are; I do not know where my child found you, and I do not know where she is going. But I want *you* to know that she is all that is left to me of my family. I am an old man, and I have spent all my years in my village, in my windmill. It was for her sake that I came to the big, strange city. I am afraid to leave my child alone. I do not know what she is looking for; I do not know what she is doing. I am afraid for her. But you do know what she is doing and where she goes. Young man, take pity on an old one. It is all, all that is left to me of my family."

He lifted my hand to his breast, and two tears came out of his wrinkled eyes and remained hanging on the lower lids.

In my heart I made an oath that I would follow Rachel like a shadow, and be her protector in the big, strange city.

VII

In the long winter nights Rachel and I read books together by the light of the oil lamp. Her old grandfather sat in a corner and watched us. The days of my first acquaintance with Rachel were the happiest of my life. All day long I wandered through the Warsaw streets, hungry, but indescribably happy. The income from my lessons was just a little more than enough to cover my half of the rent of a garret which I shared with a friend. With what was left over I could sometimes buy myself a midday meal of bread and herring and provide myself with a clean collar to visit Rachel. But my evenings in Rachel's home were purest, unalloyed joy. Her grandfather began to take to me. I did not know why it was that

I found favor in his eyes; I wondered whether it was because I had a little learning, or because of something else. It was only later that I discovered that my first guess had been the right one. For once, when we were alone, he said to me:

"A young man who has some learning won't do a wicked thing. The sacred books, once you know them, guard you from evil deeds, whether you believe in them or not."

And I must confess that both Rachel's faith in me, and the confidence which her grandfather displayed, injected a special spirit of purity into my relations with her. I repressed every flicker of the impulses which such a situation might arouse in me. In many other respects, too, my life at that time was ennobled and purified. Something in her, shining out of her childlike eyes, made me want to be a better human being, made me want to believe that beyond our narrow, earthly joys there was a world of high, unbounded bliss. It was good to have this belief. But I did not find it easy to maintain this level at first. My desires, and my habit of yielding to them when occasion offered, asserted themselves, and there were nights of wakefulness and longing which it had not been my wont to endure. But the more I saw of her the more I understood about the happiness which lies beyond desire. I learned the taste of the bliss which is born of the renunciation of the flesh, and I discovered in myself unknown ranges of emotion and perception.

It was thus that I passed the whole winter in Rachel's company. We read a great deal during those months, and talked a great deal, too. Rachel displayed quite extraordinary gifts of understanding; they issued not from the limited field of the intelligence, but from the much wider field of instinct, of the intuitions which produce poets and prophets. Often I was astonished by the penetrating observations of which Rachel delivered herself with regard to the character of people. She formed her opinions quickly, sometimes just looking at a man for a few moments; once the opinion was formed, nothing could change it. As far as I myself can testify, her judgment was unerring; and where we others needed weeks or months to reach a conclusion with regard to someone, she obtained the same result in a flash. This intuition of hers was focused on the externals of people, and read from them to their internal nature: in particular she read the color and luster of their eyes. Her extraordinary instinct made one think of animals of the finest breeding. You would have thought she heard nothing, saw nothing, but all the time she was on the alert; she seemed to know what was going on behind her back—seemed even to guess at events which had taken place in her absence.

In the company of our friends she was shy and silent. She shrank into a corner and hid from people. Unseen, unheard, she was often ignored; and when she was noticed, many fell into the profound error of imagining that she did not understand the conversation. Just the same, they were happy to have this child among them; even when they thought they had been unaware of her presence, they discovered afterwards that it was from her, somehow, that the stream of cheerfulness had flowed into the company. It was more than cheerfulness; it was gaiety, courage, faith in ourselves, so that our conversation suddenly became a matter of cosmic importance.

As long as winter lasted Rachel's grandfather managed one way or another to reconcile himself to the city. He seldom went out. Most of the time he sat at the window, reading, or looking out at the snow and muttering into his beard. But when the pre-Passover season came, and the mild spring airs melted the snows, he became restless. He began to hanker after his mill. He heard in the night the creaking of its wings. The wind drove them round and round, and the stones had nothing to grind; so they caught at the wind and ground that, and the old man heard the wailing of the trapped wind. A great sadness came on him. He would say to us:

"A miller mustn't leave his mill in loneliness; if he does, the demons come and grind their demon flour between his stones."

He began to talk of returning, and at first he insisted that Rachel return with him. It was an unhappy time for him. Rachel would not hear of leaving Warsaw. Once, when Rachel was out of the room, her grandfather called me over into his corner, and said to me:

"I must go, whether Rachel comes with me or not. I must go, because the mill is sick for me. I'm leaving my little girl to you"—and he suddenly called me by the familiar "thou," which he had never done before—"I know you're a good friend to my granddaughter; I know that you'll look after her, and I'm putting my trust in you."

Because of his tone of voice, and because he had addressed me with such intimacy, I realized all at once that the old man looked on me as Rachel's suitor, her future husband. With reason or not, I was quite astonished; and I had enough presence of mind to try to rectify the grandfather's mistake, lest he should later make unjustified claims.

"I don't know whether I can influence your granddaughter," I said, uneasily. "I'm a stranger, after all, no relative, you understand."

He did not let me finish.

"I know, I know—a stranger, no relative. But you're a good friend of hers, aren't you?"

It was clear to me that the old man was trying to reassure himself, hold on to something, so that he might leave Warsaw with a mind at peace and return to his lonely mill. There was nothing more that I could say. Two or three days later we saw him off at the station, and from the manner of his leavetaking it was clear to both of us that he regarded me as his future grandson-in-law.

VIII

All the way back Rachel laughed at the picture, and kept repeating, "Why, granddaddy looks on you as my *fiancé.*"

The question was on my lips: "And how do you look at me?" I did not give it utterance. I only said, laughing with her:

"The old folks can't imagine any other kind of relationship between young people."

Rachel kept the little apartment and lived there alone. Her grandfather left a sum of money with her, "Enough," he said, "to see you through till you get over this foolishness and marry and settle down."

Then suddenly a change came over Rachel. Two or three days after her grandfather's departure she disappeared. That is to say, she retained her old address, came home to sleep, but was always out when I came to look for her. And if I happened to meet her on the street she was always in a great hurry. Where was she going? Oh, somewhere. She evaded my questions, but her big eyes sparkled with happiness. I was puzzled and disturbed, but I could not be insistent.

At last I did manage to find her at home, but it was just as she was preparing to move away, for she was packing her valise. I looked at her in astonishment. She cried out:

"Simon! I'm so glad you've come. I'm moving out of here, and I don't want granddaddy to know. It would make him uneasy, and he'd perhaps come back to Warsaw. Please write him that I'm still living here, and that you see me every day, and that I'm well and happy."

"Rachel, what has happened?"

"Why, nothing! I've decided to start working, that's all. I don't want to live on someone else's money any more. You know the Steinman sisters; well, Rosa Steinman is going to teach me their trade, artificial flowers. I'm going to live with them, too. I've wanted to become a worker ever so long. I'm tired of books, and I'm tired of being one of the 'intelligentsia' and of eating up granddaddy's money. I think that if you really want to do something, you've got to start with yourself, and earn your own keep. Besides, that's the only way you can come in contact with life."

A light broke in on me. From the manner of her speech, from the names she mentioned, I understood all at once what had been happening, and under whose influence she had fallen.

"Joey Rosenberg!" I blurted out. "Joey, the new apostle!"

She started back, and her eyes filled with tears. She did not look at me, but turned her gaze down on her small, delicate hands. I regretted my hasty words.

"Rachel," I said, "are you angry with me?"

"No, Simon. But you of all people shouldn't have said that. Bad and stupid people who haven't a spark of God in them think that every man who has an ideal is crazy, or else he's a swindler. But you aren't like that. And you don't know Rosenberg. If you knew him you wouldn't have said what you did."

"Perhaps," I muttered.

"Simon!" She took my hand. "Please do come this evening to the Steinmans'. Rosenberg is going to be there. He comes there every evening. You'll get to know him, and I know you'll love him, too."

She said "love him" so simply, that I did not know what to read into it. I was ill at ease and did not want to stay. A minute later I turned to go, saying as I did so, "Please forgive me if I hurt you by what I said before."

She sprang up and took my hand again. "Simon! What is the matter with you? Aren't you going to help me pack? And won't you see me to my new home?"

She used the familiar "thou." She had done that before, in the way of friendship; and never was I more grateful for her friendliness than at this moment.

And yet—I could not conceal from myself my bitter disappointment that she should have fallen under the influence of "Joey the apostle." It was true that I did not know Joey Rosenberg personally, but I had seen him, and I knew a great deal about him and his way of life. He was a man in the early thirties, the son of a wealthy manufacturer, married, and the father of two or three children. But he had the reputation of being able to make any girl he wanted fall in love with him; and there were many such. In person he was tall, pale, with the face of a Christ. He was very proud of his appearance and worked it for all it was worth. He let his hair grow, so that the locks covered his neck; he affected a little beard; and there were some who said that he even painted shadows under his eyes. He had once been a socialist and had served a prison term of six months. After that he had disappeared a while from the public eye. Now he was back again, but in a new role. He believed now in a mission of "personal influence." He became an apostle, and all his disciples were young women. He "gave up everything"—which meant that he became a worker in a factory; but this did not prevent him from letting his wife and children live with his father, the rich manufacturer. He regarded all this as a "sacrifice," even a kind of martyrdom. Half a dozen girls, daughters of well-to-do families, had, under his influence, left their homes and gone to work in factories. More than one mother who had looked forward to a happy marriage for her daughter was now calling down the wrath of heaven on Rosenberg's head. His mission ended among the well-to-do, Rosenberg had shifted his operations to the poor districts, to the workers of the Grzybov Street and the Old City. His ministrations were concentrated on the seamstresses. He picked out the best looking among them and visited them evenings. He went for walks with them and preached to them of the beauty and dignity of their working-class status. The girls did not know what he meant by all this, but they were happy to walk with him, happy to look into his face and to listen to his sweet words.

I had seen him more than once—and who had not?—strolling down the Marshallkovska in Warsaw, surrounded by a bevy of girls, and towering above them with his long hair and his apostolic face. We disliked him and considered him not only vain, foolish, and dull, but vicious to boot. He had become bored with the rich foods of his mother's home and had turned for amusement to the girls of the Jewish working classes.

And now Rachel had fallen under his influence. How was it that, in this one, crucial instance, her faultless intuition had so betrayed her? How was it that she had not perceived, with her usual swiftness of penetration, the utter shallowness and emptiness of Joey the apostle?

Then, for a moment, I turned the question on myself. Was it possible that I had listened to slander, that all my friends and acquaintances were mistaken in the man? Was it possible that Rachel was right this time, too, and that behind the apparent shallowness, behind the facade of moralistic coquetry, there was a depth of character which we were all blind to?

It must be so, I told myself. Rachel was not the kind of girl to be taken off her feet by that sickly-sweet face. And suppose I was in reality jealous of Rosenberg? Something hateful and resentful was stirring in me. It was I who was shallow and mean-spirited; it was Rachel, with her fine instinct, who had glimpsed the soul of the young man who had left the rich home of his father, had sacrificed comfort and career, to be with the workers and of them. Yes, I was jealous for many reasons—and one of them was that my own life was pointless and aimless.

So I stayed, and helped her pack; and I carried her valise through the streets, and into the Old City, where the Steinman sisters lived. And all the way I had the feeling that I was taking Rachel to him, to Joey Rosenberg, whom she had said she loved.

IX

The home of the Steinmans was by "the Iron Gate," in the heart of the Old City, over the fish and meat market; and yet it was the quietest home in Warsaw. About the building seethed the turmoil of men and women, of horses and carts; a furious clamor of haggling, of quarreling, of cursing, went up into the air: and with it a thick aroma of decaying fish, tallow, and naphtha. The three sisters lived in a garret apartment and made their artificial flowers out of violet and grass-green bits of linen. A fourth in that tiny home was an old father who had lost the use of his legs. No one knew what was wrong with him; to all appearances he was a strong, well-built, heavy man, with a full, round face; nor was there any symptom of disease in his legs.

Once he had been a prominent merchant, always to be seen running in and out of the Stock Exchange. But for the last seven or eight years his legs had refused to serve him. They might just as well have been two leaden weights attached to his torso. There he lay on the sofa, a fine figure of a man, with a handsome beard and a face that seemed to radiate health, and he had to be looked after like a child. He was ashamed of his condition, ashamed that his children had to work for him and ashamed of his healthy appearance. Once during this stretch of eight years a miracle had occurred with him. He had suddenly felt that his legs were ready to serve him again. Without a word he had risen from the sofa, and a cry of amazement went up from his daughters: "Daddy's walking!" Stiffly he had taken five or six steps; and then his legs had refused to carry him further, and he had fallen to the floor. Since that time he had been preoccupied with one thought: "What is it? I walked, didn't I? I walked five steps, one straight after the other." And his life was filled with the problem of the five steps which he had taken that day.

This was Nachman Steinman now, the Nachman Steinman whose wealth had been the envy of half of Warsaw and whose wife today lived away from home because she was superintendent of a second-rate Jewish orphanage. She still wore the black velvet dresses with lace collars which she had saved out of her days of affluence; she still spoke Polish with a strong Warsaw accent, and a Yiddish which was half German—likewise a remnant of the days of social prominence. Every Saturday she read a Polish book and recited some of the poetry of Mitzkevitch. She had brought up her children in her own spirit, had taught them love of the Polish fatherland and poems by Mitzkevitch and Slovatzky.

When the disaster came, when the father, unable to run about the Stock Exchange, had lost all his money, the daughters did not know what to do. Untrained as they were, nothing remained for them but to "go into service"—the ultimate humiliation. Better to die of hunger than to become a servant girl. With the last remnants of the family capital they opened a café on the Grzybov; but their customers were not of the right sort—sporty barbers and shady characters, who spoke impudently to the young women. The mother realized that this was not the kind of business in which to keep her daughters if she wanted them to retain their reputations and marry decently some day.

They struggled along until one day Joey Rosenberg, the rich manufacturer's son, "the new apostle," came into the café. It was he —the story ran—who advised them to give it up, lent them the money to move, and installed them in their present quarters. The girls learned to make artificial flowers, and now they earned barely enough for their own keep and their father's. The mother lived in the orphanage.

The oldest daughter, Rosa, was as quiet as a dove, a saintly character. She was no longer young, but it was clear that she had once been very beautiful. Her face was delicately formed, and on it rested an eternal expression of gentleness. Those who did not know her story surmised that some tragedy had taken place in her life, some disastrous love episode, and that it was for this reason that she had not married. But her indifference to men—indifference in which there was a touch of quiet distaste and contempt—was not the result of her own unhappy experiences. It was the tragedy in the life of a girl friend which had fixed Rosa Steinman in this attitude.

It was because her nearest and dearest friend, with whom she had grown up and from whom she had been inseparable, had been betrayed by a man and had died of shame and wretchedness, that Rosa Steinman had learned to think of all men as potential murderers, the natural enemies of woman, forever planning her betrayal. Her friend's lover had taken two lives: that of the woman who was dead, and Rosa Steinman's.

The love which she had once been prepared to give to a husband, the tenderness and thoughtfulness which were part of her, she now poured out on the children of Grzybov and on her father. Along the whole street she was known as "the mother"; if a child was sick, if a mother had to leave her little ones at home, Rosa Steinman was sent for. And in her own house she was not only nurse and companion to her father—she was maid of all work. She took the heaviest tasks on herself, scrubbed the floors, did the laundry, washed the dishes. If the house sparkled with cleanliness, it was because of Rosa. And it was all done so unpretentiously, so good-humoredly and tacitly, that no one realized what was going on. Perhaps it was some girl like Rosa Steinman who gave rise to the legend of the mice which come out at night and do the household work when everyone is asleep. Rosa had no complaints, no claims; and, oddly enough, even her hands entered into the conspiracy of concealment, for they remained soft and delicate, as if they were occupied only with the making of artificial flowers. No one remarked on the queer circumstance that, with all her labors, Rosa found time to help her sisters at their work, to carry the finished flowers to the factory, to bring home the raw material, and to do the famliy marketing.

If Rosa was the dove in the household, her younger sister Bertha was the raven. Bertha was a dark, powerfully built girl of twenty-two or twenty-three. The ripeness of her will shone from her round cheeks and full lips. She was ready for marriage and knew it. But her sister had instilled into her something of her own fear, if not of her revulsion from men. Rosa had no desire for a husband. Bertha had every desire; she wanted a husband, a home, children; but she had an unnatural terror of being betrayed. She had to be certain, beyond all shadow of a doubt, that the man she chose was of "fine character," and would not, like the husband of Rosa's dead friend, run away soon after the marriage. Bertha was not afraid of poverty; she was prepared to assume the heaviest burdens—as long as she was sure that she would be together with her man. And that was the dread question: would not the man leave her when she was no longer young?

Bertha had no lack of suitors, and she was friendly with all of them in turn. But always she shrank back before the intimacy could ripen into a proposal, because she had not convinced herself that she had found a "fine character." And so every month it was another young man who was invited to the house, and every month it was another conference with her sisters—and chiefly with Rosa. And Rosa was hurt; she was deeply offended by her sister's marketing expeditions; she tried to conceal it, but she did not always succeed. More than once Bertha said to her:

"What do you want? That everyone should be like you? You're a saint, and it's easy for you to be a saint. You don't want anything any more. But I do. I want to get married. I don't want to live all my life like this."

Only once did Rosa venture on open remonstrance. During one winter Bertha had managed to keep company steadily with a young man; and when spring came she cashiered him abruptly and brought another young man home. That night Rosa said to her, with unwonted vehemence:

"Bertha, what are you doing? What do you want?"

"I want to get married," cried her sister. "I don't want to be an old maid like you."

"But don't go around marketing and bargaining," said Rosa, "if you really want to get married. I know, I'm afraid to take the risk, so I've given up the idea of marrying. But you haven't given it up, and you don't want to take the risk either. You can't keep up this picking and choosing for ever."

Bertha did not answer. Her eyes filled with helpless tears, and Rosa was filled with remorse. It occurred to her that she herself was at fault, because she had instilled her own terrors into her younger sister. She drew Bertha to her, kissed her, begged her forgiveness, and promised never again to reproach her or be impatient with her. But since that time her sister never again consulted her about her young men.

Very different from Rosa and Bertha was the youngest daughter, Matilda.

The favorite name by which they called Matilda at home was "Goldfingers," because of the marvelous skill which lay in her little hands. There was no comparison between her work and that of her sisters. The little pieces of colored linen, violet and pink and green, flew out from her scissors, and before you knew it the flower had been twisted and sewn, and it looked as though it had just been pulled, together with the surrounding leaves, from some garden bush. She was just as quick and clever with her dresses. She made them herself, and not from some fashion book, but out of her head. She had only to take a length of silk, drape it about her lithe little body, pull in a fold here, let out another there, and she had a dress of which the most expensive modiste in Warsaw would have been proud. She would loosen her hair, pass her hands through it, and there grew up, as of itself, a perfect coiffure. She seemed to walk always in fresh winds; she made one think of a young tree in a dewy field, every leaf and twig bathed and freshened. She carried the spring with her.

X

No one who knew about Joey Rosenberg's interest in the Steinman family had to be told that it centered exclusively about his latest infatuation, the youngest daughter. I, who in a moment of self-abasement had been ready to revise the popular opinion about "the new apostle," saw the situation a few hours later. I had taken Rachel over to the Steinmans', and left her there. I returned at her bidding the same evening. I realized several things: first, that "the new apostle" was concerned only about the youngest member of the Steinman family; second, that young Matilda was very much in love with "the new apostle"; and third, that it was at his request —should one say command?—that Rachel had moved to the Steinmans'.

Little Matilda made no attempt to conceal her feelings. She was so proud that Joey Rosenberg had turned his apostolic attentions toward her that she would have liked all the world to know. She prepared for his visit this evening like a bride preparing for the visit of the bridegroom. Rosa gave more than her usual attention to the living room. And the helpless father, lying on the sofa, tugged convulsively at his beard, while a dull flame smoldered in the deep-sunken eyes under the heavy brows.

The door opened at last, and "the apostle" entered. Since I had last seen him he seemed to have grown a little taller, and paler, too. Perhaps that was the effect of the dramatic, long, black cape which swung from his shoulders. But the trimmed black beard was the same, and so were the curls which hung down the back of his neck. Naturally he carried a book. Seeing me, he started slightly and could not suppress a faint grimace. But he forgot me, and his chagrin and everything else, when little Matilda ran up to him and, taking his hands, looked up lovingly into his face. The grimace yielded to a gratified and conceited smile. I noticed that Rosa, too, was strangely affected by Joey Rosenberg. The look in her eyes was one compounded of fascination, fear, and—yes—adoration. She removed the cape from his shoulders, carefully, slowly, as if she were privileged to perform a ritual. Rosenberg was a trifle confused. Some time passed before he noticed that Rachel was there; but as he sat down at the table, little Matilda at his side, shamelessly leaning her head on his shoulder, he looked up.

"Rachel! Are you living here already?"

"Yes, I've moved my things. Tomorrow Matilda's going to start teaching me how to make flowers."

"Yes, Joey," and Matilda lifted her head like a bird peeping out of its nest. "I'm going to love it, too. Look at her hands, and at those long, delicate fingers. I love her hands." She took Rachel's hand and kissed it.

Rachel blushed, glanced at me, and withdrew her hand timidly. I must have smiled, for I noticed that Rosenberg looked at me uncomfortably. I was obviously introducing a discordant note into the evening. I left the table, went over to the sofa, and began a conversation with the father. He answered me distractedly, for his angry eyes were fixed on the table where Rosenberg, happy to be rid of me, was reading from the book or manuscript he had brought with him, while the three girls—Bertha was not at home—listened with bated breath. The sick man on the sofa changed color and bit his lips. Of his three daughters he loved the little one most; he could not bear to see her snuggling close to this womanish man; he could not bear the thought of their going out together, to places he knew nothing about and could not ask about either. For he had to bear in mind that if this household was somehow being maintained, it was because of the start that Rosenberg had given it.

It was idle for me to try to delude myself into a good opinion of Joey Rosenberg. He revealed himself with appalling clearness. Whatever he did for or to anyone was in his eyes a benefaction; good or bad, he regarded it as a sanctity. It did not occur to him that it was a criminal thing to encourage so many girls in their foolish infatuation, for which he could not make any return and which could lead to nothing because he was already married and a father of children. He regarded himself, instead, as the bestower of a special kind of grace; and even when the relationship with his "sacred brides" took on a definitely unsacred character, there was always that unique "something" about him which lifted it into a higher sphere. Nor did he dream that in neglecting his own wife and children he was committing a baseness. His exalted mood was never penetrated by the suspicion that he was torturing the sick father who lay helpless on the sofa. He moved in a bright, hazy halo of self-satisfaction which nothing could disperse. He was serving a high, humanitarian ideal.

It was not only rage that tortured old Steinman; it was jealousy. His sickness, whatever it was, had affected only his legs. In all other respects he was still a strong and healthy man. He longed for action and for the out-of-doors. His only solace was the company and the friendship of his daughters. He had reached a stage when their attentions and their tenderness had become a necessity for him. But ever since Rosenberg frequented the house, his favorite daughters, the oldest and the youngest, had become—it seemed so to him, at least—quite perfunctory in their attentions to him. In any case, they now had less time for him. No sooner did the stranger enter than they clustered about him, their eyes fixed on him, their ears strained to catch every word of his.

I did my best to entertain the old man. I was not successful. The sullen fire did not die in the deep-sunken eyes. I did not know what Rosenberg was reading; I could not catch his explanatory remarks. But I could not help observing how the three girls kept drawing closer to him, as if they wanted to become one with him. Out of the corner of my eyes I could see how Rosenberg's pale face grew paler; I could see the smile on his lips, an earnest, almost pious smile, which, when he was not reading, was directed now to this one, now to that one, of the three girls. Old Steinman was watching, too; and when his eyes, withdrawing from the hateful scene encountered mine, I was frightened. There was in them a torment which no man could long endure without an explosion.

I cannot tell what would have happened if the door had not suddenly burst open to admit Bertha. She came in like a whirlwind, pulling in her wake an embarrassed young man who clutched at his collar, as if he was afraid that it would fly up and engulf his chin, and coughed uninterruptedly.

"Daddy!" shouted Bertha. "I want to introduce my beau, Moses Silberstein!"

It was like a thunderbolt. And indeed, the three girls at the table sat petrified, as if a thunderbolt had struck them. They stammered something in reply to the introduction. Joey Rosenberg picked up his book and fled.

Later, when I tried to speak with Rachel she did not seem to understand what I was saying. An odd, dreamy expression was fixed on her eyes; her mind was elsewhere.

XI

Joey Rosenberg lived up to his record. It was not little Matilda alone who fell in love with him. Rachel was drawn along, as if by a magic compulsion, and the oldest sister, too, with all her dread of men and their criminality. Rosa, who had so long remained indifferent or contemptuous toward the masculine world and could by now almost be classified as an old maid, underwent a disturbing transformation. Her face and her spirits brightened; her fingers became more nimble. But the most remarkable circumstance—and this really constituted the mystery of Joey Rosenberg's hold on women—was that not the slightest sign of jealousy was to be observed in any of the three women. On the contrary, one would have said that they were the happier for being in love with one and the same man.

In particular, Rachel and Matilda were drawn closer to each other by their common adoration. Their souls ran together, as if they had found simultaneous salvation in a new religion. I saw them sometimes when Rosenberg was not there. They sat with their arms round each other, exchanging secrets. They shared the same bed, they ate from the same plate. And on evenings when Rosenberg was due, they washed and combed each other's hair, lent each other dresses and ribbons, as if each one was content that the other should be more attractive.

I saw all this, and was silent. I was eaten up by anger; my old passion for Rachel returned and released a hot flood of jealousy. My nights became one long torment. Ever since Rachel had gone to live with the Steinmans I could not see her except by visiting the house, and when I did see her her conversation was exclusively about "the apostle." She would ask me, again and again:

"Simon, tell me, honestly, isn't he fascinating?"

Or else she would say:

"Simon, don't come tomorrow evening. He wants to read us

something he's written, and he'd rather you weren't there. He's not comfortable with you around."

And whenever she mentioned his name, "Joey," it was with infinite tenderness, though she never failed to call me by my first name and to use the familiar "thou" to me.

I did whatever she asked. When "Joey" did not want me to be there, I absented myself. I would walk to and fro for hours on the pavement in front of her house. I saw the light shining upstairs. He was there, with Rachel, *my* Rachel, and my presence made him "uncomfortable"; so I walked to and fro, hour after hour, on the sidewalk.

There was still another remarkable circumstance in all this. I could not hate him. I could be angry with him, but I could not summon up a feeling of hatred. Ludicrous as he was, the man had a certain pathos about him, a naïve, primitive pathos, which made hatred impossible. You could work yourself into a frightful rage about him in his absence; the moment you confronted him you forgave him.

On one such evening, when Rachel had forbidden me to come up because I disturbed her Joey's mood, I made up my mind to wait for him. He came down close to midnight, and when I approached him took off his broad, soft hat with a friendly gesture.

"I'm really glad to see you," he said. "There's something I've long wanted to ask you. About Rachel's grandfather, the miller. She told me that you and he are good friends, and that you've often talked with him."

His friendliness, his frank approach, choked back the words I had been rehearsing. But at the same time the picture of the old grandfather rose before my eyes, and I remembered the promise I had made him—tacitly, it was true, but nonetheless definitely— to look after his granddaughter.

I said, apropos of nothing, as it seemed:

"Rosenberg. You are married, aren't you? You have children."

"Why, certainly," he answered, and his tone was actually joyous.

"What are your relations with Rachel?"

Rosenberg stopped dead, fixed two big, sad eyes on me, and waited.

"I ask this," I continued, "because Rachel's grandfather, the old miller, entrusted his granddaughter to me before he left Warsaw. He also told me that Rachel is all that's left to him of his family. If something happens to her—I tell you this in all seriousness—it will be the death of him."

Rosenberg maintained silence for more than a minute, then suddenly seized my hand, and said, solemnly:

"I can't tell you how grateful I am to you for telling me this."

Then again a silence. I imagine he was looking at me earnestly, but the street was dark, and I could not be sure.

"Look," he said, "let's go into a café and sit down. I want to talk with you."

We dropped in at the nearest café. Rosenberg sat down opposite me and stared into my eyes. You could have sworn that the man was honest through and through.

"Do you know why I asked you here?" he said. "Because I want to see your eyes. If I want to speak with a man, I've got to see his eyes." He paused. "You said something a few minutes ago: that I'm a married man, and have children. You meant to say, of course, that Rachel might fall in love with me, lose her heart to me, and—well, as you pointed out, I have a wife and children. You are right, of course."

What was he driving at? I did not answer, and he continued:

"I'm grateful to you for raising the subject. I'm grateful to you for your interest in Rachel. But let's be frank with each other. You're a man of free mind, you're modern, you're liberated from old taboos. You understand quite well that it's not just the fact that I have a wife and children that moved you to speak to me. You understand that having a wife and children doesn't mean that I've lost interest in the warmth of the sun and the scent of flowers. It was another reason that impelled you to speak. Yes, let's be open and frank with each other."

These reiterations of a desire for frankness, these long preparations, were making my blood run cold. Why didn't he come out with it?

"Tell me," he asked, "are you in love with Rachel? Are you jealous of me?"

"Yes," I answered, curtly.

"Very good! Now we know where we stand. And now I can tell you this: the fact that you're jealous of me brings you close to me, establishes a bond between us. And I want that. Bonds of emotion are good things. Human beings shouldn't stand clear of each other, like rooted trees which can't approach each other. Human beings should be bound to each other. Is your jealousy, after all, nothing but pain? Doesn't your realization that we love the same person bring you nearer to me? Is there only anger against me in your heart? Isn't there also, behind that anger, and even in it, the softer music of a certain satisfaction? And do you know what that music, which is part of jealousy, springs from? It springs from the human love for all human things! It springs from our common humanity. You don't hate me in your jealousy; you love me. I have become nearer, dearer, more important to you because I love the same person you do. Why should I seek to deprive you of this feeling? No, I am happy to have enriched you with it. Yes, I love Rachel, and the fact that you too love her does not diminish or disturb my love for her. It makes my love deeper and finer, because love is the highest expression that man possesses, and there can never be enough of it. Love always binds, and our love for Rachel binds us to each other. I have been enriched by your love for her. Do you understand me?"

What was it that prevented me from flinging my cup of coffee in his face? Was it the driveling appeal to my "modernity," my "free-mindedness?" I mumbled a question at him. Had he spoken like this to Rachel? Did *she* understand his theories?

"Of course I've spoken to her about it. Those evenings together, with Matilda, and Rachel, and Rosa, we always speak about it, about the universal bond of love which ought to exist between all human beings. I don't know whether Rachel understands me entirely. Or Matilda, for that matter. But those children feel what they don't understand. They're nearer to the pure primitive in humanity, which was always and everywhere more communal. It's the egotistic human intelligence which has destroyed this feeling of commonalty and made of happiness a personal and individual and selfish experience. Among young girls there is always a readiness to understand a shared love, a common love. They haven't yet been corrupted by the egotistic strategy of adults. Rachel and Matilda may not understand as clearly as I, but their feeling is deeper."

So this was his new line. No more talk about the dignity of labor. Dry-throated, I asked:

"May I ask what your feelings are for Matilda? Or is this a secret?"

"Between me and those who have become bound to me through love," he said, solemnly, "there are no secrets. All the feelings which enrich me are part of their feelings. And for you"—to my positive horror he addressed me with the familiar "thou"—"for you, who are bound to me through Rachel, everything is open. I am bound to everyone who loves Rachel. And so it is with Matilda, too. Whoever loves her enters also into the sphere of my love. And the bigger the number, the larger the sphere and the freer the world. This love will spread to all humanity, and beyond, to the beasts and birds, yes, and to the green things of forest and field. And so my wife's love, or Rachel's, is no hindrance to my love for Matilda, or for another. Love begets love. The more I love, the more I am ready for love. My heart ripens and opens and grows. It becomes like the sun, which shines everywhere, like the dew, which falls everywhere, on all things. All individual love must be taught to expand, until it embraces the earth, and every race of man. No one must feel that his love is a personal possession; it is part of the commonalty of human love."

"You mean," I asked, "that in these human relations there should be no such thing as 'belonging.' All should belong to all. Is that the idea?"

Rosenberg did not answer. The spate of words had suddenly stopped. He called over the waiter and paid for the coffee. Then he rose, extended his hand to me, and said:

"See it how you will. You will understand me only if you will stop thinking badly of me. All I can say now is, that I'm not sorry we've had this talk. And I'm not sorry that we both love the same person. No, it makes me very happy."

With that he left me.

XII

A little time was to pass before I discovered the nature of Joey Rosenberg's new line. After our slightly nauseating conversation he disappeared, and neither I nor the Steinman household knew what had happened to him. When I came up to visit Rachel, she and Matilda were for ever whispering to each other; they were very sad, and very perplexed. But they had no information for me.

And this sadness of Rachel's, her absorption in Rosenberg, and the fact that he had spoken to her—according to his own account—about his theories, which she had "accepted" emotionally if not intellectually, all this combined now to deaden in me the feeling I had had for her. My visits became less frequent, then stopped for a time, and I had about made up my mind never to return. Against this resolution, however, there was the tacit promise I had given her grandfather. But then, what could I do for her? What had I done for her? It occurred to me that I ought to see Rachel once more and talk matters over with her before I wrote to the old man to come and take his daughter back to the village. I was by now neither hurt nor disappointed. Rachel, who had once overwhelmed me by her loveliness, had lost all charm for me. It seemed to me that I had talked myself into my state of mind about her and her qualities. I had, at bottom, only felt a certain responsibility for her. Even that sense of responsibility was now formal, the result of an unspoken promise; as to what happened to her, what she did, whom she met in the great city, I had no genuine concern.

Before I went to see her for the last time I rehearsed carefully the sentences which would both discharge my responsibility and make evident to her that I no longer had any tender feelings for her.

"The promise which I made your grandfather," I was going to say, formally (I had made no explicit promise), "compels me to have this talk with you. Please believe me that I have no personal motive." And then I would tell her, simply and coldly, that I considered it my duty to write to her grandfather and ask him to take her home. It was all very clear and very definite in my mind; and I repeated the cool statement several times, with considerable relish, when I made my way to the Steinman house in the Old City the next forenoon. But no sooner had I crossed the threshold, no sooner did I see Rachel seated at the work-table with the others, and hear the laughter of her voice, than the words died in my memory, so that I did not know what had brought me on this visit.

"Look!" cried Rachel, joyously. "Look who's here. Simon!" She sprang up from the table, ran over to me, flung her arms round me, and kissed me. I blushed.

"Where have you been?" she asked. "Do you know that I came to look for you, at your house, and didn't find you? What happened to you?"

I stared down at her. Her wide-open eyes shone with innocent happiness, that pure joy which may be seen only in the eyes of children. Her voice was as free, as unshadowed, as in the first days of our meeting, when I could not hear it without thinking of the fields and meadows in which she had grown up.

I muttered something about work. She did not hear me, but went on delightedly, "Do you know, Joey's going to be here this evening. He's been sick. That's why he hasn't been here. Look! That's in honor of his visit tonight," and she pointed to a bouquet of real flowers standing in a vase.

Then my resolution came to mind again.

"Rachel," I stammered, "there's something I have to tell you."

My manner startled her.

"What is it?" she asked. "What's happened?"

"Nothing's happened. There's only something we have to talk about."

Rosa lifted her head from the flowers she was working on.

"Simon, won't you eat something with us first?" she asked. "I'm just going to set the table."

"Thanks, no, I'm not hungry."

"No, Rosa, let him tell me first," said Rachel. And she pulled me into the common bedroom, sat down on the bed, and made me sit down beside her.

"Now. What's happened."

"Nothing's happened, I tell you. It's just this." I forced out the words. "I don't like Joey Rosenberg."

She would not take me seriously. "Jealous, eh?" she laughed, shaking a finger ludicrously under my nose. "Is that nice of you, Simon? Joey isn't the kind of person one can be jealous of."

"And why not?"

"Because he's an angel, that's why."

"Rachel—"

"Oh, I know that he had a talk with you. Joey told me all about it."

"But how could he have told you? You just said he's been sick and he's coming back this evening for the first time."

"But I saw him just the same. I went to him. I had to go."

"What? You went to him? Have you been visiting him long?"

"No, only since he was sick. He wrote that he wanted to see me, and his wife brought me the note. She took me to him. That's when he told me about his conversation with you."

"What? His wife? His wife knows about his visits here?"

"Of course she does. She herself asked me to visit Joey. She likes me very much; she loves me. She's asked me to come and live with them."

"And does she know that Rosenberg loves you, and Matilda?" I asked, horrified.

"Simon! Don't use that tone of voice! Joey is permitted to love, because he loves differently from all of you, because he's purer and finer than any of you."

"Listen, Rachel—"

She interrupted with a long, breathless, raving speech. "Yes, yes, I might have known that you wouldn't understand, because your sensuality blinds you. But Joey can love his wife, and Matilda, and me, and none of us is jealous. Not a bit jealous. On the contrary, we only love each other all the more. And I'll tell you what. Joey has a great plan for us all. He's going to take us to Palestine, or to America, somewhere, and start a colony, which we're going to call 'Link of Love,' because we're all links of love. And Simon, I want you to come with us, and be one of us, I'll be there, and Matilda, and Rosa, and Joey's wife, and other good people and fine spirits. Wherever we hear of a fine spirit, of a noble person, we'll try to get him or her into our colony. Come with us! You'll see how beautiful we'll make it. We'll live together like brothers and sisters. Each one's child will be everyone's child. There'll be no fighting, and no envies, and no jealousies. I want you to come! You were my friend, weren't you? I know I've been bad to you. You loved me, and I loved you, too, and wouldn't show it to you. We hide our loveliest feelings because we're bad. And it was Joey who taught me not to be ashamed of love. Simon, I always loved you, yes, I did." And suddenly she flung her arms around me and kissed me on the mouth.

It was not so much this action as the wild, babbling nonsense —the echo of Joey Rosenberg's insanity—which left me paralyzed. Before I could come to, Rachel cried out, loudly, "Matilda! Rosa!" and the two Steinman girls came running in.

"Look, Simon," said Rachel. "These two are my nearest and dearest. They are my family. Joey has made us into one family by his love for us. They're my sisters. And you're my brother, whom I kept away from me and shamed by hiding my feelings from him. But that won't be any more. And now I want you to kiss your sisters, Matilda and Rosa."

I looked dumbly at the three women, loosed myself gently from Rachel's hold, and went from the room.

XIII

I returned that evening, to Joey's reception, and learned there and then of new developments in the complicated family situation. Mrs. Steinman had the evening free and had come home in order to help in the preparations. Exactly how this foolish woman saw the situation, I cannot tell. Certainly she knew of Rosenberg's reputation and of his attentions to her daughters. But she liked Rosenberg. It might very well be that she could not help liking the son of a wealthy manufacturer. Perhaps she entertained the hope that Rosenberg would divorce his wife and marry one of the Steinman girls and already regarded him as her future son-in-law. Whatever the case, she was as excited as her daughters that evening. I arrived ahead of the guest of honor and saw Mrs. Steinman flitting to and from the kitchen, whence came the mingled odors of cooking and baking.

Old Steinman lay on the sofa, eating his heart out. But he did not dare to enter an open protest, for, in addition to being a dependent in the household, supported by his wife and daughters and therefore without authority, he could not be sure of the relationship between Rosenberg and the girls. He lay there, muttering into his beard and sometimes letting his voice rise so that phrases floated across the room:

"Look at them! Look at them! What a celebration! You'd think Count Pototzki was expected!"

His wife turned on him, furiously.

"Look who's talking! You're not being asked for your opinion. If you don't like it you can move to the old people's home."

The sick man crimsoned with shame. He motioned me to come and sit near him on the sofa, and in a bitter whisper he said. "He's a married man, this Rosenberg, isn't he? And look at the preparations they're making for him. Wait! Something's going to happen. You watch."

I thought this was just vague, impotent talk. But as old Steinman calmed down a little and became more coherent he told me of a new element in the picture. Bertha was affianced at last—definitely and "irrevocably." Her young man, whose name was

Hershel, worked in a spats factory; and he took his relations with the Steinman family very seriously, had, in fact, gradually assumed the role of family protector, in view of the old man's incapacitation. Hershel had come to Warsaw, as a little boy, from some obscure village. Living always among strangers, he had developed a deep longing for family ties; and now that he was affianced to Bertha he plunged into the responsibilities of a ready-made family with great gusto. He took a proprietory and affectionate interest in old Steinman, in Rosa and in Matilda. He had actually introduced into the house a fellow-worker of his, with a view to making a match for Rosa; but the latter had received Hershel's friend so frostily that there had been no second visit.

Hershel was bewildered and perturbed by the queer situation in the Steinman family. One of his first acts had been to take Bertha away from flower-making and to get her a job in a shirt factory. But he did not begin to interfere vigorously until the formal engagement was announced.

"I'm waiting," he said once to the old man. "A dog mustn't bark before he's a year old."

These and sundry other observations he let fall, to old Steinman's delight. He spoke of "the poor, helpless, neglected children, without father and mother" and of "the cheap swindlers of a big city, ready to take advantage of any girl."

He began by questioning Bertha about Rosenberg.

"Who is this fish?" he asked.

"Just a young man," answered Bertha.

"I can see that. But what's he doing here? And who's he after? As far as I can see he can't make up his mind whether it's to be Rosa, or Matilda, or your boarder."

"Why, he visits all of them," said Bertha. "He's just a visitor here."

"What do you mean, a visitor? You don't have visitors just so in a houseful of girls. They're always after something."

"But he can't be," protested Bertha. "He's a married man; he's got children of his own."

"What?" bellowed Hershel. "Married, and has children, and hangs around here? Well! Now I know what he's after."

"Hershel, what do you mean? He's after what?"

"He's after what's going to get him a broken neck."

This conversation Hershel had repeated to old Steinman; now Steinman repeated it to me. And so the anticipatory "you watch" was not without substance.

While I sat listening to old Steinman the door flew open, and Hershel burst in, with Bertha in tow. Immediately he sensed the air of expectancy and preparation. The odor of baking floated in from the kitchen. Matilda, Rachel and Rosa were dressed in holiday clothes; the room shone; a bouquet of flowers stood on the table; the faces of the girls were illumined by a subdued radiance.

Hershel glanced around, came over to us, and took out a package of cheap cigars.

"Here, father," he said. "Have a smoke. Good stuff—a kopeck each."

Steinman looked apprehensively toward the kitchen, took the cigars, and shoved them under his pillow. "I'll keep them for a holiday," he said, apologetically.

"Oh, no, you don't," said Hershel. "You're going to have a good smoke right now." He snatched up the package, took out a cigar, put it into Steinman's mouth and lit it for him. Steinman drew in heavily, with something like a groan of pleasure.

"Don't you be afraid of her," Hershel went on, indicating the kitchen. "And now tell me; what's all the fuss and excitement about?"

"Rosenberg," whispered Steinman. "He's visiting this evening."

"Oh. Rosenberg." Hershel nodded and pursed his lips. "Thought we were through with him. Coming this evening, is he? Very nice. Very nice indeed. *Very* nice."

There was a glint of fury in Hershel's eyes. Old Steinman grinned, half in apprehension, half in hope. Clearly he was very fond of this good, simple working man, with his sound instinct and his healthy body.

Mrs. Steinman flounced in from the kitchen and wrinkled up her nose.

"There's a stink!" she said. "Who's smoking cheap, nasty tobacco?"

"Nobody," stammered her husband, hiding the cigar.

"Now, now, dad," said Hershel, unabashed. "Just you go on smoking. I'll take the responsibility."

Mrs. Steinman glared at her daughter's fiancé, who returned her gaze steadily and goodhumoredly. Mrs. Steinman did not like Hershel. She thought him vulgar; she despised his low origins. She had not forgiven her daughter Bertha for fastening, after such long hesitation, on this low creature. All this Hershel knew, but he did not let it disturb him. He was biding his time. Once he was safely married to Bertha he would have something to say about the old lady's snobbery. Meanwhile he cultivated the friendship of old Steinman, which only infuriated his future mother-in-law the more.

This question of Steinman's smoking was a battleground between Hershel and Mrs. Steinman rather than between husband and wife. Mrs. Steinman insisted that her husband would never recover the use of his legs if he smoked. Where she had obtained this piece of medical information she did not say. But in addition, she loathed the smell of cigarettes or cigars. Old Steinman was a passionate smoker, but without a kopeck in his pocket he had not been able to get cigars even surreptitiously before Hershel came into the house. Now it was Hershel's delight to make the old man happy, and reduce Mrs. Steinman to speechlessness, by insisting on the good which a cigar did a sick man.

"So you go on smoking," he repeated now, in a soothing voice. "It's healthy, for a man who's lying down all day."

While old Steinman clutched his cigar helplessly, divided between defiance and fear, there was a knock at the door, and Joey came in, in his long black cape and big soft hat; and of course there was a book or manuscript under his arm. Mrs. Steinman ran to greet him.

"*Panie* Rosenberg!" she exclaimed, in enthusiastic Polish. "What a joy!"

Rosa, Matilda and Rachel clustered round the newcomer. They were pale with excitement. Of the girls, Bertha was the only one who did not greet him. She, at a sign from her fiancé, had withdrawn to the kitchen, whence there suddenly issued the plebeian odor of frying liver and onions. This was Hershel's favorite dish.

Mrs. Steinman whipped round, her nose wrinkled once more.

"What *is* this?" she exclaimed, in horror. "Onions!" She darted to the kitchen door. "Have you no sense?" she cried at Bertha. "Don't you know who's here? Don't you know Mr. Rosenberg can't *stand* the smell of onions?"

"And what of it?" snapped Bertha. "Hershel can, and that's all I care about."

Her mother stamped her foot. "*I* know. It's your guttersnipe of a Hershel, and nobody in the world besides him."

Hershel, who was still sitting by old Steinman, smiled. "The time has come," he said softly. "Watch this. There's going to be some fun."

"Don't drag me into it," whimpered old Steinman. "I didn't do anything, I didn't see anything."

Mother and daughter were both in the kitchen now, carrying on the dispute behind the closed door. Joey Rosenberg, apparently not knowing what to do in this situation, sat down at the table and opened his book. Immediately the girls sat down near him, their heads close to his. A moment later Mrs. Steinman came in again, and when she saw the picture, a smile of happiness spread over her features. "They're *so* cultured," she murmured.

Apparently Hershel had been waiting for her return. For now he rose, went over to Rosenberg, and put a heavy hand on his shoulder.

"Young man," he said, "what are you doing in this house? What brings you here?"

There was dead silence. The girls, Rosenberg, the mother, were petrified.

"Mother!" screamed Rosa, and the other two girls burst into tears.

Mrs. Steinman came to.

"How dare you!" she gasped at Hershel. "How dare you? Do you know who that is? That's Joey Rosenberg! Ask his pardon, at once!"

"Ask his pardon nothing!" answered Hershel, lifted Rosenberg to his feet, and, holding his shoulders, shook him vigorously to emphasize what he was saying. "Listen, you! What are you hanging round this house for? Do you want to marry one of my sisters-in-law? Answer me. I have a right to ask. I'm a member of this family. These girls are my sisters-in-law."

Rosenberg's lips trembled, but no sound came out of them. He was as white as chalk.

"How dare you!" Mrs. Steinman kept repeating. "How dare you! That's Joey Rosenberg. How can he marry one of my daughters? He's got a wife already. He's a friend of the family." She pushed forward to interfere, but Hershel detached a powerful hand from Rosenberg and with it held off Mrs. Steinman.

"Well, then, if he's already got a wife, he has no business coming here, friend or no friend. These girls have to get husbands. And don't you know that the visits of this married man are a nuisance and an interference? Don't you know the whole town is talking? They're talking about my bride, too—and I won't stand for it!" Therewith he lifted Rosenberg bodily, as if he were a sack of straw, and carried him to the door. "Out! If you haven't got sense enough to stay away from here, somebody's going to teach you." He pulled open the door, deposited Rosenberg in the lobby, went back, and threw Rosenberg's book, cape and hat after him. Then he turned back into the room. "Nobody leaves this room!" he thundered. "As for you, ma, you kindly sit down at table, and we'll all eat." And very politely he led Mrs. Steinman to the chair at the head of the table.

From Mr. Steinman, on the sofa, I heard a trembling voice: "I didn't do anything! I didn't see anything!"

"Don't you be afraid, father," said Hershel. "Ma isn't going to be angry. And if she is, it'll only be with me, and we don't mind that, do we? And now, Bertha! Let's have that liver and onions. We're all at table!"

XIV

Rachel was the first to rise in rebellion.

"What kind of house is this, and what kind of people are you?" she exclaimed, snatched her hat, and ran out after Rosenberg. He was still there, in the lobby, probably unable to move after his fright. We heard him:

"Go back, Rachel. Where will you go? I forgive him. He didn't mean any harm."

"Joey, I'll go with you. I can't be without you."

I went out into the corridor.

"Rachel!"

She turned on me. "What do you want of me?" she cried. "Why do you follow me like a shadow?"

"Now, Rachel," protested Rosenberg. "You're behaving just like that man inside. You mustn't talk like that to Simon. I know you're fond of him." He hesitated, straightened up, and said at last: "Come with us, Simon."

The three of us went down into the street. Rosenberg had recovered completely. He began to talk about principles and ideals, but Rachel interrupted him:

"Joey, won't you come to see us any more?"

"But of course I will, Rachel. I'd have gone right back to have it out with him, but you can't talk to him now, he wouldn't understand. He's in the grip of his ego; he's bewitched by the will to dominate. He couldn't have thrown me out of the house otherwise. But he'll quieten down, later on, tomorrow, or the day after, and then he'll understand what he's done."

"Joey, Joey," wept Rachel, "why should people be so wicked?"

"People aren't wicked," said Rosenberg. "They always want to do good, even when they're doing evil. You see, he thinks I'm doing harm to his future wife and his future sisters-in-law. He chased me out of the house out of love for them. Hershel is a good man, a decent man. I've nothing to forgive him. From his point of view, it's he who has something to forgive. And if he doesn't come to me tomorrow, or the day after, I'll go in search of him."

Rachel was silent.

"And now, Rachel, go back. Matilda and Rosa will be anxious about you. They'll be sad. They'll think you're leaving them. Give them my greetings and tell them I'll be there soon."

"Good night, Joey," she murmured.

"Good night, Rachel." And as they kissed, he added: "Be good to Simon, Rachel. He loves you and you love him. Don't be ashamed of that. Love is something to be acknowledged, and nurtured, and cherished, so that it may grow and develop. Don't stifle it. Good night!" And he disappeared.

Rachel and I did not go back to the Steinmans'. We walked hand in hand a long time. Again that inexplicable effect was on me: Rosenberg's presence, his words, made him seem so different from the picture he presented to the memory and to reflection. As long as he was there, the fatuity of his talk, the craziness of his ideas, were concealed from you. The truth was that at this moment I felt nearer to Rachel than I had ever felt before. And it seemed that Rachel had the same feeling about me. She said, at last:

"Simon, you know, don't you, that our love for each other is bound up with Joey? And that if he were to leave us, then the bond between us would be sundered? Because, if you don't know this, we don't understand each other at all."

I understood, or seemed to understand, for the effect of Rosenberg's presence was dying; a protest rose in me, the protest of my body, my being, my personality:

"But what am I, Rachel, what am I to you, without this man? Who am I? What sort of existence have I for you, in myself?"

"I don't know, Simon. I haven't thought about it, I didn't want to think about it. At first you were a friend; you know how we use that word—one has so many friends. I didn't see you clearly. It was Joey who made you visible to me; and if he goes away you'll be invisible again."

I struggled to understand. "You mean," I said, "like a dead plerate, which you see only by the light of the sun."

"I don't know," she repeated. "I try to tell you everything. I have to be honest with you. I don't love you without Joey. I don't want to be with you at all, if Joey is gone. It may not be something in you. It may be in me."

We walked in silence the rest of the way.

XV

Rosenberg did not come to the Steinmans' the next day, nor the day after. He never came again.

Rachel and the other girls were astounded and then alarmed. They thought something had happened to him, perhaps the after effect of the rough handling. They sent me to his home, to make inquiries. But Rosenberg had disappeared from his home too.

But when a long time had passed—months, it seems to me—I ran into him on the street.

Unreflectingly, I rushed toward him, with outstretched hand; and then stood still in amazement. He did not recognize me! He frowned, touched my hand, and at last identified me after a fashion. "Ah, yes, yes, your name is Simon, isn't it? You're a friend of that girl, aren't you?" He nodded, remotely, lifted his hand in greeting, and walked on.

I had not the courage to tell Rachel of this encounter. The child had become a shadow of herself. She could not understand why Joey had disappeared without leaving a trace, why he had never come back to speak to Hershel of his great ideas.

Her feeling for me became cooler with the passing of the weeks. I believe it reached a point of positive dislike. Except when Matilda was with her, she had nothing to say. She would sit at her working table, making artificial flowers, or she would walk back and forth in the living room, her face drawn, her eyes lowered. Sometimes she would stand at the window, staring down at the people in the street like one astonished at the spectacle of human beings still interested in life; and sometimes she would sigh, "What's the use?" and turn back into the room.

All that remained of the old bond was her affection for Matilda. The two girls clung to each other as if they were afraid of losing the last link with that which had once filled their lives. What they loved best was to sit quietly, hand in hand, in a shadowy corner of the room, and whisper to each other. Even Rosa was excluded from their intimacy; and when she would try to break in, and seek comfort, they would look at her strangely.

I was there once when Rosa made a despairing effort to find admission to the closed circle. She asked suddenly:

"What are you two whispering about? Why mayn't I know?"

Matilda answered softly: "Rachel was telling me of the prince who will come some day and preach the great love. He will be so beautiful that whoever encounters him will love him. And all those who love him he will bind to each other in love. He will have great eyes, which will pour out love on all; and he will only have to look on people to make them his. His heart will be as big as the heart of the world. He will be the prince of love, and he will come to free the world with love."

"Foolish children," answered Rosa. "The prince of love is dead, and you're waiting in vain for his return. He is not in the world any more. Look at me! I have waited so long for him that my hair is turning gray. Now I know he can't come because he's dead. Those who come have only heard of his name. They repeat his words, but they haven't his power; and when they utter his words, and feel themselves to be powerless, they take fright, and run away and hide themselves among crowds. And when somebody asks, 'Who uttered those words' they do not come forward, because they are afraid."

We all understood whom Rosa meant. Rachel cried out: "I won't believe it. He's somewhere, looking for us. They won't let him come to us. And we don't know where to find him." Then she added: "Rosa, if what you said were true, why should we go on living? Do you think we were born to do nothing, nothing but make little linen flowers? Aren't there hands enough without ours to do this slave work? Don't you know that the prince of love *can't* be dead? Doesn't the longing in your heart tell you? What is that longing? It is his voice. Could you hear it if he were dead, and gone from the earth? I am waiting for him who is afraid of no one. He is near to us, Rosa." And, bursting into tears, Rachel hid her head in Matilda's breast.

"Little sister, sister Rachel," Matilda consoled her. "Don't cry."

"It's so dreary," sobbed Rachel.

"But he'll come. You've just said it yourself," Matilda went on, soothingly, and kissed Rachel's head. "He'll come, young, strong, lovely, to bind the hearts of all human beings. He'll draw you into his heart, which is the heart of the world, and he'll put his strong arm round you."

And the two girls clung to each other in the half darkness.

. . .

Not long after, Rachel was taken away from Warsaw for a time. Her grandfather came for her and made her return to the village. But the old man had not many days left, and when he was dead Rachel was seen in Warsaw again.

She told me neither of her departure nor of her return. When we met by accident on the street, she looked at me strangely, kept her gaze on the ground, and spoke to me by my second name. Thereafter I avoided her.

But Rachel and Matilda were seen together for many years. It was as though they had grown into each other, for never was one of them seen alone. They were always dressed in black, and an air of mystery attended them. When they walked in the street their dark eyes were fixed on space, as though they sought someone invisible to others.

All His Possessions

I

NO sooner had the factory opened in the village than the Jew appeared on the scene.

The workers, who were mostly Poles from across the border, were returning from work the first evening when they unexpectedly came across the little shop—if one could call it that: just an old door put up on trestles and displaying for sale a few jars of candy, a few bottles of soda water, handkerchiefs, socks, and similar trifles. Near the shop stood a tall, lean Jew with a sparse beard. He had a little girl on one arm; the other he kept free to serve with, and as the Polish workers passed on their way from the factory, he smiled at them and addressed them in broken Polish mixed with Russian:

"Please, Mister, *gospodin, prosche panye. . .*"

The sound of Polish words, however mutilated, pleased these workers in an alien land; many of them stopped, and before long there was a crowd gathered around the improvised open-air shop.

"Where did you spring from?" they asked the Jew. "Are you from Poland?"

"I've been living in this village ever since I can remember myself," said the Jew, indicating his right to be where he was. "I lived here long before the factory was opened. See these woods over there? My parents lived on the other side of that. Their parents, too. We didn't see many people—there weren't many people around." He strung his sentences together in confused

Polish and Russian. "But now, what with the factory, and you workers—it's different, eh?" he grinned amiably at his listeners.

The workers who came from these parts were somewhat surprised. The place had been a wilderness before the opening of the factory. What had this Jewish family been doing here? But the problem did not worry them long. They, like the foreign workers, the Poles, were delighted to have the Jew around. He was not only a source of supplies—he was a touch of color, company, amusement, and variety in the gray monotony of their surroundings. They spent their money with him, and both sides felt that they had the better of the bargain.

But on the very day of the Jew's appearance in the village, a great movement began among the precinct and district police offices and agitated the entire structure of the law right to the center, namely, the capital of the province. Documents were drawn up, reporting that a Jew had appeared in such and such a village, and inquiries were formulated concerning his status and his rights. From the governor to the nearest precinct captain, through every stage in the hierarchy, the reports and inquiries moved in stately procession. And it was finally established in the capital that such and such a Jew actually and indubitably was conducting a business in such and such a village.

When it came to the test, it appeared that the Jew had prepared himself for exactly this situation, for he produced papers dating back to the days of the old Emperor, proving the right of his parents, and even of his grandparents, to live in this part of the country.

They asked him: "But what did you do here before there was a village? For the village was built by the industrialist who owns the factory; he dried the swamp, put up the houses. Before that it was a wilderness. What were you doing here?"

"Getting along," said the Jew.

"What did you live on?"

"Is there no God in heaven?" asked the Jew.

They were not satisfied with the answer, but they were satisfied with the three rouble note which the Jew furtively shoved in their hands. At any rate, it was enough to keep things quiet till the inquiry made another round trip between the village and the capital—no little enterprise in those days.

Meanwhile the table on trestles expanded and became a regular store. For the workers needed a store, and the Jew found someone who would register the store in his name; and to the store was added a little inn, where, on Sundays, the workers could get a glass of beer. A community of interest bound the Jew to the workers; and there was something more—a community of transgression of the law.

For the situation was a complicated one. The Polish workers, who were Roman Catholics, had no freedom of worship in this territory, Russian Lithuania, where the Russian Orthodox Church was supreme. Nor could they be persuaded to attend other services than their own. They sent deputation after deputation to the provincial capital for the right to open a house of worship, but always the deputations returned emptyhanded. They had given up hope; and as they lost heart they also lost interest. But one day a Roman Catholic bishop, a Pole, paid them a secret visit and upbraided them bitterly for their neglectful attitude toward their religion. The Polish workers could only weep and point to the law as their excuse; which was not good enough for the bishop, who was a zealot. Then a certain worker, who lived with Samuel the Jew, hit upon an idea. Why should not the Polish workers meet for secret services in Samuel's inn, on Sundays? No one would dream that they went thither except to drink beer; and no one would dream of looking in the Jewish inn for the image of the Madonna.

It was not easy to win Samuel over; he would not, could not, harbor an image in his house. Then he bethought himself that after all the inn and shop were inscribed not in his own name, but in that of a Christian. His own part of the house, attached to the inn, he would keep pure; the other part was, in a sense, not his. And so the ark with the image was put up in the inn and was cunningly constructed so that, when the doors of it were closed, you could not have guessed that the wall was broken there. Thus, six days in the week the Poles boozed and swore before the closed doors. And the Jew, whenever he passed the wall, would feel a twinge of remorse at the thought of the alien image behind it. And he saw to it that his little girl never uttered a Hebrew benediction in that room.

On Sunday too the workers assembled in the inn. The floor was freshly swept. The bottles of whisky and beer and brandy were hidden behind curtains. The doors of the ark were opened, and the image shone forth; a light was kindled before it, and one of the oldest workers, a pious Christian, led the prayers.

The Jew stood in front of the inn and kept a lookout for the local policeman. When he perceived him at a distance, he ran in and gave the word. At once the ark was closed before the image, the curtains were withdrawn from before the bottles; glasses were set on the table. And when the policeman entered he saw workers drinking.

In exchange for this service, the workers protected the Jew: as soon as the policeman came, they hid in their midst all his earthly possessions, a little three-year-old girl, and a goat.

II

I do not know how much truth there was in the claim of the Jewish innkeeper that he, and his forefathers, had always lived in these parts; but I do know that he had a great affection for the little plot of land behind his inn and was deeply attached to it.

It seems that he had no wife. Or perhaps he did have a wife, and other children, somewhere in the city. Here, at any rate, he had with him only little Rachel and the goat; and the goat was their chief source of nourishment. For kosher meat was unobtainable, except on rare occasions when he could visit the city and buy himself a piece from the Jewish butcher. The goat provided him and his daughter with milk, and from the plot of land behind the inn he obtained his vegetables.

Whenever Samuel looked out from the back of the house and saw little Rachel playing with the goat on the strip of meadow, his heart was flooded with joy. There they were, his two possessions, with all the room in the world to romp in. What more could a man ask?

In the spring he worked his field like any other peasant. And the first thing he did every morning was to go out into his garden and to see how the vegetables were coming along. He was impatient. He asked every peasant that visited him:

"Why isn't my garden growing?"

"It isn't time yet," they reassured him.

"I don't see a thing," he complained.

"When the time comes, you'll see plenty."

Sure enough the time came, and with the time came carrots and potatoes and radishes. It seemed to the Jew that he was growing with his vegetables; he took on height and fullness with them. Once, in the city, he tried to explain himself: "It's a very different thing," he said. "Here you see radishes lying in the shop, in great big heaps. You put down your money and you pick up your radishes. But at home I go into my garden and I pull my radish right out of the ground—fresh and crisp." Speaking thus he understood the meaning of the verse: every man under his own vine and his own figtree.

And as often as he remembered the city in the summer, the heat, the crowding and the dust; as often as he thought of the two and three families crammed into a single cellar and saw his Rachel playing on the meadow with the goat, he praised God for the mercy He had shown to him and his.

III

But the documents, once set in motion, could not come to a halt. The case of the Jew was reported in the Imperial capital itself, in St. Petersburg. Thither the Jew transferred his struggle, for he had his own even there. He was determined to hang on to the little plot of earth as long as the breath of life was in him. He did not blench or tremble when he heard the dread word: "Petersburg." He girded up his loins and betook himself thither, leaving goat and daughter in the safekeeping of a friendly peasant. And it was no light thing for a Jew to venture in those times into St. Petersburg; a lion's den was safer.

In St. Petersburg they directed him to the Jewish deputies of the Duma. But it transpired that Samuel the Jew had relatives in the capital. Or at least one relative, but that a highly important personage, intimate in the Imperial counsels, though in a rather indirect way. For this man, this relative, was connected with the Imperial Theatre, and that too in a rather indirect way; actually he was a dramatic critic on one of the newspapers.

So one fine morning this dramatic critic, hearing a noise at his door, came down and found his rustic relative engaged in loud dispute with the doorkeeper, who refused to admit the stranger.

Then the battle with the documents was joined. The critic had a friend, a certain actress; the actress had a lover, a certain officer; the officer had a friend, a certain official in the Department where the documents of the Jew were reposing at the moment.

The village Jew had his way in the end. He pleaded with his relative, the dramatic critic; the critic pleaded with the actress; the actress with the officer, the officer with the official. The answer, a favorable one, flowed in reverse, from the official to the officer, from the officer to the actress, from the actress to the critic, and from the critic to Samuel the Jew; who thereupon returned to the village and related his triumph to the policeman, the peasants, and the workers.

But the favorable reply was marred by one painful condition. Samuel the Jew was permitted to live in the village, and that was all. "His possessions" could not remain in the village. As far as the store and inn were concerned, there was no trouble, for they were inscribed in another man's name. What, however, was he to do with his daughter and his goat?

Here the peasants came to his rescue. One took the child, another the goat; and all went well until one fateful summer day when the policeman descended on the store and inn just when daughter and goat were paying a visit to the Jew. The policeman had strict orders to carry out to the letter the ukase delivered from St. Petersburg.

178

All His Possessions

There was no denying the kinship between Samuel and the little girl; her black hair, her dark eyes, her features, were too much like his. Once this kinship was uncovered, the goat went along too; for the goat refused to play with anyone but Rachel.

It was late in the afternoon, and the evening shadows were drawing on; but the policeman had his orders, and the Jew's possessions could not remain in the village for more than two hours after their discovery. So he put a switch into the girl's hand, and bade her betake herself from the village, driving the goat before her. Thereupon the villagers at their doors beheld a strange scene: a policeman accompanied by two subordinates marched in stately order behind a little girl, who walked weeping toward the woods, behind a goat. The women wrung their hands and asked each other what had happened. "Has she been taken in witchcraft?" they wanted to know. But there was no answer.

IV

Samuel the Jew went along perforce and delivered "all his possessions" to a friend in the city; then he returned to the village, but could not stay. What was the good of his garden, his little stretch of meadow, the blue sky above, the green earth beneath, if Rachel was not there to play and the goat to graze? The garden lost its charm, and he even forgot, in his loneliness, the difference between a radish which you pick up from a heap in a city store, and one which you cut, fresh and crisp, from the ground where it grows. Before many days had passed he closed store and inn and went off to the city.

But summer in the city was intolerable too. He kept dreaming of the inn, and of the garden, and of the stretch of meadow. And when he saw his little Rachel romping with the other children in the filthy yard, smeared with garbage from head to foot, his heart contracted and he almost fainted. Before long Samuel the Jew disappeared with his daughter from the city, and where they went, and what became of them, I do not know.

The goat wandered about the city streets, to the delight and mockery of heartless children; it could not understand what had happened to the green ground; and after a time the goat disappeared too.

And what happened to the Catholic Sunday services?

On this we have a definite report. When Samuel the Jew was driven from the village, the workers became law-abiding. They no longer conducted illegal Catholic services, but boozed the Sundays away, from morning till night, without interruption.

De Profundis

I

I can think of no other way of opening this record than with the following observation:

It did not matter whether you came in Boruch Pompe's covered wagon, or in the modern bus which shuttled to and from the nearest railroad station: if you wanted to enter the townlet you had to get off at the abattoir and chase away the slaughterer's sow and her farrow from where they lay sprawling in the blood which oozed out upon the road. It could not be done with yelling, or whistling, or honking. It needed a strong right hand and Boruch Pompe's whip, or the stick which the bus driver carried for this purpose. When the grunting, squealing horde had been temporarily dispersed, you jumped back on the wagon, or the bus, and proceeded on to the main street.

Opposite the church with its live hedge, where the peasants hitched their carts, stood a tumbledown house—more ruin than house—dominated by a tremendous, crooked chimney. Here Grabski, the old carpenter, or, as he was better known, Grabski the husband of Yadviga the washerwoman, occupied the cellar; and hard by the ruin stood the little shop of Long Leib, or, as he was better known, Leib the husband of Malkah with the goiter. The dark blue doors of the shop were covered with tin shingles, on each of which was painted a picture of some commodity: a bolt of cloth, a herring, a sack of salt, or a candle.

Children of Abraham

The two houses had been standing cheek by jowl as long as anyone could remember—and longer. With the passage of the years the roofs had begun to incline toward each other, until they touched and held each other up, like two ancient gaffers at the end of their strength. The crumbling rainspouts had run together, so that you could not tell from whose roof the water gushed to the street; and in some places a single mantle of moss covered the walls, so that without pulling the two structures down you could not have known where one ended and the other began. But the most striking bond of unity between the houses was the gigantic chimney, which in far-off forgotten days must have been built to accommodate a baker's oven and which now served both Yadviga's and Malkah's kitchen stoves.

The common chimney was a great trial to the neighbors and had more than once threatened their friendly relations. When a Christian festival came round and there was a great roasting of pork sausages on Yadviga's stove, the chimney, which had a habit of reversing the draught, would blow the odor into Malkah's kitchen; and all day long Malkah would feel sick and would keep a piece of candy in her mouth to drive out the taste of the abomination. As against this, when Malkah was preparing the Sabbath fish on a Friday afternoon or was frying potato pancakes for the Chanukkah festival, they would be holding their noses in Yadviga's kitchen, and muttering: "Jewish onions!" The greatest strain was at Passover time, when the Jewish woman brought home the *matzoth,* or unleavened cakes, and the Christian woman would gather her children into the house, lest something befall them.

Except for these minor periodic difficulties, injected into their lives by their rival faiths, there was complete harmony and friendship between the neighbors. Their common poverty, their common needs, made a bond between them. When Yadviga had to spend a whole day doing the laundry in some well-to-do home, she left the children in the Jewish woman's care. When Malkah had to do the big spring cleaning for Passover, the Christian woman lent a hand. They would also lend each other a bundle of faggots, half a loaf of bread, or a few groschen—everything, in fact, but dishes and eating utensils, these being within the province of their rival faiths. Sometimes it would happen that a child of Yadviga's would toddle over to where one of Malkah's children was eating something on the doorstep and stick an unkosher Christian spoon into a kosher Jewish dish. Then Malkah would have to run to the Rabbi with the dish and ask whether the dish could be purified and kept. Sometimes the Rabbi would say yes, and the only damage done was the shock to Malkah; and sometimes he would say no, and then the dish passed into the keeping of the Christian woman. That happened with other things, too, such as ducks and hens which the Rabbi had declared unkosher. But the Christian woman did not accept these windfalls as gifts; if she could not make a return in kind—money payment was almost always out of the question—she did a day's washing for her Jewish neighbor or helped her with the cleaning. The rivalries of their faith had no more serious consequences than these.

That was how it used to be once upon a time. Here is the way matters stand now:

Market day is drawing to a close. One by one the peasant's carts are unhitched from the hedge about the church. There is a neighing of horses, a squeaking of wheels. The stallions strain their necks longingly toward the mares harnessed to other carts. The shopkeepers, men and women, sit at their stalls—often nothing more than an old door mounted on trestles—in front of their shops, with their blue, green, and red shingles; they sit waiting, as they always do, for one more peasant, one more customer. The wind lifts the dust stirred up by the cartwheels, mixes it with flying feathers and the chaff of oats, and lays down a gray blanket on the exposed goods, drives it into the faces of the watchers at the stalls, puts a dull coating on the scraggy wigs of the women and on the beards of the men. Still they sit there; they will not carry their goods in and dismount their stalls until all hope is gone. They look dully at the hens fluttering around in the dust, picking here and there at a grain of oat. "Our earnings for the day!"

Across the way, where the light of an ikon lamp falls on the new-painted sign of a Christian shop, two or three carts still linger.

Who knows? Perhaps some peasant, dissatisfied with the goods on display there, will have the courage to go back to his old Jewish merchant. There is not much hope. For these are the days of the boycott. Once upon a time the "shop" across the way was just the village inn. Now it is the emporium for Christians. Willingly or unwillingly, the peasants cluster about its doors. Now the last sounds of the market float across the square—the voices of quarreling peasants, the squealing of pigs. A barefoot peasant woman drags a drunken peasant away from the emporium. The Jews watch, suck their tongues in their dry mouths, and wait for what they know will not happen.

"Let's go in," says Long Leib. "There'll be nothing more. I'll take the goods in."

"Just a few more minutes," urges his wife. "There are some peasants still inside there." She finishes with a half sob, and the goiter in her throat flies up and down, distending a blue network of veins. She digs out of her bag a piece of candy wrapped in dirty paper, unwraps it, and puts it into her mouth. She always does this when she feels faint.

And while Malkah sits with the face of a mourner at the stall, someone comes out of the inn opposite; not a peasant, but a queer young fellow in a dirty raincoat, with a dirty, rumpled, square-shaped student's cap on his head. He carries a heavy stick and is accompanied by Stefan, the cobbler's apprentice, whom everyone calls, behind his back, Meitik, after a murderer once famous in these parts. The young fellow in the student cap comes straight over to Malkah's stall and points with his stick at the cloth rolls.

"Foreign goods?" he asks, sharply.

"God forbid! Here! Look at the official labels!" she answers, terrified.

The student picks up the cloth measure lying on the stall.

"Has this measure been stamped in the magistrate's office?" he asks, without looking at the woman.

"God help us! Of course!"

"Where's your dealer's license?"

But instead of answering, Malkah looks with sudden closeness, out of her shortsighted eyes, into the face of her stern interlocutor. She recognizes the narrow, conical forehead, the broad, upturned little nose, and she puts her hand up to her face in a gesture of astonishment:

"Oh, dear, oh, dear, if it isn't *Panie* Stash! Why, look! You wouldn't know him! He looks like a regular doctor, or an official! What a pity that his mother isn't alive to see him in his student's cap. How happy she would have been! Dear God! The poor have no luck! If their children rise in the world, they themselves aren't here to see it!"

The student is unmoved by the gush of words. He snaps:

"The license!"

"It's in the shop, of course. How would I be doing business without a license?"

The questioning continues:

"Have you paid your income tax?"

"*Panie* Stash! How can you ask? Of course I've paid it."

The student walks away, stations himself before another stall.

"Who's that?" asks the woman on the other side of Malkah's stall. "An inspector?"

"And what young Pole just out of school *isn't* an inspector over Jews these days?" answers her neighbor in a tearful voice.

"But that's the Grabski lad who's come back from the university!" says Malkah, as if she couldn't get over it.

"Used to eat my bread!" mutters Long Leib. "Was brought up in my house, you might say." And he shakes his beard incredulously in the direction of the retreating student.

"And his mother was my crony," croaks Malkah, and digs out of her bag a piece of orange peel, which she puts into her mouth. "She couldn't live without me."

"Bad days!" says a Jew, darkly. "If you helped to bring him up, you've done the Jews no service."

"Here's my day's takings!" cries Long Leib, savagely, showing two empty hands. "Here's what I'm going to pay my taxes and licenses and stamps with!" In his rage he grabs up two armfuls of cloth and carries them into the shop. Leah, the oldest girl, helps him. Pinchas, the oldest son, is not at home. He has gone away to train himself on a farm so that he might be accepted as a pioneer for Palestine. Malkah sucks at the piece of orange peel and helps the other two.

II

Even in his childhood Stash Grabski had been definitely queer, not a bit like Yadviga's other children, Malkah would relate in later days. "He was the only one I had a hard time with. He used to dirty my pots and pans, whenever he could get hold of them, with a piece of swine meat, or with a fork that had been used for swine meat. He knew I wouldn't be able to use it after that. Or else, on Passover, he'd try to bring a piece of leavened bread into my house, though he knew very well that that would defile the whole house. We had to watch him as if he was seven devils. You might say he was born hating Jews. He couldn't stand Jewish children! When our little boys went past his house on the way to Hebrew school, he'd set their big dog, Burak, on them. We couldn't make him out! He wasn't like a human being!"

"Mind you, I always said that he'd grow up into nothing good!" added Long Leib.

Stash gave early confirmation of Leib's dismal prophecy. When the lad was eight years old he climbed up one day, during the Festival of Booths, on to the roof of the house and flung a dead, putrefying cat into Leib's booth, just when Leib was making the benediction before the meal. The filthy carcass landed right in the fish soup and, besides desecrating the ritual booth, ruined the festival meal. One of the children, running out of the booth, caught sight of Stash scampering away on the roof. That night there was the devil to pay. Old Grabski, a decent, friendly soul, who often used to do odd jobs for the Jewish draymen, was beside himself with rage and nearly killed his son with an ash switch. The mother, Yadviga, came weeping to Malkah, and beating her breast: "How can such a demon have come out of my belly? Why, you're like a sister to me; better than a sister. A mother couldn't be as good to me." And when Grabski entered, dragging his tight-lipped son

along, Yadviga turned on the child with a scream: "Why did you
do this to me?" And she fell on Stash with her fists, tore his hair,
insisted that he go down on his knees and apologize to Leib and
Malkah. The lad stood there, grim-faced, bitter, wordless. The
sweat ran down from his forehead, making dirty runlets on his
cheeks. He did not weep; he did not remonstrate; he did not
apologize. Even when his father took him in hand and flayed him
with the switch, which whistled through the air, there was no
change. In vain did Leib and Malkah plead with Grabski to let
the boy go. "No!" yelled the father. "No! He's going to beg your
pardon! He's going to beg your pardon!" It became a matter of
pride with Grabski; he would not be defied in the presence of
strangers. The lad stood there, unmoving, biting his nails.

"Neighbor! Neighbor!" gasped Leib, "that's enough, he won't do
it again. I promise you he won't." And, thrusting himself between
father and son, he received several blows of the switch before
Grabski realized what he was doing. But little Stash had his way;
he did not apologize to the Jew.

The incident was, however, a turning point in the lad's life. It
left its mark on him. From that time on there were no more wild
pranks. He gave up playing around with dogs and dead cats. He
began to take school seriously and even became a model pupil.
He learned slowly, but once he had learned something it was
part of him. His behavior had something unnatural about it; he
walked quietly, a morose, brooding expression on his face, a silent
fury in his eyes. He had nothing to do any more with Malkah or
her children, did not throw pieces of pork into the dishes or bring
bread into the Jewish house on the Passover. Whenever he met
Malkah he turned away silently.

"I like that quiet of his even less than his crazy tricks," Malkah
would say, uneasily. "Those eyes of his!"

"Mark my words," answered her husband, "he'll grow up into
nothing good."

When Stash was graduated from preparatory school with fair
marks, the town doctor encouraged him to go to the local high
school, and, since old Grabski was by then unable to work and

the family subsisted on whatever the mother and the oldest daughter earned, a stipend was collected for the fees. The rich owner of the slaughter house (who was distantly related to Stash's mother), the town magistrate, the captain of the fire-brigade, the doctor himself, and a number of others contributed. It was agreed to see Stash Grabski at least through high school.

III

Neither the passing of the years, nor the change in his status, softened Stash Grabski. If anything, his promotion intensified his silent hatred of his Jewish neighbors. Whenever he saw his mother standing on the doorstep chatting with Malkah, a spasm would contract his features. But there was little friendliness in him for anybody, and he had no comrades.

His appearance, it must be said, was far from prepossessing. The thick, coarse skin which came to him from his peasant ancestry—the sign manual of their laborious destiny—was sallow and sickly from the monotonous diet of cabbage and potatoes which was the mainstay of the Grabski household. Malnutrition and privation were written on his face and in his bearing; more than once he had been on the point of leaving high school because the few groschen he could earn by physical labor were badly needed at home. As it was, he made a trifle now and again by coaching younger students, and somehow or other he completed his course. But pupils were not always to be had; and the father, who was much older than his wife, became weaker and weaker, so that even when work was obtainable—which was not too often—he could not take it on. The rich butcher, who had been willing to participate in the glory of creating a scholarship for a student, was not the kind to help poor relatives. The mother went out washing, the oldest daughter became a seamstress, and in their spare time they worked the little field behind the house. The soil was sandy and niggardly; they were lucky to get out of it a few bushels of potatoes and a basket or two of cabbages. Stash could not afford new clothes; his trousers were patched and repatched, till they threatened to fall to pieces. He could not take part in the social and sports activities of the school, because he had not the clothes and could not afford the trifling entrance fees.

Nor was he by any means a distinguished pupil. There was nothing about his accomplishments or for that matter about his character and bearing to lift him out of his painful mediocrity and focus friendly attention on him. He made no special progress. His teachers promoted him grudgingly from class to class, more in order not to disgrace him than because he had really merited it.

Even his poverty did not make an exception of him; he could not make a special play about that, for there were students at the high school who suffered as much, or even more, for the sake of an education. There was, for instance, Anton Striga, of whom it was told that he helped his father, the janitor, to clean the outhouses every morning before he came to school. And though Anton's clothes were as threadbare as Stash's, and his food no better, there was nothing deliberately plaintive or tragic about his bearing. You would have thought, from his spirits, his good humor, that he had just left a well-to-do house, after a solid breakfast and after the maid had carefully cleaned and brushed his clothes. Anton did not make a high virtue of his poverty; he mixed naturally with the others, and his naturalness made him popular. He was often invited to the houses of his well-to-do comrades and had once spent a whole summer on a country estate. With all his poverty, with his obviously mended clothes, he could be seen now and again taking a stroll with the sisters of one of his comrades.

No such thing ever happened to Stash. He carried with him, into school and everywhere else, not merely the necessary physical consequences of his poverty but a spiritual counterpart of it. It lay on him like a burden and made itself externally visible in his heavy gait, in his black mood, his touchiness, his nervousness. It was this nervousness which always made him perspire, so that his narrow forehead and his thick hands were always wet. When you shook hands with him, you wanted to hurry away and wash your hand. It was impossible for him to make friends, for he did not know the meaning of give and take in human contacts. A harmless jest filled him with fury, as if it were a premeditated insult. He was contemptuous of his comrades and yet longed for their friendship and admiration. Above all he was in a constant rage against the boys of well-to-do families, and he was forever muttering under his breath: "You wait; some day *we're* going to be on top."

In his later high school years he joined a student socialist group, and even frequented communist meetings. He was all on fire within for something which would drag him out of the sea of mediocrity which had engulfed him. He wanted somehow or other to make a terrific impression on his fellow-students, and particularly on the richer ones; and whichever of the radical groups he approached, his first idea was to become the leader. It did not work; he could not even remain a member of the group. He had not the abilities of a leader, nor the discipline of a follower. He had his own explanation. "It's privilege!" he muttered. "There are privileged classes among the leftists, too." He became a bitter enemy of socialists and communists.

About that time certain students were called before the director of the high school; some Jews were expelled for socialist activity, and one was even sent to prison. The rumor spread rapidly that Stash Grabski had been the one who had handed in the names. Thenceforth his fellow-students avoided him more than ever. Even those among whom he had expected to win approval for his new, anti-socialist, anti-communist opinions, the nationalists and members of the N.-D. (National-Democratic) party, were suspicious of him. A dreadful feeling of persecution began to haunt Stash Grabski.

There ensued a religious interlude. Stash came under the influence of a young priest who had recently come to town. For a time Stash even entertained the notion of withdrawing from the world and of devoting his life to God's service. The idea soothed him, and during that period he would spend hours in the church, working on his religious enthusiasm. There were some who believed that the lad had found himself at last in the religious life. But most of those who knew him at all well found his conversion unnatural and extreme, especially as he made a great to-do about his salvation and went about radiating piety and spiritual counsel.

De Profundis

"There's Stash," they would say. "He's got a new act. He's gone churchy. Anything to make an impression on us." He would catch remarks like these the day after he had been seen at the head of a religious procession, carrying a banner all by himself through the length of the town. He tried to ignore the snickering voices. But when his conversion had worn thin—and it did not take long for this to happen—he would turn round at his tormentors with a yell of fury, to their amusement rather than their alarm.

The religious episode came to an early end and was followed by what turned out to be Stash's real vocation. About that time there emerged among Polish student bodies a new type of patriotic organization, the first local echo of Hitlerism. Stash had belonged to patriotic organizations before and had withdrawn from them because they had not brought him to the fore. There had been something about them, certain limitations to their jingoistic spirit, certain ethical associations, a demand for more than mere hatred of foreigners and the desire to run amok. These limitations and qualifications, which had pushed Stash into the background, were not found in the new organization. All ethical rules were suspended; for the sake of the fatherland everything was permissible, or rather commendable: the utmost hatred, the vilest means, the most criminal conspiracies. All bars were dissolved, all rules suspended; viciousness became an integral part of the patriotic program.

From the first moment of contact with these "principles," it seemed to Stash that here, at last, was the movement which had been destined for him and for which he had been destined. He felt in himself a capacity for unchallenged leadership in such a field. There was in him a hunger to outrage all scruples, smash at all inhibitions, and, by the perfection of his break with the trivial rules of the bourgeois concept of political morality, make a unique place for himself. There was a double attractiveness about such a career. He would put the fear of God into the Jews—they would encounter a hatred the existence of which they had never dreamed of; and he would stagger his comrades by an exhibition of ruthlessness which not one of them would dare to imitate.

IV

The Organization was secret, or semi-secret; for though the school directorate sympathized with it, the law forbade it among high school students. Stash threw himself into the activity with all the energies accumulated in him by years of frustration and gave evidence of a skill and persistence which no one had suspected in him. He drew in workers by the ingenious device of giving them highly "important" work to do: namely, to go out to the village fairs and markets and agitate among the peasants against the Jewish shopkeepers. He obtained, from Warsaw headquarters, quantities of leaflets to distribute. His fellow-students found their assignment exciting, and when they had become intoxicated with their work, Stash encouraged them to more "activism." He instructed them to "create incidents," to start arguments in the middle of a busy marketplace, and to take advantage of the noise and confusion in order to move the vortex of excitement toward the Jewish stalls and shops. He also introduced the first anti-Jewish "pickets"—which were not content with picketing but actually prevented customers from entering Jewish shops or stopping at Jewish stalls.

A Jewish delegation finally waited on the director of the high school and lodged a complaint. Nothing could have pleased Stash more than to hear that he was the subject of such a demonstration. He declared heroically to his comrades that he was ready to sacrifice not only his high school career, but his very life, in the sacred cause. He suspected, however, that the danger was very small. And in fact, the director received the Jewish delegation politely and dismissed it with soothing promises. Stash's sacrifice was a minor one: he had to listen to a reprimand delivered tongue in cheek; he had to promise to be either more "moderate" or more "circumspect" in the future.

He was neither. His hatred grew by what it fed on. The more he tormented the Jews, the more he needed to torment them. All the joys of youth which he had missed, all the dreams of prominence and domination which had been his miserable consolation, now found expression. And the more outrageous his behavior became, the more it seemed to him that he was sacrificing himself, that he was "contributing" his youth, his health, his leisure hours, to a great and exacting enterprise, to a noble cause which none but he really understood. When he was not organizing his groups or conducting "field operations" in the villages, he was brooding on new methods of intensifying the boycott; he was thinking up detailed techniques for the provocation of riots at markets, for precipitating quarrels between peasants and Jewish shopkeepers.

His nights were filled with the same obsession as the days. The normal reveries of adolescent boys were unknown to him. Malkah with the goiter could not understand this indifference of his to the opposite sex. More than once, when he paced up and down before her shop, on picket duty, she would approach him and say wheedlingly:

"A young man like you shouldn't waste his time on such things. A *panitch* like you, a handsome young fellow, should give the young ladies a chance, go for walks with them in the town gardens, instead of standing all day long in front of a Jewish shop. It's not worthy of you, *Panie* Stash. It's the sort of thing we expect from hooligans, with nothing better to do, not from an intelligent young student who's going to be a famous doctor some day."

Of all the Jewish shops, Malkah's seemed to draw upon itself the most consistent measure of attention. It was hard to say why. Perhaps he remembered that incident with the dead cat and the unmerciful beating his father had given him, all because of those Jews. Perhaps his memory went back further, and he resented, without knowing it, a far-off time when he had played freely and happily with Malkah's children and had been looked after by her when his mother had gone out washing. On the other hand, it may have been the fact that Malkah's store had been a favorite with the peasants, because she had been known as a helpful, good-natured, accommodating soul. If a peasant had brought a child with him to market, and couldn't drag it around while he made his purchases, he could always count on Malkah with the goiter to take care of it. He could always leave his packages in her shop and be certain that when he came back nothing would be missing. He could even hitch a hog to the post in front of her door while he went off on business.

Or perhaps there was something about Malkah herself which awakened a special fury in Stash, something about the sad, long, weatherbeaten face, the tight lips, the faded wig, the goiter. Perhaps, again, it was her husband, Long Leib, whom he saw leaving the house, in the early morning hours, summer and winter, with two bundles of cloth goods, one on his right shoulder, the other under his left arm. Long Leib would take the path across the field at the back of the house, because that was a short cut out of the town toward the road leading to the villages.

He knew the whole family, Malkah, Leib, every one of the children. Once upon a time, long before the incident with the dead cat, Stash had been a playmate of theirs. With one of them, in particular, a boy, he had used to play at soldiers. Stash tried to repress this recollection. It disgusted him to think that he had once been intimate with a Jew-boy, especially as he watched this boy, Pinchas, grow up. He hated the sight of him, with his Jew face and his earlocks and the books under his arm when he went to learn queer things in the Jewish school. He knew the oldest girl, too, Brochah, who had gone away to serve in a household in Lodz and who came back on Jewish holidays, always bringing with her a bundle of dresses and linens for her mother to store away for her trousseau. In fact, he knew everything that went on in the neighboring household.

Every Friday night, as surely as the sun rose in the east and set in the west, the Jewish shop would close for twenty-four hours. The shutters would be put up and would remain there, no matter what happened, until sundown on Saturday. Through the two little windows of Malkah's living room and kitchen the Sabbath candles would shine, and the odor of the Sabbath fish would float back down the Grabski half of the chimney. And that odor had a curious effect on Stash. It brought back with it a childhood, almost a babyhood, that he yearned for and yet wanted to forget; it had something homey about it, something intimate and soothing, and at the same time it angered him. It brought back a queer feeling of comfortable hours spent in the Jew woman's kitchen, in the company of her children.

When these thoughts came to him, Stash made a furious gesture, as if he were chasing away an irritating, buzzing fly. When the smell of fish frying in the Jewish kitchen next door came to his nostrils, he would not permit the old nostalgic recollection to overpower him. He would get up angrily and say, "The fish in our rivers were meant for us, not for those filthy Jews. They eat up everything—our fish, our cattle, our geese and hens. Wait!"

V

The first time he picketed Malkah's shop and had to look into Malkah's protesting eyes, he felt uncomfortable and cursed himself for his weakness. He had two comrades with him, and he was teaching them the technique of the boycott: how to approach a peasant who lingered before the Jewish shop with intent to enter, what to say to him, how to reply if he became obstreperous—all the instructions he had received from headquarters in Warsaw. When Malkah, hearing the commotion in the street, came out to discover the cause, and her eyes fell on Stash, she was more astonished than frightened: "Why, goodness me, its *Panie* Stash! What's he doing there? I knew him when he was a baby! And a pretty little baby he was, too." She seemed to be appealing to the bystanders and to Stash's comrades, to bear witness to Stash's sweetness as a baby, as if that would make impossible his participation in such activities.

Stash turned his eyes away from her.

"Why, he even—he even fed at my breast," babbled Malkah, "just like one of my own children. When his mother used to go out for the day, to earn something, she'd leave him with me. And he'd be hungry, and he'd cry, so I'd feed him, like one of my own babies. Because that was the time I was suckling my boy Pinchas. How can he do such a thing to me now?"

Stash recovered a little self-confidence. Shaking his fist in Malkah's face, he shouted:

"Shut your mouth, you filthy Jew woman. If you don't, I'll shut it for you!"

The coarse bravado of his language restored Stash's courage. And from that time on he was no longer afraid to meet Malkah's look. Malkah, in turn, became afraid of him.

Not long after this first encounter Stash left town, and the Jews breathed more easily and hoped that he was gone for good. They heard that he had entered the University of Warsaw. Stash's mother died in the meantime. There was no particular reason why he should return, and without him there was some prospect that the local boycott organization would fall to pieces. In any case, the university would keep him away for several years; in the meantime much could happen. All these hopes turned out to be vain. Stash did not finish his course at the university. He came back after a certain time, in a filthy raincoat and a filthier student cap, and took up where he had left off. But now he had acquired a certain authority. Stefan, the shoemaker's apprentice, and the rest of the gang, looked up to him as the unchallenged leader. Even Malkah, when she saw him the first time after his return and failed to recognize him, was aware that this was no longer the small-town hobbledehoy: he had about him the self-assurance of the big city tough.

Nor was Stash content now with his old terroristic methods, though he intensified them, so that not only the Jews, but the peasants themselves, were intimidated. It was not enough to picket the Jewish stands and shops on market days. Jewish peddlers, who, in the immemorial tradition, wandered with their packs from village to village, were accosted and told to go home. Farmers who had been accustomed to making their purchases from the itinerant peddlers were warned not to admit them. On top of this, Stash co-operated with national headquarters in opening Christian emporiums in the market towns; and suddenly there sprang up, opposite the Jewish shops, brand new stores, with big signs "Christian Shop," and holy lamps for those peasants who could not read.

The peasants had been accustomed for untold generations to dealing with the Jews. They were at home with them. They did not like these queer, modern establishments, where they had to wait cap in hand, and where the shopkeeper made them feel that he was doing them a favor. Besides, the old Jewish shops had been something more than shops. A peasant could always ask for a favor there, deposit his bundles in a corner till he was ready to go home, have his youngsters looked after, hitch his pig to the door post.

Because of this, Stash and his henchmen had to bring force to bear in the boycott of Jewish shops and stands. Peasants who refused to be persuaded or intimidated into putting up with the inferior goods or service of the new stores had to be taught a lesson. Altercations arose, no one knew exactly how, and a peasant who did not comply with the boycott found himself in the midst of a brawl. Jewish stalls were overthrown. It became dangerous for Jews to venture into the villages on market days.

But it was not enough to chase the Jewish dealers from the marketplaces on fair days. Stash maintained a regular technique of persecution and discouragement throughout the week. Jews sitting in their wretched little shops, their eyes glued on the door, would suddenly perceive, instead of the longed-for customer, Stash, accompanied by his "adjutant." Stash demanded to see the dealer's license—perhaps for the third time that week; he demanded to see the weights, the labels on the goods, the tax receipts. The Jews were so intimidated that they complied, though they knew very well that Stash had no official standing, could not legally enforce his demands, and had no other backing than that of his gang.

Thus, by the habit of submission, the Jews themselves conferred a semi-official status on Stash Grabski, so that in the course of time the regular officials, the mayor of the town and the appointed assessors, began to be afraid of him. Apart from the submissiveness of his victims, Stash used as a weapon his fiery patriotism and backed that with dark hints concerning the central organization in the big city, "which was keeping an eye on local officials." There were, in this Polish townlet, many respectable Christian families which had lived on the friendliest terms with the Jews for as many generations as could be remembered; they had neither reason nor inclination to quarrel with the Jews now. But for the first time in their lives they found it uncomfortable to be known as friends of Jewish families. This young Stash . . . one could not tell what position he might be occupying tomorrow . . . he was not just the son of poor old Grabski, the half-paralyzed carpenter . . . he was one of the men of tomorrow. . . .

VI

For the Jews generally, and in particular for Leib and Malkah, Stash's special victims, the breaking point was approaching, the point of revolt, the point at which there was nothing to be gained by continued submission, nothing to be lost by resistance—and, it may be said, the point at which caution and calculation were thrown to the wind, and outraged human nature asserted itself blindly.

There came a market day on which Leib and Malkah no longer put up a stall outside the shop but waited for peasants to come sneaking in for a purchase, without exposing themselves to the public gaze. And out of ancient habit, or actual need, or obstinacy, or all three, peasants did come in from time to time. At one moment, in fact, the shop reminded one of the good old days. There were several customers—peasants and peasant women—demanding attention; Long Leib was handing down bolts of cloth from the shelves and Malkah was measuring off and chaffering with the women; the children were playing in the living room behind the shop, and Malkah had to call in the oldest girl to help serve the customers. In the midst of this unusual flurry, Stash Grabski and his adjutant, the shoemaker's apprentice, entered. Stash banged his heavy cane on the counter, so that there was sudden silence, and declared in a loud voice that on the previous night smuggled goods had been delivered to this shop. It was therefore his duty to look through the goods and to make sure that every bolt of cloth had the official label on it. And without waiting for permission, he began to pull down bolts of cloth and tearing open packages for his adjutant to examine.

Malkah and Long Leib watched. Malkah's goiter rose, swelled, became bluish. "There you are," she said to her husband. "The one chance we had to earn a groschen." She put on a submissive smile, which sat ill on her dark, wretched face, and turned to Stash Grabski: "*Panie,* good, dear *Panie,*" she wheedled. "Why don't you let a poor old Jew woman alone? Your mother—God rest her soul in heaven!—was my best friend. Why should you do these things to me?"

"What's in that package?" snarled Stash, poking about with his stick.

Long Leib was a patient man. Years of suffering and humiliation had made him hard and given him endurance. More than once, when Stash Grabski had marched insolently into the shop, Leib had felt tempted to pick up something heavy and smash it into the head of the young hooligan. To hell with everything, he said to himself. Things can't be any worse than they are. But Long Leib would pull himself up. It was not only himself he had to think of. He had to remember the effect which such an incident would have on the Jewish community generally, on other Jewish communities, in other towns and villages, too. It was this thought, rather than the fear of what might happen to him, that tied his hands. And so he swallowed his bitterness and with his one seeing eye grinned wheedlingly at Stash Grabski, just as his wife did. Sick at heart, he repeated her words:

"*Panie* Stash, we're old neighbors, aren't we? Has *Panie* forgotten how he used to play with my children in the old days? Has he forgotten what good friends we were with his sainted mother?"

"Hold your tongue, you filthy sheeny!" bellowed Stash. "And hand down those packages."

But even Long Leib's iron patience has its breaking point. And even the thought of the consequence for the Jewish community is swept away by the torrent of resentment which rises in him. Long Leib jumps down from the ladder with the agility of a boy, throws himself at Stash, hurls him away from the packages he is handling:

"Who the devil are you? Are you an inspector, or an official? Show me your badge and I'll let you examine my goods."

"Leib!" gasps his wife. "Leib! What are you doing? You are playing with fire! God help us all! We're in this boy's hands!" And Malkah thrusts herself between her husband and Stash Grabski and breaks into a suppliant wail: "It's nothing, *Panie!* These are packages of goods left over from last year. I'll show them to you."

Long Leib has had enough. He pushes his wife aside.

"I'll show him nothing," he yells. "Does he think he can boss us about because he put on a student's cap? Does he think he frightens everybody? Does he think we've forgotten who he is and where he came from? I'm not going to open packages for every hooligan that comes in here."

Fright paralyzes Malkah. Her goiter swells, so that the veins in her throat, bluish, distended, seem ready to burst. The beating of her heart has become almost audible.

"God help us, Leib! What have you done? Do you want us all to be murdered, or driven out of the town? *Panitch!* Dear, good *Panitch!* Don't pay any attention to him. He didn't mean it! Take pity on a poor old Jew woman! I haven't had a bite to eat since early this morning." She hardly knows what she is saying. In the extremity of her despair she slaps herself on the cheek, and turns on her husband. "Leib! Keep your mouth shut. Think of your children!"

"No!" screams Leib. "I've had enough. Why should I be afraid? Have I got stolen goods here? Hasn't every bale got the stamp on? Aren't they taking the life out of me anyway with their taxes? What more do they want? My blood? They can have it. For God's sake stop pleading with him. It's only old Grabski's lout of a son. And now"—he addressed himself to Stash—"Get out! Because you can stand here all day, and I won't let you see my goods. If you can bring an inspector, or an official, you can look at the goods. Not before!"

Stash had turned white. It was the first time that he had met with resistance, and he was not prepared for it. The conceited, arrogant smile died on his lips, and his eyes seemed to lose their light. His narrow forehead contracted, and the sweat began to pour out from under his student's cap. But he said nothing. He only lifted an unwashed fist toward the Jew's face, turned on his heel, and left the shop. His adjutant followed him.

"Leib!" moaned Malkah. "I'm afraid. Something bad's going to happen."

"I'm not a bit afraid," said her husband, calmly. "Let them do what they like to me—it's all one now. I haven't got the strength to put up with it any more. You can kick a dog around just so long."

That evening they returned: not Stash and his adjutant, but the official city inspectors, with badges and identification papers. They turned the shop upside down and left it looking as though a hurricane had visited it; they searched every corner of the house, tore open the cushions, broke the furniture. They found nothing—but Stash had had his revenge.

As the winter approached, things went from bad to worse. The peasants became weary of resisting the boycott. They preferred to accept the inferior goods and services of the patriotic stores rather than run the risk of getting their bones broken by the Stashes and their like. Besides, as the cold weather set in, they came less frequently to town. The harvest had been a poor one; there was no money in the villages. The last market days were desolate. The peasants could not afford a pair of shoes or a measure of cloth. All they could bring to town was a basketful of small eggs, a bundle of hog's hair, a little bale of flax, to exchange for a piece of salt or half a liter of petroleum. Their last stores of oats and potatoes they kept at home, to carry them through the winter.

The Jewish shops looked like mausoleums, and as the season drew to a close, bills and i.o.u.'s of the Lodz merchants fell due, and the loans of the Benevolent Association were called in. It was useless to wait for customers. If a penny was to be earned, and even if supplies were to be scraped together in kind for the winter days, it could be done only by going out to the villages, taking to the road. The peasant would not come to town, but tempted at home by goods he needed, he might part with a few potatoes or eggs or cabbages. This had always been the winter practice; Jews had ventured out in the early morning, under their heavy packs, and had returned covered—in spite of the bitter cold—with the sweat of labor and of fear.

But now Stash's organization spread a network of terror about the town. When the last market day came, Stash openly proclaimed that thereafter no Jewish peddlers would be permitted to circulate in the surrounding villages. If one of them made the attempt, he would return sooner than he expected, and not on his own feet, but carried by others, and wrapped in a sheet.

Stash was as good as his word. The first Jew to defy him was Samuel the butcher. Samuel left town early one morning, not to sell but to buy; there was no meat left in his shop, the Sabbath was approaching, and there was a peasant in the village of Sanczev who had a calf to sell. But Samuel got no further than the town limit. A hail of stones broke on him from behind a fence, and he had to be carried home.

That day there was a terrible outcry in the Jewish community. "We're done for! It's the end!" A delegation was hastily gathered and sent to the mayor. The Rabbi put on his festival clothes, his black satin gaberdine, and his velvet skull cap, and went to see the Catholic priest. But priest and mayor had the same reproach to make: the Jews were Bolsheviks, enemies of Poland and destroyers of religion. In particular the priest told the Rabbi that instead of running around he ought to stay with the Jewish youth and persuade them to a new course, so that they should cease to be traitors to the fatherland.

"Does every young Jew have to become a Trotzky?" asked the priest, sternly.

The next day a delegation was sent off by train to the Jewish group in the Polish Sejm. The delegation was told to go back quietly; everything would be attended to. The delegation returned, to find that Stash was carrying on as before.

The mayor finally "took steps." He sent out a couple of armed men to watch the roads. But the effect was nil, and the mayor admitted that he had not anywhere near the number of men he needed. Privately he advised the Jews to keep off the roads for a little while, until Stash's organization would be exhausted, as it soon would be.

That Sabbath, at the services in the synagogue, when the scrolls of the Torah were being lifted out of the ark, and the hoarse voice of the cantor, shaking with suppressed tears, began the appropriate prayer, a scream rang out from the women's section behind the curtains:

"Men! Why do you permit this? One lad has made up his mind to starve the Jews of this town—and all of you can do nothing against him!"

For a time it seemed that the woman was right, that nothing would be done and that after the attack on Samuel the butcher no one would dare to defy Stash Grabski's ukase.

For some days the Jews remained indoors, Malkah and Leib with the rest. At that time of the year it was not unusual for families to stay abed for a week on end, getting up only for meals. The snow fell steadily, the roads were impassable, no customers would be on hand before the spring. There was nothing to get up for—and it was warmer abed.

Leib's shop, like all the other Jewish shops which catered to the peasants, was locked. The shelves were almost empty; what had not been sold by the end of the season was returned to the Lodz warehouses. A little stock was held for the winter, to be peddled in the villages when the storms subsided; that, at least, was the usual procedure. But now, with Stash Grabski's prohibition against Jewish peddlers, it looked as though it had been a folly to keep even this last remnant of stock.

But how long could this go on? As long as the storm continued, as long as the ice laid a seal on the doors, Leib and his family submitted incidentally to Stash Grabski's orders. When the storm let up, when travel became possible, it was another matter. It is not easy to die passively, least of all in the company of loved ones. And not only need, but pride, outraged manhood, egged Leib on to action. On the morning the snow ceased to fall, and the howling of the wind declined to a whimper, he sprang out of bed, and called to the oldest girl:

"Leah, where have you put my boots?"

"What are you going to do?" cried Malkah.

Leib pulled on the heavy boots, wrapped them round with rags.

"What I'm going to do?" he muttered through set teeth. "You'll see soon enough."

He drew on his coat, girdled himself with a rope, and went into the shop. He took out of their tattered newspapers a bale of cloth, a couple of shawls, a handful of kerchiefs and socks, and wrapped them over. He thrust the bundle into a sack.

Malkah watched him, terrified, hoping he would change his mind. When she saw that he meant it, she got out of bed, and began imploring him to wait. Not that day, at least.

"Let be!" he answered. "I'd rather be finished with it than drag it out like this. I can't stay in here any longer, do you hear? I can't sit still. There's nothing to wait for but starvation."

"Leib! Leibel! You're a father of children!"

Leib did not answer. He passed the rope round the sack, pulled it tight with a vicious jerk, slung the sack over his shoulder.

"Nothing will happen," he said at last. "I shan't let myself be starved to death by a young hooligan." Accoutered and loaded he made for the door.

"Father in heaven," moaned Malkah, "be with him, and guard him, and bring him back to me!" And she raised her arms to heaven, then remembered that she had not washed her hands yet, and that she was therefore unfit to address herself to the All-Pure. She passed her fingers hastily over the ice on the door latch, and washed the tips hastily.

"Nothing will happen," repeated Long Leib. "This evening, God willing, I'll be back with a sack of potatoes."

Malkah wanted to keep her eyes on him after he had left the house. She tried to rub away a patch of ice from the windowpane, but the seal of winter was too thick and heavy for her, and by the time she caught a glimpse of the street her man was gone.

"God be with him for my children's sake," she wept. "Let him return soon, even if with empty hands." And with that she re-

membered that the youngsters, still in bed, had literally nothing
to breakfast on.

"Stay under the covers," she called to them. "I'll go out and get
you something."

She came back with a small package of rice, made the fire, and
put the pot on to boil. But the meal was not ready yet when she
heard a commotion in the street. There were running footsteps,
shouts, and answering shouts; and to her horror she thought she
heard the name of her husband being called.

Her heart stood still, and the few remaining hairs under her
dilapidated wig seemed to her to be crawling out of their roots.
For a moment she was incapable of motion. She only stared with
glassy eyes at the frightened children. Then she snatched up a
shawl, left the pot on the fire, and ran out into the street. Far away
to the right, in the direction which Leib had taken not so long ago,
she saw figures, and she knew at once, beyond all shadow of a
doubt, that calamity had overtaken her. She tried to say something,
but the goiter rose in her throat, and only a gurgling sound came
out as she ran up the street in the direction of the retreating figures.

Less than a kilometer from the crossroads, a little distance beyond
the last ikon. Long Leib was lying, with his face buried in his sack,
and the blood oozing from his body had cut a red gutter in the
snow. A group of men and women was already assembled about
him—Christians as well as Jews, women in shawls, men in long
boots. Others were running in this direction from the town.

No one greeted Malkah. There was only a silent parting of the
crowd; a way through was made for her. She drew near, saying
nothing, and looking round her with a kind of mild surprise in
her eyes, as though unable to understand what was happening.
Then she bent down over her man and shook him gently, as
though to awaken him from sleep.

Voices broke in on her. "Don't move him! Don't touch him! Let
the police come first!" The words were uttered in Yiddish by some,
in Polish by others.

The silence once broken, the women burst into a loud lamenta-
tion. One of them, beating her breast hysterically—it was the

woman who had screamed in the synagogue—directed her re-proaches at the men. "Look! This is our lot! Our blood is given to the dogs! It is the great destruction again, and there is no one to help us!" The infection of her despair spread to the other women, some of whom began to tear their hair and scratch their faces. One woman seemed to have lost her mind completely, for she stood by the dead man shaking her body like a pious Jew at his prayers before the Ark. Malkah alone seemed to be calm, and this was more dreadful than the hysteria of the others. She did not weep, or tear her hair, or scratch her face. She stood there as if she could not understand what moved the others so. But her goiter had swelled up horribly, and her eyes were sinking deeper and deeper into their sockets.

The police arrived, in great numbers, a captain, a lieutenant, and several sergeants. There were also some civilians, including the town doctor and Stash Grabski.

They all got out of the way for the police, and they gave Stash an even wider berth. They let him come close to the man lying in the snow. There was a secret feeling that Stash Grabski belonged there more than anyone else.

Stash Grabski stood there like one of the officials and listened to the doctor's report: "The bullet entered here, at the back, near the side; it traversed the lung; it is undoubtedly lodged in the heart. Death was instantaneous. The murderer must have been standing over there, behind that clump of trees. That's where the shot must have come from. No use looking for footsteps now, though."

Stash listened gravely, said nothing. His face was very earnest. From under his student cap the sweat poured down, plastering a wisp of hair to his forehead. He had pulled down his eyebrows so that his eyes were almost invisible. And yet it seemed to some, who cast a glance at him now and again, that a flicker of sadistic pleasure passed over his tight lips.

Suddenly he was aware of something fastened on him, not the gaze of a pair of eyes, but the concentration of an entire being, something that poured simultaneously from the face, the throat, the head of a woman. Malkah had perceived, as from a distance, the figure of her husband's murderer, and she was staring intently at him. There was neither anger, nor bitterness, nor self-pity in the look. Instead, Stash read there, uncomprehendingly, a profound mother-pity for him. What was still more incomprehensible to him was that the look came in the oddest way from the woman's swollen, bluish goiter, which seemed to be bursting through the distended throat, as if it were trying to spew forth the gathered gall and poisoned blood of all the years of her suffering.

Stash started away from her instinctively. He was astounded by his own reaction. He had not thought it possible that a wordless glance should have such power. He would rather have had the woman scream something at him. But she refused to scream. She refused even to show anger. It was pity, and pity for him rather than for herself, which spoke from the extinguished eyes and from the sallow, weatherbeaten face, from the locked lips and from the swelling throat. Pity, without a touch of reproach in it, without any demand for an explanation or a reckoning, was poured out on him, sank into him, and penetrated to the depths of his heart.

"*Pshakrev!*" he cursed under his breath and shifted his ground. "That Jew woman has a way of looking at you!" But his bravado failed to bolster up his spirit. He felt something rising from deep within him, in response to that flood of compassion, something akin to the sensation he had known years before, in the early time of his brief religious experience, something that softened him, made him weak, thrust him into a dark mood. He looked away from the Jew woman, but it was too late. She had evoked in him the memory of something that went back further than his religious experience. He was suddenly afraid of these ghosts within him. He turned on his heel and left the crowd.

VII

There was an investigation, of course, not only by the local authorities but by special officers sent down from district headquarters. On the very day of the death Stash himself was called in and cross-examined. But he had a perfect alibi. Very early that morning he and a fellow-student had been sitting together in the home of the latter, reviewing a course in Roman law. The entire family of the student testified to this effect. Others testified that he had been seen leaving the house of the student at about the time the crowds began running toward the scene of the murder. There was no way of connecting Stash with the crime. Stash having thus been cleared, the investigating officers turned their attention to a rumor that a peasant had been seen early that morning slipping out of town. The peasant had carried a gun and was undoubtedly going out hunting. There had in all probability been a fatal mistake: the peasant had seen the dark, bent figure of the Jew and had fired, mistaking him for game. And, queerly enough, this talk went on without anyone being found who had actually seen the "hunter."

Again the Jews organized deputations, to the mayor, to the government, to the Jewish deputies in the Sejm, to the priest, to anyone who would listen. But the mayor, and the government, and the priest, and the Jewish deputies, while all promising to co-operate in clearing up the incident, warned against exaggeration. After all, it did look like an accident; it would serve no good purpose to turn it into a political incident when there was no proof; things like this were best forgotten as soon as possible. In any case, there was much restlessness in the villages; the Jews were suspected of seizing on any pretext to give the Poles a bad reputation; if they were not careful, something serious, a great explosion of popular anger, might ensue. And not against the local Jews only.

So it went on, until between weariness and despair the Jews quietened down. Before long one heard such phrases as "Well, the world isn't coming to an end," and "We've got to live somehow with these people," and "Let's think of tomorrow," all uttered very sagely and patiently. Long Leib had hardly been buried, the snow had hardly concealed his grave, before the town had settled into its routine.

There was one man in the town who did not recover his equanimity with the rest, and that was Stash Grabski. From the first day on, from the hour when Long Leib fell near the crossroads, from the moment when he had felt rather than seen the Jew woman's face turned on him, he found no peace of mind. Since he had stared back at the twisted lips, sealed with pain, and at the sunken, light-less eyes, with their strange expression of infinite pity, it was as though a patch of blood disfigured his own face and could not be washed off. But what haunted and persecuted him most was the recollection of the goiter rising in the woman's throat, showing bluish through the distended skin, filled with accumulated gall. He could see it straining the veins, threatening to burst through and to drench him from head to foot in its poisoned blood. The first night after the murder he had a hideous dream, which returned on later nights with increasing persistence. From where he slept, in the garret of the ruin which was their home, he could look down on the window of the woman's shop. He dreamed horrible dreams, that the goiter had detached itself from Malkah's scraggy throat, had acquired legs, and was crawling up the walls toward him; it entered the room and stationed itself in the corner where his clothes were hanging. The goiter was a sort of bag, made of bluish skin, and filled with a mixture of human miseries, which had dissolved into a thick liquid pus or bile; and in the thick liquid there was a squirming of leeches, which were continuously swallowing each other. Then somehow the goiter acquired eyes, and these were bent on Stash. There was no reproach in the look, no complaint, only a dumb request: "Murderer, have pity on me, take a knife and cut me open and let the pus and bile flow out of me." Then the goiter would change appearance and would become the stretched-out neck of a young bird, which had fallen from a branch before it had grown its feathers, and which was begging someone to stab it through.

The first time this visitation came on him, Stash managed to tear himself out of his sleep and to leap from his bed. He lit a candle, to drive the shadows out of the corners; for it was from these, it seemed to him, from these shadows clustering in a con-spiracy, whispering to each other, that the abominable vision had arisen. He spat, crossed himself, and tried to fall asleep again. But sleep would not come. Now, instead of the goiter, it was his mother that he saw.

On the second and third night the experience returned. Most extraordinary of all, when his mother appeared to him, she was invariably followed, in a few moments, by the Jew woman. His mother was dressed in her Sunday clothes; she had her prayer book under her arm, and from her hand dangled her prayer beads. Or else she carried a taper, as she had used to do in church. But she was not in church at all. She was standing on the threshold of the Jew woman's shop, and the two of them were in intimate conference. The picture troubled him: why should his mother hold the candle, as she had done in church, and as she had done when she lay on her deathbed, why should she hold the candle now while she conferred with her neighbor? And what was it that they talked about, so intimately, so earnestly, in low, eager, scared voices? They were undoubtedly talking about him, about Stash, and also about Long Leib. Their faces were somber, distraught; it was a matter of life and death; someone was sick, in his last agony; and that someone was Stash himself; and it was also Long Leib. Both of them were sick and on the point of death. The women were taking counsel. And in the midst of this dream or hallucination, it occurred to Stash that for ever and for ever, as long as the world would last, he and Long Leib would be linked together.

"Hell!" he screamed, and sprang from his bed to light the candle. He lay down again and kept his eyes wide open, fearing sleep. But that picture of his mother, side by side with the Jew woman, would not vanish. No longer in a dream, but in a clear, waking vision, he saw her, as he had seen her in childhood. The picture was normal. His mother did not wear her Sunday best, she was not carrying a prayer book or a taper. She was in her daily rags, and she held on her arm a baby as raggedly dressed as she. The Jew woman was in the same wretched case. His mother was weeping and complaining and wiping her eyes with a corner of her ragged dress. The Jew woman comforted her, thrust her hand into the pocket of her dress, took out two copper coins and gave them to his mother. ("Extraordinary!" thought Stash, by habit. "No matter how poor those Jewies are, they've always got something in their pockets!") His mother thanked the Jew woman.

"You can leave the child here, *Pani* Stepanova," said the Jew woman, clearly. "He'll play with my children till you come back from work." She took the child from the mother's arms. The child would not go at first, but cried and struggled. The Jew woman set it down amongst her own little ones, who were rolling about like a brood of ducklings in a corner of the shop. Then the Jew woman took out half a loaf of bread, cut off several slices, one for each child, including the little stranger. "Now, Stash," said his mother, "you stay here till I come back from the day's washing, and I'll cook you some nice, warm gruel." The child became quiet; it ate the slice of bread hungrily.

"What?" asked Stash. "Was that what mother said? She mentioned my name? No, that's impossible." He could not bring himself to believe that he, Stash Grabski, had been helped and fed by the Jew woman. It must have been his sister Zasha. He could not have remembered it of himself. No, not he! He could never have accepted the Jew woman's charity, not even as a baby. All his blood protested against the suggestion.

And yet, despite himself, the picture worked on him. Somehow the Jew woman, with her goiter, changed for him; even the shop, which he loathed more than the woman herself, because of the peasants he had seen going in there to buy accursed Jewish goods, yes, even the shop became somewhat different. The disgust which had convulsed him when he had smelt the onions frying inside the Jewish house, and which recurred whenever he thought of Malkah and her brood, tried to assert itself now, but it was not the same as before. The children, too, the Jew children in their rags, presented themselves in another light. He looked in himself for the customary revulsion, the loathing which they always inspired, and could not find it.

There was a hammering of queer ideas in his mind. "No," he muttered, "they weren't exactly Rothschilds either." Not that he had ever seen a Rothschild or knew what a Rothschild was. But he had a picture in his mind: a Rothschild was a fat Jew who sat in a counting house filled with bags of gold and spent all his days and nights counting the gold coins. "No, they never saw a gold coin in their lives, you've got to admit that. They were poor, yes, just as poor as one of our own." For now it occurred to him that although there were bolts of cloth in the shop, the Jew woman's children went in rags and crept about with naked behinds on the earthen floor. They didn't dare to take an inch of cloth for themselves. He repeated, vaguely, "No, they were not Rothschilds, not by a long way." He reflected: "They hungered all week, lived on dry bread —when they could get it. Only for their holy Sabbath they prepared the one meal of the week—whatever they could scrape together, onions and chicken fat, a piece of fish, a loaf of white bread—and that was what they lived for from one week end to the other."

And then, for no particular reason, he wanted to know what had become of the oldest boy—Pinchas, wasn't it?—with whom he had used to play as a child. They had rolled about together in the sand on the sunny side of the shop. Once they had arranged a little cemetery for dead beetles and flies and birds. When they had been toddlers, just able to run about, they had gone into the autumn fields, dug up potatoes, and roasted them over a fire of sticks. Once they managed to find a piece of netting and went to catch fish in the river. He even remembered how he and this boy, Pinchas, had, on a certain Jewish holiday, collected fir branches and sold them to the Jews, who used them for their booths.

That was a long time ago. They had ceased to play with each other even in childhood. The time came when he, Stash, couldn't stand those Jews, couldn't stand Pinchas, either, couldn't stand that Jewish cap of his and those earlocks dangling out from under it. It had always enraged him to see the little Jew boy, going with his companions to the Hebrew school. One afternoon, when the Jewish children had gone down to the river to bathe, he had crept up with Burak, their big dog. He had snatched away the clothes, thrown them behind a bush, and then sicked Burak on the children, who had had to run all the way home naked and weeping. What had happened since then to Pinchas? He had heard it said that he had gone to Palestine, or that he was working on a farm somewhere in Poland, preparing himself for the life of a pioneer in Palestine. He had also heard that those young Jews were pretty good workers, at that. They wanted to build up their homeland and take all the Jews there.

"Well, the sooner the better," he muttered. "Why should they take away our jobs, eat our bread? We need our fields for our own peasants. There's no room here for Jews. We need everything, fields, animals, for ourselves. Let them get out of Poland instead of settling down in it like pigs in a sty. And that's what we're working for—to get them out. That's what it is! It's because they won't get out that we have to use these methods against them!"

He was relieved to find himself thinking normally again. "Yes," he said eagerly to himself, "we've got our own troubles. We can't waste time on them. The quicker they get out the better for all of us!"

VIII

To make up for the tormenting uncertainty of those nights, he made desperate efforts to strengthen his position during the days. He was ashamed of the womanish sentimentality which assailed him after his nightmares. It was this half-witted humanitarianism which was the ruin of Poland; and who were the chief protagonists of humanitarianism if not the Jews themselves, who used it as a weapon against Poland?

There was a new driving force in him now—his anger with his own weakness. The more he questioned himself in the nights, the more brutally he spoke and acted during the days. He called together his group and delivered a long and furious harangue against the timidities which were creeping into the organization. No one was to think that because of that incident of the dead Jew there was going to be a letup in the pressure. Now that the Jews had been taught a lesson, the weaklings in the organization might be inclined to say, "Enough!" No! This was just the moment for intensification of the boycott.

All day long Stash Grabski ran around organizing his gangs of highway watchers; all day long he was accompanied by his adjutant, the shoemaker's apprentice with the name of the famous local murderer. But though he did his best to hide the fact from himself, Stash was aware that a sudden change had come over the attitude of the townsmen. Yes, they were still afraid of him, Christians as well as Jews. He smelt it, and he did not dislike it wholly. And yet, when he saw a Polish mother instinctively clutch her children when he came down the street, it was not exactly gratification that he felt. Nor was it pleasant to catch a frightened, horrified whisper: "There he is!" And very often, it seemed to him, the name of Long Leib was included in the whisper. It was no use: the two of them were going to be linked together for ever. Stash tried to pass it off with a sneer. "I'll put the fear of God in them, I will." It did not quite work. Nor could he carry it off with mere bravado when, on entering the café which had recently been opened in the town and which was a sort of political center, he noticed distinctly that some people kept their eyes averted from him, and others drew their chairs away from his vicinity.

It had been quite different only a few days before. His entry had been the signal for a kind of demonstration. A murmur of approval had run through the room. There he was, Stash Grabski, the savior of his country! They had clustered about him to hear his views on the latest political developments. The room had brightened up with his entry, become livelier, more alert. And now there was this sudden change. Not that they dared openly to snub him. They just did not see him. Or, if they greeted him, it was with the kind of gesture which invited no intimacy. The older people in particular, who had always hailed him warmly and had shaken hands with him cordially, were now the coldest. And it was not so long since Dr. Poznanski, the town doctor and one of its most respectable citizens, had had him to dinner in his home.

The clearest indication of the decline in his status came from the doctor's daughter, Elizabeth, whom Stash had for some time regarded as a political pupil and who had been on the point of declaring herself a member of his organization. He met her on the street the third day after the death of Long Leib. She acknowledged his greeting, but she did not stop. She lifted her hand, she even smiled at him, and it was a cold, forced smile which was more offensive than a complete snub. Later in the day he saw her in the political café, and went over to her. She turned pale, stood up, and stammered something about having to rush home because her mother had the migraine. And she was gone!

Stash kept his countenance; nor did he permit himself to take this and similar incidents too much to heart during the day. At night it all came out. "Blast them all!" he raged, in his garret. "For whom am I doing all these things, if not for them? For Poland! For the fatherland! There's no pleasure in it for me, God knows. And they turn up their noses at me! Those lousy Philistines! Those bourgeois lice! Those pot-bellied middle classes! They want *me* to do the dirty work, so that they can keep their hands clean and refuse to shake mine. *I* clean out the garbage, get myself bespattered with muck, and *they* have their pure consciences—*they* have nothing to do with that sort of thing. They employ a hooligan for that, and he's not good enough for them. Oh, wait! Wait! Their turn will come, too. Wait till *we* arise, the new masters of Poland. You think we'll labor and you'll collect, you think there's nothing to pay, but you'll learn—"

He stopped, terrified by the tenor of his thoughts. What did he mean, "pay?" Wasn't he doing all this from a sense of duty and loyalty, from unreflecting, unselfish devotion to Poland? But on the other hand, if it was all for Poland, why this sense of guilt?

And now his terror deepened. Who had said that he had a sense of guilt? Admittedly he was doing things which did not—how should he put it?—did not look well. But what had he to gain from them? And what did his relations to the "victims" matter? He was acting like the soldier on the field of battle, who has nothing personal against his fellow-soldier in the enemy army. Duty had put a gun into his hand. "I'm a soldier, a volunteer in the army of the fatherland. And this is a war to the death."

A sudden resolution formed in his mind. He would fight fire with fire, he would beat the devil at his own game. He would confront the Jew woman, to show her that he dared to look her in the face. That would put an end to his abominable dreams.

He had noticed that on the days which followed the burial of

Long Leib dark groups of Jews assembled every morning and night in the house of the widow. A candle was lit for them, and they stood together—so much he knew from glimpses through the window—but what it was that brought them together he did not know. They came regularly, morning and night, dark, stooping, black-bearded figures, conspiratorial, sinister, their bodies shivering with the cold, their hands thrust into their sleeves. What did they want? What plots were they hatching? Would it not be well to break in on them and at the same time to outface Malkah and her goiter?

On the evening of the day after Long Leib was buried, he stationed himself with his adjutant outside the Jew woman's shop. They let the conspirators gather, and then Stash crossed over and entered the shop. But he got no further than the door. This was what he saw: the Jew woman sitting in torn stockings on a low stool; near her stood a guttering candle, and she was muttering to herself as her body shook to and fro. In the room beyond Stash caught a glimpse of Jews clustered about a candle. They seemed to be praying. The children, who were seated by Malkah, were the first to observe Stash. They became stony with fear. Malkah looked up. She did not start with surprise; she did not betray fear. It was as if somehow she had been expecting this visit. She nodded toward Stash, her lips tightened, and the goiter rose in her throat and distended the skin. Stash could not take his eyes off it. Now it made him think of the swollen breast of a mother whose child has died and who cannot get rid of her milk. The sickening, nightmarish idea came to him that the swollen breast-goiter was for him. Had not the Jew woman said that he had fed at her breast in his babyhood?

He left the shop without saying a word. He walked up to his companion, slapped him on the back, and said, with a loud laugh:

"The Jew men are bringing down a curse on me. They're making arrangements with the devil to deliver my soul to him."

His companion laughed with him. But a few minutes later, as they were leaving the marketplace, Stash said:

"Stefan, what do mothers do with their milk when the baby happens to die?"

216

"What the hell's the matter with you? What kind of question is that?"

"I just wanted to know, that's all. They've got cups, haven't they, to draw off the milk till the swelling goes down."

"Sure they have. They say that when a woman's that way, with a lot of milk in her breast and no baby to feed, she suffers terrible pains—burning pains, like when you stick a pin under your fingernails."

"It's a lousy business, being a woman," said Stash, assuming an indifferent tone of voice.

Stefan's tongue was loosened.

"They say," he continued, "that women like those pains—I mean from the milk in their breast when the baby's dead. They try to keep the milk as long as possible. The pain gives them a kind of satisfaction. But it hurts them. That's funny, isn't it? You know what happened once in the village where I come from? There was a woman who had a baby, and it died. And she didn't want to lose the milk in her breast, so she used to steal at night into the sty and suckle the newborn pigs. And one night she was caught at it and they nearly killed her. But the other women saved her; they said she couldn't help herself; she had to get the milk out, because that soothed the pain."

Stash shuddered.

Coming home late that night, he hesitated to mount to his garret. He felt a curious need to pray, a need which, except for the brief religious episode in his high school years, he had not experienced since childhood. It was a sudden, incomprehensible hunger for protection.

He stopped at the foot of the stairs, turned back to his sister's room, and very carefully, very slowly, thrust open the door. No, she was not there. In a corner of the room stood the big, heavy bed in which his parents had slept in years past. On it were piled pillows and quilts; and above it, on the wall, burned the lamp before the holy picture of Jesus, bloody and emaciated, in the lap of the Virgin. Black and gold the picture glimmered down at Stash; he remembered that his mother had loved it; she had prayed before it regularly, and on Ash Wednesdays she had adorned it with flowers and had put it before the door of the house to greet the procession as it went by.

Stash closed the door behind him. He did not want to be seen. He knelt down on the floor in front of the picture and looked at it closely. He did not pray; he only looked at the picture. After a time it seemed to be looking back at him in the dim, sorrowful light of the little oil lamp; and it seemed to take on life. The great, mournful eyes sank into the face; the face itself acquired lines and furrows, became filled with years and sadness and suffering. The body of her son lay in her lap, the nails were still in his hands and feet, and from these wounds, as well as from his side, the blood poured out upon her. Motionless, fascinated, Stash watched the shifting of the lines and shadows on her face, which now began to resemble the face of the Jew woman. For the expression of suffering was entirely without reproach; and the pity which spoke from the eyes was not for herself, and not even for her son, but for him, for Stash. And now something dreadful began to happen. The throat under the folds of the dress was swelling, rising, exposing itself; it was like the breast-goiter of the Jew woman. And at the same time the blood that was running out of the son's body was making a little crimson valley in a snow-covered road, just as the blood of Long Leib had done.

"My God!" whispered Stash. "Am I going mad?" He wanted to rise and found he could not. He was fastened to the place; and in spite of himself his open eyes were directed at the transformed sacred picture. Something told him that he would kneel here for ever and that the sacred picture would not resume its own form, until he had confessed—until the words, "I have sinned," had crossed his lips. It was useless to invoke the memory of his cynicism, useless to revile his own weakness. Here he would stay, kneeling, horrified, his eyes wide open, until he had broken his pride and uttered the words.

Some time later, he did not know how long, he was lying in his bed, his eyes directed into the darkness of the night. He was not sleeping, but neither was he visited by hallucinations. The room was lightless, yet he did not think of shadows congregated in the corner. The devil was gone! Stash's heart was lighter; it could feel; it was able to weigh human deeds and human suffering.

IX

"God," he whispered, "it seemed to me that I meant well; why did evil come out of it? It seemed to me that I wanted to help my fatherland, my fellowmen, my peasant brothers, who live in such wretchedness. It seemed to me that I did what I did out of love for Poland. It *seemed* so to me."

But now he knew better. "For in truth," he went on with his confession, "that which I did came not out of love for my fellowmen, but out of hatred of them. Not their sufferings moved me, but my own vile need to dominate. If I stooped to the meanest acts and did the evil that others did not dare to do, it was not for their sake, but for my own. Now they start away from me, and loathe me. But that is not the worst—for I am forsaken by God.

"What horror there was in *her* eyes when she greeted me today! How reluctantly she spoke to me!"

He sprang from his bed and knelt down on the cold floor. He felt better this way. It seemed to him that he could more easily disentangle his thoughts in the posture of prayer; and indeed, whether it was this posture, or the result of his confession, he found himself pursuing a train of ideas which led to the prime cause of his wretched condition.

"It came to pass this way," he whispered, excitedly. "I would not think of other human beings as human beings. No. I would not consider that they were like me, with my hopes and fears and pains. I would not let myself feel the *reality* of the life which surrounded me. I considered human beings only as *things*. That's it. Or else as animals, at best as animals. No, not even that; because we take pity on animals. As *things,* then. I would not let myself remember that when they bleed they suffer, when they are hungry they suffer, just as I do. And why would I not let myself remember? Because, if I had remembered, my pride and ambition would have been paralyzed. I would not then have followed the orders given me by leaders who had the same pride and ambition as I had and who also would not think of human beings except as things. So I obeyed them and became their dupe; for I too was a thing to them. They would not and will not understand that I too have feelings and that it sickens me now to have oppressed those that did good to me, those who are poor and wretched, as my mother was poor and wretched. We lived in the same street, almost in the same house, on the same patch of earth, under the same patch of sky.

"But when I looked at them I would not see them; I wanted to see only worms which it was my duty to crush into the earth. So I used the words 'fatherland,' 'duty,' 'sacred cause,' to cover up my not-seeing. I spoke of the hunger of our masses, the needs of our peasants, of our stinking cities, our starving children; but never once was there in me a feeling of pity for anyone. Had I felt pity, I would also have pitied these, my neighbors, whom I saw every day struggling with hunger, want, nakedness, oppression. But instead I added to their wretchedness; I besieged them, I made them tremble at the sight of me, I poisoned their sleeping and their waking hours. And this delighted me. I said that this was good, it was noble. I swelled up with righteousness, I knew myself to be a great man. Fool that I was! Wherein was I great, and before whom? Did not those who egged me on to these acts despise me for them? Did they not applaud me *only* until I had accomplished their vileness, whereafter they cast me off like an unclean thing? And they did not even despise me because they despised my wickedness. No! They despised my folly and my filth, my willingness to be their tool.

"God, have pity on me, and let me be clean again!"

.   .   .

When, at the end of the seven-day period of mourning for her murdered husband, Malkah reopened her shop, the first customer to cross the threshold was Stash Grabski.

Two children who were already up fled from the shop with a cry of terror. Her endurance at an end, Malkah began to beat her breast with her fists.

"End it now!" she sobbed. "Persecute me no more! Kill me and I will be at peace."

Stash did not answer. He moved slowly toward her, fell at her feet, and seized one of her hands. He pressed it to his lips and let his tears fall on it. Then he rose and ran from the shop toward the church.

Kneeling in the darkness of the confessional, his head sunk on his chest, he poured out the story of his sins, from beginning to end, the full recital of his vanity, hatred, cruelty. And when he could speak no more he listened eagerly for words of consolation.

"This world of ours is imperfect," murmured the priest. "Therefore our deeds must be imperfect, too. Because of the sin of Adam we are all impure, and what we do must therefore be impure. Only the Son of God is pure, who came to take upon himself the imperfection of our deeds. But God looks into the heart of man and takes account of the intent more than of the act; He weighs the purpose rather than the means. Therefore pray, and mortify yourself, and beg forgiveness, and you will be consoled. Peace be with you, my son."

Stash listened closely and tried to draw comfort from the words. He found only confusion. Even while the priest was speaking, Stash's heart answered with obstinate dissatisfaction. "Something is wrong in what he says. I chose the purpose, and I chose the means, and the means and the purpose are of a piece. Was my sin against God, that I should ask *His* forgiveness? And if *He* forgives me will that purify me toward the human beings against whom I turned my wickedness? Shall I flee to Him with fasts, and mortification of the flesh, and prayer, and leave behind me the misery I created? Shall I not flee to those whom I have wronged and obtain *their* forgiveness? What will it help them if I pray all day long, and fast from morning till night? I have lit a fire. Who shall put it out?"

He left the confessional without feeling himself cleansed. But the first onrush of his repentance had exhausted itself, and he did not know where to begin the undoing of his wicked life. So it was for several days. Devoid of any will power, he let himself be dragged along by the forces which he had set in motion and which no longer need his co-operation. He said neither yea nor nay; he only knew that of itself the monster he had created would not let go of him; and he had not the strength to break loose.

There was one man in particular who personified the monster and its relentless hold on Stash Grabski; that was Stefan, the shoemaker's apprentice, who had once been known as Stash's "adjutant." It was the change in Stefan's relationship to his "leader" which most disgusted and horrified Stash.

Since the day of the murder of Long Leib Stefan had cast off the role of the follower and inferior. The distance between the student and the street hooligan was eliminated; in its place there came not simple equality within the organization, but a revolting claim to intimacy, as though the murder had made Stash and Stefan soul mates.

Stefan had once been content to listen respectfully, as became an illiterate villager in the presence of a university man. Now he did most of the talking. And it seemed to Stash that his companion deliberately emphasized the vulgarity of his speech and manners, which put one in mind of big city gangsters and their wenches. He had a way of winking at Stash, and of hinting at low secrets which did not exist, which was especially infuriating. And without invitation or provocation, without any intermediary intimacy, Stefan began speaking to Stash in the familiar second person singular. It was intolerable, utterly intolerable; and Stash felt impotent to free himself.

It happened that one day Stash had, as by a miracle, shaken off the company of Stefan, and as he passed down the street he saw as through a mist Elizabeth Poznanski, the doctor's daughter. He raised his cap, not daring, however, to stop. To his amazement it was she who stopped; she even seemed to smile in a friendly way. Wide-eyed, Stash heard that she had a message for him. Her father wanted to see him that evening—but as late as possible, so that no one should know of the visit. It was not an encouraging message, yet Stash's heart jumped. He wanted to ask the girl something— he did not quite know what—when Stefan hove into sight, with his open shirt, which displayed his unwashed throat, with his filthy hat, and with his big stick which he slapped boisterously against his top boots as he came striding along.

Stash prayed in vain that the wretched fellow would have the grace to leave him alone.

"Hey, there, Stash!" roared Stefan, came up to the two of them, and looked impudently into Elizabeth's eyes. "I got something to tell you," he said importantly, to Stash. "Got to see you right away."

Stash nodded, and motioned him off. Stefan ignored the gesture. The girl was blushing. Hurriedly Stash took leave of her, and walked on with Stefan.

He was choking with resentment.

"Couldn't you see I was talking to the lady?" he asked. "Couldn't you wait a minute?"

"What's the matter, Stash? Are you ashamed of me? Couldn't you introduce me to the lady?"

Stash had not the courage to speak out. No, he said, he was not ashamed of Stefan, but that wasn't the way to behave; that wasn't —and as Stefan grinned at him, half goodhumoredly, half contemptuously, he stopped. For if he said more, he would say too much. He would say that he was sick of Stefan's company, sick of the way Stefan shadowed him, clung to him, degraded him.

It was not unusual now for Stash to come home in the evening and find Stepan stretched out on his bed in the garret, without even having taken off his muddy boots. Stash had known little privacy in his life, and the lack of it had not irked him particularly. Even now he was not quite accustomed to the privilege of a separate room and his own pitcher and wash-basin. But what he could tolerate as part of family life he could not tolerate from a stranger. It made the bed unclean to have had Stefan even so much as sit on it. And for that matter he always felt unclean now when Stefan was about. It filled him with revulsion to have to shake hands with him, to have to touch the coarse, foul fingers, with their horrible nails underlined with grime. He felt the need to go and wash immediately after the contact. And the more hateful he found Stefan's company, the more closely Stefan clung to him.

As they walked along after the encounter with Elizabeth Poznanski, Stash made up his mind despairingly that there was no way of ridding himself of his past and of freeing himself from Stefan—for these had become the same thing—save by leaving town, going away somewhere to start afresh. But that evening he had his appointment with Dr. Poznanski, and the brief interview gave another turn to his resolution.

By a piece of unexpected good fortune Stefan left him at the door of his house, so that he did not have to cast about for an excuse to be alone. Late after dinner, when the streets of the little town were deserted, he made his way toward the Poznanski house. He had been there before, more than once, not a furtive visitor, as now, but a welcome guest. He had sat at their table, next to Elizabeth. He had been listened to respectfully, as the authority on politics, on nationalism, on patriotism and the Jewish question. That was all gone. When he rang the bell, it was not Elizabeth who came to greet him with a smile. The maid opened the door for him. She showed him into the bleak waiting room, with its peeling walls, and bade him wait. Dr. Poznanski was expecting him.

But Dr. Poznanski was not in a hurry. Heartsick, Stash tried to take his mind off his changed status. He picked up the old newspapers lying on the table and read them grimly. He heard a sound of voices from the dining room. There was laughter, argument, high spirits. Perhaps the doctor would invite him in there again, after he had imparted his private message to him. Stash felt a great longing to be in there again, the center of attention, with Elizabeth's eyes fixed on him.

The doctor entered at last, shook hands with Stash, and motioned him toward the consulting room. Dr. Poznanski's voice was friendly, but reserved. On his face, with its carefully trimmed Napoleon goatee, there was a look of anxiety. After shaking hands, and saying "How d'you do?" perfunctorily, he asked whether anyone had seen Stash enter the house.

"Why do you ask that?"

"I don't want it known in town that I'm mixed up in politics. You understand, a town doctor has to be neutral, has to have good relations with all respectable citizens. It's not a question of money, you understand. I don't care if I lose all my Jewish patients. It's got to do with the standing of the medical profession. It's a matter of professional ethics and professional duty. You understand."

Oh, yes, Stash understood. He understood more than the doctor thought he did.

"And since that business with the damned Jew, you know—mind you, not that it has anything to do with us, or with the movement, or with the work that has to be done—but since that damned Jew was found out there—and, mind you," the doctor babbled on, "it was obviously his mistake, I mean his own fault, crawling about in the morning darkness, can you blame anyone for shooting on sight? —but since that time, the town's been in an absolute turmoil, the Jews made such a stink in their papers, here, in Poland, and abroad, too. You know their international power and unity, I don't have to talk to you about that, there's been such a stink that I think the best thing for you to do would be to leave town for a while, till things quiet down, and while you're at it, take along your assistant. You see, it's winter now, there isn't much doing, when the spring markets reopen, you can come back, you understand."

"Yes," said Stash, irritated by this repetition of "you understand." "Yes. I understand everything." But he did not say that he himself had been thinking of going away. For, as he left the house, his heart hot within him, he was quite certain that he was going to stay.

A line from a play he had learned in school came back to him:

The Moor has done his task, the Moor can go.

He repeated it bitterly. Stash had done the dirty work; Stash could now be dismissed. "No," he said to himself. "I can't be dismissed just so."

When he entered his house he discovered his sister bent over the sewing machine. She lifted her face to greet him, and he saw on her face signs of tears. What had happened? She told him that Stefan, his adjutant, had broken in an hour or so before, dead drunk. He had demanded money. Failing to get it he kicked up an awful row.

Stash became white.

"Where is he?"

"Up in your attic. The people you hang around with!" she cried. Stash fled up the stairs as if a demon were pursuing him. His garret was dark. He lit the lamp, and there Stefan was, lying, boots and all, in the bed, sunk in a drunken stupor.

Stash tugged at him viciously, rolled his body on to the floor. "Blast you!" he panted. "Get out! Get out!"

Stefan staggered to his feet. His dribbling mouth was wide open with astonishment. "What's this?" he gasped. "What's this?"

"Get out!"

Stefan came to slightly. "Oh no," he said. "Oh no. We're pals, we are. If I was good enough to help kill a Jew, I'm good enough—"

At any other time these words would have struck Stash dumb. He was beyond fear now.

"Get out," he repeated grimly, "or I'll break your jaw."

"Oh!" said Stefan, blankly. "You will? H-m. And suppose I tell our comrades that you were seen on your knees before the sheeny-woman, kissing her hand and begging forgiveness. Eh? You didn't know that I knew, did you? Fine thing for the leader of our movement. Crawling like a dog to an old Jew woman and begging her forgiveness."

Stash's heart began to drum. The anger went out of him.

"Yes, I did it," he said, rapidly. "I did it and I'm glad of it. Beasts that we are, murderers! We should have been hanged, if there was any justice. You, me, the whole gang of us. Go and tell everyone that I kneeled to the Jew woman and asked her forgiveness. I'll do it again, in the presence of everyone. I won't leave her till she forgives me. Because I was among the murderers of her husband. Her husband, the father of her children. Swine! Do you understand that? Do you see what we've done?"

Stefan looked at him for a moment, broke out in a bellow of laughter, and clumped out of the room.

Stash heard the door open and close downstairs.

"God," he whispered, "I thank you for the strength to do what I did," and he crossed himself three times.

226

De Profundis

X

That was the worst winter Malkah could remember. She had believed that she had known the lowest levels; but the death of Long Leib revealed depths below depths. For while her husband lived there had been not only the comfort of his presence but a last resort which now failed her. Between the closing of the fall markets and the opening of the spring markets, there was nothing for it but to go out among the peasants. This Leib had done in winters past; and somehow or other they had managed: a bag of potatoes here, a half sack of grain there, an occasional fowl, a handful of eggs. Now that was ended. For when Malkah, in desperation, tried to take her husband's place, she found the work too much for her.

There was a peasant family in a village near by which had always been on friendly terms with Malkah and her husband. On a day when the snow had stopped falling, Malkah wrapped herself up to the eyes in layers of clothes, covered her tattered shoes with burlap, and set out with her daughter for the village. The two women staggered along under the burden of the goods they had taken along; they managed the journey both ways, bringing back a half bushel of potatoes. But they were laid up for several days after, and since that time the girl, Leah, spat blood.

There was left now only the charities, against which Malkah struggled till the last moment. Hunger and cold triumphed. She who had always thought of herself as a "merchant" now became a public charge. She stood in line for a loaf of bread, a bundle of wood, or a bottle of medicine for her sick daughter. It was no consolation for her that half the peddlers of the town were in like plight and were making their daily pilgrimage, not to the villages, but to the offices of the charities. Poverty she thought she could endure; but beggary, literal beggary, did more than hunger and cold to undermine her health.

And still hope did not die. "Let me only live through this winter," Malkah would murmur. God had punished her enough. The wave of anti-Semitism might recede a little. The market days would return. She would, one way or another, replenish her empty shelves, and become a merchant again.

This sustained her and, after a time, she had the help of Stash Grabski. For Stash the effort at atonement moved in cycles. When he had broken with Stefan, he fell into a stupor. He lacked the energy to make the atonement complete. He knew what was happening in Malkah's household, knew of her sortie into the village, of her decline into sheer pauperism; and yet he did nothing. He brooded over the wrongs he had committed; and it was as though this constituted a process of accumulation within him. For in time the stupor passed, and he began to cast about for some practical expression of atonement.

Then, in the dead of winter, he became sick of his futile self-reproaches. Late one afternoon he took his sled from the house and went out into the Lonkicz woods. In the darkness of the early evening he brought home a sledful of firewood, not for himself and his sister, but for Malkah, the widow. Still he could not bring himself to make the gift openly or even to face her. He waited till a late hour and deposited the bundle on the doorstep of the shop.

When Malkah opened the door the next morning, she started back with a cry of joy. A good soul had remembered her! And perhaps Elijah the Prophet himself, the protector of the poor, had taken pity on her. But even as she stooped to pick up the wood, so that she might hasten with it into the house and build a fire for the little ones, she reconsidered, and her joy was replaced by terror. What if this was the work neither of a good soul nor of Elijah, but of an enemy? Jews were forbidden to pick up firewood in the forest; the privilege was reserved to Christians. How did she know but what the enemy was lurking behind a post, waiting for her to take the wood in, so that he might follow, and accuse?

"Listen," she said to the children. "There's some wood on the threshold of the shop. Let it lie there. Don't take it in even if you're dying of cold."

That day Stash sat at his window and watched the snow cover the firewood on Malkah's threshold. He suspected what was in the Jew woman's mind and could not make up his own to speak to her. He would have liked to ask his sister to go over and tell Malkah that the wood was a gift from him, that she had nothing to be afraid of. He could not do it. Then his accumulating energy burst out, and he said, aloud: "I was not ashamed to do evil, I am ashamed when I want to do something good." He ran from the house and knocked at Malkah's door; and without waiting for her to come out, he shouted:

"Mrs. Leib, that bit of wood's for you, do you hear?" There was no reply. He opened the door, and shouted again, "That wood's for you."

Still Malkah did not reply. She stood watching, her heart a-flutter. Long after Stash had withdrawn she remained standing behind the door, afraid; and when Stash looked out the next morning, the bundle of wood was still there.

He went across again, opened the door, and cried, half in despair, half in anger: "Didn't you hear what I told you yesterday? Why don't you use the wood to make a fire and warm the children?" And leaving the door open he flung the wood in piece by piece, pulled the door to, and fled.

"I think it has happened," said Malkah, slowly, to her children. "God has awakened in his heart. Who can tell if this is not the work of his mother; perhaps she came to him in a dream. Was she not my best friend all those years?"

This was the beginning of the change for Stash. His shame died in him; he was not afraid to face Malkah any more, and he was not afraid to let his sister know. He told her of the firewood, adding:

"She did us more than one favor when mother was alive, that Jew woman."

"I wish to God you'd never started with your politics," answered his sister. "And I wish to God you'd go back to Warsaw now, to the university, and take up your studies again. Your hanging around here will only bring misfortune."

"I've brought the misfortune already," said Stash. "I want to make some of it good."

But that evening his sister went down into the cellar, gathered up a small sack of potatoes, and carried it over to Malkah.

"When you'll have it, you'll return it," she said.

Malkah burst into tears.

"Like in the old days, with your mother," she sobbed. "God rest her soul in heaven! We always helped each other in times of need."

XI

The change that had come over Stash Grabski was soon reflected in the attitude of the party members toward him. The word went round: "Stash Grabski has turned traitor." It was known that he had gone to Malkah the Jew woman, and had begged her forgiveness on his knees. It was known likewise that, not content with this degradation, he had taken to bringing the Jew woman gifts of firewood and potatoes. Of course he was no longer seen at the meetings of the patriotic organization which he himself had founded. It was reported further that Stash Grabski was trying to link up with the Jewish communists, the socialists, the Marxists and all the other internal enemies of Poland.

"Judas Grabski!" The first time he heard the appellation thrown at him, Stash stopped dead in his tracks. By the time he looked round he saw no one. "Judas! So let it be!" he muttered. He walked along the street staring straight in front. He would have to get used to this. He would have to get used to sneering looks, to quick whispers of contempt, to a multitude of lies.

In the loneliness of those days he did, indeed, make some effort to find new links. He soon discovered that he belonged nowhere now. The old associations were broken; the patriots despised him; but the leftists, the workers, despised him no less. His timid efforts to approach the latter were viewed with suspicion. Who could tell what a man like Grabski was up to? He came one evening into the reading room of the worker's club and asked for a book. The librarian, a young woman, asked him politely to leave. "We don't permit strangers here," she said. "It's against the law to admit anyone but members."

He went out little, for no house was open to him, and on the street he was recognized only to be avoided or hissed. He stopped greeting people, for fear of being insulted. Dr. Poznanski passed him on the street one day and kept his eyes fixed away from him. His daughter Elizabeth did not even bother to pretend that she did not see him. And once Stefan, with a gang of young hooligans, stopped him. They did not touch him, but Stefan spat in his direction, shook his fist, and cried: "Wait! You'll get what's coming to you! Judas!" Even the priest treated him like a leper, for when Stash forced him into conversation, he said, coldly: "God does not like people who overdo things. To be a good Catholic means to be a well-balanced person, to live amongst your own kind, not to show off with your charity to strangers, and not to run from one extreme to the other."

His sister pleaded with him to give up the struggle, to leave town, return to Warsaw, resume his studies. It was useless. A stark, somber obstinacy took hold of Stash. He would not budge. No one could make him budge. It was the same mood of obstinate and wordless defiance as he had felt and shown in his childhood, when his father had almost flayed him in the vain effort to make him apologize to Leib and Malkah. They could despise him, cut him, spit on him, hiss after him—he was staying put. He felt now like some watchdog which stood guard over a door and which robbers were trying to frighten away. Neither the threats of Stefan nor the cool insolence of Elizabeth and her father could change his mind.

He felt he owed Malkah something more than the occasional bundle of firewood, or handful of potatoes, which he and his sister carried across to her. The winter was drawing to an end. Malkah had hopes—how else could she have lived?—of better times; and Stash encouraged her though he knew what she did not know, that the organization which Stefan had taken over was planning a new drive against the Jews with the opening of the spring market days. Who would stand by her now, if not he himself, Stash Grabski?

He was in her house nearly every day now, made no attempt to conceal his friendly relations with the Jew woman, came and went freely.

"It won't be long now, Mrs. Leib," he said, heartily. "The holidays are coming, the markets will begin. No time to waste. I advise you to get in whatever stuff you can, from Lodz."

"It will be all right?" she asked for the hundredth time. "Nothing will happen?"

"Nobody will lay a hand on you," growled Stash. "Not while I'm alive. Listen to what I'm saying: go to Lodz for the goods. I take the responsibility."

It was not as simple as all that. Before she could visit Lodz Malkah had to obtain a loan from the Benevolent Association—and she was not the only applicant. But she was a widow, and this pleaded for her more than her own tearful words; Long Leib, dead and rotting in the ground, still helped his family. He helped Malkah in Lodz, too, where she had to stretch the slender loan to cover her needs. But she came back with several bundles of cotton goods, calico prints, shawls, head-dresses, set to work in the desolate shop, and by the time the first market day came could call herself a "merchant" again.

It was a marvelous spring, big with promise. The air turned mild unusually early, the iron hold of winter was loosened from the buds, and a shimmer of green appeared, almost as soon as the snows began to melt. The ice on the river broke up overnight, and the earth, which had been like frozen rock, became a soft, steaming, spongy mass. The skies burst into sudden radiance, and across the fresh blue the raveled fleeces of tiny clouds drove before the wind. It was a young, whispering wind, which played with the beards of the dark-faced, worried-looking Jews, and fondled the tattered wigs of their womenfolk, as if trying to inspire them with its own certainty of happiness to come.

Early on the first market day the peasants' carts began creaking into town, stiff with the long enforced idleness of the winter. They rattled noisily across the bridge, drummed softly on the damp earth, drawing in from the four points of the compass and bringing with them the accumulated produce of the winter: sucking-pigs nourished for four or five months, chickens grown into handsome pullets, baskets of fresh white eggs, bundles of cheese, as well as the remainders of their winter stores, potatoes, oats, and vegetables. The Jewish shopkeepers watched the stream of carts, rubbed their hands, and prayed. The stalls had ventured into the open again, doors or planks on trestles, racks on spindly legs, and, everywhere, bundles of cloth, peasant shoes, peasant hats with flashy black brims, linens, ribbons, suits, coats.

But early on that same day the watchers at the doors observed, among the crowds streaming in, queer individuals who had never been seen at markets before; they wore the white cloaks of the peasantry, but they were definitely not peasants. Something in their walk, in their posture, betrayed the city. Among them were also familiar figures, the local riff-raff; but most of these men were new. They were quite peaceful, it seemed. They circulated only among the peasants, gathered them into little groups, addressed them earnestly. Sometimes they strolled past the Jewish shops, peered in, walked off without saying anything.

They were peaceful, at any rate during the early part of the day, so that the famished shopkeepers, facing their first prospect of earnings in half a year, became hopeful. There was every promise of a big day. If the shopkeepers were famished for earnings, the peasants were famished for city goods. The shirts had rotted on their backs during the winter, the frosts had eaten their overcoats, the iron ground had worn away their boots. Shocks of hair stuck out through tattered caps, elbows through burst sleeves. The peasant women were thinking of the approaching festivals, and their mouths watered at the sight of the bright blouses and shawls. Long before noon the crowds had gathered round the Jewish shops and stalls, the eager chaffering had begun, the loud handslapping of completed bargains rang in the clear air. It was almost like the good old days.

Almost, but with one significant difference. Those sinister figures in the white cloaks went to and fro among the peasants. The shopkeepers tried to ignore them, but could not. There was no picketing, no remonstrating with peasant buyers at the Jewish stalls. And that made it all the more ominous; it was as if forces were being gathered for one major and decisive attack. Where would it come? No one could tell. And so, as hope struggled with fear in the heart of the Jewish merchant, he kept one eye on his customer, the other on the marketplace; one ear listened to the customer, the other was focused on the crowd. The baskets were held ready near the stands, for a quick getaway.

The tranquillity became oppressive.

"I don't like it," said one merchant to the other. "It's *too* quiet. This can't last."

Nor did it.

From the cattle market across the way there came a sound of running feet, an echo of shouting. Hands are frozen in the midst of gesticulation, words are cut in half.

"What is it?"

No one knows. There's been some fighting. A Jew has been killed. "Killed!" The word, launched no one knows by whom, is enough. Instantly the bolts of cloth, the blouses, caps, boots, ribbons begin to fly into the baskets. And right in the midst of this panicky retreat, not yet properly under way, there descends a rain of blows. They seem to have come up from underfoot, these sinister men in the peasant coats. And before anyone knows what has happened the ground is strewn with Jewish merchandise which is being trampled into the black, spongy soil. A storm of feathers arises, as if someone had shaken out a huge pillow over the marketplace. There is a frightful confusion of mud, merchandise, screams, human bodies.

In front of Malkah's store Stash stands, as he has been standing since early morning. He holds in his hand the thick, gnarled stick with which he once used to tumble Malkah's goods off the shelves. He looks excited, but the old obstinate glitter is in his eyes. He will not be moved from this place.

The hours have passed, and there has been nothing for Stash to do. There have not even been pickets to drive away. Peasants and peasant women come and go; they seem to have a partiality for Malkah's shop; it may be compassion, it may be habit. But they are here in larger numbers than elsewhere. And Malkah is in a fever of activity. She hardly knows what she is doing; while she pulls down a bale for one customer, she is chaffering with another and holding on to a third. Leah, the sick daughter, must perforce help this day. Her thin arms lift and set down the bales; she adds her childish voice to her mother's. If only this day passes peacefully and ends as it has begun!

Between eager offer and entreaty addressed to her customer, Malkah gulps a prayer to the Almighty. "Father in heaven, sweet Father, my punishment has been enough." She reminds herself that she has mentioned the All-Pure Name with unwashed hands, and she passes her tongue hastily across her finger-tips and dries them on her apron. "Father in heaven, remember my little ones, my orphans." She runs to the door of the shop, looks out hastily. Yes, Stash is there! "Look, good people, what God has done for me! My enemy stands before my door and guards me from evil!" She runs back to her customers. "Good woman! I swear to you, I swear by my orphan children, that I can't sell it for less, and it is worth twice what I ask. What? Haven't I been honest with you all these years? Will I trick you now?"

And suddenly the blow fell.

They did not break into her shop, as they did into others. Stash saw to that. With his big, gnarled stick he held off a crowd of them—the men in the peasant cloaks, the strangers. All that Malkah saw was a flashing of black hat brims, a flailing of sticks, a whirl of bodies. There was a confusion of shouts, groans, curses. Then Stash Grabski's body lay on the ground.

The assailants scattered, the horrified crowd stared at the body. They did not know whether he was seriously hurt till he made an effort to rise, fell back, and rolled over. Then they saw blood running out of his ripped clothes and forming a red pool on the black earth.

When Malkah drew near, she heard that familiar admonition: "Don't move him! Don't touch him! Wait for the police!" So they had shouted when she had drawn near the dead body of her husband. Now, as then, she said nothing, and only looked round with a mild surprise in her eyes, while her goiter swelled up horribly and distended the blue veins on her throat.

The Stranger

THE story of "the stranger" belongs to the traditions of one of Poland's oldest Jewish communities. Who "the stranger" was no one knew. He was somebody who for a long time had been a familiar figure in the local synagogue and yet still had retained the name of "the stranger." Apparently he had taken a vow of a special kind, in connection with the fragments of holy books. For whenever he entered the synagogue, in between prayer periods, he made a regular search under the benches and in all the corners, for torn or lost pages of psalters and sacred books, and deposited them reverently in the large wooden box kept for that purpose, so that they might afterward be given formal burial, according to the custom. When not thus occupied, "the stranger" sat in a corner, by a lectern, and repeated psalms.

The man was without family and without a history. He had arrived once in the village, on a Friday afternoon, and had claimed shelter, over the week end, it would seem, as many wandering Jews did. But he did not depart when the week end was over, and why he elected to remain in this particular community was never discovered. Sunday morning the beadle still saw him lingering in the synagogue house. The beadle, who had one eye and belonged to the Aaronic line, was a choleric man, lacking in the spirit of hospitality. Tradition and law gave wanderers at least the right to a week end in the village; whoever overstepped this minimum, however, was made to feel unwelcome by the beadle.

"What? Still here?" he said, surlily. "Isn't it time for you to be going?"

"I've been thinking of staying here."

"What's that? Staying here? That's all very well over a week end, from Friday to Sunday. But not longer, oh, no."

The Jew smiled, picked up his sack, and left the synagogue house. But he did not leave the village. He took shelter with a poor Jew on the outskirts of the village, a man much given to the practice of hospitality, so that his humble cottage was never without its wayfarer. Then, to make room for another, the stranger betook himself to the house of the baker. Daily he came to the synagogue, and the beadle never failed to shake his staff at him and to remind him that it was time for him to be gone.

"One more Sabbath I'll allow you. And then be off with you!"

But by the time the next Sabbath came the stranger had taken shelter with the village shoemaker. It appeared that he knew a little about cobbling, and the village shoemaker could make use of him, and on the Sabbath the stranger came to the synagogue as the shoemaker's man, and the beadle could not threaten him any longer.

And thus he had settled in the village, and had become a familiar figure without ever losing the name of "the stranger." Indeed, he was so familiar a figure that people forgot all about him. There was nothing about him to attract attention. He had a short, thick, white beard; the hair that grew out of his ears was white, too; he had heavy eyebrows, and tear-sacs under his eyes. This Jewish community, like every other, had its troubles and its problems, over and above the regular struggle for daily bread. What difference did it make where this unimportant stranger came from, who he was, who his family had been? They did not bother to find out his name, either. Maybe he was a little queer, but what of that? He was first every morning in the synagogue, starting the day with a search for fragments of books and pages. He wore his prayer shawl and phylacteries longer than anyone else. He spent every free moment saying psalms. Then he would resume the search for fragments and torn pages; when he found one

he would kiss it, carry it over to the wooden chest, and deposit it
there.

He was a humble, retiring sort of man. He had no regular place
in the synagogue during the official hours of prayer. He stood
among the poor, among the laborers, near the door. He was
never called up to the reading of the Scrolls on a Sabbath or
high holiday. The notables of the village, the well-to-do householders, never conversed with him. Now and again he exchanged
a few words with his like, the workers and beggars. Year after
year he remained in the employ of the village shoemaker, was
content with whatever pay he received, and was never seen anywhere except at his work or else in the synagogue, praying, looking
for sacred fragments, and placing these regularly in the wooden
chest.

Sometimes, when evening prayers had been said and darkness
was drawing on, he would sit awhile near the wooden chest and
listen to the talk of the workers and of the peddlers who made
the rounds of the villages. They told of their experiences on the
road and at the fairs; they told of hostile villagers who set their
dogs on Jews, of drunken peasants who attacked them, of robbers
who specialized in despoiling Jewish merchants. Then the stranger
would sigh deeply and murmur:

"What wonder that such things happen? The gentiles have lost
their religion."

There was nothing remarkable in these words, and no one paid
any attention to them or had reason to believe that the stranger
had something significant in mind.

Sundays the peasants would come to the village. Sunday mornings the stranger would linger at the door of the synagogue, to
mark the behavior of the gentiles. If he saw them streaming in
the direction of the church, from whose spire came the sound
of the bell, he would be at peace, would turn back into the synagogue and resume has psalm-saying; but there would be a warmer
note in his chant, and his eyes twinkled. And as the sound of
the church bell came in through the window of the synagogue, he
would say to a neighbor:

"Every man serves God in his own way."

That was all he said. The neighbor did not know what was behind the remark and made an impatient gesture, to indicate that he was in the middle of prayer and could not interrupt himself to answer.

There was a certain time when the spirit of the stranger was overcast; for a change had come into the behavior of the peasants. They streamed in Sunday mornings as always, and in the direction of the church, too; but they did not enter the church. They hitched their horses to the railing, left the carts standing, and betook themselves to the village inns. One of these was kept by the village postmaster on the northern side of the marketplace, the other was kept by a Jew on the southern side. The peasants filled both inns, the church bell tolled, and the church remained empty. Then the stranger turned back from the door of the synagogue, picked up his psalm book, and said to his neighbor:

"Something dreadful is going to happen. The gentiles have lost their religion."

Again his neighbor did not understand; he only put his finger to his lips, impatiently, to indicate that he was in the middle of a prayer and could not interrupt himself. The stranger fixed his eyes on his psalm book, but could not read. He lifted his eyes heavenward and said, in a broken voice:

"Father, Father, take pity on the peoples of the earth, turn not Thy face away from them."

The instinct of the stranger had been right. When a few godless Sundays had passed, doleful reports were brought to the village. Robberies had increased on the highways; Jews had been beaten; a gang had attacked a Jewish merchant, stripped him, taken away his merchandise and his horse, and left him with the empty cart on the road; a Jewish peddler had been found half dead in the middle of a field. A wave of fear passed through the Jewish community, for unrest in the land meant starvation for them. Worse followed. Somewhere in a village a Jewish butcher had dared to defend himself against a drunken peasant. The insolence of it was reported throughout the countryside, and a general uprising against the Jews was planned. On a certain Thursday the Rabbi called the entire congregation together in the synagogue for a day of fasting and prayer. They stood in their prayer-shawls from dawn to dusk; they repeated the prayers of the Minor Day of Atonement and wept before the Ark of the Scrolls. The stranger, a pale and sorrowful figure, mingled as always with the poor, whose place was near the synagogue door, and kept on repeating:

"Such things may mean the end of the world, God forbid! The gentiles have lost their religion. . . . There is neither judge nor judgment when the world has forgotten God. . . ."

They paid no attention to him; they did not hear him when he murmured over his prayer book.

"Father, Father, let Thy Glory rest upon all the world! Make Thy Name known to all the peoples of the earth."

They did not see the tears which rolled down his cheeks; they did not hear his plaint, they did not know what his special fear was—that the world of the gentiles had lost its God, that the nations were wandering in darkness, that drunkenness and lust and rage were sweeping over the earth. Nor did they note when, toward the end of that day, the stranger slipped out of the synagogue, hastened down the lane of the Catholics, and disappeared somewhere.

Very soon after, a tremendous announcement was made in the village, namely, that a great Rabbi was about to convert to the Catholic faith, and that on the Day of the Assumption of the Virgin there would take place the procession of his baptism. Two bishops were coming from Warsaw to officiate at the ceremony.

The Jews of the village did not know, and could not discover, the name of the "great Rabbi." They knew that their own Rabbi had not, God forbid, taken leave of his senses. No one was missing from the community, and no rumor had reached them of such a calamity from any other community. Assumption Day came and with it the procession. Immense crowds had congregated from the surrounding country, and they marched down the village street headed by the two bishops and the priests of the locality. All day long the church bell tolled. The peasants were dressed in their

Sunday clothes, and carried lighted tapers. The priests were clad in white, and acolytes carried censers before them. Others carried amphorae with sweet-smelling spices. Then followed the bishops, under canopies, and after them came little girls attired like brides, holding aloft sacred banners. The procession halted before the church, the air was filled with incense and music, with flags and sacred images. And when the priests and acolytes and little girls and peasants knelt down on the earth, the Jews beheld, in the center of the throng, "the stranger," dressed like a Rabbi, in a satin gaberdine and a great fur cap on his head. He carried a silver cross in his hand, and his eyes were upturned to heaven.

The Jews stared at him and at each other. Was this the great Rabbi over whose conversion the Catholic world was rejoicing—this unknown little cobbler's assistant? That evening, in the synagogue, they laughed bitterly at the deception, and said to each other:

"How much do you think he got for it?"

But before long they learned that "the stranger" had been accepted into the priesthood and that he preached every Sunday in the Catholic church. They learned, moreover, that vast crowds assembled to hear him. They wondered where the little cobbler's assistant had learned their language; but there was no doubt about it that he spoke it, movingly, that every Sunday he exalted his listeners and strengthened them in the faith of Jesus and the cross. The peasants wept to hear him, threw themselves on the ground, and, broken-hearted, confessed their sins.

From that time on a spirit of piety reigned in the village. Sunday mornings the inns were empty; the peasants who hitched their carts to the church railings went inside to pray, and the church was so crowded that many prayed in the churchyard outside. And when the "Rabbi" passed through their midst, holding aloft the cross, they threw themselves down before him and prayed fervently.

Nor was it only on Sundays that they displayed such piety. The villagers went to church morning and evening, on week-days, too. There was no more drinking in the inns. The attacks on the

Jews ceased, and the roads became safe. The Jewish peddlers were
no longer molested. Instead of setting their dogs on a wandering
Jew, peasants welcomed him into their home; or if they encountered him on the road, they gave him a lift in their cart. And one
day a peasant came to the Rabbi with a purseful of money which
he had taken away from a Jew; he asked that the money be restored to its owner, and that he be granted forgiveness.

No longer did the Catholics grimace when they saw Jews entering their house of prayer. They said:

"Everyone to his God; we to ours, they to theirs."

Thus it was for a long time; there was peace between the Jews
and the gentiles.

Many years had gone by when the Jews were assembled in their
synagogue on the eve of the Day of Atonement. They had just
begun the dread Kol Nidre prayer when suddenly there staggered
in a man in the attire of a priest. The Jews, clad in their white
robes, shrank back, and their hearts were filled with dread. The
priest managed somehow to thrust his way through them, and to
reach the foot of the pulpit. There he fell to his knees, lifted his
arms to heaven, and cried out in a sobbing voice:

"Hear, O Israel, the Lord Thy God, the Lord is One."

And with that he rolled over and died.

Terrified, they approached the dead priest and raised his head.
By the tear-sacs under his eyes they knew that he was a Jew. And
some of them, looking closely, suddenly recognized, across the
years, "the stranger" who had collected the fragments of old prayer
books in the synagogue. Then their terror was increased tenfold.
They did not know what to do with the dead man. The Rabbi
declared that the man was a Jew, and that they were in duty
bound to lay him to rest in the Jewish cemetery. Therefore they
hid the body until the end of the Day of Atonement. When night
came, two Jews, a butcher and fisherman, who were eager to
straighten out their heavenly accounts by the performance of a
good deed, risked their lives in order that the dead Jew might
be with his own. They carried the body from its secret hiding

place to the Jewish cemetery, and there they buried it at dead of night.

The name of the stranger was unknown, even as were his family and the place of his birth. When the tombstone had to be put up over his body, the mason asked what he should inscribe thereon; and the Rabbi answered that he inscribe "Abraham, the son of Abraham," which is the name given to one who has entered the Jewish fold from without. The tombstone with the name "Abraham, the son of Abraham" inscribed on it, may be found in the cemetery of the village till this day.

The Footsteps

"MUMMIE, is it far yet?"

"No, darling, only a little way."

Little Solomon took a stronger grip on his mother's apron, and his weary legs, thin as match-sticks, picked up speed. In a few moments, however, they began to drag again, and the sand seemed so heavy to the child that he could not lift his feet out of it.

"Mummie! Sit down for a while, won't you? Mummie, please!"

"Where, child? Where shall I sit down? Don't you see all the Jews walking on? How can we sit down in the middle of the road?"

"Mummie, no, I don't want to walk any more." And the child let go of the apron and stood still, weeping.

The woman glanced ahead to where the expelled Jewish community was strung out along the road. She was a long way behind. Every day it was so—she would start out with the rest, and during the day she would fall behind because of little Solomon; and she was afraid that some day she would fall so far behind that she would lose them altogether. It was late in the afternoon, the sky was beginning to redden; she could not let darkness overtake her with the others so far ahead. With the last of her strength she picked the child up and plodded on, sobbing for breath. It was the third day of wandering, and what with her fear and her exhaustion she felt a cold sweat breaking out on her forehead and running down from under the black kerchief. And though the sweat was cold and an autumn wind was blowing across the open fields, the mother was burning as with a fever. She was wearing all the holiday dresses she had been able to save and put on, one above the other; and as she stumbled along she pulled her head up, to catch her breath, and the skin of her throat became taut and stringy. Her arms and hands were numb. But it was good to have the little boy's hot face snuggling into her shoulder. So she carried him a distance, till the weakness in her knees became dangerous and she feared she would fall down with the child. Then she called in a hoarse voice to the older boy, who was plodding along ahead of her.

"Joey! Joey!"

It was hard for her to do this, and only extreme fear enabled her to overcome her pity for the older one. Joey, staggering under a double load of bedding and of sacred books, was keeping pace with his father. Because he was already a Talmud student, he wanted to carry the burden of an adult, and for three days he had kept to his resolution.

Joey fell back, letting his father continue alone.

"Joey, there's no more strength left in me. And Solomon can't walk any more."

"Give him to me, mother, I'll carry him." And Joey shifted his load, stooped, and picked up the child. He carried him a dozen paces, and had to set him down.

"Solomon, don't you want to see the Messiah?" he asked.

"When will he come?" asked the six-year-old, eagerly.

"Soon, very soon. When we get to the village. That's what grandpa said."

"Yes! I want to see him. I'll walk now."

The little one suddenly began to run down the road, picking up his thin legs out of the sand, and crying, "Look, Mummie, I'm running."

"I'm looking, darling," panted his mother, wiping the sweat from her face and following.

Before long they reached the next village. Evening had fallen, and the leaders of the exiled community decided to pass the night in this place, for the nearest town was still ten versts off and the women and children could not have continued for half that distance. The horses were unyoked from the one cart which accompanied them, in which they carried the sacred Scrolls. The men and boys laid down their burdens, the women untied their bundles and took off layer after layer of coats and capes and gaberdines; they spread these on the damp grass for the children to lie on. Two of the men, cattle merchants who had acquaintances in this village, set out to get a supply of milk from the peasant women, and within fifteen minutes a crowd of villagers had assembled about the refugees. They came carrying pails of milk or of fresh water, which they distributed among the women and children. But the men assembled under a tree, unwrapped their prayer-shawls and addressed themselves to their Father in heaven; the cool wind carried the melancholy words, mingled with the humming of autumn insects, across the empty fields.

Like the other women, Hannah Leah had peeled off cape after cape, to unburden herself and to make a bed for her children. Joey, the Talmud student, stood with his father and the other grown-up Jews, under the tree, and prayed earnestly with them. Goldy, the older sister, who had carried bedclothes and linens all the way, was waiting her turn to fill the pitcher with milk. In a few moments she came running back joyfully, crying:

"Mama, mama, I got some."

The mother poured the milk into cups, for Goldy and little Solomon.

"Drink, Solomon," she whispered. "Drink up every drop and don't spill any."

But Solomon was not listening to her. He sat with eyes fixed on the sky, on which the darkness was gathering from every corner of the horizon. It seemed to him that he caught from a distance the strains of the cantor's violin, floating out of the cantor's house in the old village where they had always lived. Or perhaps the violin was playing somewhere under the water of the lake near by, playing by itself. And he listened intently.

246

"Solomon, darling, say the benediction and drink your milk," the mother urged.

Out of habit Solomon murmured, "Blessed art Thou, O Lord, King of the universe . . ." and held the cup to his lips. He did not drink. Instead he turned his eyes toward his mother and said:

"Mummie, where are we going?"

"Why, Solomon, you know, don't you? The Messiah is coming and so the Jews have to be assembled all in one place."

Solomon took a gulp of milk, and before he had taken the second lifted his head again and asked:

"Mummie, is he a very big man, the Messiah?"

"He's very big, Solomon, he's taller than any Jew in the world."

Solomon could not drink. A feverish interest burned in the great eyes which had been watching the unfolding road for three days. He asked:

"Mummie, is the Messiah a king, too?"

"Yes, darling, he's a great king, over all the Jews, and over all the kings of the earth."

Solomon went into a trance.

"Child, why don't you drink?"

Without knowing what he did, Solomon sipped at the milk. He lifted his eyes again.

"Mummie, has he got soldiers too, the Messiah?"

"Angels are the soldiers of the Messiah, angels of heaven with fiery swords."

"With fiery swords," Solomon repeated softly and joyfully, and the assembling darkness veiled the smile of triumph on his tired lips.

By this time the sacred service under the tree was over, and Joey came back with his father. In all the years of his married life Chaim Zorach, the grain merchant, had never observed whether Hannah Leah, his wife, was eating properly or not, whether Hannah Leah had a new cape or not, or whether anything in particular was worrying her. He took it for granted that Hannah Leah would worry about him, not he about her. Calamity had changed him suddenly. He went up to his wife and asked her compassionately whether she had eaten anything yet. The question was so strange that something in her throat prevented her from answering. She only made a gesture with her hand, to indicate that it did not matter, she was quite well, and not hungry. But Goldy, foraging for the family, turned up with a loaf of bread; and a fire had been built, over which now swung the community caldron in which potatoes were boiling. Hannah Leah cut the bread and held out a slice to Solomon. The child started, and asked:

"Mummie, why did he tell the policeman to hit you?"

"Who, darling?"

"The Messiah?"

"Child, he couldn't have told the policeman anything; he hasn't come yet."

Chaim Zorach groaned. He held the slice of bread in his hand, looked up at the sky, and muttered:

"Yes, these are the agonies which herald the coming of the Messiah. There is no other explanation."

Joey, the Talmud student, who knew the tradition, now asked: "But, father, mustn't the Messiah son of Joseph come first, and mustn't Elijah the Prophet be the herald?"

"Perhaps these have already come. Who can tell?" answered the father.

"And if they've come," added Joey eagerly, "then all these expulsions have a divine purpose and the Jews are being brought together to greet the Messiah."

"God grant it!" sighed the mother, wiping her eyes, and looking wearily at the dry bread she held in her hand. "It is time!"

"It's time and past," agreed the father bitterly, chewing on the dry peasant bread.

By now the last glimmer of light had withdrawn from the western horizon. The stars grew larger and brighter; the murmur of field and stream became louder, as though a million souls had been waiting in the depths of the earth and water for the light

248

to fail so that they might utter their lament. A penetrating chill set in, and all the extra capes and mantles which the parents had brought along were needed to keep the children warm. The fire on which they had cooked their wretched evening meal was kept going, and around it young and old huddled, so that from afar off they looked like a strange assembly of conspirators. Soon a mournful chant arose from one corner and was taken up by the others. It was the second Psalm: "Why do the heathen rage . . .?" Here and there glimmered the white patches of bed linen, cushions and quilts, on which the little ones were laid to sleep. The congregation became quieter and quieter, the chanting of the Psalm became lower, so that there rose over it the murmur of the million souls which lamented from the depths of earth and lake. The peasants who had come out to greet the Jews had gone home. The fire sank into a dull glow, and the space of the fields and heavens seemed to expand about the cowering band of exiles.

They slept the sleep of exhaustion, all of them—except little Solomon. He was afraid to sleep. The wailing of the insects and the croaking of the frogs did not lull him to sleep; it filled him with fear. Nor did he want to sleep. He burrowed deep into his mother's cape and felt hot and cold at the same time. There was something he wanted to say, but he did not know what it was. He kept his eyes fixed on the sky, and he began to perceive that the stars, growing larger and brighter, were the soldiers of the Messiah, and the light which they radiated came from the swords of fire in their hands. And these stars, these soldiers, were sentinels guarding the congregation of sleeping Jews, while about them, in the veiled fields, in the hidden lake, policemen were murmuring and snarling, and waiting for a chance to attack the sleepers. Soon a great battle would begin, between the soldiers in the sky and the policemen concealed in the fields and the lake, those policemen who had hit mother, and who had driven all the Jews out of their homes, and who were now lying in ambush. And Solomon watched the sky intently, waiting for the Messiah to appear among his soldiers, on a great fiery horse, with a fiery rod in his hand. He would give the signal and come charging earthward, and his soldiers would come riding after him.

The night became colder, but little Solomon's head became warmer. Every one was asleep. The last two logs of the fire, incompletely burned, were sinking into each other among the ashes; they too were falling asleep. On the other side of the fire someone awoke. It was the old Jew who had begun the chanting of the Psalm. In a low voice he resumed the lament: "Why do the heathen rage . . . ?" But father and mother were fast asleep, so were Goldy and Joey. They were all asleep, and here the Messiah was about to descend and there would be no one to see him or greet him. Oh, that would be dreadful! Neither father nor mother nor Goldy nor Joey would see the Messiah!

"Mummie! Mummie!" he called, and there came no answer. His head became still warmer. It seemed to him now that someone had lifted him up and put him astride a fiery horse. But everyone still remained asleep. "Mummie! Mummie!" he called again, and still they slept on.

He looked upward desperately. The stars were growing bigger and bigger, brighter and brighter. He saw them clearly now, fiery horses, and the angel soldiers on them, blazing swords and blazing lances in their hands. Suddenly their ranks were divided, and from behind them a star a thousand times larger and brighter than any of them flashed forward. No, it was not a star, but an eagle, and on the eagle a huge man was seated, dressed like a Rabbi, save that on his head, instead of a skull cap, there was a dazzling crown, and he held a sword in his hand.

"Mummie! Mummie!" screamed the child. "He's coming! I hear footsteps! He's coming!"

Hannah Leah, starting out of a deep sleep, clasped the child to her, and, only half awake, cried in anguish:

"Who, my darling? Who?"

"He!" whispered the child. "The Messiah!"

Sanctification of the Name

WHITE lies the snow on the roads and fields. The light of the moon is thrown back by great white stretches as by frozen seas; the stars are so densely sown in the heavens, they sparkle so restlessly, that you would think they are elbowing each other for room. And from the distance comes the sound of a Jewish melody, punctuated by the crack of a driver's whip:

> Hey, hey, clear the way,
> Jews are coming, stand aside,
> Come, my friend, come, my friend,
> Let us go to meet the bride!

Beards and earlocks, tangled gaberdines, shining eyes, merry voices—where are these Jews coming from? From a wedding, of course. The covered cart is jammed with celebrants, the father of the bride, the father of the bridegroom, the uncle of the bride, the uncle of the bridegroom—the four chief celebrants, they— and a host of other villagers. In front and on top sits the driver, jovially tipsy. The whip curls and crackles in the air. "Hey, hey, clear the way, Jews are coming, stand aside!" His hat executes a dance of its own on his head. The horses, infected by their master's gaiety, forget the daily yoke; they feel they are coming from a wedding, it is proper to rejoice, to let go, to throw off the burden of care—and they cease to be drayhorses, they become racehorses, they streak down the white road like phantoms.

Inside the celebrants, and among them the four chief celebrants, the two fathers, the two uncles, sit rocking, with arms interlaced, with beards waggling in the dark, with hats slipping to a side. They sing joyously. What do they sing? Songs of drink or of love, songs of youth or of the chase? Not they! They are Jews! And in a time of merriment they sing snatches of the Talmud, fragments of prayers, reminders of the sacred books and of the commandments.

> From the sages let us learn,
> From the holy men of old,
> Let the fool for riches yearn,
> Piety outshineth gold;
> Come, my friend, come, my friend,
> Let us go to meet the bride.

White shines the road, white lie the fields; and the melody of the Jews, half gay, half mournful, carries across the night.

> Come, my friend, come, my friend,
> Let us go to meet the bride.

Neither the driver on his seat nor the Jews rocking inside the cart, see advancing toward them the carriage of the Pan, the nobleman of their village, the master and landowner; they do not hear the bellow of the driver behind the three horses harnessed in length: "Hey, filthy Jews, off the road! The Pan is passing!" They cannot hear the words because their hearts are full. And why should they not be full? One more Jewish pair wedded, in defiance of disaster! One more Jewish home set up, to be as the house of Jacob and as the house of Abraham, a place of learning and prayer! They do not hear, they do not draw off the road, they do not take their hats off with a frightened, "Yes, sir, good morning, sir, your servant, sir, excuse us, sir!" Still more loudly the postilion bellows: "Jewish dogs! Off the road when the Pan is passing!" Now they hear, and they stick their heads out. They answer him in their own tongue: "Who are you to bid the world off the road when you pass? We are the worshippers of the living God, you worship an image, an idol." They do not yield: it is

the Pan's carriage which must stand still while they pass: and
back from the road drifts their melody:

> From the sages let us learn,
> From the holy men of old,
> Let the fool for riches yearn,
> Piety outshineth gold.

. . .

The next day the liveried servants of the Pan were in the village,
seeking, questioning: "Who came back last night along the road,
in a cart? Whence came they? What were they doing?" Likewise
they brought report, true or false, of the body of a dead peasant,
found that night in the empty inn along the self-same road.

And before the day was ended five Jews had been carried off
in chains and flung into prison: the fathers and uncles of the
bride and bridegroom, the four chief celebrants, and the drayman who had driven them.

These four chief celebrants were the four leading householders
of the Jewish community.

. . .

The Jews of the village are assembled in the synagogue. The
tall white candles burn as on the Day of Atonement. From the
women's gallery overhead comes a sound of stifled weeping, a
continuous, subdued refrain. Now and again a voice rises above
the dolorous chorus, the voice of the wife or mother of one of the
prisoners. The old Rabbi, in white robe and prayer-shawl stands
before the Ark of the Scrolls and intones a Psalm:

"Why do the heathen rage, and the people imagine a vain
thing?"

The whole congregation, in white robes and prayer-shawls, repeats tremblingly after the venerable Rabbi:

"Why do the heathen rage, and the people imagine a vain
thing?"

There is sudden silence in the crowded little house of prayer.
A sound is heard by the spirit, the sound of passing souls. These

are the souls of all the martyrs of all the generations, an invisible procession; for the Psalms are being said now for Jews who are being tortured to death.

In the prison human demons tear the flesh of the prisoners, to force a confession from them; in the synagogue Psalms are being said to strengthen the prisoners in their resistance, so that they may endure and not be broken, so that they may remember the Name of God, and sanctify it. It is a bitter trial of alternating torment and temptation. The Pan has promised that the first Jew to confess to the crime and to convert to Christianity will be rewarded as no man in these parts was ever rewarded before: he will be made the overseer of all the taxes paid by the Jews, he will be given the franchise of all the inns in the district, he will be made the ruler of all the Jews. And as for the rest, they will be beheaded, their corpses will be quartered and denied Jewish burial.

Behind the sound of the procession of the martyrs, the spirit catches another, horrible beyond endurance: it is the screaming of the men whose flesh is being torn from their bodies.

Concerning four of the tormented Jews there is utter certainty in the hearts of the assembled: these four will assuredly not desecrate the name of God either to escape from passing pain, or for the sake of the vanities and frivolities of this earth. In the lamentations of the wives and mothers of the tormented ones there is never a suggestion of a desire for such weakness; when their eyes have wearied of shedding tears, they look forth into space with pride. And when the women about them dare to look at them, their eyes, too, betray pride, and even a reverent envy of those, the wives and mothers of the men who are sanctifying the Name of God.

But concerning one, the fifth among the prisoners, the drayman, the community is not sure. A gross, ignorant lad he is, the driver of the village; impious, God help us; more than once has he been known to desecrate the Sabbath in the sight of others. He is not seen every day in synagogue for afternoon and evening prayers; but he has been seen, on a Sabbath, strolling down the village street with his horse. The Rabbi has rebuked him more than once; and there was even talk once of imprisoning him for a few days in the vestibule of the synagogue, that he might learn godliness. But it is said that when this was threatened he counterthreatened that he would run away to the Christians and have himself baptized. So they left him alone.

In a corner of the women's gallery the mother of the drayman stands alone, her kerchief drawn over her face, ashamed to look at the other women. But they cast glances at her, glances of pity and bitterness. "To have brought forth such a son!" For there is a rumor in the village that the drayman is ready to confess, that he has obtained a respite, that the wall of resistance is about to be broken. The mother of the drayman stands alone, for the others have withdrawn from her. She says no Psalms, for she does not know the text; she holds no prayer book in her hand, for she cannot read. But she murmurs a prayer of her own:

"Father in heaven, be his strength! Father in heaven, be his strength!"

The tears run down her cheeks into the kerchief. No one sees her tears or hears her murmured prayer; for they have withdrawn from her, and look at her with pity and bitterness: "To have given such a son to the Jewish fold!"

• • •

Once again the Jews are assembled in the house of prayer. This day no Psalms are said. All are seated on the floor. The lecterns will not be used for study or prayer. The candles are ranged along the floor. The Rabbi, in stockinged feet—symbol of mourning—reads the Book of Lamentations—supreme utterance of mourning. The congregation repeats the words after him, quietly. For now it is the end, and the time of official mourning is at hand. The executioner's block stands in the marketplace, the men are being led out. Four memorial candles burn in the synagogue, and about each candle sit the nearest of kin of the martyrs. In a corner of the synagogue, in a lowly place near the entrance, stands a fifth candle, which has not been lit. Near this candle sits the

255

mother of the drayman. It is not known yet whether her son has withstood the trial, and whether he belongs to the martyrs. Still they look at the mother with pity and bitterness: "To have given us such a son!"

The murmurous repetition of the Book of Lamentations is suspended as the sound of hoofs comes closer down the street. Something is thrown down before the door of the synagogue, and a fist smites on the door. One, two, three, four—five. Five knocks. And at the sound of the fifth the mother of the drayman springs from her place by the unlighted candle, and tears open the door. Five heads lie on the ground before the synagogue door.

She sought out the head of her son and lifted it in her hands. Holding it high before her, she entered the synagogue. It was as if she wanted the whole world to see. A fierce pride shone from her eyes. She had lifted the kerchief from her face, so that she might look back at everyone of the assembled. And the assembled moved away from her reverently, made a space for her, when she began to dance.

Lightly her footsteps moved over the floor as she danced with her son's head before the Ark of the Scrolls. She uttered no word, her lips were locked, but her eyes passed from face to face over all the assembled. And they all moved away from her reverently, envy and wonder on their faces:

"The mother dances with her son! The mother dances with her son!"

She laid down the head of her son at the foot of the Ark; she brought the memorial candle from its place by the door and placed it in the midst of the memorial candles in the center; and with her own hands she lit the candle, so that it burned among the others.

A Letter to America

THERE were assembled that evening in the synagogue of Yuzepov, all the notables of the Jewish congregation, or, to be exact, all those that were still left in the half dismantled townlet. Even so, they made up a galaxy of names which had shed luster on their province, and whose brightness had penetrated to the ends of the Russian empire, names which were sought in matrimonial alliance wherever learning, piety, and achievement were cherished among Jews. There was, for instance, Reb Israel Ashkenazi, the openhanded Jew who had inherited a great fortune from his parents and had spent it all in innumerable small benefactions. There was Reb Yechiel Meir Salant, the man of incomparably high descent, whose forefathers had been famous Rabbis for fifteen generations in an unbroken line; there was Reb Meir Alter, the super-pietist, of whom it was said that on Sabbath days no candles would burn in his house except such as were made of kosher chicken-fat. And then, of course, there was the Rabbi himself, a light in Israel; not to mention a host of lesser personalities. Yes, it was the glory of Yuzepov—or the remnant of the glory of Yuzepov—which would have sufficed for many a larger city in its prime—which was assembled that evening round the table of the study house, by the light of the half candle left over from the evening prayers. The flickering candle beams shone on broad, wrinkled foreheads, long and venerable beards, sad and dreamy faces. The shadows concealed the want and privation which daylight would have revealed in their bearing and clothes. They sat listening as the Rabbi dictated to the scribe, who, with steel-frame glasses on his nose and long goose quill in hand, was writing a letter to America—to the Association of Yuzepov Jews of America, via Jake the Sponge-Cake Baker, the son of Toibe, the butcher's widow.

"To the illustrious benefactor, famous in the four corners of the Jewish world, Reb Jake Toibenschlag, by profession sponge-cake baker," the Rabbi began.

"Not enough," interrupted Reb Israel Ashkenazi, a small man with a little face, like a child's. "After all, he's a man of wealth. He may feel offended with such brevity, and we need his help. You might at least add: 'The prince among his people.' What harm can it do?"

But Reb Meir Alter, who had a merited reputation as a choleric man, would not have it. Poverty had not broken his pride nor softened his temper. "What? 'Illustrious benefactor' and 'famous in the four corners of the Jewish world' not good enough for Toibe the butcher-woman's son, who used to catch pigeons in the streets of Yuzepov?" Reb Meir stuttered for a moment. The whole idea of writing to Jake the Sponge-Cake Baker, and of applying such titles of honor to that ignoramus in America, whom Reb Alter would not have admitted to his house, made him speechless. He turned his thick, bushy brows upon frail Reb Israel Ashkenazi, who shrank from the challenge. "How much honor would you like to impart to him, Reb Israel?"

"A whole town in hunger, Reb Meir," answered Reb Israel, timidly. "Famine in the streets and houses. Women and children. And our only hope is over there, in America, with the Jews of Yuzepov on the other side. And he's their president, isn't he? What if, God forbid, he should take offense because of a few words more or less."

"It is written," said the Rabbi, formally, "that Rabi, the great teacher, treated all men of substance with honor. Therefore," and he turned to the scribe, "add those words: 'The prince among his people.'"

"Pah!" exploded Reb Meir Alter, made a disgusted gesture, and relapsed into silence.

"And now add the following," continued the Rabbi. "We, the notables of the holy congregation of Yuzepov, turn to you with faces clouded with sorrow and hearts filled with pain. Let your compassion be awakened. Our children fail before our eyes, because they lack food, and there is none to take pity on them. Our wives and sisters and mothers faint with hunger, and there is no one to succor them. And the old men of Yuzepov, yea, even the noblest and most distinguished, the learned and the famous, they who yesterday were givers to a world in need, must today stretch out their hands in order to receive a piece of bread, and—"

But here Reb Meir Alter could no longer contain himself. He smote the table with the palm of his hand and exclaimed: "Notables of our holy congregation of Yuzepov! Men of learning and piety! This is a shameful thing that you do. Why—"

Reb Israel Ashkenazi, pale, diminutive, plucked up courage and interrupted the outraged notable. "But is it not true? Is it not? Do we not stretch out our hands today for a piece of bread, we who were once the givers of nourishment to congregations? The Lord of the universe has desired that it should be so, and we must take His decision upon ourselves in patience and humility."

"But does the Lord of the universe desire that we humble ourselves to the ignorant and impious?" raged Reb Alter. "Does He desire that we crawl on our knees to this—this ragamuffin, who broke the laws of the holy Sabbath in the eyes of all the congregation? Does He desire that we heap honor on cobblers and pants-pressers who happen to have gone to America? No! That I will not believe." And rising from the table, he strode away into a dark corner of the study house. "I will not listen any more to what you write," he called back.

Reb Israel smiled his childlike smile at the graybeards gathered about the candle. "It must be God's will that we shall be shamed and humbled. We must take shame and humiliation upon us because He so desires."

The Rabbi dictated further:

"Yea, the noblest figures of your ancient mother town, Yuzepov, even Reb Israel Ashkenazi, and Reb Meir Alter, and the Rabbi of Yuzepov, are barefoot, clad in tatters, and have not wherewith to cover the nakedness of their bodies."

The scribe wrote on. Suddenly there was heard the thunderous closing of the door, as Reb Meir dashed out into the night.

.   .   .

Brother-President Jake Toibenschlag, in his capacity as chief officer of the organization, had already sent out the call for the routine meeting of the Members of the Congregation of the Men of Yuzepov when the letter arrived from the old home town. The agenda on the circular mentioned, among other business on hand, "the discussion of ways and means to assist the folks on the other side of the ocean." But there had been such discussions before, and ways and means had been devised, without anyone really understanding what had happened in the "old home town."

The Congregation of the Men of Yuzepov held its Friday night and Saturday morning services in Professor Landau's dance-hall. There, likewise, the Y. Y. M. A. (Yuzepov Young Men's Association) held its regular meetings on the first Wednesdays after the 7th and 15th of each month, in accordance with the Constitution and the By-Laws. And on occasion all the branches and divisions of the Men of Yuzepov came together on Saturday nights—if an important dance did not make them homeless—in the same locale.

Brother-President Jake Toibenschlag received the letter on Saturday morning, just before he left for synagogue services. When these were over, he invited home with him, for the Sabbath benediction, and for the drinks and cakes and the meal by which the benediction was followed, Reb Notte, officially known as Brother-Beadle. When they had intoned the benediction with the proper flourishes, swallowed the drink with gusto, and done handsomely by the Sabbath meal, Brother-President Jake Toibenschlag remembered the letter. Seated in his comfortable armchair, he drew it forth from his breast pocket and handed it to Brother-Beadle to read.

Brother-President Jake Toibenschlag had done well in America. He was the owner of three stores famous for their white bread, their cookies, and their *knishes* stuffed *à la* Warsaw. You had only to mention the word *"knish"* in the presence of a Polish Jew, and he would respond, automatically, "Jake Toibenschlag." The master-baker himself was a broad-boned thickset man, whose yellow skin, wherever visible, was thickly dotted with shining freckles which the week-long accumulation of white flour never dimmed. His yellow beard, after dropping solidly for a short distance, bifurcated toward each shoulder. A solid, respectable picture he made, as he waited comfortably for the reading of the letter.

Reb Notte rolled out the preliminary Hebrew phrases: "The illustrious benefactor, famous in the four corners of the Jewish world, the prince among his people, Reb Jake Toibenschlag, by profession sponge-cake baker!"

"What's that? What's that?" asked Brother-President, catching only his name.

"That's just the Hebrew greeting. It's nothing," answered Brother-Beadle.

"Translate," ordered Brother-President.

Brother-Beadle translated the titles into homely Yiddish.

"Is that me?" asked Brother-President.

"It certainly isn't me," answered Brother-Beadle, with complacent flattery.

Reb Jake Toibenschlag had so strange a look on his face that Reb Notte suspended the reading. Reb Jake had suddenly been carried back to the townlet of Yuzepov. He was living once more with his mother, the butcher's widow, in the narrow alley off the marketplace. He could see himself lugging the butcher's block from his home to the shop.

"Read on," he said to Reb Notte.

When the end of the letter was reached, Reb Jake Toibenschlag sat like a stunned man. The whole townlet now rose before his eyes. He saw them all, the notables, the princes of the congregation, the men of nobility and learning and tradition, in their gaberdines of silk and satin, in their heavy fur skull caps. It is late Friday afternoon. The Jewish notables of Yuzepov are strolling down the synagogue alley toward the synagogue. The silk and satin and fur glitter in the waning sunlight. In the windows of the homes of the rich shine the great silver candlesticks. Behind the notables stroll their daughters, remote as stars from little Jake, the son of the butcher's widow. Him too Reb Jake Toibenschlag, famous for cakes and *knishes,* now sees across the years, a ragged urchin lugging the butcher's block home, down that same Synagogue alley. They, Reb Meir Alter, and Reb Israel Ashkenazi, are on the way to prayers, while he is bringing home the block from the store. The sons of the notables, white-collared, new-washed, carry their fathers' prayer books. Little Jake shrinks into the wall and turns his face away, to let them pass.

And now they were writing to him, calling him "illustrious" and "a prince among his people." They were begging him, little Jake, for help.

"Who signed the letter?" he asked Brother-Beadle again.

"The Rabbi of Yuzepov, and Reb Israel Ashkenazi, and Reb Meir Salant. And there's a postscript, on the other side, in another handwriting. The Rabbi's, I think."

"Read."

"And in particular I address myself to the donor and benefactor, Reb Jake Toibenschlag, on behalf of the mighty who have fallen, the givers of yesterday who are the takers today; for their condition is pitiful, and they suffer more because they are ashamed to take. Such is, above all others, the plight of the one-time man of valor and substance, the proud Reb Meir Alter, who walks around in rags and hungers from week end to week end, because he will not accept charity. And for the good that you will perform toward us, God will help you, as the Talmud says—" and Reb Notte went on reading, though the other was no longer listening.

For Reb Jake Toibenschlag was looking about him in a queer way. He recognized the familiar surroundings, the furniture, the pictures on the walls, the cut glassware twinkling on the side-board, the heavy carpet on the floor, the overstuffed, velvet-covered armchair he was seated in; and yet—it was not his own house. He stood up distractedly. It was all a mistake. The house and the furniture did not belong to him; it belonged to those Jews in the frayed and tattered satin gaberdines, whose letter he had just heard. It was their house, and he had stolen into it and was trying to pretend that it was his. Reb Meir Alter should be sitting in the armchair he had just vacated, Reb Meir Alter, the great man, the scholar, the giver of charity. And he, little Jake, the butcher-widow's boy, should be standing outside, peering in, as he had always done when things were as they ought to be.

It was in this confused state of mind that Brother-President Jake Toibenschlag turned up at the meeting that evening; and after the letter from Yuzepov had been read forth to the Congregation of the Men of Yuzepov, he rose to make a speech, and found himself saying something that he had never intended to say:

"Fellow-members, fellow Yuzepovites! There's been some kind of mistake somewhere. I don't know what I'm doing here and what you're doing here. We're not supposed to be sitting here, listening to a letter written to us by them, the notables of Yuzepov, begging our help. I'm not supposed to be President, and the letter should never have been addressed to me. It's all a mistake, I tell you. The President ought to be the Rabbi of Yuzepov; and he ought to be here; and the meeting ought to be attended by all those fine Jews in the silk and satin gaberdines, like Reb Meir Alter, and Reb Israel Ashkenazi, and Reb Yechiel Salant. And we ought to be begging them to help us, we ought to have written that letter, because consider who they are, and who we are. Something's gone wrong, that's what it is."

The Heritage

IN the evening Dr. Lazarovitch returned from the hospital and, as was usual with him of late, locked himself in his cabinet. He was sitting there when the servant knocked and announced that supper was served, whereupon the doctor grunted in reply, and this was now understood to mean that he would wait until everyone else had finished and would eat alone. But this time the knocking was renewed, and to his astonishment Dr. Lazarovitch heard his wife's weak voice. "Boris, we're waiting," she said in Russian. The sound of his wife's voice had a curious effect on Dr. Lazarovitch; it seemed to him to be laden with a strange, uncomfortable significance.

For it was more than a year now—that is, since the time when his eldest son, Mikhael, left for Moscow and was admitted to the medical school of Moscow University—that Dr. Lazarovitch had been avoiding contacts with his family. This contained, apart from the son mentioned, Dr. Lazarovitch's wife, Anna Izakovna, who was always sick, a daughter, Zhanka, and a younger son, Salomon, who was in the fifth class in the local Gymnazia, or high school. The last was, in a way, Dr. Lazarovitch's favorite; but for all that the doctor rarely saw him or the other members of the family. In the morning he received patients; in the afternoon he was at the hospital; and when he came home from the hospital he locked himself in his cabinet ostensibly to do some work. But he did no work; he had not held a book in his hand since he had left the university. He only sat and thought of his

264

eldest son, who had gone away to Moscow and through the influence of family friends had been accepted as a student at the university. That was the story; but Dr. Lazarovitch knew, and his family knew, and all their friends knew, that it was not by the use of influence that the boy had obtained admission. Mikhael had simply had himself baptized. No one ever spoke about it, not even within the family circle. But from that time on a shadow had fallen on the family. Anna Izakovna went to bed early every evening; the children retired to their rooms, and Dr. Lazarovitch would come out for a late supper, eating hurriedly and abstractedly at a corner of the table. Then he would return to his cabinet, pick up an old copy of the *Retch,* and read the year-old report of a speech on the budget made in the Duma by a member of the Cadet Party; and thus reading he would fall asleep. Sometimes the old servant, who had been with them a great many years, would come in and wake him up. Dr. Lazarovitch would undress and pass the remainder of the night on the couch which he used by day for the examination of patients and above which hung a picture cut from an illustrated magazine, Rembrandt's "School of Anatomy."

And therefore Dr. Lazarovitch was very much astonished, and filled with uneasiness, when he heard his wife calling him to supper. He knew at once that something had happened, and he dreaded the news without knowing what it was. He found his family seated at the table, and the first effect of the now unaccustomed picture was so pleasant, that it suddenly occurred to him that he ought to resume the practice of eating with them. But his dread returned on the instant. He had barely taken his place before he turned to his wife and said, "What has happened?" The children exchanged glances silently, and Anna, who was looking somewhat better that evening, answered, "Nothing has happened." The silence of the children, the evasiveness of his wife, exasperated Dr. Lazarovitch, and he repeated his question harshly. Then Anna Izakovna said, in a voice she might have used to impart the news of a great calamity: "Mikhael has written that he's coming home for Passover." And with that a gloom settled on the assembled family, as though some dead person were lying in one of the rooms.

That night the doctor did not fall asleep over the report of a speech delivered in the Duma. He sat thinking of his son. Actually he himself did not understand why his son's abandonment of Judaism should have produced this effect on him. Neither he nor his son had ever been particularly interested in Judaism. He himself remembered very little about it. The Passover and the Day of Atonement still lingered in his mind out of the childhood which he had spent with his father, a pious Jew, a shopkeeper in a little town. But after leaving home as a boy, in order to pursue his studies in Moscow, he had never seen his father again and had dropped all observance of the Jewish festivals. Anna Izakovna, whom he met in Moscow, and whom he later married, had never known anything at all about Jewish customs and festivals; and they had brought up their children exactly as most of their friends had brought up theirs, without any Jewish tradition. The only festivals observed in the house were those which everybody else— that is to say, the Russians generally—observed. And as a matter of fact Mikhael had been brought up as it were with a view to being ultimately baptized. He was an exceptionally able boy. In his fifth year at the Gymnazia he had begun to show a special aptitude for mathematics; and when it was decided that he would continue his studies beyond the Gymnazia it was taken for granted by everyone in the house that he would have himself baptized, in order to avoid the thousand and one difficulties and restrictions which handicapped a Jewish student in Russia and stood in the way of his subsequent career. The doctor, his wife, Mikhael himself, had long thought about it, though they had not so much as mentioned the subject. Why was it then that when it came to the thing itself, when Mikhael had achieved his ambition by the accepted means, why was it that he, the doctor, could find no peace? What was the force which worked on him now and which was alienating him from his home and from his entire family?

Of late he had been trying to think the matter through; he had exerted himself to bring up the memories of the past years and to seek among them the cause of his discomfort. But he found thinking difficult. When he began to probe deeply he felt himself growing exhausted, and his big, broadboned body hungered for sleep. For in the twenty years which he had spent in the provincial city which lay within the Jewish Pale of Settlement, Dr. Lazarovitch had forgotten how to think. Once upon a time he, like many other students of that era, had been an "idealist." When he completed his studies he would—according to the formula of those days—"go to the people," move into some remote, forlorn village, cure the peasants and the peasant women, teach reading and writing to the village children. That was how students talked in his time, and that was in fact what many of them had done. But when Dr. Lazarovitch completed his studies he did not "go to the people" or move into some remote and forlorn village. He fell in love, instead, with Anna Izakovna, the daughter of "Director" Salomon, an elderly, retired factory manager, who had four daughters and whose house was frequented by the Jewish students of Moscow. All the girls played the piano, and the house was conducted in a very aristocratic manner. The butler, an old Russian, wore white gloves when he served at table, though there was not much to serve. But the butler with the gloves, and the girls with the pianos, made a great impression on young Lazarovitch. To him fell the sickliest and plainest of "Director" Salomon's four daughters, Anna.

No sooner had Dr. Lazarovitch married the daughter of an aristocratic house than he forgot about his ideals. He went with his young wife, whose health took a permanent turn for the worse immediately after her marriage, to settle in a town in the Jewish Pale of Settlement, where his father-in-law had many relatives and acquaintances; and there he began to practice. For a time the line was taken that in the Jewish Pale of Settlement, too, much "good work" could be done, and that "light" still had to be spread not only in the villages but in the towns too. But Dr. Lazarovitch soon became acquainted with the local intelligentsia—the pharmacists and schoolteachers—and became a member of the club, where he sat into the small hours of the night playing cards. He spent little time at home, and soon lost his taste for his aristocratic wife, which did not, however, prevent him from begetting five children with her. Two of the children died early, the other three grew up with only occasional attention on his part. Then came the apostasy of his oldest son, Mikhael, and it was this that brought to an abrupt end his card-playing days.

As the time of his son's return drew near, Dr. Lazarovitch became more and more restless. He began to feel that he did not belong to the house. Nor had he the slightest inclination to go back to the club. He could not sit still in his cabinet. At first he thought that his restlessness was due to the fact that with his son's return the whole town would learn of his apostasy; and this gave him the hope that when the worst was over, when everyone was accustomed to the situation, things would resume their normal course and he himself would find peace again. But he soon discarded this view, perceiving, in spite of himself, that his discomfort came from deeper sources than he cared to admit. He was afraid of something, and he did not know what it was that made him afraid. A thousand times he said to himself that nothing had really happened, that in permitting himself to be baptized his son had not become a different person. Dr. Lazarovitch was absolutely free from any taint of religion or superstition, and therefore he could not admit that an external change in religious affiliation had the slightest inner significance. The truth was that neither he nor his son believed in a God. What difference, then, could an external change of classification make to the internal psychic situation? And then, to look at the business from a purely practical point of view, was there any sense in letting the boy throw away his career, his gifts, his future, for the sake of a superstition? Had not Mikhael acted with complete logic when he had, once for all, removed the obstacles which threatened to hold up his career? And so Dr. Lazarovitch kept arguing with and at himself, without any appreciable results. He could not find peace. He knew that something deeper was involved than a mere externality; he knew that a wall had risen between him and his son, that they were separated from each other forever, and that his son was no longer a continuation of himself. Within himself, within Dr. Lazarovitch, something had changed; and within his son something new had begun; they were moving toward two different worlds. And it was the wall between him and his son which frightened Dr. Lazarovitch and filled him with discomfort.

Two days before the Passover the young man arrived. Dr. Lazarovitch did not see him immediately; he was terrified by the prospect of facing him. Between visits to patients he stole into his own house without announcing himself, and once he actually approached the living room and peeped in through a crack, hoping to get a glimpse of his son and curious about his appearance. There was no change in the boy; the same smooth face, the same childlike eyes. And the doctor was filled with astonishment that the apostasy should have produced no change in his son's appearance. Mikhael still looked like his son, and still the doctor was afraid of him.

There was no bustle, no liveliness in the house on the day of Mikhael's arrival—or for that matter at any time later, during his stay. There was, in fact, less noise than usual; it was as though people were walking about on tiptoe; it was as though they were ashamed in each other's presence; and when evening came they were in their rooms, or else they were all in the living room, but each one reading in a separate corner.

Coming home that first evening later than was his wont, the doctor looked in through the window before he entered, and he saw his oldest son, the apostate, sitting alone in the living room. It seemed to him that there was a great sadness in the boy's face; and a pang of helpless father-love shot through Dr. Lazarovitch's heart. It seemed to him that he had never felt so close to any of his children as he did at this moment to the apostate; and he was glad that he could still feel something like paternal love. The boy was such a dolorous figure that Dr. Lazarovitch almost cried out to him. Somehow the blue student uniform did not properly belong to him. His face was pale, and on it rested a strange expression, which made Dr. Lazarovitch think of a girl who had lost her innocence. With all his sophisticated convictions the doctor asked himself whether it was right for the boy to begin life under the shadow of such a sin. And then, unable to restrain himself any longer, he entered the house hastily and went into the room where the boy sat alone.

Mikhael was so deeply absorbed in his thoughts that he did not notice his father until the two heavy hands rested on his shoulders. Then he started up convulsively.

"Mikhael, how are you?"

The boy sprang to his feet, and cried out, "Father!" The blood had withdrawn from his face. He was about to say something, remembered, and was silent.

Suddenly, as if to force the issue into the open, Dr. Lazarovitch adverted to the forbidden subject.

"How did you manage to enter the university?" he asked, in a harsh voice.

The boy bit his lips, and stammered: "I didn't know you'd take it so hard." Then, when his father made no comment, he added: "If you want, I'll quit the university and become a Jew again. The whole thing makes me sick, too."

"No, don't do it."

"Why, father?"

Dr. Lazarovitch moved closer to his son, and said, in a low voice: "This isn't a question of religion. You know I'm not religious. It's a question of principle, and you've already broken the principle. What difference will it make if you become a Jew again? The situation won't be changed by it. A girl who's lost her innocence can never get it back. Do you understand?"

And then Dr. Lazarovitch took his son's head between his hands, and perhaps for the first time in his life, kissed the boy.

• • •

A few days later Dr. Lazarovitch learned that when Mikhael had been baptized, his closest friend, Joseph Kalmanovitch, had been baptized with him. The two boys had graduated together from the local Gymnazia. Everyone knew that Joseph was in love with his friend's sister, Zhanka, and that the young people were as good as engaged. When Dr. Lazarovitch learned of Joseph's baptism, he wondered whether he would dare to come to the house on his return from Moscow, and if he did dare to do such a thing, how he would try to carry it off. But the young man actually showed up, greeted Dr. Lazarovitch as if nothing untoward had happened, asked after Zhanka, and when she appeared, invited her to go out with him. The incident passed off in the quietest, most normal way. And Dr. Lazarovitch, stupefied by the matter-of-factness of it all, began to ask himself whether it was not he alone who was such a reactionary, and so superstitious, whether it was not he alone who saw any importance in this business of religious "apostasy." And yet he could not reconcile himself to the idea that after what had happened with his son, his daughter should want to marry an apostate and his wife should be completely indifferent. He thought he might clear up the confusion in his mind by speaking openly with his daughter; but when, finding her alone, he raised the subject, she answered him with a decisiveness which left him aghast. She said that it did not make the slightest difference to her whether her husband was a Jew or a Christian; she had fallen in love with Joseph, and if her father would not let her marry him, she would live with him without benefit of marriage.

It was only then, at long last, that the doctor began to understand all the implications of the situation. His children were leaving his house and his faith; he would be left alone, in his old age, in an alien faith; he might yet see himself living with one of his children, and dandling strange, baptized grandchildren on his knee; perhaps his children would even prevail on him to baptize before his death, so that he might be buried in the Christian cemetery which they had already chosen for themselves. All this came home to him now, and the disillusionment was so sharp and so bitter that it seemed to him that something had to be done about it.

And the first thing he did was to persuade himself that he had suddenly discovered a great need for religious conformity. He began to haunt various little Jewish prayer-houses scattered throughout the city, dropping in for afternoon and evening prayers when he left the hospital. For a time this interested him, but he soon realized that whatever it was he wanted, it was not the same thing as the religious practices of plain, everyday Jews, who came to prayers because they felt that they owed God something and were anxious to pay it off as quickly as possible and hurry off home. There was no inspiration or satisfaction in this attitude of theirs. Nor, for that matter, did he understand the content of the prayers, which he read or followed with difficulty. The gabbling, the gestures, the bodily motions of these habitually Yiddish-speaking Jews, at their devotions, struck him as outlandish. But he did not give up hope of finding what he sought. He was quite certain that somewhere or other there waited for him the great, powerful Judaism which offered both explanation and consolation, which made it worth while for Jews to put up with the torments and humiliations of their exile, the persecutions and discriminations, and gave them the strength to endure through it all. This Judaism would also recompense him for the loss he had sustained in his children.

He actually made a systematic effort to introduce the Jewish festival customs into his home. Not that he really knew much about them. He did not remember the details clearly out of his childhood, and he felt rather ridiculous, in the midst of his preoccupation, to see himself running about obtaining kosher meat or the white Sabbath loaves with which to adorn the table on Friday evening or, when Passover came around again, boxes of *matzoth,* or unleavened bread. The family took him seriously, or pretended to. The *matzoth* were served up ceremoniously on a special platter; but the other members of the family seemed to be afraid to go near them. Anna Izakovna and the three children made earnest faces—but he knew, in his heart, that the whole business was a comedy. There had never been such a thing as a Jewish festival in his home. There were festivals, of course, but only those which the Russians observed, or others than the Russians—but not the Jews. The Lazarovitches observed Easter with the Orthodox Church and had a Christmas tree like the Polish Catholics in their vicinity, but never Chanukkah candles or a booth on the Festival of Booths. Hence these new ceremonials were meaningless to the rest of the family and his insistence on them bewildering.

The Heritage

What Dr. Lazarovitch had in mind particularly was that at least his youngest and favorite son, Salomon, who was only fourteen years old, would as it were catch on. The boy was on his mind, because he perceived him to be different from the others. The doctor had had to overcome a great many obstacles before he had secured Salomon's entry into the Gymnazia. This was the period in the first decade of the twentieth century when anti-Semitism was becoming fashionable in Russia and was even penetrating to the Russian masses. The boy suffered much from the attitude of his Christian schoolmates toward him. Often he would come home from school with red eyes, in whose frightened pupils was written the immemorial Jewish question: "Why?"

At first, indeed, the boy even turned to his father and asked him outright: "Why do they torment us like that in school? What is it that the Jews have done? And why do we remain Jews?" But receiving evasive or meaningless answers, the boy stopped asking questions. He learned rapidly what it meant to be a Jew—at least, what it meant externally. He aged, as Jewish youngsters did, before his time and like an adult bore his persecutions with patience and humility. He asked no more; but to his father it was clear that the question had not disappeared from his mind. It was there, in fact, more than ever; and finding no expression in words, it found expression in his face, in the sad eyes and wrinkled forehead. Salomon turned very early to serious books, passing from a child to an adult almost without an intervening period of boyhood. His lips habitually wore a slightly contemptuous smile, the only protection of the impotent against a malevolent world.

For Salomon's sake, then, as much as for his own, Dr. Lazarovitch persisted in his search. His youngest child awakened in him a feeling of peculiar responsibility; him at least he would save, and him he would keep from the path of apostasy. Very often the doctor wanted to discuss with Salomon the subject of Mikhael's baptism, but he was afraid of hearing the truth from the boy's lips, namely, that he, the father, was much more responsible for this situation than the son. He had done nothing, as Mikhael's father, to anticipate or prevent the act.

It was, however, as if Salomon was aware of the special aim in his father's newfound religious and ceremonial enthusiasm and would not permit himself to be ensnared, for as the father became more insistent on the festival observances, the boy developed an aversion for his home. He began to stay away, spending afternoons and evenings at a friend's house; and after a time he stayed away nights as well.

Dr. Lazarovitch felt this to be a personal rebuke. "He's avoiding me," he said to himself, and was wounded. Now that he was trying to do something for his son, his son was turning against him. "Why?" he asked, pretending not to know the answer. And once, when Anna Izakovna told him that Salomon had not been home for two nights in succession, he sought out the boy at the house of a schoolmate, and began to upbraid him bitterly:

"Why do you stay away nights? Why are you always running away from your home?"

"Why do *I* stay away?" asked the boy, stung. "It's you who's always been running away from home!"

The direct, simple answer stunned Lazarovitch. This was the second great shock, as his daughter's defiant answer had been the first. All the emptiness and poverty of his inner life rose again before him, starker and clearer than before. Again he realized that something had to be done, something drastic and fundamental, before it was too late.

The failure of his religious approach was all too apparent. He shifted ground and began to study the problem from quite another point of view. He began to inquire into the general condition of the Jewish people, to read the Russian-Jewish periodicals, and to attend meetings. He became aware that there was a serious movement on foot for the creation of a new Jewish life in Palestine. Numbers of Jews had already settled there, were tilling the soil, were giving reality to the ancient dream of the restitution of their people to a land of their own, where Judaism could develop in freedom and joy. Yes, he recalled now that this dream had haunted the Jews he had known in childhood, his father, the shopkeeper, and his father's friends. And thinking deeply on that time, he recalled more clearly than ever before the festivals and celebrations which had filled that life. They came back to him more sharply now than when he had pursued the illusion of a religious impulse; he saw more vividly the Sabbaths, the Friday evenings with their candles, his mother making the benediction with closed eyes and uplifted hands; he saw the little Chassidic prayer-house to which his father had taken him daily, the elaborately prepared table of the Passover *seder* ceremony, with its multiple symbols, the eager, shining faces, the glowing wine-cups. It seemed to him that all this was closely connected with Palestine; it seemed to him that over there, in Palestine, the warm, heartening life of his childhood, with its comforting fullness of meaning, was being reconstituted once more, stronger than before, in greater freedom. There the Jewishness which explained, consoled and strengthened was coming into its own. It was like a vision. In the midst of the restored ceremonial and the reawakened tradition, pictures of the Bible and of his father rose like an accompaniment. The life of that obscure little shopkeeper took on a pattern and a meaning; there was a direct connection between those forlorn little Jews, the shopkeepers of the villages, his father and others, and the heroes of the Bible. The connection expressed itself through Palestine, the land of Israel, which created the universal bond. His father, the shopkeeper, had issued thence, and had longed to return to the land of Abraham, Isaac, and Jacob; his father had loved the faith and the customs of the patriarchs, and had wanted to preserve and practice them. But here, in exile, where persecution never relaxed, it was impossible to live the life of the patriarchs and to be shepherds and tillers of the soil. Here the Jews could only preserve the ceremonial of the Sabbath and the Passover. There, in Palestine, they would be able to revert to the old life, and live in every respect like the patriarchs. They were tilling the soil, watching their flocks, and maintaining the old, lovely piety. There Judaism was whole, pure, solemn; there the Jews were showing how essentially moral and clean they were. There the festivals took on once more their pristine grandeur. Yes, and he, Dr. Lazarovitch, would go to Palestine, join the other Jews, live with them and like them, feel as they felt. He would recapture the taste of the Sabbath and the Passover, the memory of which lingered in the far-off pictures of his childhood.

For a time Dr. Lazarovitch kept this discovery to himself, as something too precious to be exposed to misunderstanding. He spoke to no one. But it was observed that he had become quieter and more self-assured. He was more patient; he was even sociable and kindly. He relinquished entirely his habit of locking himself in his cabinet at the end of the day's work. To the habit of taking his meals with the family, which he had resumed in pursuit of his religious plans, he added the habit of lingering with the children after the meal. He was no longer irritable with his wife. He did not speak much, but there was an affectionate light in his eyes, something that radiated from a hidden happiness, and no one in the family could understand what it was that had produced this extraordinary change.

The temptation to speak out, to unburden himself, was strongest in respect of his youngest son. The doctor was quite certain that Salomon would understand him, though in fact he could not have said why this should be so. Perhaps it was because this dream, this Palestinian vision, was what the boy needed, much more than ceremonials and festivals, in order to heal the inner hurt. And why, the doctor asked himself, should not he and his younger son go to Palestine? Why? And the oftener he asked himself, the more joyously certain he was that now, at last, he had found his way out of the labyrinth. Thus it was that one evening, after Salomon had gone to his room, the doctor followed him and without preliminaries put the question to him:

"Salomon, have you ever thought about Palestine?"

The boy flushed, fixed two shining eyes on his father, and exclaimed:

"Father! What makes you ask that?"

"Why shouldn't I ask it?" answered the doctor, astounded.

His feelings had not deceived him! It transpired that Salomon had long been thinking about Palestine. Without speaking of it at home, he had joined the youth Zionist organization of his Gymnazia and knew all about the Zionist movement and its achievements. He knew the names of the Jewish colonies. It came out now, in a burst of grateful and amazed intimacy. The father listened, scarcely believing his ears.

"Salomon," he asked suddenly, putting his hand on the boy's shoulder, "would you like to go to Palestine with me?"

An expression of incredulity came into Salomon's eyes.

"Father! Are you serious?"

"Of course I'm serious, Salomon. Don't you see how we're being choked to death here? What is there left for me?" He felt a great need to unburden himself of all that oppressed him. But he restrained himself for fear of frightening the boy. He took a calmer tone, and tried to smile. "Yes, Salomon, there Jews live a great and pure life. Will you go with me?"

"Of course I'll go with you."

"Even if mama and the others want to stay here?"

"Let them stay here if they like it here!" answered Salomon, without hesitation. "I want to live there, where Jews are like other people, free men, the equals of everyone."

"Where Jews are free men," the doctor repeated, under his breath. "Good, my boy. Let them stay here if they like it here." And the doctor turned and almost ran from the room, afraid that he would not be able to hold back the tears which were welling into his old tired eyes, welling up out of the old tired heart which he had thought incapable of feeling.

From that day on father and son made a group apart in the family. They felt richer and luckier than the others, they felt more privileged; they looked with compassion on the mother and the sisters and above all on the apostate son. Often they sat together in the doctor's cabinet when the rest had gone to sleep. They studied the map of Palestine. Salomon showed his father the locations of the new colonies, and taught him their names. They even began to study Hebrew, the new-old holy tongue. Actually the doctor went along for the first two or three lessons, and then found that his tired brain was no longer capable of study. But Salomon persevered alone, and when he talked with his father of the life that awaited them in the land of Israel, the old man felt that his own

youth had returned and he was once more a child listening with
wondering eyes to the stories told by his father, the shopkeeper.

Then, on a certain evening, when the whole family was assembled, and the dinner things had been cleared away, Dr. Lazarovitch
cleared his throat and announced that he had something important
to say. He had prepared a speech, in which he had set down all
the reasons and principles and purposes involved in his decision.
But the speech did not come off. At the last moment, when all eyes
were turned expectantly on him, he brought his palm down on
the table, and asked excitedly: "Who will go with me to Palestine?"
That was all.

Mother and daughter looked first at him and then at each other,
petrified. They had nothing to say. After waiting through a painful silence, the doctor turned to his sick wife, and asked her, in a
louder voice: "Will you come with me to Palestine, or will you
stay here with the apostate children?"

His wife answered, terrified, stammering:

"I don't know what you mean. I don't know what you want.
Wherever my children are, I'll be there too."

"Very good! Very good!" said Dr. Lazarovitch, sternly. "I'll sell
out everything, divide up with you, and the youngest child and I
will go to Palestine."

Anna Izakovna's first impression, like that of her daughter, was
that this was nothing more than a queer outburst of rage on the
part of the doctor, whose newfound family interest and general
solicitude had seemed unnatural to them. They were quite sure that
by the next day he would have forgotten his threat. But they soon
discovered their error. Dr. Lazarovitch did not go to the hospital
the next day. He was not at home for patients. He was busy looking for a purchaser for his practice and for the two houses he owned
in addition to his own home. But before he had found a purchaser,
he had scraped together all his available cash, turned over his affairs
to a broker, and left for Palestine.

He took with him only his youngest child Salomon, to find a
home for the two of them in the midst of the peace and beauty of
Palestine.

A Peculiar Gift

IN the Valley of Jezreel, within the shadow of Mount Gilboa, a Jew was following a plough pulled by two horses. The Jew guided the plough; his ten-year-old son, Solomon, whipped up the horses, one red and one black; and Sarah, his eight-year-old daughter dropped the seed into the fresh-turned furrow.

"Drop them down straight, little one," he sang to the girl. "Right to the bottom of the furrow. God's over us, and he'll return thirty-fold, forty-fold, fifty-fold. Such returns have been and may be again. Whoa, Solomon, not so fast with the nags! Hold the red one! Hold the black one!" The Jew stopped and peered into the furrow. "Take them, good earth, and multiply them! God gave you to us, and we are back with you. Dear earth, do God's bidding, and you, little seeds, fall in good places where you will not die and rot; fall comfortably and well, so that you may sprout and feed me and my wife and my children. I have prepared a bed for you, a warm, brown bed, a bed that flows with milk and honey, as the great teacher said."

Panting as he followed the plough, the Jew kept up his breath-less, ecstatic monologue. He wiped the sweat from his face. The sun blazed down on him, the wind lifted up the corners of his gaber-dine and the points of his beard; it fluttered the tips of the kerchief round the little girl's head. And all five of them, father, daughter, and son, the red horse and the black, labored joyously along the hard, sloping field, turning up the earth in the ancient Valley of Jezreel.

I, a visitor in this lonely place, sat on a stone and waited for the family to make the last furrow for that afternoon. I was worried for the Jew behind the plough; I was afraid for him. For I knew him from of old, knew the kind of man he had been. Was not this Noah the dry-goods merchant, whom I saw now after many years, Noah who had given up his business in Ekaterinoslav and who now, with son and daughter and two horses, one black and one red, was toiling along the slope of the field, disguised as a farmer? And what a farmer! A lyrical farmer such as never was on land or sea. As he came back toward me his voice was still uplifted.

"It's good, Mr. Jew," he chanted. "Do you hear me? It's good."

"It's good and hot, Reb Noah," I answered.

He halted.

"Hot? Did you say it's hot? Maybe it is. What does the Book say? 'In the summer the heat shall not burn you, and in the winter the cold shall not consume you.' What if it is hot? It's good, I tell you."

In the old days, when I had used to visit him in Ekaterinoslav, Reb Noah had been a merchant of standing, dealing with cities as wide apart as Warsaw, Kishineff, and Lodz. He was said to be worth between fifteen and twenty thousand roubles, and his credit rating was even higher, for who knew as well as Reb Noah the value of a rouble, and who guarded a coin with the same vigilance? When he came to Warsaw as a buyer, he stayed always at a third-rate inn, a rouble a day, meals and all. He welcomed a rouble with jubilation, parted with a kopeck only under duress. He always defended himself by saying that he was saving his money for Palestine; yes, some day he would close his shop, wind up his business, betake himself to the Holy Land, and become a laboring man, a tiller of the soil, which, as all the world knew, was what his ancestors and all the ancestors of the Jews had been. Of course nobody believed him, for if Reb Noah was sparing of his cash, he was most generous of his words. It was remembered, moreover, that in his boyhood Reb Noah had sung in the choir of the famous cantor of Berditchev and had become a businessman against his will; and it is a well-known fact that frustrated singers are the most talkative of mortals. But the unbelievable, or at any rate the unbelieved, came to pass. Noah the dry-goods merchant disappeared from Ekaterinoslav, in the height of the season, and the places of his business knew him no more. They waited for him in vain in the warehouses of Warsaw and Kishineff and Lodz. And soon he was forgotten, as businessmen are apt to be. Other customers took his place. Reb Noah had really gone to Palestine; and here he was, in the Valley of Jezreel, wearing, instead of the perky little bowler of the Russian Jew, the stately fez of the Turks, and talking to me as he leaned upon the plough which I had watched him guide.

"But—but—how could you really bring yourself to do it?" I asked, convinced and yet incredulous.

"I'll tell you what it is," he answered, thoughtfully. "I've always believed, deep down, that I was a gifted man, a man of peculiar gifts. My only difficulty was that I didn't know what I was gifted for. Till one day it came to me suddenly that I was *gifted for Palestine.*"

"What's that?" I said. "Gifted for Palestine?"

"Why, certainly. Some Jews have a gift for this, some for that, some for the other—and some for Palestine. Take Baron Edmund Rothschild, for instance. A great man, isn't he? But who knew what he was great *for* until he discovered his peculiar gift? He had a gift for Palestine. And so did I. Not as great a one as Baron Rothschild. I'm gifted for Palestine in a smaller way. But then, I'm a smaller man, and it's all I need."

"It's a laborious talent, Reb Noah," I suggested. "A sweaty talent, if I may say so."

"Not a bit of it," he retorted, and contradicted himself by wiping a freshet of perspiration from his face. "A talent for dry-goods is a lot sweatier. You should have seen me trying to persuade a peasant woman that a length of calico was what she needed, and that she was getting it dirt cheap—which she was. Now, *that* was a sweaty job. But this? Pooh!"

"But the horses, Reb Noah? How do you get along with the horses? I knew you when you wouldn't come within a mile of a horse."

"I daresay you did. And yet—well, how was I to know? See that red nag there? He's the sweetest horse in the world, an absolute saint of a horse. Never kicked anyone in his life. Click your tongue at him, and off he goes; call 'Whoa!' and he stops. A saint, I say. The black one, I admit, was different. A lowdown horse, mean, unfriendly—an anti-Semite of a horse. A grand worker; but he loved to kick. They told me, when I bought him: 'Reb Noah, you'll never manage that horse. You'll never get round him.' 'I won't, won't I?' was all I answered, and took my horse home. And I said to myself: 'Noah, get this into your mind. The first day you handle him, he'll kick you ten times.' But did he? No, he did not. He kicked me only six times. So there I was, four kicks to the good, the very first day. The second day I counted on six, and got away with three. How's that for progress? Today he doesn't kick any more. He's learned the verse from Isaiah: 'The ox knoweth his master, and the ass his owner's crib.' I'm boss, he's servant, and we're at peace. I give him his food, he gives me his labor."

"And your wife, Yetta," I went on. "How did she take to being a peasant woman."

"Ah, that now—that was a hard business." Reb Noah became reflective. "Things are brighter today, but the beginning—" and Reb Noah tightened his lips, drew his mouth to one side, closed one eye and nodded several times. "When we came out here, my wife and I and the little ones, the place was a wilderness. *Tohu-u-bohu.* Without form and void. Eight Jewish families in all, in this 'Arab hole' which we took over. That's what my wife called it. 'Noah, you murderer,' she cries, 'what are you doing with me and my little chicks? How do you expect us to live here?' And what could I answer? The first thing I got here was a good dose of malaria. There was no water in the place; you had to bring it by the pailful from the nearest well, miles away. The children were sick, too. And my Yetta! The things she said! And me shivering with the fever. 'Yetta,' I answer, 'don't talk that way! It's blasphemous! This is the Holy Land, of the Prophets and Kings and Priests. It's forbidden to speak evil of it. Wait,' I say, 'this "Arab hole" is a paradise. Wait till the fig trees blossom—our own fig trees now, ours. And wait till we eat the bread of our own planting. Don't you know the story of the twelve spies Moses sent into Palestine, how they brought back an evil report?' No, she knew nothing about the twelve spies. So I told her the story. And soon after that I got better, and took my two horses, and went out to the ploughing, and ploughed all day. And when I come back, she's in tears. 'What is it, Yetta?' She says she's lonely, she hankers for company, the kind she had in Ekaterinoslav. 'What have you done to me and my chicks?' she starts all over again. 'I've done nothing to your chicks,' I says. 'They've been out ploughing the fields with me. And as for your Ekaterinoslav company, a rotten fig for that. Today you're a peasant woman, and peasant women don't have company. And if you're lonely,' I say, further, 'you've only to step out of doors and take a look at our Valley of Jezreel. Look, there's Mount Gilboa, where the glory of the great King, Saul, was brought low; that's where King David pronounced his curse in olden days, no dew and no rain should fall on the hills of Gilboa. And over there is Mount Tabor, where the Prophetess Deborah sang her song of praise to the Lord, for the victory over Sisera. And way up yonder's the summit of Mount Hebron. Isn't that company enough for you? And you talk about that silly Ekaterinoslav company, which always cost money to entertain and wasn't worth a broken eggshell. Why, Yetta,' I say, 'you ought to be ashamed of yourself.' And she answers: 'Oh, you've always had plenty of words to spare. You can talk a stone into a pair of legs, and you've talked me into coming here. God help me, what's going to become of me?' What could you say to a woman like that?"

I could only echo his question: "What *could* you say?"

"Well, there's a God in heaven," he answered, elliptically. "She began to get used to the life. Bit by bit. Bit by bit. One morning I caught her standing at the door, looking out at our little field, shining with dew, and there was a smile on her face—she didn't know I saw her. And then, one evening, I see her go out into the garden, and she's murmuring to herself. And I see her bend down and pull out a weed. And I said to myself, 'Ho, ho, it's getting you, old girl. The soil's getting you, the good mother earth.' And I went out to her and said, 'Pull 'em up, wife, pull 'em up, all the weeds. The mountain up there is still wild, and wild things grow there, and the wind carries the seed of them down, and the wild things grow in our field. But in the time to come our brothers will live up there, on the mountain, and wild things won't grow there any more. So when the wind will blow this way, and bring seed, it'll be the seed of good grain, and we won't have to tear it out.' But she didn't give in so easily, the old woman. She says: 'I wish I could tear you up by the roots, the way I'm tearing these weeds up.' But I knew she was half won over; that's why she talked that way.

"No, after that I wasn't afraid any more. The land got her. There's something in the land that gets everyone. It pulls you. And why? I'll tell you why. You come here in the beginning, and it's a howling wilderness. No people, no friends, no house, no water. Nothing! And you want to run away! You feel you won't be able to stand it twenty-four hours. But if you hold on, till the first things grow in your garden, and you've got the first loaf from your own fields, then you'll never want to leave. All land is like that. And this land of ours, the Holy Land, more than any other land in the world. Think of all the history in it, think of all the blood that's gone into it—think of—"

Reb Noah was becoming rhetorical, and that was a pity. So I interrupted him:

"And how do you get along with the Arabs, Reb Noah? They say, back there in Ekaterinoslav—"

He interrupted me in turn.

"How do I get along with my neighbors? Why, perfectly. Best of friends. When I came out here the young fellows in the neighboring colony said to me: 'Reb Noah, you've got to get yourself a revolver and a knife. If you go without them, the Arabs will find you in the middle of the field, unhitch the horses, and drive them off, leaving you there with the plough.' And what did I answer? 'My lads,' I said, 'I'm not afraid of your Arabs. See this Turkish fez? That's my revolver. And see my little boy Solomon here? That's my knife.' Because the first thing I did when I got to the Holy Land was to buy myself a fez. 'That'll show them,' I said, 'that I'm a Semite, just like them.' I went out into the field, ploughing, and my fez was on my head and my little boy by my side. I'd like to see the Arab who'd attack a father when his six-year-old boy is along with him. There is no such Arab; because the Arabs are Semites, and Semites are merciful. I'll tell you what happened once. I was out there"—he pointed to the furthest end of the field—"I was way out there, one day, under the hill. I was ploughing with my little Solomon, when along comes an Arab on a horse—an Arab with a gun on his shoulder and a sword by his side. When he drew alongside I passed my hand over my forehead and my breast, which is the way they greet each other here, and I said: *'Ni habik said,'* which means, 'Let your day be beautiful.' And he passed his hand over forehead and breast and answered, *'Tahbadnik,'* which means, 'Let your morning be fresh.'

"Because as soon as I came out here I learned to say 'Good morning' in Arabic. I'd like to see the murderer who's going to attack you after you've said 'Good morning' to him. Especially a Semite. Well, the Arab on the horse points to the little boy, and asks me in Arabic whose he is. So I press little Solomon to my heart, to show he's mine. Then the Arab gets off his horse and begins to finger my plough, because he'd never seen one like it before, his people still using wooden ploughs, like our ancestors ages ago. Then I touch the plough, and I point way over the hills, to show that in the place I come from they use iron ploughs. So he shrugs his shoulders, and smiles, and nods. And now, seeing we were good friends, I say to him, 'You, me, *achim,* brothers, Semites'; and he smiles again, showing all his teeth, and bows, and says *'Hawadji,'* which is their word for *'gospodin,'* or mister. Then he jumps on his horse and rides away. So I ask you, do I need a revolver, or a knife?"

I stared at Reb Noah, not knowing what to say now. And he, a little ashamed of his garrulity, said, "One more furrow, there and back," and turned his horses toward the field.

I stood watching him as he steered the plough; I watched the horses pulling, the children helping. It was not too straight a furrow that he drew—but it was a good one, deep and even. And I could not help thinking:

"How did this Jew find it in himself to throw away his comfortable business, his security, his ease, his Ekaterinoslav, and come out here into the wilderness? How did he throw off the habits of the city, the money curse, and take to guiding a plough under a blazing sun?"

Then I remembered what Reb Noah had just said. "I've a special gift. I'm gifted for Palestine." Undoubtedly he was; how else could he have come through? And I reflected further: "Perhaps that gift belongs not only to some Jews, but to all. Perhaps the gift for Palestine slumbers in the whole Jewish people."

The Last Jew

HIS parents had died and had left him a synagogue, and he did not know what to do with it.

Every morning, after he had swept the sidewalk in front of his house, he would cross over to the synagogue which he had inherited from his parents and sweep the sidewalk there, too. Then he would open the synagogue, and bring out from the vestibule the stands loaded with slippers, gaiters, sabots. He would carry them across to his store and arrange them for the day, in front of his store. His wife and daughter would bring out other stands and load them with pots, jugs, plates, cups and saucers—all kept in the vestibule of the synagogue. Every evening, when they closed their little shop, they would carry the merchandise back into the vestibule of the synagogue, lock up, and return home.

Sometimes, in the middle of the day, a Cook's Tour guide would come from a near-by city, bringing in his wake a couple of long and lean English misses who were "doing" the quaint little old French town, and who, having duly inspected the medieval church, the remnants of the Roman wall, and all the other local antiquities, would recall that they had heard about a synagogue too.

"Monsieur Crémieux! Sightseers for the synagogue."

Monsieur Crémieux pretends to be very busy with his shoes and sabots. The guide comes over, and adds, confidentially: "They've promised a decent tip. I told them. They agreed."

If the sightseers are men and look like good tippers, Monsieur Crémieux waits for no assurances from the guide, but takes down the keys from their nail, opens the doors of the synagogue, and displays his inheritance. And if the sightseers are elegantly dressed, or come in a private automobile, or look like Americans, Monsieur Crémieux is very friendly, almost effusive. He even opens the drawers of the bureau, and pulls out a few old books, which are not as old as they look, and have no antiquarian value, being in fact, tattered reprints of Amsterdam missals in wide use a generation or two ago. The sightseers handle the books very respectfully, holding them upside down, and making a face of wonder at the mysterious Hebrew letters. Monsieur Crémieux tells them that these are genuine finds, for which he has been offered enormous sums by American collectors. He replaces the books in the drawer with a great show of reverence.

But if the sightseers are English misses, who never give more than a few sous for the privilege of inspecting the synagogue, Monsieur Crémieux calls to his wife or daughter:

"Open up the synagogue for the visitors!"

Then the Cook's guide acts as the cicerone and blossoms into an authority on Judaica: he dwells at length on the candelabra, and explains the peculiar traditional features of the pulpit; he goes over to the Ark, pulls away the faded curtain, opens the shaky doors, and uncovers the sad-looking Scrolls in their old and dusty covers. He also "interprets" the various Hebrew inscriptions scattered about the synagogue, reads the religious almanacs, and the names on the Eternal Lamps left about by forgotten Jewish householders of the past. The greater the prospect of a generous tip, the more elaborate and interesting become the explanations of the guide, the stranger and more exotic the details of the Jewish faith.

Such was the synagogue, such its owner and keeper. Monsieur Crémieux himself observed the same festivals as his neighbors, that is to say, the Christian festivals. He regarded them as his own, and his wife prepared the house for them exactly like the other good women of the little town. The only difference between Monsieur Crémieux and his neighbors was that now and again they went to church, while he never went except to attend the funeral of some friend.

The Last Jew

Monsieur Crémieux knew that he was a Jew; he knew that his neighbors had nothing against this and that they saw nothing wrong in his abstention from church services, though he himself would have preferred to attend them.

For Monsieur Crémieux was very much like his neighbors, an ordinary and unassuming sort of person, completely absorbed in his livelihood and in his little pleasures, a man without time or inclination for agnosticism or heresy. For that matter he was no pietist, either, having just as little time or inclination for this extreme. He would, indeed, have liked to attend church services, but not in a regular, systematic way. For, after all, Sunday was the only day of rest, and when was a man to spend a few extra hours in bed if not on Sunday? Monsieur Crémieux merely recognized the necessity of God, especially in a time of tribulation: sickness, for instance—doctors and medicines were frightfully expensive, the "holy bread" was cheaper and probably more effective. God was useful, too, in a legal dispute, as a last resort.

The older Monsieur Crémieux grew, the more convinced he became of the usefulness of God; like all who have passed through the economic struggle and emerged into calmer waters, he felt the need to belong to a church; not ostentatiously, not intensively, as it were, but for social purposes.

But Monsieur Crémieux knew that he was a Jew, that he therefore belonged to another "church," that in the little town he was the only one left to represent his church.

He remembered as in a dream the time when there used to be services in the synagogue. He was a very little boy. He remembered the light of many candles. All the old Dutch candelabra in the synagogue, which visitors generally regarded as the most interesting of its possessions, were then filled with blazing candles. A man sang, leading the congregation in prayer. The little boy stood next to his father, who wore a white prayer shawl: white shawls, lights, singing. And then somehow the praying in the synagogue faded away; householder after householder died or went away to a big city; the children wandered away, too, became baptized, married Christians. Then there was no more praying in the synagogue. Two Jews remained in the little French town—Monsieur Crémieux and an elderly cousin of the same name.

As long as this cousin lived there was one day in the year (the cousin knew the date; he had a Jewish almanac sent him regularly by the Paris Rabbinate) on which they observed a certain ritual. Toward evening they would come into the synagogue, light all the lamps hanging before the Ark, and stroll up and down the aisles. Of the prayers which belonged to this or any other Jewish occasion, they knew nothing. The cousin, however, had a prayer-shawl and would walk about in it, while our Monsieur Crémieux would walk about in everyday attire. They remained in the synagogue as long as the oil in the lamps lasted; then they would douse the smoldering wicks and go home. On that day they kept their shops closed, and the cousin ate nothing until noon; he only permitted himself a drink of water. He said that this was the Jewish law for this day: you could not eat till noon; you could only have a glass of water.

When his cousin died, our Monsieur Crémieux wanted to continue the observance of the day, but he did not know how to do it all by himself. Besides, after the first year he forgot to renew the subscription to the almanac of the Paris Rabbinate. Ever since then he had let this last observance lapse.

But Monsieur Crémieux could not live without a religion. He was a citizen of standing, and the finest people in town came to buy his sabots and slippers and his wife's crockery. The Curé was a steady customer of theirs. All his acquaintances—which included the magistrate of the town and his circle—were fairly religious; several times a year they attended church, if only to set an example and give their moral support to the Curé. Monsieur Crémieux knew as much about the church services, the festivals, and the local politics of the church, as anyone else. His customers discussed such matters freely with him; even the Curé himself would tell him of his troubles, would complain of the mounting wickedness of the world, and the spread of heresy and atheism. People did not go to church to pray, said the Curé, but to gossip, or to show off their new clothes. The confession box was empty from one year's end to the other, and no one ate the holy bread save on the death-bed.

The Last Jew

Monsieur Crémieux was public spirited. Having no religious congregation of his own, in whose affairs he could take an active part, he took one in the affairs of the local church. He was generous in his counsel to the Curé; it was at his suggestion that the latter put up a cross of electric lights before the door of the church; his, too, was the idea of bringing down a special organist from Lyons. Monsieur Crémieux went further: he helped to raise the money for the organist's expenses. He was the leading spirit in the famous bazaar for the benefit of the church and donated several pairs of sabots and slippers, while his wife and daughter came forward with a set of dishes. He also peddled raffle tickets and headed the list with his own contribution.

On a certain night Monsieur Crémieux lay down to sleep and found that sleep would not come. A disturbing idea haunted him. It had occurred to him, all of a sudden, that he was older than he admitted to himself; his time was approaching; and if he died a Jew he would have to be buried in the Jewish cemetery in Lyons, which would mean no little expense for his heirs. The thought hurt him, for his heirs were very fine people: there was Monsieur Graves, the electrician of the town, who had married his older daughter; there was the younger daughter, who helped her mother in the sale of crockery; and then, of course, there was his wife. Why should they be put to this extra expense? He would get himself baptized, become a member of the Catholic church; then, when he died, he would be buried in the local cemetery, among his own. It would be cheaper, and more comfortable too.

So Monsieur Crémieux meditated, tossing about on his bed. Then a doubt occurred to him. What would happen to the synagogue if he ceased to be a Jew? It could not properly go on belonging to him, since he would be a Catholic. That was a pity; the synagogue was such a good place for keeping his stocks of sabots and slippers and his wife's stocks of crockery. Besides, who would look after the synagogue when it no longer belonged to him?

He repressed his own doubt. Who was to prevent him from keeping shoes and crockery in the vestibule of the synagogue? He had been doing it so long that he had at least squatter's rights. In any case, no one else had a right to the synagogue; it had been left to him by his parents. They had said nothing about his religion.

The next day Monsieur Crémieux went to the priest and opened his heart to him.

"*Monsieur le Curé,* I've come to ask you to receive me into the Catholic faith. Am I not to all intents and purposes one of you? There is no one of my faith in this town but myself, and it is a hard thing for one man to maintain a religion all by himself. The nearest Jewish center is the Rabbinate in Lyons, and that's a long way off. *Monsieur le Curé,* I think I ought to become a Catholic."

The reaction of *Monsieur le Curé* was not at all what Monsieur Crémieux had expected. The dignitary bit his upper lip and drew forth his snuff-box; but he did not offer Monsieur Crémieux a pinch as his custom was; and this indicated that *Monsieur le Curé* was angry.

"And what will happen to the synagogue, Monsieur Crémieux? Who will look after it? To whom will it belong? To no one?"

"Why, the synagogue is mine, as long as I'm alive. My parents left it to me in their will," answered Monsieur Crémieux warmly.

Monsieur le Curé shook his head sadly. "I must say, this is the last thing I expected of you, Monsieur Crémieux. A decent, respectable citizen like you! It is wholly unexpected! Shocking, if I must be frank."

Monsieur Crémieux was astounded. But before he could utter his feelings the Curé descended on him in a torrent of words.

"You *dare* not cast away the religion of the noble people called Israel! It is the people chosen of God, the Father, concerning which it is written: 'The remnant of Israel shall not be cut off.' These are the words of the Holy Book, and you, Monsieur Crémieux, propose to do exactly that, cut off the remnant of Israel! You, a decent, respected citizen, are prepared to cast away the faith of your fathers and abandon the synagogue which is the pride of our city. No, Monsieur Crémieux. You must remain faithful to your religion, you who are, for this town, the remnant of Israel which shall not be cut off. You cannot change your faith. You must remain a Jew, and continue to guard the synagogue which your parents left to you as an inheritance." And here the Curé lifted his hand, with two admonitory fingers extended, exactly as if he were in the pulpit.

That same day the rumor spread through the town that Monsieur Crémieux wanted to cast away his religion and enter the Catholic fold. The effect was instantaneous and profound. Before the day was out, Monsieur Crémieux noted a distinct change in the attitude of the respectable citizens of the locality.

Acquaintances of his, householders of standing and reputation, walked past his shop without greeting him. Some ignored him, others ostentatiously turned their heads away. A few stopped to remonstrate with him.

"What's this we hear about you, Monsieur Crémieux? You want to stop being a Jew, and turn Catholic? It is incredible!"

On the Sunday following, the Curé preached a sermon on the subject. Monsieur Kravan, the town notary, called on Monsieur Crémieux on Monday, and did not mince matters.

"Monsieur Crémieux! What you propose is nothing more nor less than desertion! You asked *Monsieur le Curé* to aid and abet in the crime of desertion! And what is it you wish to desert? It is the beautiful old synagogue, our synagogue, which your parents left you as an inheritance."

Monsieur Crémieux was staggered. He set a high value on the good opinion of the town notary, which he had always done his best to earn.

"But, Monsieur Kravan, I don't even know how to pray in the synagogue. It's years and years since anybody prayed in it. I've forgotten completely the little I knew about my religion."

"*Cela m'est égal,* Monsieur Crémieux," said Monsieur Kravan. "I tell you that's all one. The fact is that you occupy an official position in this town. You are our only Jew; and I say you cannot leave your post. It is your duty to stand guard over our lovely old synagogue. I did not think it would come to this. I had, indeed, heard that you were negligent in your duties, that you do not look properly after your holy documents, and that you even make use of the synagogue as a storehouse. If that is true, it is most regrettable, Monsieur, most regrettable. However, I did not think it would come to this."

Something boiled up in Monsieur Crémieux.

"Monsieur Kravan! I do not think it is anybody's business what I do with my synagogue. *My* synagogue, Monsieur"—and Monsieur Crémieux smote himself passionately on the chest. "*My* synagogue, which my parents left me. I will do with that synagogue whatever I like. If I want to, I shall pray in that synagogue; and if I want to I shall keep my sabots and my crockery in it. I am not obligated, Monsieur, to listen to anyone on this subject. Moreover, let me tell you that if I want to baptize, I shall do so, and I shall not thereby relinquish any of my rights in the synagogue. Why, it has never even occurred to me to relinquish my rights in it." Monsieur Crémieux, the mild Monsieur Crémieux, became more and more excited. "I'd rather burn it first. *Oui,* Monsieur, I'd rather see it burn down. What is more, before I die I *will* burn it down. *Pas de juifs, pas de synagogue!* No Jews, no synagogue! I'll burn it down."

"In that case, Monsieur Crémieux, you will go to jail."

"Oh, will I? Because I choose to destroy my own property? Mine, mine, left to me by my sainted parents." Monsieur Crémieux's voice had risen to a squeak. "I will defend this right with my blood! I will carry the case to the highest court of France."

And with that Monsieur Crémieux turned his back on Monsieur Kravan, flung into the shop, and began to quarrel with his wife. He quarreled with her and with his daughter all evening, after the shop was closed; and when he was not quarreling with them he was striding up and down, muttering a slogan. *Pas de juifs, pas de synagogue!* No Jews, no synagogue! After a time, he took down the keys, strode across the street, and entered the synagogue. Stumbling through the vestibule, he kicked a pile of dishes out of his way, and heard with savage pleasure the sound of smashing crockery. Moonlight flooded the building—a huge desolation, with its high little windows above the women's gallery, and with its strange, towering pulpit, which somehow or other looked as if it had just been occupied by a ghostly figure. The stained glass above the Ark caught the pallid blue of the moonlight and transformed it into a web of dark hues.

Silence and emptiness! Monsieur Crémieux heard the thunder of his own footsteps crashing back upon him from the walls and pillars. He strode back and forth, from pulpit to door, from door to pulpit, and did not know what to do with himself; nor did he know why he had rushed into the synagogue. He climbed up the high pulpit and climbed down again. He went up to the Ark, drew aside the curtains, opened the creaking doors, and looked in at the forsaken Scrolls of the Law, in their dusty mantles. And suddenly an unidentifiable childhood memory stabbed him, and there flashed upon him a vision of candles and prayer-shawls, a sound of singing. He leaned his face on the Scrolls and began to weep.

"Oh, Dieu d'Israél! Oh, Dieu d'Israél!"

After a few minutes he collected himself, stood up straight, smote himself again on the bosom, and shouted: "It is *my* synagogue, is it not, God of Israel! I will not give it away to the Christians. *Non, non, Dieu d'Israél,* it is mine, it is mine!"

The moon had disappeared; the shadows which had lingered in the corners had swept forward and taken possession of the entire synagogue. He could barely make out, in the black emptiness, the outlines of the Dutch candelabra. Here and there he caught the faint glimmer of the golden lettering on the walls. Monsieur Crémieux suddenly remembered that strange evening, recurring once a year, when he and his cousin used to light all the lamps in the synagogue. What was it now? What was it? Yes! He had it! It was called *Yom Kippur,* the Day of Atonement! That was it!

Why had he remembered, he asked himself. Was it because this was perhaps the very evening? Why not? This very evening! Certainly! It had always come at this time of the year, toward the close of the summer.

Monsieur Crémieux dashed out of the synagogue and across the street. Bursting into the living room, he told his astonished wife that he would not eat dinner that evening. He would only drink a glass of water. For this was the Jewish holiday he had been wont to observe, the holiday on which one sacrificed a meal and took a glass of water instead. Having delivered himself of this information, he took a bottle of oil from the kitchen, returned to the synagogue, and laboriously filled the lamps. When he had lit them, he looked in the chest behind the Ark, and found there the prayer-shawl which his cousin had used to wear; this he draped about his shoulders, and began to march back and forth along the aisles.

He went home that night in a mood of exalted contentment, and from then on decided that this was too fine a thing to restrict to one evening in the year. He would make *Yom Kippur* whenever he wanted to. He would light the lamps, he would put on the white prayer-shawl, he would walk back and forth along the aisles whenever the mood seized him.

The good citizens of the little French town were astonished by the behavior of Monsieur Crémieux. At diminishing intervals they would see the synagogue illumined at night, and they would learn from Madame Crémieux that her husband was inside. No one tried to enter, nor would Monsieur Crémieux have admitted anyone. The last Jew, he walked back and forth as long as the lamps burned, murmuring, over and over again, *"Dieu d'Israél! Dieu d'Israél!"*

Monsieur Crémieux was as good as his word. Years passed, and the incident of his attempted apostasy was almost forgotten. But Monsieur Crémieux felt that he had not much longer to live—and he remembered. One night he went into the synagogue to "make a *Yom Kippur*," as he called it. This time he put in new, large wicks into the lamps, and filled them to overflowing. Hour after hour he walked back and forth, with the tattered prayer-shawl drawn over his shoulders, mumbling to himself. When his old legs would carry him no further, he took off the shawl, soaked it in oil, and hung it under the guttering lamps above the Ark. He did not douse the lamps before he left; he only locked and double-locked the doors of the synagogue, went home, and crawled into his bed.

Late in the night he started up. There was shouting, there was a sound of footsteps, there was a thundering on his door. He looked out through the window, and saw a great pillar of flame enveloping the synagogue. He lifted up his hand triumphantly and shouted, with his last living breath:

"Pas de Juifs, pas de synagogue!"

White Roses

WE sat one evening at a table on the Boulevard St. Michel, in the quarter which the tradition of twenty generations has made the heart of Paris, the center of its dreams, the proverb of five continents—the Latin Quarter. There were three of us, sons of the ancient Jewish people, and we talked of how the old gods were dying and no new gods were being born. The crowds poured back and forth in front of the café; young people mostly, drawn hither from all the corners of the world, young men and young women with rich hearts and empty pockets, laughing, gesticulating, arguing in a dozen languages. It was wonderful to observe how, in spite of the Babel of tongues, there seemed to be a spirit of universal understanding; for the foundation of all their discussions was for ever the same, something which made itself understood across all linguistic barriers. Here, in the midst of this sea of love, we three young Jews sat, and talked of the dying gods. Like all of our kin, we had inherited too heavy a burden from our forefathers; like all of our kin we were preoccupied with our God. Such is the way of Jews: if they are not quarreling with their God, they are lonesome for Him. Here too, where young girls paraded before us, their bodies wrapped in silk, their lips and cheeks bright with cosmetics, and tempted all who were hungry for love, we were absorbed in a discussion of the death of the gods.

"We never know the ways of God, and the instruments He chooses for his purposes. We may be sitting here, among the street girls of the Boulevard St. Michel; and God may be active in the midst of us and we completely unaware of it."

"The God of Abraham?"

"None other."

Two of us looked at the one who had made the first statement. He read incredulity in our eyes.

"Would you like me to prove it to you? Just a little indication of what I mean?" said our friend.

We nodded.

"Just a minute."

He lifted his hand and beckoned. The elderly woman whom we had seen on other days carrying her basket of flowers, appeared before us. She was a familiar figure here. She had been standing near the girls at the next table; and they had been listening to our conversation, conducted in a language they did not understand, indifferent to its content, and merely hoping that we would call them over and invite them to dine with us. The flowerwoman addressed us in French.

"You don't have to speak French," said our friend, in Yiddish, smiling. "We all understand Yiddish."

The woman looked at us, startled, and a little suspicious.

"Jews?"

"And are you a Jewess?" two of us chorused.

"I used to be," she answered, with a touch of shame.

"What? Converted?"

"God forbid!" The woman spat in horror. "I'm not sunk as low as that!"

"Then what do you mean, 'used to be'?"

"How can I call myself a Jewess?" she said, with a heartbreaking sigh. "I go out selling on the Sabbath, do business on the holy days, never see the inside of a synagogue, never hear the prayers —how can I call myself a daughter of my people?"

"How is that?"

"How? Simply enough. What am I to do? My husband is gone —they needed him in the better world. He left me with my little ones; my little ones have to be fed, haven't they? They must go to school, mustn't they? If I don't go out with my flowers on Saturdays, others will take my place, and keep it for the weekdays, too.

299

Then I'll have to fight for my route; and the waiters will chase me away. I'll be called the trouble maker—it's always the Jew who's the trouble maker, isn't it? So on Friday evenings I light my Sabbath candles, pick up my basket of flowers, and run to my beat."

"And Sabbath mornings?"

"What can I do? Only my oldest child, my boy, works. So on the Sabbath morning I have to wake him, and I have to see him take his bag of tools, and on the holy day of rest go off to the workshop. And I, the Jewish mother, wakened him for that purpose. What shall I do? Not waken him? Have him lose his job?"

"And aren't you afraid of what will happen to you in the world to come?"

"Certainly I'm afraid. I know that a day of judgment will come. Before long the great festivals will be with us, the New Year, and the Day of Atonement, when the gates of heaven are opened, and our lives are judged. But I won't take it lying down. No. I'll have my say, I'll have it out with God Himself. 'Father in heaven,' I'll say, 'it's not easy to be a Jew, especially in a big city like Paris. Maybe a Rothschild finds it easy to be a good Jew here, and to have his own private synagogue in the yard of his house. If you want me to be a good Jew, why don't you find me a decent livelihood, so that I won't have to run around with my basket, selling flowers? And if you let me run around selling flowers on the streets, you mustn't expect me to be a good, observant Jew; because I have to run around on Sabbaths and holy days, I never see the inside of a synagogue; because where I live there isn't a synagogue, there's only a church, where you wouldn't want to see me, would you? Oh, yes, I could perhaps go on the Sabbath to the synagogue on the Rue de Rivoli, but then I'd have to take a trolley, and you've forbidden us Jews to ride on the Sabbath, so rather than ride on the Sabbath, and offend you with that, I don't go to the synagogue. And that's how my Jewishness falls away from me, week after week, year after year, till there's no more Sabbath and no more festival for me.' That's what I'll tell the Judge of the world."

The woman fetched a deep sigh; and before she went she offered us a bouquet of the white roses in her basket.

White Roses

"If it weren't for these roses," she added, "I wouldn't even know there's such a thing as the Sabbath in the world."

"The roses?" asked one of us. "What have the roses to do with it?"

The woman looked down shyly, and lowered her voice, as if she were afraid that the girls at the next table would hear and understand.

"Yes, these roses. You see—all week long I sell red roses, but I've made up my mind that on Friday evenings, on the eve of the Sabbath, I'd sell only white roses; and that would remind me that it is the Sabbath, and that I'm sinning against the Sabbath."

We looked away from the woman at the crowded tables. On the bosoms of the young women with painted lips, white roses: in the hands of others, walking to and fro, alert and expectant, white roses, white as doves: white roses in the midst of gay, dissolute throngs.

The woman with the flower basket left.

"Well," said our friend, "was I wrong when I said that the God of Abraham pursues His purpose everywhere, even here, on the Boulevard St. Michel, in the midst of its lusts, in the maelstrom of its youth and passion. He is everywhere, and everywhere He finds His instruments; if it isn't a synagogue and prayers, it is a flower-woman and her roses."

And from that day on, whenever I visited the Boulevard St. Michel on a Friday evening, and saw the white roses on the bosoms of the street-girls, I remembered that it was the Sabbath; and it seemed to me that the courtesans of the Boulevard St. Michel were no longer what they were, but had become purified, had become quiet, modest brides. It seemed to me that I heard the wings of doves above the Latin Quarter, and all the tumult died into the murmur of the restful and holy Sabbath.

So the Jewish flowerwoman lit her Sabbath candles with white roses; and perhaps her benediction was just as acceptable to the God of Abraham as the ceremonies in the homes of the pious.

The Magic of the Uniform

ON a Parisian boulevard Gershon Rabinovitch, one time building and supply contractor to the Russian army in the "good old" Czarist days, ran into the former Governor of his home province and recognized him immediately in spite of his shocking attire.

Every government official whose daily bread consists of the miseries of other human beings has the cold and slippery eyes of a fish. When the Governor of Ekaterinoslav turned his on you, the temperature of your blood at once dropped ten degrees. The gray, glittering, jelly-like pupils seemed to convey just one devastating message: "If you drop dead right in front of me, it won't make the slightest difference."

Years of exile, humiliation, and want had stripped the Governor of all evidences of former glory; but the chilly, annihilating gubernatorial eyes had remained the same. Contractor and Governor stopped at the same instant, as though they had suddenly been subjected to a magnetic force.

Quite instinctively, and even though he knew he did not have to do it, Rabinovitch raised his hat and forced a humble smile to his lips; and the Governor, responding likewise to the habit of years, forced a colder film across his eyes, though he too knew that it was quite pointless. Then, passing his tongue over his withered lips, the Governor said:

"Rabinovitch the contractor, I believe."

"Yes, Your Highness," answered Rabinovitch, and for sheer joy passed his hand caressingly over his bared head. "As you see me."

The Magic of the Uniform

"Have you been here long?"

"No, Your Highness. I moved over from Berlin about eight months ago."

"Ah, you're not like one of us. Where they fling us, there we lie. You Jews always manage to adapt yourselves. If it isn't Berlin, it's Paris. We ought to take lessons from you people in refugee technique. You've got it down to a fine art. You've been practicing it for thousands of years. Not like us, ducks in a desert. You ought to teach us."

The Governor was trying to be friendly, but in his voice there was something of an official rebuke. He really did not want to play the Governor; he knew it would do him no good; he did not even like it. And the truth was that with other Jewish acquaintances he was quite human. But whenever he encountered a Jew out of the old days for the first time, the ancient relationship asserted itself, and had to be overcome all over again.

"Adapt ourselves?" repeated Rabinovitch, with a sigh. "If you can call it that. A wife, three children, a mother-in-law, and a widowed sister-in-law. The few marks I brought with me from Berlin are almost gone. And what I'm going to turn to next, I haven't the faintest idea."

The Governor was silent. He twirled the blond moustache which, miraculously, had not yet turned gray, thought awhile, and then said:

"Rabinovitch, I have a business proposition for you. A first-class proposition. There's a fortune in it." Successive films withdrew from his eyes, which, like his voice, gradually became quite human.

Rabinovitch's first reaction was naturally one of complete scepticism. If he listened at all it was because he experienced a queer pleasure in entertaining, or seeming to entertain, a business proposal from a Governor. He wrinkled his brow in sign of attention, tried to impart a fishy glitter to his eyes, and said:

"I am very curious, indeed, to hear what plans Your Highness has in mind." And even Rabinovitch's voice had taken over some of the tone which had disappeared from the Governor's.

"My plan, Monsieur Rabinovitch, is a very serious one."

The Jew was quite startled by the Monsieur.

"I suggest," went on the Governor, "that we retire to a café, sit down at a table, and discuss the matter in detail."

But Rabinovitch's pleasure in the reversed roles died as suddenly as it was born. He became impatient to hear the plan.

"Why a café, Your Highness? Tell me the outline of the idea."

"Briefly, it's this," answered the Governor. "As you know, Paris has gone crazy over Russian dishes. The Russian restaurants are full to overflowing, and there aren't enough of them. They're making money hand over fist. Well, I happen to be an expert in Russian dishes, dishes which no one in Paris, except me, even knows about. Marvelous *blintzes* and pies with fillings of all sorts which simply melt in your mouth. And then twenty varieties of *pirozhkes* which my wife, Elizavet Ivanovna, invented—her own recipes. I tell you, Monsieur Rabinovitch, we can make our fortune. All you have to do is fit out a little restaurant, and provide the initial capital. The first customer will bring a dozen the next day. All Paris will be at our doors in a week. There won't be another restaurant like ours; we shan't have a single competitor."

Quite to his astonishment Rabinovitch found himself listening with the closest attention. The business instinct in him was awakened, and drove out the last remnants of his silly pose. He said to himself: "Be damned if the man isn't talking sense." The frown on his face was now natural. He lifted the edge of his beard into his mouth and chewed on it meditatively.

"But who is going to prepare those dishes, Your Highness?" he asked. "Who's going to do the cooking?"

"What do you mean, who?" responded the Governor. "I, of course."

"But for heaven's sake, Your Highness isn't going to put on a white apron and stand at a stove baking *blintzes* for a Jew?"

"Forget that nonsense about My Highness; it's long since been driven out of my head," said the Governor, and his gray, wrinkled skin colored a little, as though he were ashamed of having capitulated so quickly. Then he added, a trifle embarrassed: "The fact is, I was always an amateur cook; and when I wanted to give my friends a special treat, I used to do the baking myself. You may not have known it, but I had a reputation as a *gourmet,* if you know what that is."

"Well, then," said Rabinovitch, coming out of his reverie, "this is worth talking over. Yes, we must sit down in a café," and he took the Governor's arm familiarly—a gesture from which His Highness did not start away.

. . .

A miracle happened. A Russian Governor had a business proposition for a Jew, and the proposition made sense. To the innumerable little foodshops of Paris, one more was added, under the name of "Ekaterinoslav Specialties." It was the Governor who insisted on this name, as an expression of patriotism.

At the rear of the restaurant the Governor stood in an alcove, a white apron over his shabby clothes, a cook's cap covering his bald spot, and prepared the dishes. His eyes were as fishy as ever; and as of old he twirled his blond moustache, which, not grayed by the years, became white with flour. Rabinovitch and he soon became accustomed to the new relationship. Indeed, there was only one minor difficulty which cropped up at the beginning and was soon disposed of. When Rabinovitch had to give the day's orders to his cook, he felt uncomfortable for want of a form of address. It was the Governor himself who noticed his embarrassment and eliminated its cause.

"Your Highness," Rabinovitch would say, "I believe we shall need today four *kuliebaks,* two with bread stuffing, two with meat, a couple of dozen *pirozhkes,* and a few *strudels.* What do you think?"

"I think the first thing to do is to drop that silly business of My Highness," said the Governor.

"I guess you're right," answered Rabinovitch. "The title doesn't seem to fit here. But we have to have some sort of order—I mean, how ought I to address you? In the regular way, with your name and your father's, Vassil Ivanovitch?"

"Just call me Kokushka," said the Governor.

"Kokushka?" exclaimed Rabinovitch. "Oh, no, I can't do that. I don't care what's happened, but after all you were once our Governor."

"Now, please," answered the Governor. "I want you to call me Kokushka. That's what we used to call cooks in Ekaterinoslav. I want it."

"If you insist," yielded Rabinovitch. "After all, what's the difference, as long as I have something to call you by. Let it be Kokushka."

And "Kokushka" it remained.

The little restaurant achieved a moderate, humdrum success. The Parisian public, Russian or native, did not make a riot round the doors of "Ekaterinoslav Specialties," as the Governor had expected. There was just a living in it, and that was enough to thank God for in those days. The Governor was the Jew's employee (it never came to a partnership) and the Jew paid the Governor his wages regularly. There was no complaint on either side. The Governor was a model employee, dependable and industrious; he came on time every morning, cooked and baked all day long, and relieved his employer in the restaurant when the latter was called away somewhere. But nothing resembling a friendship sprang up between the two men, and they did not see each other outside the restaurant. Nor could anything else have been expected. They belonged to two different worlds. The restaurant brought them together, and there the Governor became Kokushka. Outside of it he was still Your Highness. But even within the restaurant Kokushka retained the cold, fishy, inhuman eyes of the Governor. Rabinovitch observed that the white apron and the white cap imparted a new hardness to the dead light in Kokushka's eyes, and often he was quite afraid of it, though he knew that there was really nothing to fear.

"It's only Kokushka," he reassured himself. "What difference does it make what kind of eyes he's got? He does his work, I do mine. I give orders, he carries them out."

One day Kokushka came out of the kitchen, when the restaurant was empty, and approaching Rabinovitch with downcast features, proffered a request—a loan of three hundred francs. His voice was broken, his manner humble. He was like a man overtaken by a disaster.

Three hundred francs was a considerable sum for Rabinovitch no less than for Kokushka. Kokushka had never before asked for an advance on his pay; his attitude had been correct, even stiff. Indeed, Rabinovitch had been slightly astonished that Kokushka had never come to him for a favor. He had also been a little uncomfortable about it. He felt that this exaggerated correctness was meant to convey a reminder: "It's true, I'm only a cook today; but yesterday I was the Governor of a Russian province."

Now Kokushka's humility made Rabinovitch uneasy. If Kokushka could so humiliate himself, it must be a serious matter. No doubt some family misfortune. Rabinovitch's pity was stirred.

"I hope Your Highness isn't in serious trouble," he said, reverting to the official title out of sheer kindness. "I hope Your Highness's wife isn't sick."

"My wife's always sick," answered the Governor. "That isn't it. I need the money for something else. A very earnest matter. I have been given a great opportunity; and I'm afraid that if I don't act quickly someone's going to snatch it away from me." The gloomy look deepened on the Governor's face.

"Well now, that's very interesting," said Rabinovitch. "A great opportunity, you say. Couldn't we perhaps take advantage of it in partnership?"

"Why, no, it's nothing for you, Monsieur Rabinovitch," said the Governor, smiling suddenly.

"Why, how can you tell that it's not for me? Let me hear about it, Your Highness. After all, I've been in a great many businesses. Why can't we be partners in this one?"

"There's no possibility of a partnership here," said the Governor. "It's a one man affair."

"What can it possibly be?" asked Rabinovitch, bursting with curiosity.

"It's a uniform."

"A uniform?" said Rabinovitch, astounded.

"Yes, a general's uniform. It belonged to General Mikhail Nikolaievitch Marteiev, who died last week. His widow's prepared to sell it to me for three hundred francs. It's of superb workmanship, Russian throughout, made in the old days, with the Czar's own chevrons on it. That's what makes it entirely suitable for a Governor. I was unable to rescue mine when I fled from Russia."

"A general's uniform!" repeated Rabinovitch, thoroughly disappointed. "Oh, Your Highness! I thought you'd dropped that silly business."

"Silly business!" The Governor started back; his eyes filmed over, the look of deadly coldness was intensified. "Silly business!" He held himself in, and made a gesture which said, Oh, what's the use? "I don't suppose you can understand. And it isn't your business, after all. All I ask for is the loan of the three hundred francs. I give you my word of honor, the word of an officer of the Czar, that I'll work off the advance to the last sou."

Rabinovitch stared at the lean, unhappy man, whose humility sat so painfully on him, and remembered the old days, and his heart softened. "Every man has his little weakness," he thought. "Mine's a holy book of wisdom in a corner of the synagogue, and his is a general's uniform."

He scratched his head thoughtfully. "You're right," he said, "it's none of my business how you spend your money. But, Your Highness, it is a silly business, isn't it? A uniform for three hundred francs! What are you going to do with it? You're not going into the army, are you? You haven't got a regiment to command, have you?"

"Monsieur Rabinovitch, for the love of God, lend me that three hundred francs," pleaded the Governor, and smote himself over the heart. "I swear to you I'll work off every sou."

"All right, all right, I'll lend it to you, only stop hitting yourself in the chest like that," cried Rabinovitch, who felt the tears starting to his eyes.

"God will reward you!" said the Governor, in a broken voice.

.   .   .

With the acquisition of the general's uniform something happened to Kokushka, the cook, something that boded no good. It did not manifest itself in overt action. As before, Kokushka performed his duties faithfully; he was punctual and dependable. But the gubernatorial look in his eye became fixed. Beneath his cook's cap the fishlike glitter of his gray pupils became colder and more inhuman than ever. Rabinovitch, serving in the restaurant, felt their icy chill at his back. He found it harder and harder to address his employee; and he began to avoid any form of address, shying away from the familiarity of Kokushka, and refusing to make a practice of Your Highness. Besides, he no longer knew who it was that stood there, with that baleful look, baking *pirozhkes* and *strudel,* the Governor of Ekaterinoslav in all his power, or Kokushka the exile, humble and industrious.

"It's the accursed uniform," thought Rabinovitch. "No doubt about it. That's all that was missing. I didn't have troubles enough without it. And this is only the beginning. God knows where it will finish."

And he could understand what had happened. After all those years of exile and humiliation, after the hunger and loneliness of his obscure poverty, the Governor had found refuge and reassurance—in his uniform. They called that "morale." The Czar's chevrons were awakening ancient instincts and ambitions. Rabinovitch could see the Governor going home evenings, to his wretched little hotel, putting on the glorious uniform of His Imperial Majesty, and sitting down on the bed where his sick wife was doing her best to keep up with her cheap seamstress work.

The horrors and privations of the last seven or eight years had undermined her health. The first flight to Constantinople, via the Caucasus, the danger, the wretched quarters they had lived in, fourth-rate hotels where the rooms were always filled with the sweet-sour of badly washed linen—all this she had had to endure, on top of the frightful shock of the revolution. When they at last got to Paris she had taken to her bed; but even in her bed she had earned part of her keep by sewing.

At first the challenge of his wife's sickness, and still more of her courage, had made a man of the Governor. He had abandoned the silly romantic dreams which were the common resort of most of his acquaintances, he had stopped hoping for miracles, such as a world crusade to restore him and his like to power, and incidentally to "liberate Mother Russia" from the hands of the infidels. In brief, he had made up his mind to earn his living. That was how he had thrown off the wolf's clothing of the Governor, put on the sheep's clothing of a Kokushka, and gone to work for Rabinovitch the Jew. He had buried his past together with his dreams of the future; and he had been driven by a single thought: how to restore his wife to health. If he could only save up a few hundred francs, he could send her south, to the Riviera. This was the thought which had kept him at his work in the restaurant, and had kept his wife working on the clothes which were ordered from her.

Until the uniform came into the picture.

Now, every evening, when Kokushka came home, he could not wait until he had put on his uniform and seated himself on the bed. He did not speak; neither did his wife. But, lying there, and staring at him out of her pale blue eyes, she saw the curious glitter of his pupils, saw the nose standing out stronger over the tensed lips. He sat there, curling his moustache with an imperial gesture, sat there, and meditated. She knew what thoughts were passing through his mind; she knew what dreams were dancing behind those hard, glazed eyes.

"You shouldn't do that," she said, weakly, without indicating what "that" was. "You'd better wash the dishes."

The Governor did not answer. He rose from the bed and began to take off his uniform. He handled it with reverence, as if he were his own orderly. He put on his working clothes again, went to the sink, and began to wash the dishes. How long had he had the uniform on? Perhaps a quarter of an hour. But who can tell how much a man can live through in a quarter of an hour?

It was this uniform which brought the Governor and his wife to the brink of disaster.

The newspapers were suddenly filled with reports of peasant uprisings in Russia; and editorial writers broke out in a rash of prophecies; the Russian government was done for; it could not last more than a few months. In the circles frequented by the Governor there was tremendous excitement. The long-awaited miracle was at hand; the crusade was about to begin!

And one evening, when the excitement was at its most intense, the Governor put on his uniform, betook himself to the house of a friend, became drunk, and went to pay an unexpected visit to Rabinovitch, who had just finished cleaning up and was about to close. One lamp was still on when the door burst open and the heroic figure burst into the restaurant, braid and epaulets and chevrons shining, medals tinkling.

"Good God!" said Rabinovitch. "What's this?"

"This," said the Governor, "is the uniform to which my rank entitles me. And I would like you to know, Monsieur Rabinovitch," —and the emphasis on the word *Monsieur* was so abrupt, that all the medals tinkled again on the General's breast—"that I still occupy the rank which was conferred upon me by His Imperial Majesty. Until I am relieved by his authority, direct or delegated, I am the Governor of the province of Ekaterinoslav. This official title cannot be detached from me by anyone else, whatever name he may assume, or by any group, whether it call itself the Soviet or another government. As long as the continuity of Czaristic authority, vested in me, has not been broken by Czaristic retraction, I am still the Governor of Ekaterinoslav. This entitles me to certain privileges, among which is the wearing of uniform of a general of the Russian Imperial Armies, such as you now behold."

The Governor's tone was tranquil, self-assured, even a little friendly. But it was cold. This was, indeed, the tone in which he used to address Rabinovitch in the old days, the tone in which he could quietly utter a "no" which might mean death to the listener.

"By God," thought Rabinovitch, "the same ugly look, the same murderous frostiness, the same courteous smile." Aloud he said: "Why, certainly, Your Highness. But I would like to know what is going to happen to our *blintzes* and our *pirozhkes*. Is it Your Highness's opinion that we ought to advertise for another cook?"

"As far as you are concerned, Monsieur Rabinovitch," said the Governor, "it is proper to inform you that you will be held re-

sponsible for the crime of *lèse majesté,* inasmuch as you have had
the audacity to engage as cook and to address with the undignified
title of Kokushka a representative of His Imperial Majesty. The
penalties for acts of disrespect toward the duly accredited repre-
sentatives of His Imperial Majesty are prescribed in the Code of
Laws."

Rabinovitch kept his eyes fixed on the General, and continued to
smile benevolently.

"That's just the way he used to talk in Ekaterinoslav, while I
would listen with my heart in my mouth, and my life in his
hands." And for the moment it seemed to Rabinovitch that he
was dreaming. Or perhaps he was really back in the old days and
the Governor of Ekaterinoslav was standing before him, curling
his moustache with an imperial gesture, while the light gleamed
on the double-headed eagle on his epaulets. "How can you do
business with a man like that?" thought Rabinovitch, looking sadly
at Governor-Kokushka.

And then, quite suddenly, quite unexpectedly, there rose out of
the inner depths of Rabinovitch the restaurateur a tide of resentment, an accumulation of fury, the repression of twenty years and
more. His hands trembled, his lips became bloodless. He turned on
the Governor in an explosion of rage.

"Get out of here!" he yelled. "Get out, you dog's body! You filthy
animal! You're getting off too easy! Your heads should have been
chopped off long ago for the way you governed Russia! Look what
you've done to Russia, and what you've done to yourselves! You've
become cheap comedians, imitation noblemen! Get out, I say,
before I kick you out!"

It was incredible! Rabinovitch was ready to suit his action to his
words. For, as Governor-Kokushka made no move, Rabinovitch
picked up a pailful of dill pickles and emptied the contents on the
General; not content with which, he seized the General by the
scruff of the neck, marched him to the door, and flung him into
the street.

"He's going to hold me responsible for the crime of *lèse majesté!*"
gasped Rabinovitch. "He's going to invoke the penalties duly pre-

scribed by the Code." He opened the door and howled after the General: "Why, you drunken bum, you old booze-hound, do you think these are the old days, when you could steal and swindle without being held to accountability? We're living in France, thank God! You dog's body, you! I gave you the money for that uniform. You haven't returned the money. The uniform's mine!"

. . .

"Ekaterinoslav Specialties" was closed for the next two days. The excitement had been too much for Rabinovitch. He lay in bed, groaning, and his wife, his mother-in-law, and his sister-in-law took turns in applying cold compresses to his heart. The Governor stayed home too, with his sick wife. He was without a job, without hope for the future; all he had was a general's uniform to which, in spite of frequent washings, there clung the sour smell of pickles.

On the morning of the third day Rabinovitch went back to the restaurant and found standing at the door, a pitiful, broken figure, with downcast eyes and wilted moustaches, Kokushka.

Rabinovitch would not even talk to him. He put the key into the door furiously; but before he had opened the door, Kokushka had taken hold of his elbow, timidly.

"Monsieur Rabinovitch, forgive me, I implore you. I must have taken leave of my senses. I can't explain my crazy behavior any other way. Forgive me, in God's name; forgive and forget, and take me back as your cook."

Rabinovitch suppressed the sudden pang of compassion which shot through him. No, he could not forgive or forget.

"You get out of here!" he said. "I don't want to have anything more to do with you. Get out!"

"Monsieur Rabinovitch! In the name of God! Have pity on a broken man! I have a sick wife at home."

Rabinovitch had never heard words like these from the Governor. The pang of compassion returned, stronger than before. He felt his resentment melting away, and he was furious with himself for his own softness. He had to think of his business. He had to think of his health.

"Do you want me to start again with a Russian Governor?" he asked. "Who knows what you'll do tomorrow? It's impossible to work with you. What's more," he added, desperately and untruthfully, "I've hired a new cook."

The Governor shrank away. He turned and shuffled off. Rabinovitch went angrily into the restaurant, not at all sure he had done the right thing. An hour later the Governor was back, this time with his sick wife, whose yellow face looked as if it had drawn into itself the pallor and sordidness of all the wretched hotel rooms in which she had lived in the last six years. It was she who approached Rabinovitch and spoke, while her husband lingered in the background like a terrified boy.

"Monsieur Rabinovitch! You are a human being! What can I say, what can I do? My husband behaved like an idiot. I know it. It's the uniform that's to blame; it's the miserable uniform. I asked him the very first day: 'What do you want that for?' But I promise you, Monsieur Rabinovitch, it won't happen again. He swore it to me on his knees, it won't happen again. Take him back, Monsieur Rabinovitch, for my sake. You're a man, you understand things."

"Yes, yes, I understand things," spluttered Rabinovitch. "But how am I to blame? Tomorrow the whole business may start again."

"No, no, it won't," said the Governor, without lifting his head. "It will never happen again."

"What assurance have I got that it won't happen again?" asked Rabinovitch, fiercely.

"Insult me, Monsieur Rabinovitch; insult me, humiliate me. For God's sake, insult me, the Governor of Ekaterinoslav! Call me Kokushka, ask me to wash the slop pails, degrade me, I implore you, Monsieur Rabinovitch!"

"But why should I insult you and humiliate you?" yelled Rabinovitch. "I don't want to insult you. Why should I insult you?"

"But what am I to do?" pleaded the Governor. "Tell me what I am to do. You see I've committed a great folly. Help me, help the son of an unfortunate and broken people."

"But I am also the son of an unfortunate and broken people," wailed Rabinovitch. "How am I to blame if misfortune has fallen on Russia? Are you going to judge me for that? Did I want it? I am also the son of a persecuted people. Can I help it if a great calamity has befallen you?"

"Yes, I know, I know," said the Governor. "But you're used to misfortune, and we're not. You've had the practice of it for thousands of years—thousands of years of exile and wandering. We're new to it. We don't know how to manage. You ought to help us, teach us."

"But how am I going to teach you if you take three hundred francs and throw them out on a uniform? You've got a sick wife at home, and instead of using the money to cure her, you spend it on a uniform. You don't want to learn. You're unteachable! All you think about is uniforms, and the Czar's chevrons, and jobs which bring you lots of money without any work. You don't want to learn."

"It's true, it's true," moaned the Governor's wife. "And it's the uniform that's to blame." She turned on her husband. "Didn't I tell you immediately to throw it away? Didn't I tell you it would get us all into trouble?"

The Governor was miserably silent for a moment. Then he beat his bosom and groaned: *"Durak! Durak!* Fool! Fool!"

The wretchedness gathering in Rabinovitch's heart became too much for him. What could you do? The man couldn't help hankering after his uniform. "My God's in the synagogue and the sacred books, and his God's in his uniform!" he thought.

And if he was going to be frank with himself, Rabinovitch would admit that he needed the Governor. He was a good cook; and good cooks were rare. Even if he found another, he would not get rid of the Governor, for the latter would surely come back, and haunt his doorstep. And perhaps the man was cured. . . .

His resentment was quite dead. After all, this was no ordinary man—a Governor of Ekaterinoslav.

"Do you know what?" he suggested at last. "If you give me the uniform to take care of, you can have your job back. Because till you got the uniform there was absolutely nothing wrong with you.

You did your work, you came on time, I hadn't the smallest complaint to make. It's the uniform that's to blame. Your own wife says so. You go home, bring me the uniform, and let me hold it—and I'll give you another chance."

The Governor bit his lips, frowned savagely, shifted his weight from foot to foot. A terrible inward struggle was taking place. Then, lifting his eyes, he saw his wife's yellow, drawn face, her spare, fading figure, and her look of supplication. That decided it. Without saying a word, he motioned to her, and they left the restaurant.

An hour later Kokushka was back. He carried under his arm a carefully tied parcel, which he handed silently to Rabinovitch. And, strangely enough, the latter observed that the glitter in the fish-eyes had been replaced by a certain softness. Rabinovitch was so deeply touched that he took the Governor's arm.

"I tell you, Your Highness," he said, affectionately, "a uniform is absolutely nothing. Today you've got it, tomorrow you haven't. The thing that matters is what's under the uniform," and Rabinovitch pointed to his heart. "If a man's heart is in the right place, he'll do the right thing, with or without a uniform, whether he's a Governor who administers a province or a cook who prepares meals for hungry people. Maybe the cook can do more good than the Governor. What good's a Governor anyhow? It's better to be ruled than to rule. Ruling is a sinful business, and the desire to rule is wickedness, while no sin ever came out of good cooking."

The Governor thought it over.

"Monsieur Rabinovitch! You're right! So help me God, you're right. But be careful with my uniform, won't you? You never know but what it might come in handy again!"

"There's nothing to be done with him," sighed Rabinovitch, inwardly. "I've got my ways, he's got his! A gentile's always thinking of ruling people! And he wants to learn the art and technique of exile!"

He shook his head, but said nothing to the Governor.

Dust to Dust

TO right and left on the table stood two shining porcelain demons, such as the Chinese station at the entrance of their temples to frighten evil spirits away. The demons had human heads, with wide open, distorted mouths and long, protruding tongues; their fingers terminated in sharp, curving nails. And between the two heads glittered a third, that of old Neufeld, the antiquarian. You would have taken him for a companion piece; for he was all forehead and skull, and the taut yellow skin threw back the light from polished curves. Only a few hairs clung behind the ears, and even they would bristle sometimes, so that they looked like the horns of the Chinese demons.

On tables and chairs, on the floor and on boxes, were heaped old Neufeld's treasures: Japanese vases, antique swords, bronze figurines, paintings, colored silks and satins, period furniture, and costumes of all epochs whose wearers had died long, long ago.

Old Neufeld sat fondling a Chinese bowl, passing his fingers over it as if it were a living thing and holding it now and again to his withered cheek to feel its coolness. He smelt it, tasted it with his tongue, to try it with all his senses. His red eyes glowed with an inward light, and his face became suffused with the loving absorption which may be seen sometimes on the face of a musician when the instrument responds perfectly to his touch.

"The Chinese, the Chinese!" he croaked. "The shades of green they conjured up! What other people had such a feeling for color? I tell you this is authentic cucumber green, stolen from nature herself. They mixed no colors; they took the essence out of grassy growths, and nobody knows how they did it."

A young man sat at another table, Bloom, once Neufeld's errand boy, now his partner.

"What do I care whether it's cucumber green or potato green," he answered impatiently. "You can't make a living out of it, and that's all that matters. Before you can sell one of your authentic Chinese porcelains your stomach will fold up. The Chinese were a great people, and nobody can imitate their colors; but how does that help you to pay the rent? Especially here, in the heart of New York. You give me good Bohemian glass, and modern Japanese trays, and porcelains which you can get from the factory whenever you like and sell at a good price, and you can keep your green antiquities."

It was not the first time that this kind of talk had passed between them; and now, as always on such occasions, old Neufeld was beside himself with anger.

"Don't you dare to talk to me like that! I won't listen to you. Modern porcelains, indeed! And why not pots and pans and toilet bowls? Only a man without taste, a complete ignoramus, could talk like that. A dealer in antiques is a scholar, do you understand? An artist. Even a scientist. Because it's art and science rolled into one. And what about feeling? Look at this." He held out the Chinese bowl with a dramatic gesture. "Think of the thousands of the dead who have looked on this, touched it! Think of the labor and skill that went into it! Princes looked on it and were delighted. It was the companion of kings. It belongs to the authentic period of the Mings. Ying Sheng the poet has written about it. Poets brought lotus flowers to place on it, while they sang their delicate love songs. Look at the shape of it, like the silhouette of a woman's breast; and the color of it! There isn't a man alive today who can reproduce the form or the color. And here you come babbling to me about your filthy modern crockery."

Bloom was not offended. He yawned and answered:

"That's all very pretty, Mr. Neufeld, but it's not going to fill my pocket or even get me a loaf of bread. What's the good of talking to my butcher about Mings and Shmings and Ching-Chung-Chang periods. It takes you years to pick up a piece like that, and years to sell it. You pay through the nose for it, then you have to sell it for a song. That is, if you can sell it at all. People have no understanding of such things; or if they have understanding they haven't a cent to bless themselves. They'll come and admire and say it's wonderful—and where does that get you? And then at last, when you manage to get rid of a piece to someone, you go blue in the face before you find another. I'm asking you, what kind of business is that, with your Ching-Chang-Chungs?"

Old Neufeld gnashed his teeth, and clung to the Chinese bowl as if his young partner had designs on it.

"If people want to sell spittoons and cheap Japanese crockery, they're welcome to it," he stuttered. "They're ignoramuses, boors, guttersnipes—I won't have anything to do with them. I'm a representative and lover of the arts, do you understand? Let them buy, or let them keep their dirty money; I'm not going to change my life for them."

Young Bloom shrugged his shoulders. What was the use of going over these arguments again? If he had listened to the old man the shop would have been closed long ago. But he had his section of the shop, which the old man ignored: the section where he sold his "Japanese crockery," his imitation Mainz porcelains, cheap bronzes, and so-called period pieces. At first Bloom had made these purchases furtively and had hidden the wares, producing them only when the old man was out and when he thought he could make a sale. Gradually he had become bolder. When someone came puttering around in the shop, and pulled a long face over the prices of authentic antiques, Bloom had produced, from the back, one of his fakes, which looked more authentic than the real antique, and sold for less than one tenth of the price. Even so there was a handsome profit on it. And had it not been for such sales, there would not have been enough for the rent.

Old Neufeld, turning his back contemptuously on these transactions, was powerless to prevent them. So the "illegitimate" business had overtaken the honest business, and old Neufeld saw his reputation dwindling. He saw first a shelf, then half a wall, then a whole wall, devoted to the vulgar, imitation "art" products which were turned out by modern factories. Occasionally he went into a rage; but always on the first of the month, when the rent was paid out of young Bloom's section of the shop, he was silent. The scholarly experts, most of them, as Bloom correctly pointed out, as penniless as they were erudite, who used to frequent the place, dropped off. They could not bear to look on the display of cut glass, dishes, bronzes and other respectable, commonplace wares which Bloom placed side by side with the treasures of the past. They were just as much hurt by the sacrilege as was old Neufeld; and unlike him they did not have to tolerate it.

And thus, month by month, the shiny brasses, bronzes and glasses pushed out the old Chinese dragons, the Persian bowls and the oriental silks, crowded them into a corner, as life crowds death into a corner. The time came when the genuine antiques were the intruders, the newcomers the masters. And old Neufeld, for all his rage, could see the end approaching, and in his heart admitted that young Bloom understood the world of reality more intimately than he.

Why be obstinate about it? he asked himself. I'll give these people what they want. I'll go in for pots and pans, just like Bloom.

"You're perfectly right," he said one day to Bloom. "There's no call these days for decent stuff. I'm going to sell out the remainder of that—that—stock"—and he cast an angry glance at his Turkish swords, his Spanish and Italian shawls, his Saxony porcelains and French bronzes, his oriental demons and Renaissance bas reliefs, pushed into the corners of the store—"I'm going to get rid of them and devote myself to your spittoons."

"Good for you!" exclaimed Bloom. "You should have done it long ago. In the old days"—he meant in the days before he entered the business—"when rents were low, and it cost next to nothing to live, a man could amuse himself with antiques. But today!" He whistled. "It's no good trying to make a pleasure of your business. You can't afford it. It's another world."

Dust to Dust

Old Neufeld shook his fist at the antiques. "I'll finish you off!" he muttered. "There's nothing to be got out of you."

But it was easier said than done. The old man's resolution carried him no further than the promise. When it came to the actual selling of the goods, on which he had reduced the price far below the original cost, he found himself unable to tear himself away from his possessions. And, queerly enough, the less he asked for a genuine piece, the smaller was the esteem in which the prospective customer held it.

"This sword?" he said. "Why, this was the sword worn by Mehmet Ali the Great, when he set out to take Jerusalem from the Christian infidels. And these beads, on the filigree of the scabbard, were worked by his favorite slave girl, the daughter of a Mongolian Khan. Every bead was washed in her tears before she set it in the filigree; she pricked her fingers, so as to color the beads with blood. No, no, come to think of it, I'd rather not sell this piece."

And he took back the sword, and clutched it to his bosom, stroking the scabbard as if it were the head of a beloved child.

"What? Twenty-five dollars for that tray and porcelain tea service? Do you know what that is? Genuine Empire! Napoleon took his last cup of tea from it before he started out on the retreat from Moscow. I shan't sell it, that's all."

And it was no better when it came to his Renaissance silks.

"This piece?" he asked. "It was woven by a master to the accompaniment of music. There's no more silk like this in the world today. Savonarola nearly burned it at the Burning of the Vanities. Leonardo da Vinci happened to be present and snatched the piece from the flames; that's why the edge is cut off—the flames got to that point. 'Burn everything,' Leonardo said to Savonarola, 'but not that.' Titian inherited this piece of silk. He draped his daughter in it when he painted her portrait. Now do you understand what that piece of silk is?"

But it was so with everything he offered for sale. The more hopeless the prospect, the more precious became the object. He felt its soul, he remembered the hands through which it had passed; and

321

it seemed to him that all those who had been in contact with the object pleaded with him not to shame them and not to consign the keeping of their memories to brutish and uncomprehending owners. Kings, princes, khans, sultans, sultanas, and slaves were at his mercy.

And as against this, whenever he tried to sell a vulgar modern piece, without shape or spirit, and without a history, there was nothing for him to talk about. The flashy surfaces and dead lines betrayed the machines from which they had just emerged: no past, no soul, no memories. Perfunctorily he offered a young woman a cut glass beaker, and when she hesitated, he brought forth eagerly, from its corner, a glowing Persian drinking cup.

"Now that's something," he crowed. "Hafiz, the greatest of the Persian poets, drank from this cup, and what you see here are verses he wrote in honor of this cup. Only it's not for sale," he added, hastily. "I was just showing it to you."

The young woman stared and turned up her nose. The drinking cup looked old; it was dusty; no doubt full of microbes, too. From the drinking cup her eyes wandered to the queer collection in the corners of the store, bent old swords, dragons, six-headed snakes. She had never heard of Hafiz, and did not know why a Persian poet should be of any importance. She was furnishing a new home —a great many customers were young women, newlyweds, who were furnishing homes—and she wanted it bright and modern and proper, with things that were recognizable and intelligible. Those weird-looking objects on which the old man's eyes rested so lovingly were repulsive to her. They spoiled the whole shop.

Young Bloom began to understand that Neufeld did not really intend to part from his treasures. Indeed, he could not; they were too much part of him. And the "treasures," together with their owner, were becoming a burden. Not only that they took up space; they were a nuisance. They interfered with the development of the shop. They brought a musty smell, literally and figuratively, into the place. The bright, snappy young women who were furnishing homes for the first time were offended or repelled by these oddities, as well as by queer old Neufeld's passionate discourses on them.

Dust to Dust

The break-up began when Bloom told his old partner that he would have to get rid of the two Chinese demons.

"You mean the demons which stood at the entrance of the Temple at Mukden, and kept away the evil spirits?" asked the old man, scarcely believing his ears.

"Those are just the ones I mean," said Bloom, dryly. "It was all right to use them for frightening off evil spirits; but the damned trouble is that they're frightening pretty young women away from our shop."

Neufeld stood like one stunned. What next, he asked himself. And he got his answer soon. It was no use, the young man told him, trying to maintain a double character in the shop. Either it was a modern art shop, where people found the kind of furnishings their friends had, or else it was a museum, and one didn't make a living out of a museum. In short, one of them could stay in the place and make it what he wanted; but not both.

The implication was only too clear. How could old Neufeld stay, when his "department" was not earning enough for the lighting and heating? After a few quarrels they reached an agreement. Old Neufeld sold out his interest. Bloom remained in possession, and the old man found himself a cellar on a near-by side street, where he paid a trifling rent and could install his cot. To this new location he transferred, as tenderly as a father carrying his sick children, or as a cat moving her tiny kittens, his demons and swords and porcelains and silks and bowls. And here, indeed, they were at home; for the dust gathered on them quickly, the darkness sheltered them; and when a few weeks had passed one would have believed that antiquities and owner had been living here a hundred years.

Old Neufeld was soon forgotten. One by one the customers or cronies who had known him in happier days were carried off to the cemetery. The young people who had seen him in the modern shop did not even ask after him. Old Neufeld missed neither friends nor customers. He walked to and fro among his possessions, his dusty, dinted hat on his head, his clothes becoming more and more tattered, and he himself becoming more and more like one of his queerer antiques.

323

Children of Abraham

He seldom ventured out. The world outside was raw, brutal, vulgar. Here in the cellar a thousand memories filled his days and nights. He lived in the palaces which his antiques had once adorned, conversed with the exotic characters who had left their impress on them. When someone came in, bringing with him a breath of the noisy, heartless, colorless and soulless present, old Neufeld felt ill at ease; he spoke his own language, pursued his own fantasies, which others could not understand.

He was without family; his wife, whom he scarcely remembered, had left him no children. He did not know whether his brothers and sisters were still living; and if they were, he had no idea where. Wife, children, brothers, sisters—all were represented by his antiques. He did not do any selling; the monthly installments from young Bloom sufficed for rent and food. At the back of the cellar, next to his cot, he kept an oil stove on which he cooked his meals. One lamp sufficed for him, and he kept it burning from morning till night; had it not been for the food he had to go out and buy, he would have forgotten what daylight looked like.

Winter came, and he spent most of his time in bed, covered with priceless old stuffs, Renaissance shawls, eastern brocades and priestly vestments. The dead became increasingly vivid to him; he saw little Chinese princesses, in tiny golden shoes, their heads modestly lowered, tripping among his antiques, putting lotuses into the vases they loved; he saw Arab chieftains striding toward the spears standing in the corner, lifting them up, brandishing them furiously and silently, before they set out for the reconquest of Jerusalem; he saw their Indian slaves fastening their swords about them. The aristocracies of later ages and other lands mingled with them, ladies in crinolines sipping tea daintily from Mayence porcelain cups, and young couples in buckram and velvet treading a measure to the sound of invisible flutes. Monks in long black mantles stood motionless, holding open books before their eyes; and wisps of incense curled out of the mouths of the Chinese dragons and formed a bluish canopy over the strange assembly; while in one corner the Persian poet Hafiz sat, and drained his beaker while he indited a love song.

324

One day the outside door of the cellar remained tight shut. It was not noticed until the afternoon, when one of the last surviving customers of former times happened to pass that way and thought of looking in on the queer old antiquarian. He knocked, received no answer, and went off, shrugging. Coming that way the next day, he tried the door again, and this time decided to inform young Bloom.

They broke in, and found old Neufeld on his bed, rigid in death, and looking like a Chinese mummy. His body was covered with shawls, dalmatics and silken scarves. The Chinese demons stood guard over him, and a spider had begun to weave its web between a corner of the cot and the near-by wall; some of the strands were already fastened on the yellow face of the dead antiquarian.

The Quiet Garden

WHEN old Simon died, his two sons, Notte and Anshel, took an oath at the grave-side that they would always look after their mother and that they would remember their father as long as they lived.

"Don't worry, Dad," cried Notte, to the dead man. "We'll make arrangements for Mom."

Notte's wife, the dead man's older daughter-in-law, was heartened by her husband's promise, and felt she could ask something in return. She cried into the open coffin:

"When you reach heaven, put in a word for your little grandson. He's my only child."

She had something more to say, but was interrupted by the second daughter-in-law, Anshel's wife, who called out:

"And not only for her boy. Put in a good word for all your children, and for all their children, too."

A pious woman who was not one of the mourners, but who happened to be in the cemetery at the moment, raised her voice:

"And why only for his children and their children? Let him plead in heaven for all good people, all over the world, and especially for the young people who have to go to war. Let him plead for them, so that no bullet may hit them." And the stranger pushed her way to the grave-side as if determined to make use of an unexpected opportunity to get a message into the world above.

I do not know whether little Simon ever delivered the messages entrusted to him by the living at his grave-side. But it is quite certain that he heard them, for at the words "We'll make arrangements for Mom" a faint smile touched the dead lips, and there was a perceptible bristling of the stiff hairs of his moustache. The smile was still visible when they closed the coffin, preparatory to lowering it into the grave. So he had smiled in life, too, when his older son, who was "well-to-do," had promised him that "If anything happens to you, God forbid, we'll make arrangements for Mom."

Out of his village in Poland, Simon had brought with him nothing but his two bony hands, his smile, his wife Nettie—a trusted and loving comrade as lean and frail as himself—and his two little boys, Notte and Anshel. The day after his arrival Simon had gone to work, and he had not stopped till the day before his death. And when there was no work at his trade, he worked at worrying; for idleness was wearisome to him, and he could not bear it. Even Sabbaths and holidays were a weariness to him, because he longed for his needle and scissors as though they had become a part of his body and he did not feel himself without them.

It was true that during the week he longed for the Sabbath, so that he might rest. But when the Sabbath came, and Simon had had a good night's sleep, he did not know what to do with himself. He was bored. He had no friends, he had no one to visit or receive. So he would stand at the window throughout the afternoon, watching for the return of the stars which announced the ending of the Sabbath.

"What are you looking for?" his wife asked him. "What are you waiting for?"

"I want to be at work again. The Sabbath is too long."

So the years passed for little Simon. The children left the home early, fended for themselves, and he was left alone with good, faithful Nettie. Evenings, summer and winter, they sat in the kitchen. The parlor was always neat and clean, with pictures on the wall. No one went in during the day, but at night it was their bedroom. Their life was passed in the tiny kitchen. There they ate, and there they sat, mostly in silence. Every now and again they would recall the village of their birth.

"Do you remember Long Sam, in the old country?" the old man asked suddenly.

"You mean Long Sam whose daughter ran away with a soldier?"

"Yes, Long Sam whose daughter ran away with a soldier?"

"Why did you think of Long Sam?"

"I don't know. Just so."

Or else it was:

"Do you remember the back alley?"

"You mean the back alley where Aunt Deborah lived?"

"Yes, the back alley where Aunt Deborah lived."

"And where the pump stood, and where you went Saturday afternoons to get fresh water?"

"Yes, where the pump stood and you went Saturday afternoons to get fresh water."

"Why did you think of the back alley?"

"Don't know. Just so."

Now and again one of the boys would remember his parents, and suddenly appear in the kitchen.

"Look, Nettie! Look who's here. Our Notte. I'd as soon have expected the Messiah. Notte! How are you? How's your wife, how's the little one?"

"Everyone's fine, Dad."

"Notte, won't you have a glass of red beet borscht? Remember, you always used to like my borscht."

"Dad, are you still working in the Brooklyn shop?"

"What else shall I do? You've got to make a living, haven't you?"

"He's not very strong," says the mother, with a sigh. "He wakes up in the night because his side hurts him."

"Don't you worry, Dad. We'll make arrangements. I'll talk it over with Anshel. You won't have to work in your old age."

Little Simon smiled; it was that faint, pale smile which was seen on his lips before they sealed up the coffin.

Another half year would pass without a glimpse of either of the children. The old people sat in the kitchen. Once they made up their minds to venture out on a visit to one of their sons; but they lost their way.

"Well," said the old man, when they had found their way home, "we'll try again next Passover."

Then another half year passed and the second son would appear. "Still working in the shop, Dad?"

"What else shall I do? Got to make a living for me and mother."

"Don't you worry. We'll make arrangements."

So it went on, till word was brought to the children that their father was dead.

He died as quietly as he had lived. One car followed the hearse, carrying the widow, her two sons and their wives. And the two daughters-in-law gave little Simon their messages to take to heaven, because their husbands had promised "to make arrangements for Mom."

Old Nettie stood at the grave-side and wept. She gave her husband no message for the other world, did not beg him to intercede for her. She stood weeping dumbly and saw through her tears the earth being shoveled over her husband. When everything had been done for little Simon, according to law and custom, when the last prayers had been said, the last rites performed, old Nettie remained standing there, her arms outstretched. The children came to lead her away; she looked around naïvely, with the patient, dull eyes of an animal, and asked: "Where?"

Her two sons soothed her: "You come with us. We'll make all arrangements."

So anxious was each son to have his mother stay in his home that it almost came to a quarrel at the cemetery gates. But for the first week, the week of mourning, she was with her older son, Notte, who was a salesman by profession and better off than Anshel. When that week was over, she was, for the next eight days, the guest of Anshel. Then she went back to Notte, for another week, after which she was claimed by Anshel. Thus she shuttled back and forth for a time, till the sons began "to make arrangements" with an old folks' home to take her in permanently. But before the application was accepted she had gone off quietly to join her husband.

It was no longer possible to get the same or an adjoining lot for her. Everything had been sold out. Besides, the area in which little Simon was buried was a trifle too expensive for a mere woman. She was therefore put to rest in a new, remote section of the cemetery, where lots were cheaper. Thus they slept their eternal sleep separately, he among men he did not know, in the more expensive section, she among women she did not know, in the cheaper section.

As they had been forgotten in life, they were forgotten in death. They were entered on the roster of "the unvisited," "the unremembered," and of their portion in the living world nothing remained but the heap of earth on their bodies and the patch of sky over that.

More they did not need. In winter all the graves disappeared under a mantle of snow; but when the spring sun removed the white covering, their graves too were exposed. The fresh wind carried the seed dust from the flowers on the graves of the rich to those of the poor. In the daytime the sun warmed the errant seeds, in the night time the rain sank in on them. Yellow daisies, bluish waterlilies, and dark-eyed jasmine blossomed above Simon and Nettie, lying apart from each other. A quiet garden, tended by the hand of nature, enclosed them both.

Sometimes the two brothers, Notte and Anshel, would meet by accident in a crowded subway car, or would run into each other at a meeting.

"Hello, Notte!"

"Hello, Anshel!"

"Say, we ought to pay a visit to the cemetery to see what the old folks are doing."

"You're right. We certainly ought. How about a week next Sunday? We could meet at Brooklyn Bridge and ride out together."

"Right! A week next Sunday. Don't forget."

Neither took the other seriously, neither turned up "a week next Sunday." They had more important matters to attend to. Years went by, and the graves of Simon and Nettie, unnoticed by any living eye, slept through the winters and blossomed quietly in the summers.

The Quiet Garden

After many years it happened that one of the brothers came out on a summer day to this cemetery. A fellow-member of his fraternal organization was being buried here, and attendance at the funeral was compulsory under penalty of a fine. It occurred then to the son of Simon and Nettie that he might as well look up the graves of his parents. The mother's he could not find; but after a long search he came across the little marker on the grave of his father, and he stood there, astounded and frightened: what secret and silent hand had planted this garden on his father's grave?

It did not occur to him that the quiet wind and the loving earth forgot no one, not even the little tailor.

Fathers-in-Law

OLD Glickstein, whom the East Side knew familiarly as "the grandfather," had not always had the same bitter and contemptuous attitude toward American radicalism and its future. Many years before, when he had been accounted one of the most brilliant orators and most active spirits in "the movement," his estimate of its worth had been very different. But this had declined with his own reputation, which was now based entirely on his past. And he affected to regret his own record, for when anyone reminded him of the days of his glory, he made a deprecatory gesture and said, angrily: "That's enough, now!" He was, of course, glad of the opportunity to make the gesture, and to exclaim "That's enough, now!"

Glickstein's own children were to blame for his embitterment and despair. In public he poured out the vials of his wrath and his immeasurable contempt on "the big shots," the parvenus who had taken over the movement, had betrayed and degraded it, so that there was nothing left for a pure spirit like himself but "to leave the field of battle." In private he was quite clear as to the real causes of his disastrous decline, namely, his children.

For actually, while he spoke derisively of "these newfangled parlor pinks," who were as ignorant as they were pusillanimous, and as hypocritical as they were egotistic, he would not quite relinquish some degree of credit for having been their teacher. If someone mentioned in his presence the name of one of the new "leaders," "the grandfather" would crow: "That man? Why, I was the one who taught him the theories of Bakunin and Kropotkin. Whatever he knows he owes to me!" He had, indeed, been the teacher of an entire generation; it was not his fault if his pupils had declined from his lofty standards.

Of his own children, however, he could not even say that he had been their teacher. To begin with, he had never had the time for it. His days had been spent in cafés and at meetings, at conventions and conferences. Apart from the matter of time, he had never been interested in his own children. He had left their upbringing to their mother; that was her business. And she, though she was the wife of the well-known public worker and had never (so it was whispered) submitted to the indignity of a formal marriage ceremony, but had become his common-law wife in vindication of the purity of their love, turned out to be an exceedingly ordinary mother; she loved her children as every ordinary mother does and let them have their own way, even when they showed an alarming interest in religion.

It must be admitted, too, that the children of the great Glickstein were not particularly interesting. First there came an uninterrupted row of daughters, who shot up with unaccountable rapidity, like strange watery growths. Glickstein always referred to them as "onions," for a mysterious reason which he never explained. In their childhood their attitude toward him was one of fear rather than respect. Glickstein had a voice which had originally been deep and resonant, but which excessive oratory had cracked and hoarsened, so that it gave forth the terrifying tremolo of an overused trumpet. He had enormous black eyebrows which completely overshadowed his eyes. His face was clean shaven, so that his nose stood forth from it without any distracting substructure. His build, too, was impressive; so that for children the first reaction was one of fear. On the rare occasions when he would be home, he would stride about with his hands thrust deep into his trouser pockets; and he had one phrase for the family: "I want quiet!" When they heard that phrase, uttered in the deep, cracked tremolo issuing from under the commanding beak, there was quiet. The laughter of the children, the chattering of the mother, came to an abrupt end. And if it happened that the phrase failed, once in a way, it was followed by a single, tremendous word: "Sarah!" That settled it. "Sarah!" was the ultimatum.

All this lasted through the years when the children were at school. Then a change began. The first girl graduated, found a job as a stenographer, and contributed seven dollars of her salary toward the upkeep of the house; the remainder she kept for clothes and pocket money. The second girl went to work in a millinery shop and also contributed something toward the upkeep of the house. Before long Glickstein began to feel that he was not lord and master in his own house; there were others sharing the responsibility and demanding a share in the authority. Without putting it into words, they presented him with an alternative; they could move to another home, where the imperious "I want quiet" would not fall on their ears. The unspoken argument sank home.

The girls had never understood what their father's occupation was and what he made a living from. Their mother had tried to explain to them that their father was "a great man," "a public figure," "a leader." The words left no particular impression. If their father was "a great man," then "a great man" was a form of occupation, a trade like any other. They would have preferred a more familiar and more impressive occupation; they would have liked to be able to tell their friends that their father was a manufacturer, or a storekeeper. One of them, the milliner, feeling uncomfortable at having to describe her father's business as that of "a great man," represented him to her boy friend as a landlord. She thought this more impressive, and more likely to win her boy friend's respect; nor was she mistaken.

The boys who followed in the Glickstein family, after the row of girls, were more interesting. The youngest of them was particularly promising. By the time he reached high school age his father mapped out for him the career of poet. The boy was quiet, thoughtful, and shy; he took after his mother in appearance and spirit. But Glickstein sustained the greatest shock of his life when, one evening, his son reproached him with never attending temple services and never making the Friday evening benediction at table, like the fathers of his boy friends.

"You aren't a good Jew," said the boy, firmly. "A Jew attends temple and makes the benediction every Friday evening."

"Who told you that? Who told you that?" asked the father in his cracked baritone. And as always when something disturbing happened in the house he let out a trumpet call:

"Sarah! Sarah!"

Sarah happened to be busy in the kitchen at the moment. When the trumpet peal came to her ears she knew that a crisis was at hand, and she came running in with perspiring face and rolled-up sleeves.

"What's the matter?" she asked, terrified.

"Go on now, tell your mother what you told me," stormed Glickstein. "Tell her. Repeat every word."

Falteringly, the boy said:

"I told pop he isn't a Jew. A Jew goes to temple and makes the benediction every Friday night."

"Do you hear that, Sarah? Do you hear it?" thundered Glickstein.

"What's so terrible about it?" asked Mrs. Glickstein. "You know what boys are? They hear something in a friend's house, and they repeat it."

"What's so terrible about that!" mimicked Glickstein in despair. "What's so terrible about that! I'm not a Jew because I don't go to temple and I don't make the benediction on Friday night. That's nothing to you!"

"Well, what harm would it do you if you went to temple once in a while, for the boy's sake, or if you stayed home Friday evenings, so that the children could stay home instead of being always with strangers?" Ancient longings spoke out of Mrs. Glickstein, also the cumulative effect of receiving most of her household money from her daughters instead of from her husband.

"What's that you said?" asked Mr. Glickstein. "Did you say temple to me? Did you suggest that I attend temple services?

335

Children of Abraham

Have you forgotten who I am?" And Mr. Glickstein took off the glasses which he had had to use of late, and worked his tremendous eyebrows up and down. The habit of years asserted itself in Mrs. Glickstein, and she shrank from her husband.

"I didn't say anything," she stammered. "I only said, for the boy's sake—I mean—I didn't say anything. You never went to temple, and there's no reason why you should go now."

"And to think," said Mr. Glickstein, "that my life has been spent with this woman!"

Mr. Glickstein had not noticed how his wife, year after year, had yielded to her children and had permitted, or even encouraged, the infiltration of the Jewish religious atmosphere into his home. It had begun with the cooking. Whenever a Jewish festival came round, there would be on the table the appropriate dishes—dumplings, *matzoth,* or *pirogens.* Whatever Mr. Glickstein's views on Jewish ritual, he had never entertained any distaste for the appropriate dishes. On the contrary, he had always enjoyed them; and his enjoyment of them helped him to forget their religious associations. But coming home one Friday evening, he was startled to observe on the table not only the stuffed fish and white bread appropriate to the Sabbath, but also the lit candles which bespoke the woman's benediction, and the glass of wine for the benediction by the master of the house.

"Sarah!" he declaimed. "What is this?"

"What do you care? The boy likes a Jewish touch about the house. What harm is there in that?"

"What *harm* is there in that? What harm is there in *that?*"

But at this point the girls interfered.

"What business is it of yours?" said the older one, who contributed seven dollars a week to the upkeep of the home. "Sam wants the Friday night benediction. I'm paying for the wine. Go ahead, Sam."

Glickstein collapsed in a corner, at a loss for words. Sam, pallid and terrified, put on his hat, turned the pages of the prayer book, and began to stammer the Hebrew words like a little boy in the first class at a Hebrew school:

336

"And—and—it was—it was—morning—it was morning—and evening—"

"Ignoramus! Heathen!" thundered Mr. Glickstein. "You don't even know how to say the Friday evening benediction!"

"Did you ever teach him how?" wailed his wife.

Glickstein strode over to the table, grabbed the wine-cup from Sam's hand, shoved the boy to one side, and said the benediction from beginning to end without once looking at the text in the prayer book.

He not only *said* the benediction. He chanted it with all the roulades and the grace notes of the tradition. His wife stared at him with shining and grateful eyes, and his children were dumbstruck with astonishment and admiration.

. . .

Coming home late one evening, Mr. Glickstein found assembled in the parlor a group of young people. He paid no particular attention to them, but passed through the room and went upstairs. He was accustomed by now to feeling himself more or less of a stranger in his own home. But before he had begun to undress, his wife burst in and imparted to him the news that Masha, the milliner, was engaged to Mr. Borenstein, a wholesale dealer in groceries and a fine, decent young man. Mr. Glickstein listened in a stupor. In itself, the engagement of his daughter seemed to him to be a matter of minor importance. He experienced a faint satisfaction in the thought of his daughter's happiness; he was also aware of a more distinct inward disturbance at the thought of the loss to the household income. But he relied on his wife to straighten matters out. The management of the house had always been her department. She had never failed to adapt herself to changing conditions; she would not fail now. And there his interest ended. However, as a matter of ordinary courtesy, he went down to the parlor and suffered himself to be introduced to the young man. Prospective son-in-law and prospective father-in-law shook hands, said "How do you do?" looked at each other awkwardly, and sat down. Glickstein could think of nothing to say

337

regarding the wholesale grocery line, and the young man had never heard of Kropotkin and Bakunin. The first five minutes determined the character of future relations between them: a remote and wordless friendliness. It was always a cordial "How do you do?" a handshake, an interval of embarrassed silence, and withdrawal by mutual consent and with mutual relief. Glickstein avoided his home more than ever before. The place had become intolerably noisy. It seemed to him that his daughter's young man was literally taking the house by storm. Innumerable young people turned up nearly every evening; all of them had loud voices; all of them laughed immoderately at nothing. It was a madhouse, and to avoid a nervous breakdown, or a quarrel with the young people, or both, Glickstein gave his home a wide berth.

He did not occupy himself with the preparations for the wedding, but left that to his wife and the young couple. Let them do what they wanted. For his part, he waited gloomily for the whole wretched, confused, noisy business to be over, so that his life might resume its normal tenor.

The bride and bridegroom hired a hall, musicians, a wedding jester, and a "reverend." The bridegroom's family, with its many ramifications, was of Galician origin, Jews attached to the traditional ritual. They insisted on a wedding in the good old style. And since Glickstein had washed his hands of the business, and his wife was only too delighted to have a real, hearty Jewish wedding, there was no disagreement anywhere.

Had it not been for his wife's insistence, Glickstein would not even have come to the wedding. Reluctantly he donned the Prince Albert which he once used to wear on the lecture platform, and just as reluctantly he entered the cab which took them to the wedding hall. The place swarmed with excited and noisy guests, practically all of them relatives and friends of the bridegroom. The young men wore tuxedos, the young women extravagantly décolleté evening dress. All afternoon and evening they danced. Glickstein wandered about like a lost soul; he knew no one, and no one knew him. Sarah was happy in the company of the other mother-in-law, a pious old Jewess who wore the traditional wig;

from time to time Glickstein caught sight of them in earnest conversation and wondered what it was they could talk about hour
after hour without a let up. As for himself, he moved about in a
vast loneliness, punctuated by occasional, convulsive "How-do-you-
do's?" Finally he sat down in a corner, and resigned himself to a
long vigil.

The moment of the ceremony arrived at last. The canopy was
erected in the middle of the hall; the two fathers-in-law were
finally introduced to each other. Glickstein saw before him an old,
trembling Jew, with a gray beard and gray earlocks. Apparently
he, like Glickstein, had been hiding in a corner, feeling equally
alien to this crowd of young people. Timidly the old Jew put out
his hand, and said:

"*Sholom aleichem,* greetings."

Glickstein was petrified. For an instant he felt like rushing out
of the hall. Who was this incredible fossil? But a feeling of compassion succeeded his first reaction of amazement. He put out his
hand, too, and answered:

"*Aleichem sholom,* greetings!"

When the ceremony under the bridal canopy was completed,
the fathers-in-law were forgotten again. A young man whom Glickstein did not know courteously found a place for him at the dinner
table; the other father-in-law seemed to have disappeared. To right
and left of Glickstein there was riotous conversation, laughter,
much eating and drinking; but he might as well have been a
thousand miles away for all the attention he received. When dinner was over and the tables were cleared away for the resumption
of the dancing, Glickstein looked for a quiet corner whence he
could slip out of the hall unobserved. And as he wandered between
the stacked chairs he felt someone plucking timidly at his elbow.
He turned and beheld the trembling old Jew with the gray beard
and earlocks, the bridegroom's father.

"The bridegroom's father-in-law seems to be all alone," murmured
the bridegroom's father.

"Certainly not!" answered Glickstein, irritably.

"I mean," stammered the other, in an imploring tone of voice, "I mean the young people have forgotten the old."

"Yes! Yes! We're forgotten," said Glickstein, dramatically.

"Let's sit down somewhere and take a drink," suggested the bridegroom's father, humbly. "We're the two fathers-in-law, aren't we, the old-timers? We belong together."

All the free-thinker, the radical, the anti-religious orator rose in Glickstein. What had he to do with this old pietist loon, this superannuated representative of superstition and reaction? Was not this the world he had been fighting all his life as a soldier of progress, liberty, and enlightenment? But from beneath these impulses of his career rose others, deeper and stronger, also released by the sight of the gray beard, the earlocks, the skull cap. Glickstein remembered something—he did not know exactly what. He took the old man's arm.

"Yes, yes," he answered, "we belong together. We don't belong to those—those—" he indicated the young people in tuxedos and décolleté—"those dancers, those ignoramuses and vulgarians. What do they know? What have they ever achieved? But you and I, yes, you and I, the old fathers-in-law, we understand each other."

Glass in hand they sat down in a corner, and with knees touching they drank to each other's health.

"Heil, Hitler!"

I HAD of course heard much about the professor; I had also dipped into his books. His fame traveled before him; not always, to be sure, "like a precious ointment," for there were people who accused him of undermining the moral sense in man. Still, it was a name to conjure with. His books were the first to be flung into the flames in Berlin—a tribute to the world conquest which his new ideas had achieved. Men who became famous always send out before them a false impression of themselves. I, at least, must confess that the picture I had formed of the professor was altogether wide of the mark. I probably expected his presence to have about it something as sensational as his reputation. I was utterly amazed by the unaffected simplicity and modesty of the man and by the strange touch of resignation in his bearing.

What struck me most, however, was the fact it was impossible to detect in him the faintest manifestation of hatred; not a single harsh expression escaped him when he spoke of the enemy. Yet I knew only too well, as did hundreds of thousands of others, what he had passed through in the last few months. Not only had they destroyed the work of a lifetime, scattering to the wind in one day what it had taken him decades to build up; not only had they stripped him of his fortune and his books; they had subjected him to the foulest tortures of which the Nazi prison cell and concentration camp have ever been the witnesses. His friends and admirers abroad had given up hope of getting him out alive, and it was only by a miraculous combination of influence and bribery that they finally obtained his release. Now he stood before me, an elderly man, bent and graying. But the gray had come on him suddenly; it had attacked him as a bandit attacks an unsuspecting wayfarer in a forest. His stoop, too, was not that of age, but of pain recently endured. Only the face was serene, completely serene, almost trans-figured, one would have said. It radiated spiritual peace and made a space of silence about itself. It made one think of the silence in which a man wanders when he has lost his way in the desert. This man, too, had lost his way in his latter years; he could not tell where he would be on the morrow and to what place he would give the fleeting name of home. But never a word of bitterness from him. When we spoke of Germany, he said, with a resignation which suggested confession:

"Yes, we've sinned a lot; our post-war generation has a lot to answer for."

It happened that shortly before I was introduced to the professor, I had met again, after a long interval, an old acquaintance of mine, a New York financier, of German Jewish origin. His English still betrayed a German accent which even Hitlerism had not been able to obliterate. This man, I happened to know, had had a hand in the refinancing of post-war Germany; together with many other American bankers he had helped to put that country once more on its feet. His first words to me were:

"I've learned to hate!"

"Whom?" I asked.

He answered, in an excited voice which brought out more sharply his German accent:

"Whom do you think? The Boches, of course."

When I told the professor this story, having first explained what role the financier had played in the post-war history of Germany, he smiled. It was a thoughtful gentle smile, which rested for an instant on the childlike lips under the overhanging moustache.

"Yes, he can permit himself to hate."

"How so?"

"Only his pocket was affected."

"Pardon me, professor, if I suggest that with this man it wasn't a question of financial loss. I think his hatred springs from something else entirely; he feels himself outraged and insulted, as all of us do. He suffered as a Jew. To be quite frank with you, professor, I am a little astonished—"

I hesitated, and the professor broke in. For the first time he betrayed a faint excitement.

"What do you mean, 'suffered as a Jew?'" he asked. "He personally didn't suffer anything, did he?"

And I, in turn: "How can you say he didn't suffer personally? Each one of us feels these sufferings personally."

"Just words," said the professor. "'Insulted,' 'outraged,' 'humiliated.' Certainly these words call out resistance, a desire for revenge. By 'personally' I mean physically."

I must have turned pale, for I felt as if the blood were standing still in my veins. I suddenly wanted to sit down.

"Why are you so startled?" asked the professor, and smiled again. "Here is what I mean. For more than a thousand years we Jews have been living in Germany, and our lives were woven into the life of that country with a thousand threads. Take my own family. Our records go back more than three hundred years. For the last three generations we've been doctors. And here a man comes along, and in the course of a brief, catastrophic period, wants to obliterate our thousand-year-old history, wipe it off the record, make it as if it hadn't been. And we let him do it! For that is what it amounts to, if we permit him to infect us with hatred of Germany. If I let myself be overcome by hatred, I am implying that Hitler is right, that we have never been part and parcel of the country, that we never really belonged to it, that we were always strangers, clinging to the land as long as circumstances were favorable to us. . . . That is what I mean by 'personal.' You, the Jews outside Germany, can permit yourselves to feel insulted and outraged by Germany, to hate and talk of revenge. But we German Jews, for whom Germany, with all her faults, was our homeland, and must remain our homeland, we German Jews can't permit ourselves to hate. No humiliations, no outrages, can sever the threads which bind us to the country, and have bound it to us for a thousand years. We have had bad times in Germany, we have had good times. This is a bad time; a good time will follow. That, too, is what I meant by 'personal.'"

What had at first been only a faint touch of excitement in the professor, had grown, to my astonishment and distress, into a violent agitation; and though he undoubtedly meant, in all honesty, what he was saying, there was evident—at least to me—in the curious over-emphasis, in the staccato utterance, an attempt to overcome the suspicion which had been aroused by the word "physical."

As a matter of fact, I would have liked to drop the subject at this point; I was glad that the professor had lifted the conversation to the level of generalities, thereby evading the painful impression which his use of the word "physical" had created. But my curiosity and my obstinacy were stronger than myself, and before I knew it I had plunged back.

"Excuse me, professor," I said, "all these considerations which you raise, as to why you should not hate Germany, are themselves generalities; they are not personal factors. However pertinent they may be for German Jewry as such, they don't explain why an abstract concept like history can affect you, the person, the individual; because you, the person, the individual, surely can't help crying out for liberation and revenge. What are the arguments based on generalities and logical considerations which can quieten the feelings aroused by the physical sufferings—yes, let me use that word, 'physical'—by the physical sufferings through which you have passed?"

This time it was the professor who paled. His lips trembled. His eyes fell, and it seemed to me that his voice had become unsteady.

"Yes, that's just it . . . the physical torment. Does physical torment always and inevitably evoke hatred and the desire for revenge? Don't we often get just the contrary effect?"

I shrank from the suggestion, but offered no comment. The professor continued eagerly:

"What I mean is quite simple. It's easy to die once; but how hard it is to die over and over again! You know that wonderful legend of Tolstoi's, of the man who is clinging to a twig above an abyss and yet feels not the slightest trace of the death-horror. Man is condemned to live in whatever situation he finds himself; no matter how imminent the danger, he looks for something, he risks everything, if only it offers the prospect of survival."

"No," I said, at last. "I don't quite understand you, professor. I would be grateful if you'd make it simpler."

"Very well. Let's take, as our instance, a certain prominent political figure, and try to explain his course of action. We all know the man. He is thoroughly honest, thoroughly decent. His life has been devoted to the progress of mankind; he has been consistently faithful to his ideal of human liberty. His hands are clean. Then the disaster comes, and this man shares the fate of the rest of his party. He's thrown into a concentration camp. And suddenly, a few months later, we hear from him; he has recanted everything he believed in; he has made public utterances which falsify everything he has fought for. Well, you can't convince me that this man has been bribed, or that he doesn't mean what he now says. No, there are deeper factors at play here, deeper human elements, which we don't want to consider, which we don't want to face. We, who stand outside of events, and who want to think of them as things that happened in a book, want to believe in strong characters, consistent heroes. We would have liked to impose on this man the role of a martyr. He is tortured in a concentration camp! What a marvelous figure he will cut in history! And no doubt if the man were given the opportunity to die for his cause, he would be able to summon up the little bit of courage which is needed for the right exit. But they didn't give him that little opportunity to die heroically, according to the pattern we've made for him. What they did give him, was the opportunity to live, that is to say, the opportunity to die over and over again. And for that sort of thing his nerves lacked the requisite strength.

"Very well, then. I listen to this man, making his shameful public retractions; and I must confess that they impress me as his honest conviction; he has discovered that throughout his life he has been following a false ideal: Hitler, and Hitler alone, is right! And I must accept one of two conclusions, it seems: either the man has been a dupe all his life, and was not honest with himself, or else he is lying now.

"But as a matter of fact the dilemma doesn't exist. He was honest before, and he's honest now; however dreadful and improbable it may sound, he is thoroughly convinced that Hitler is right. That's why I've tried to make it clear that a man can't go on living without some sort of ground under his feet; and if that ground doesn't exist, he invents it in his own mind. . . . For instance, let's look into the following situation. The majority of men are quite courageous, combative, even heroic, on one side of their bodies: that is, when they face the enemy and do their fighting frontward. But the vast majority of men would be utter cowards if they had to fight an enemy whom they did not face, but to whom they had their backs. The backbone is an extremely delicate and nervous organ. It has much less power of resistance than a man's front—his face, for instance. It therefore often happens that a man who is capable of the highest heroism and endurance when his enemy is in front of him, collapses and sells out when he has to protect his rear."

"Am I to understand that figuratively, professor?"

"By no means. You must take it quite literally. There are certain sicknesses which manifest themselves in an exaggerated sensitivity. The chief symptom is that the patient won't permit his back to be touched. When he gets into a crowd, or when he has to stand in a queue, he becomes frightfully nervous. He is afraid that someone will touch his back. And if someone actually does it, he leaps round like a wild beast—as if someone had thrust a hand into an open wound. A man like that is capable of any amount of heroism frontward, or faceward. But suppose he happens to be taken to a concentration camp, where they discover his particular weakness—as they discover similar weaknesses in others. What do they do with such a man? Well, they strip the clothes from him, and they make him stand with his face to a wall, and his hands in the air. And they tell him to shout 'Heil, Hitler!' The man doesn't know, of course, what's going on behind his back, and what they're going to do *to* his back; whether they're going to touch it with a redhot iron, or whether they're going to turn a stream of ice-cold water on it, or bring down on it a lash loaded with leaden weights; or whether—and this is the most horrible of all—they're going to touch it with their fingernails. His entire backbone is tensed like a harpstring—one touch, and it will snap. . . . Now let's assume that this man is by nature honest, that he has deep-seated convictions, for which he's prepared to suffer, even to offer up his life. He isn't a young man, who could begin life anew. Most of his life is behind him, the future affords little prospect. He's a conscientious man; he knows that if he endures these tortures without yielding, his life will retain its significance; whereas if—God forbid—he fails himself, he has denied and destroyed his own past. It is clear to him, then, that there is only one course for him to follow; and that is, to die, and with his death to place an honest seal on his own life. And he's ready to do it—if only they'd give him a chance to do it frontward, faceward. With his front he could endure anything. He would throw himself, frontward, into a boiling caldron, or leap into a blazing furnace; and the last word on his lips would be one of defiance and affirmation, just as it was with the martyrs of old. But don't you see, they withhold just that opportunity from him; they won't let him die a heroic death. They've discovered his weakness, his back; and they've stripped, and put him with his face to the wall. And now there's only one thought in his mind. *They mustn't touch his back.* Not with a hot iron, and not with ice-cold water, and least of all with their fingernails, their naked fingernails. Everything in him concentrates on that one frightful idea—all his thoughts have this one hideous fear— no, he has no thoughts; he has only open wounds in his brains, and the wounds are like mouths screaming this one demand. *Don't touch my back!* Honor, honesty, consistency, faith, decency—all these things have become a single, squirming confusion; shuddering waves of sensitivity pass up and down his spine, yes, with some sort of sexual overtone in them. But it always amounts to that one thing: *They mustn't touch his back.* And the only protection that he has is: 'Heil, Hitler!' 'Heil, Hitler!' His voice is the only shield which he can interpose between his back and the poised horror.

And so his voice becomes clearer, louder, more and more sincere; it takes on faith and conviction. 'Heil, Hitler!' Yes, 'Heil, Hitler!' 'Hitler, the savior, the Messiah!' *'Jude, verecke!'* And 'When Jewish blood flows from the knife!' 'Heil, Hitler! Heil, Hitler! Heil, Hitler!' "

"Professor! In God's name!"

His face had become an ashen blue. A thin line of foam came out on his lips. He continued to shout, in ever louder tones: "Heil, Hitler! Heil, Hitler!" And then suddenly he collapsed in my arms, in a dead faint. I put him down in an armchair and ran for a glass of water. In a little while he came to. He even mustered a faint smile.

"Yes," he murmured, "If only you don't have to fight with your back, you can manage."

"Professor, we won't talk about it any more."

"It doesn't make any difference now," he said. "I only wanted to make it clear that a man who's been shouting 'Heil, Hitler!' day after day, week after week, whether he does it willingly, or against his will, has no right to hate."

"But what?"

"I don't know. I haven't a word for it. But it's quite different from hate, quite different."

We were both silent.

A Royal Table

JOE slept through the night in a single, unbroken stretch. When he awoke in the morning, it always seemed to him that an invisible hand had wrapped him in a parcel and shipped him through the darkness from one day to the next. But it was his habit, since the time he began to work—and that was when he had entered his adolescence—to wake up not at the last moment, but with an interval before him in which to gather the determination needed to get him out of bed. He had acquired this technique in the old country, during the winters; in the village of his birth central heating was unknown, the fire in the stove died out in the night, and when the gray dawn began peeping in through the ice-covered windows, you needed a hero's heart to poke your leg out from under the warm covers and put it down on the frozen floor. And if you hadn't a hero's heart, you needed at least an interval of preparation, in which to work up your courage. Now that he was in America, and recently married, the habit and technique still clung to him.

When he emerged from sleep, he could never remember where he was. But soon there stole in on him the delicious awareness of a young body lying next to his; the realization of his marriage came over him like a flood of warmth, and tore him out of the instinctive surliness of the first waking moment, the heritage of the nights of his bachelorhood. In a gesture of bliss he put out his powerful arms toward the source of the flood, and whispered:

"Sarah, darling!"

349

The soft-breathing freshness beside him drew away with sleepy, capricious resentment, murmuring:

"Let me sleep! The percolator's standing on the stove!"

But he would not let her be. The fullness of the night's sleep had released the tension in his nerves and muscles, the accumulation of a heavy day of labor. His energies were renewed, and he remembered suddenly how he had come home the night before, so exhausted that he had scarcely put away the meal his wife had prepared, only to collapse on the bed like a felled ox. He remembered how she had pouted, teased him, called him an old gaffer, pleaded with him to take her to a movie. Then she had become quite angry, half seriously, half in jest, saying that she had pictured their marriage quite differently.

Only now he remembered, too, the red-black gypsy bolero she had put on for him when he came home—the bolero which she had undoubtedly brought with her from the old country and which she had been wearing when he had first seen her at the fancy dress ball: red-black bolero, thick black plaits hanging down her back—they had taken his breath away when he had set eyes on them that night. And ever since then he had followed her about like a shadow. He called out to her, at the ball: "I know a piece of home goods when I see it," but he had kept his eyes not on her lovely dress, but on her lovelier face. "Your mother's work, I'll bet, every bit of it."

"Where were my eyes last night?" he reproached himself now. "She's right, bless her. She's young. She wants to live. And I come home like a broken-down old horse, and flop down on the bed, so that she has to pull my shoes off. What kind of way is that?

"It's my blasted job!" he continued. "That's what it is." A well-paid job it was, but a strenuous and dangerous job. All day long you had to be on your toes, with a thousand eyes about you: one false step, one slip of the foot, and that was the last of you. (He closed his eyes to drive away the picture.) A dirty, dangerous, exhausting job, riveting those iron girders on the twenty-second floor of a rising skyscraper; nothing to hold on to; you've got to hop from girder to girder. Acrobatics, that's what it is; and if you miss one leap—good-by! There's nothing in the world can save you.

To hell with it! He wasn't afraid; he knew nothing could happen to him. He was as light as a cat, as sure of every jump. He didn't know the meaning of dizziness. In the old country, before he came to America, he had been a tinsmith and roofer. Steeples meant nothing to him. And the job he had now was well paid. Nine dollars a day. No, he wasn't afraid. That wasn't it. But the tension was getting on his nerves; it was wearing him down. He brought home, in the evening, not the sturdy, jolly young man his young wife waited for, but a man used up and useless. Well, he'd stay on this job just a little while longer, till they'd paid up for the furniture, till he'd put by a few dollars extra. Then he'd take time out to look for another job. Of course, if his wife had taken a job, too, after their marriage, it would have gone faster. But he pulled a face at the idea. He didn't like the thought of her still in the shop, when she'd become his wife. "I'll get by," he thought. "Nothing's happened to me so far, nothing's going to happen. I don't want her in that blasted shop. Let her get the feeling of it out of her bones. Thank God, it didn't eat her youth up—it does to so many. You see them wilting, year after year. The shop gets what belongs to a husband. No, let her stay home like a lady, do the little bit of housework, go walking in the park afternoons. And then, maybe, before long, there'll be a kid to look after. I'm old enough to be a father, I guess."

Pride and delight filled him at the thought of "a kid." He put his rested, muscular arms round his wife, saying:

"Don't you want to look at me, Sarah? Last night I wanted to sleep, this morning you want to sleep."

She muttered sleepily: "Go on, Joe, it's time to get up, you'll be late."

This time the repulse stung him. He lay silent—there was still time. And she, half asleep as she was, felt that she had hurt him. She turned round, burrowed her head into his shoulder, and said, in her deliciously dreamy voice: "Go on, Joe, darling, get dressed, and

go to work, and try to come home not too tired. Listen, darling—"
she lifted her head, and drew his ear to her lips: "You know how I
love to make a royal table for you."

That phrase, "a royal table," intoxicated him. She had the queerest terms of speech, the loveliest ways of expressing herself. She'd
brought them with her out of the old country—the girls here did
not speak a Yiddish like that. "A royal table for you." It was as if
she had poured something into him, a heavy, glowing liquid which
ran into every corner of his body. And she had such a way of saying it, too, a playful, meaningful way. All sorts of pictures, vague,
alluring and nostalgic, floated up at the back of his mind. "A royal
table for you!" What a gift she had for making a lovely, significant
secret out of the most trifling fact.

He kissed her again and again for the words, and she pushed
him away lazily. "Go on now, Joe, you've rubbed half my face off
with your beard. You didn't shave last night."

"Oh, I'll shave this evening!" he promised her. Who wouldn't,
for a royal table? He sprang out of bed singing the phrase to himself, and he was still singing it, like a schoolboy, when he ran into
the street.

He strode along with the crowd, his lunchbox under his arm.
The crowd streamed along with him. Mechanically he dodged in
and out between slower moving pedestrians, across streets, behind
buses and passenger cars. There was a magic liveliness in his limbs,
the result of his young wife's words to him. With hundreds of
others he was sucked into the wide-open jaw of the subway station.
He saw nothing, heard nothing: he was repeating to himself, with
a joyous, secret smile: "I *love* to make a royal table for you." He
was jammed close with others, elbows and knees, bodies, faces,
until it seemed that he was a brick in a building, unable to assert
himself any more. But his eyes and senses were alive, alive and
separate, and the magic phrase was working in him, keeping them
busy.

Still smiling inwardly, he wondered what she would be wearing
that evening when he came home. Would she have on that same
darling, black-red gypsy bolero, crimson flowers on a black back-

ground; or would she think up another reception for him. These tricks of hers! Why, once, when he came home, she had put on a wimple, like those he'd seen his grandmother wear, many, many years back, in the old country, on Sabbaths and festivals, going to synagogue; and she'd made her hair in coils, like a great, big Sabbath loaf. It staggered him when he looked at her; he could have eaten her up. She said: "Mother used to dress like that when she was a girl." And once they were at the movies, and they saw a movie-star wearing slacks, whereupon his Sarah wouldn't leave him alone until the two of them went to Macy's, and she got herself the material for slacks. She made them herself, of course, and when he came home one evening she was lounging around in them, and be damned if she didn't look a thousand times more charming than that movie actress.

In ever-recurring amazement he kept asking himself what right he, Joe the tinsmith, had to such a woman?

"By God," he muttered, "the moment I clapped eyes on her at the fancy dress ball, I said to myself, 'That's a home-made piece of goods, that is. I've got to get to know her.'"

His friends could not understand him. What did he want with that uncivilized greenhorn of a girl, that Galician hick who couldn't speak English properly yet, had no idea of American ways, didn't know how to handle American boys? What did he think he was doing?

"Oh, I knew what I was doing," he chortled, inwardly. "Yes, *sir,* I knew what I was doing."

"Wait now," he began again, with a baffled feeling. "I bet she's going to put on that cute dressing gown, which you can wear either buttoned or unbuttoned; blue silk, and heavy, really for Sunday mornings. But she wears whatever she likes whenever she likes. Now that dressing gown, there's something about it when she puts it on . . ." And he smiled again. That girl couldn't wear a dress without making you feel she was born with it, it's part of her. Oh, yes, Joe the tinsmith had his eyes about him; *he* knew what he was doing when he ran after that Galician greenhorn and wouldn't look at anybody else. And in the pride of his insight he felt himself a master of life; he had achieved riches which made a Rockefeller look like a pauper.

He did not see his fellow-passengers, mostly young people like himself, who had been torn out of the arms of sleep and love and exiled into the coldness of the raw morning. The sweet taste of their night-refuges lingered in the corners of their lips and eyes; their eyelids were still heavy with dreams. But there were others, who had risen out of hard, lonely beds, and brought with them on their journey only the cold resentment of the empty night; girls well on in years, on whose faces the factory had worked those unmistakable, hateful lines; men whose faces were hungry, and whose needy bodies even now, half unconsciously, stole a pretended friendliness out of the unwilling proximity of women. There were some women who, aware of that hunger, shrank into themselves; but others, in the same case as the men, felt the same wretched need for physical companionship.

And then the subway, which had pulled them and kneaded them into a single mass, spewed them out and scattered them once more into a thousand separate, hurrying fragments, each intent on its own destination. Joe too detached himself from the mass into which he had been absorbed and where he had dreamed his separate dreams. The cold air of the street drove away the feel of the night, the charm of the morning encounter, the magic of his young wife's words. He walked swiftly, dodging in and out, till he came to a gate in a long wooden wall which cut off half the block.

He was late. Only by five minutes—but still, late. The last elevator had already gone up to the twenty-second floor where he was to take his place that morning with the other steel-riveters. Now the elevators were being used only for materials, and were carrying up bricks, cement-wires and marble blocks to the fifteenth floor, from which point they would be lifted further by the derrick. The head foreman in the wooden booth at the entrance heard Joe's excuse, that there had been a traffic delay, and told him that if he wanted to get in on that morning's work he would have to go up with one of the elevators to the fifteenth floor, and mount one of the girders as it was being swung up on the derrick. That wasn't

Joe's job of course; it was the job of special workers who got higher pay because it was the most dangerous kind of work. They had to sit astride the girder and help to swing it into the right position when it reached the proper floor.

But Joe was only too glad to take it on. First, he would secure his morning's work; and second, perhaps more important, he would show those fellows up on the twenty-second floor that he could swing a girder just as well as the younger men who had that job. Why, only a few months ago he had done a little job on the steeple of the Thirty-ninth Street church, refusing to wear his safety-belt—for which he nearly got himself fined. He leapt on to the elevator, feeling in his limbs the flush and strength of Sarah's words to him. Between the eleventh and twelfth floors a protruding wire caught at him, and ripped away half his coat. Had he been standing an inch closer to the open side of the elevator, the wire would have dug into his flesh, and perhaps lifted him out and dropped him a hundred and twenty feet.

"God damn fools!" he yelled at the workers on the twelfth floor, leaning out to shake his fist at them. "Why the hell don't you cut that wire?"

His voice was swallowed up in the ringing of hammers and the sustained thunder of riveting machines. Those that saw him had no idea why he was shaking his fist. That was a bad thing. Someone ought to send word to the inspector about the wire.

But he forgot about it the moment he set foot on the platform of the fifteenth floor. The danger which now confronted him wiped out of his mind the danger through which he had just passed. But he was not afraid. He was a steel-worker: that was enough. And it wasn't the first time, either, that he had ridden a girder in mid-air. He was going to show those boys that he could handle the job as neatly as any of them. He should have been among them, by rights, getting twice the pay he was now getting as a riveter.

He swung out on to the narrow framework beyond the platform.

"Hey!" yelled the foreman of the fifteenth floor. "Your belt!"

"To hell with the belt!" shouted back Joe. "Here's my belt"— and he waved his two powerful arms in the air.

355

"You can't go!" the foreman yelled back. "If the inspector sees you I'll get the sack."

"O. K." Joe leaned back, took the belt with a grimace, and moved over to the girder waiting to be lifted. He slipped the belt round the girder, and fastened the ends to his body. The foreman watched, nodded, waved his hand to the man in the derrick. An instant later the girder was lifted into the air, and swung about like a macaroni on a fork. Below him Joe saw the street, and the human pigmies, the toy cars. The scene flashed on him and flashed away. He had no time for sightseeing. His attention was absorbed by the movements of the girder; nerves and muscles were on the alert, adjusting his body to every new position. One instant he swung around, and hung with his head down; the next instant he was up again. The derrick played with the gigantic girder as if it were a straw. Then came the crucial moment, and Joe needed all his senses, all the elasticity and rapidity of response that his body could summon up. Above him the workers were waiting on the already riveted girder. Joe hunched himself like a cat, threw his weight right and left, imparting a swinging motion to the rising girder. Now was the time to loosen the safety belt, crawl forward to the tip of the girder, fit it into the waiting notch, and hammer it in. Joe drew the steel hammer out of his seat pocket, loosened the belt, fasened his legs round the girder, worked his way forward; the end slipped in perfectly. One powerful, well-directed blow with the hammer was enough. Strong arms were stretched out to the girder; a new thunder of hammers and of air-compression riveting machines filled the air; the girder became part of the vast skeleton of steel.

"Atta boy, Joe!" he said to himself, as he scrambled off the girder, his body drenched with sweat.

The frightful tension of a few minutes, the fierce concentration of energy and alertness, had wiped clear out of his mind the last remnants of dreaminess which a magic word had distilled into him. The maelstrom of work sucked him in. No thinking now, no re-membering. His flesh threw off the recollection of the warm, loving body which had strengthened and renewed it in the night. He was

had the strength for it. Sometimes she had even made him take a bath before dinner. "I hardly ever see you bathed and shaved," she said.

She was full of the queerest and most delightful notions, and if an idea struck her, she could suddenly make a weekday into an unexpected Sabbath. One evening he came home and found that she had put candles into the brass candlesticks which she had brought from the old country; she had put in candles, she had lit them, she had spread a fancy tablecloth—just as his mother had used to do on the eve of the Day of Atonement, before they went to synagogue for the *Kol Nidre* prayer. "What is this, darling?" he asked, baffled. "But don't you know?" she answered. "This is Friday night! It's the Sabbath eve!" And it was true. Since he had come to America, since he had started working here, he had lost count of the days; or, rather, the days were all alike to him; no Sabbaths, no festivals, such as had been observed in the home of his parents. There was only Sunday, when you could stay in bed longer. And here, all of a sudden, the sweet lights of the Sabbath, the fancy tablecloth, the twisted Sabbath loaves. And she wouldn't let him sit down at table till he'd bathed and shaved, and changed his clothes. And then came a meal which he never forgot: fish, and boiled peas, and a carrot-and-honey-stew, which he hadn't tasted since he left his mother's home in his boyhood.

"You wait!" she said to him. "When we have a baby we're going to have a regular Sabbath in our home, the kind my mother used to make. Our little one won't grow up a heathen; he'll remember that he had a father and a mother who kept the Sabbath."

Well! Hadn't he known what he was about, he, Joe the tinsmith, when he got it into his head that he was going to marry just this Galician greenhorn of a girl, this "hick"? Hadn't he been right to fall in love with her at first sight—his girl whom everybody laughed at "because she didn't understand American ways"?

And it wasn't only on Fridays that she got the fancy to make a great evening of it. Once he came home in the middle of the week —a Wednesday evening—and there it all was, the royal preparation. There was a fresh-baked cake on the table, and candles stuck in it, and flowers—like at a wedding. And she came to the door to greet him, shining in a new waist. "Congratulations, darling," she said. "Congratulations?" he said, puzzled. "About what?" "It's your birthday, darling! You're thirty-three years old today! Many happy returns!" But where had she found out that it was his birthday? And where had she found out that it was his thirty-third? Because, as a matter of fact, he couldn't have told whether this was his birthday or not, and he wasn't even sure how old he was within a year or two. The days and years had run into one long, monotonous stretch, without milestones, without reminders. There were times when he was ready to believe that he was three hundred and thirty-three years old. His mother did not know when his birthday was. She'd lost the record, and she had so many children that she'd lost track of the dates. He had come to America without a passport—that was in the good old days when such things happened. His Sarah had just picked on a day, and had decided that henceforth this would be his birthday. She told him, so to speak, when he was born, as if she were his mother, not his wife. Well, now, had he made a good bargain, Joe the tinsmith, or hadn't he?

So there was his birthday. And after that there was their wedding anniversary. And if it wasn't the one or the other, if it wasn't a Sabbath or a festival, well, she was capable of making a great evening of it for no reason whatsoever, except that she felt like it. She'd suddenly proclaim a special evening, put on a new dress, make him take a bath, change his clothes—as if they were going to a wedding. And they were, indeed, forever going to a wedding; their own! They became bride and bridegroom all over again. So now he began wondering what kind of wedding-feast she would prepare for this evening, and what new setting she would have for it. Not that she spent any money on these impromptu celebrations. She only moved the furniture around, put the lamps in different corners—and it was a new house he came into. But it was no use trying to guess what she was up to.

He was torn out of this sweet dreaming by the shrilling of the siren. A few seconds later he was in the thick of the tumult again, edging along the planks to the new positions, riveting new girders into the vast spidery steel framework. Once again eyes and ears, muscles and nerves, were concentrated on the fierce task.

The minutes dragged along with a strange hostile slowness. It seemed to him that he had never been aware, until now, of their reluctant passage. He felt an unaccustomed exhaustion, which did not belong to this hour of the day. And then something happened to him that had never happened before. Suspended between heaven and earth, he suddenly cast a glance downward, and was overwhelmed by the consciousness of danger. It was a totally new experience. Since his boyhood he had clambered on roofs and steeples; and he had lost—perhaps he had never had—the perception of altitude. Now it penetrated him, and filled him with a dreadful dizziness.

He came to with a gasp. "I'm in a bad way today," he said, quickly. He would have to quit, find some excuse, go home early. For the moment he had to go on, pretend to himself, and to others, that there was nothing wrong; finish the riveting he had begun and then get out of it.

His hands were trembling when he stepped off the boards and felt the secure steel framework under him. "What the hell are they going to say?" he asked himself. "What's this holiday all of a sudden? And what about tomorrow? It's going to be the same thing all over again."

Yet he could not return to the outside boards. He was actually afraid. Then it occurred to him that he could work on the inner side of the incomplete platform, where a man did not need to watch himself so closely. There a man could stand up freely and rivet the uprights instead of the horizontal girders. He went over to the foreman and said:

"Look, I'd like to work over there, on the platform. I'm not feeling so good today. Headache, I guess."

"If you're getting dizzy," answered the foreman, sharply, "this is no job for you. Better look for another."

"Who said I'm dizzy?" snapped Joe, seeing his job disappear.

"I've been working on these jobs since I was a kid. I've only got a bit of a headache. I'll be all right tomorrow. I'm all right now, in fact. Forget it." And he turned on his heel.

The foreman stopped him. "No, sir. You can't go back on that job when you're dizzy. It's against the rules, and I don't want anything to happen, because I'll be blamed, see? You can finish the afternoon on the platform, working on the wires, and in the morning we'll have the doctor examine you to see if you're fit for a riveter's job."

"What do you mean, doctor?" answered Joe. "I'm absolutely all right. I've been doing this work ever since I can remember. I did it as a boy, in the old country."

"Listen, I don't care how long you've been doing it and where you started. I said you're going to work on that platform on the wiring. The pay's lower, but it's either there or you quit right now."

Joe turned away, feeling a chill at his heart. "What kind of Goddam mess did I get myself in now?" he muttered, as he climbed down toward the platform.

The advantage he had thought to gain by working in a safer place was gone. Worry for his job, for his future, more than offset the easier position; and what would have been child's play to him a day before, or even that morning, became desperately difficult. On top of it all, he was determined to regain his status. He refused to stay put on the platform. As a new girder came swinging in, he swung out to meet it.

He heard the foreman's voice, faint but insistent through the uproar.

"Hey, you there, quit that! If you want to stay on that platform drop the riveter and work on the wires." The foreman came puffing toward him. "What's more, you're working on your own responsibility. That's the rules, and you've got to observe them, and if you don't like 'em you can go home right now."

With a heavy heart Joe dropped the riveter. Well, it was no use arguing now. Besides, there was only an hour or two more to work. The next morning he would have the doctor examine him.

There wasn't the slightest doubt in his mind that he would be pronounced fit, and sent back to his regular job. And no sense in worrying, either. He remembered, too, that he had promised Sarah he would come home fresh and lively. This, at any rate, was easy, simple work, this weaving of the wires for the cement; you made one net, lay down on it, and made another net. It was like lying in bed and working. You could think your own thoughts, you could go back to your dreams.

"What time is it?" he asked the worker beside him.

"It just blew four."

One more hour. "To hell with it!" he thought. "If they won't put me back on riveting here, I'll get myself another job. There's always work for a good riveter. And maybe I'll give it up anyhow." It was not at all a bad idea. Sure, he'd be making less money if he were a wire-worker; but then he wouldn't be using himself up the way he did. And he wouldn't come home every day like a worn-out old horse. Sarah would like it better; yes, she would, even if they had to manage on less. If you married a young, pretty, lively girl, he argued with himself, you've got to see that she's satisfied; she's liable to look somewhere else for what you can't give her.

He pulled himself up. No, not Sarah. She wasn't that kind of "modern" girl. Just the same she had her rights; and one of her rights was a husband, instead of a wreck of a man.

No, he wouldn't worry about it now. Time to think it over later. Just now he would take it easy, he would prepare his mind and heart for "the royal table" she'd promised him. And he tried again to guess what she'd be wearing when she opened the door for him; the black-and-red bolero, and her plaits hanging down on her breast; or the cute slacks, which made her more attractive than the movie star. No, he was ready to bet that she'd put on, out of contrariness, the high waist with the decorated, standing collar, and her hair done up in a coil on her head, the way the student girls in the old country used to dress and make their hair. He loved that affectation of hers; and he pictured her now, sitting opposite him, at "the royal table."

"Hey! Inspector!"

A sudden yelling pierced the tumult of hammers and riveters. The siren shrilled again. A rush of workers along the platform; from below, in the silence which had fallen, a howl of rage:

"God blast that puller!"

The workers sitting astride the unriveted girders did not dare to turn their heads. They could only call out:

"What is it?"

"The riveter who was sent to work on the platform slipped through. He's lying down there with his head split open."

"How did it happen?"

"He lay too close to the elevator. One of the heavy wires was sticking out, and it pulled him off."

"Listen, fellers!" That was the foreman's voice. "I want you to witness that I wanted to send him home. He stayed on his own responsibility. I told him that. He's got no insurance claim. He said he was dizzy, and I told him he couldn't stay except on his own responsibility. You fellers heard me."

At home everything was ready, just as Joe had dreamed about it. After preparing the meal, Sarah had washed and combed out her long, black hair. Then she had braided it, but she had not coiled it on her head; she let the plaits hang down over her shoulders. And after long thought she decided against the high-collared waist which made her look like a European student girl and chose instead the exciting, black-red gypsy bolero in which Joe had first seen her at the fancy dress ball. Then she sat down and waited for Joe to ring the bell. She had managed the time beautifully, and he would be here any minute now to take his place at "the royal table."

The Pull of the City

I

BEHIND the broom-like tangle of the bare willow branches the sloping, snow-covered fields stretched from the farm buildings to the valley. Across the fields ran the black double thread of the railroad line, which was indicated even more clearly by the bleak telegraph poles. Now and again a crow came to rest for a few moments on the telegraph wires and sent down a tiny shower of snow. A cluster of stunted trees stood on a little elevation surrounded by a red fence, and behind the elevation was the farmhouse. Its dead white walls and blue shutters relieved the monotony of the landscape and brought into the desolate scene a suggestion of home. For Moishe Mordecai, engaged at the moment in chopping down the trees, house and shutters were something intimate and familiar, as if he had been born here and had lived here all his life. Perhaps it was their peculiar, inexplicable appeal which had prevented him from abandoning this accursed village of Silverton and returning to New York, where his yellow-faced brother-in-law Beinish had tried to imprison him for ever in the even more accursed workshop.

It was a cold afternoon. The heavy clouds hung low, and through them the sunlight filtered as through a thickly frosted window. Across the icy silence echoed the strokes of Moishe Mordecai's axe. A tattered woman's kerchief was wound about his head, and his boots were wrapped in burlap, after the fashion of peasants in the old country. Near him, on the snow, lay his sixteen-year-old son, Arontchik, who was trying to build a fire out of frozen twigs. The motionless air was filled with a stinging cold which cut the skin like a knife and penetrated gloves and burlap and clothes.

Wielding the axe, Moishe Mordecai panted like an exhausted horse. The agony of his effort sent drops of sweat down from under the woman's kerchief; they did not fall from his face but were arrested half way and frozen in his beard. At intervals he stopped chopping, hopped from one foot to the other, breathed on his hands and murmured:

"Father, Father in heaven, have pity on me, help me!"

He looked at his son struggling to build the fire, and his heart contracted. If he had not been ashamed he would have cried his prayer aloud. But he kept his voice low, though he could not keep back all his tears, and murmured, again and again:

"Father in heaven, I cannot endure it! My lot is bitter, I cannot endure it!"

Then at last the full flood of his tears burst from his eyes. For an instant they warmed his cheek, and then turned into ice. The boy heard him sobbing, looked up, and saw him resting his head on the handle of his axe.

"Father!" he cried, horrified. "Father! What is it?"

"Nothing!" replied Moishe Mordecai, passing his sleeve across his face. "Nothing! Only Czar Nicholas should come to this, for driving me and my little ones out of our home! Oh, God, teach him what it means to chop wood in the forest on a winter's day!"

The boy was silent. He had not realized that things were so bad. He wanted somehow to console his father but could not find words, and in his embarrassment he left the smoldering twigs and began to gather up the fallen branches.

"Enough," said his father. "We'll go home and see what mother is doing. Maybe tomorrow God will help us and drive away the frost. Then we'll make up a wagonload of wood and take it to the village to sell."

Father and son heaped the branches on the two sleds which they had tied together. Released from the torment of his labor,

The Pull of the City

Moishe Mordecai felt his hope rising again slowly. Yes, he would persist! He would still become a free worker on his own land, in a free country.

"My son," he said, "there will be better times for us."

When they had tied the wood on the double sled, they began to pull it homeward across the hard, pitted fields. Side by side they staggered along, the perspiration turning to ice on their faces.

When they came into the half-furnished house, with its thin walls from which the summer wallpaper was peeling away, they felt even colder than in the fields. It was as though the frost had entered with them in a vain effort to find a warm spot. In the living room they found Hannah, Moishe Mordecai's wife, busy over the stove. She seemed to have covered herself with every piece of cloth she could lay hands on, and from out of the midst of the blanket which was wrapped over head and shoulders, she was blowing into the smoke and cursing the frozen faggots which would not catch fire. She was not surprised at all to see husband and son coming back in the middle of the day. She was used to it; and without turning toward them, she said, bitterly:

"A farmer! He's got to be a farmer! Nothing else will do!"

Her husband did not reply and she, angry with herself because she knew how he suffered and yet was unable to hold herself in, went on, still addressing some invisible person:

"There's no sense to it! Everybody says so! Because if there was any sense to it wouldn't everybody be a farmer instead of a tailor?"

Still silent, Moishe Mordecai drew off one of his boots and began to fan the fire with it, as he had been wont to do in the old country.

"Oh, yes," said Hannah, in a louder voice, "it may be a good thing, but for gentiles, not for Jews. I say it's no sort of work for Jews."

This last remark was too much for Moishe Mordecai. It wounded him where he was most sensitive, in the principles which had moved him, as it had moved so many other modernizing Jews, to go back to the soil.

"That's exactly what the anti-Semites say," he burst out. "That

367

the Jews are no good for the soil; that they're fit for nothing but peddling."

The accusation that she was, God help her, repeating what the "anti-Semites" said, silenced Hannah. Moishe Mordecai followed up his triumph as he fanned the fire:

"And I'm going to show the gentiles that a Jew can work the land just like them. I won't let myself be driven away, not by frost, not by heat, not by hunger. I've sworn to become a farmer, and that's what I'm going to be!"

"Who's stopping you?" asked his wife. "You don't have to become a farmer. You're a farmer already."

She went over to the table and began to knead a heap of dough made out of flour which her daughters, employed in the New York workshops, had sent to their father, "the farmer." For although Moishe Mordecai spoke with the utmost contempt of the workshops and never alluded to them otherwise than as the instruments of "blood-sucking exploiters," it was still his daughters, the city workers, who were sustaining the farm.

When Moishe Mordecai, who had been a grain dealer in the old country, landed in America, he had tried to adapt himself to the workshop. But he had been forced to give it up. It was not merely the physical effort, hard though that was on a man in the late forties; nor was it merely the physical confinement, which was equally hard on a man who had lived all his life in the open. These handicaps he might have overcome. What struck him down was the spiritual humiliation. Moishe Mordecai was a man of principles. In his youth he had been caught up in the Haskallah movement, which had swept up thousands of Jews; its aim had been to lift the Jews out of the ghetto, modernize them, transform them into artisans and workers on the soil. Moishe Mordecai had read all the modern Hebrew books and periodicals. He had been a man of intellectual and social standing, descended from a family of scholars. And he had found himself in a New York sweatshop, doing a woman's work which needed neither intelligence nor learning and which could be done just as well by an ignorant peasant girl. It was this debasement that he could not stand; this, and the frustration of his lifelong dream of ultimately becoming a farmer. So he had applied to an organization which existed for the purpose of settling Jews on the soil, and the organization had obtained this farm for him, for a small sum down, the remainder to be paid off over a number of years.

He had known in advance that it was no light undertaking. He had been told so by any number of people; he had read about it in any number of articles, in the Hebrew periodicals. It was a hard way to get your bread; but this was the kind of bread that tasted sweetest. Therefore Moishe Mordecai had sworn to put up with every torment and privation, and to come through. Besides, Moishe Mordecai had always fancied himself as an authority on agriculture, though he had never wielded a spade nor guided a plough. After all, he argued, what was there to know? If an unlettered peasant had the brains for it, would he, Moishe Mordecai, be baffled by it?

He took the farm over in the autumn, on the basis of encouraging calculations. The potato crop would net him the three hundred dollars for his first payment on the mortgage and carry him over till the next harvest. But it turned out that the potatoes were planted in damp soil, so that most of them had rotted. If it had not been for the flour which his two daughters sent him regularly from the city, he would not have been able to live through the winter. On top of this assistance, he earned a little from time to time by chopping down his trees and selling the wood in the village.

Another than Moishe Mordecai would long ago have fled from the flimsy farmhouse with its peeling wallpaper back to the city. But not Moishe Mordecai. He had read too deep in the modern Hebrew books. He understood too well how important it was for Jews to prove that they could work the soil just as diligently and successfully as the sons of any other people. Moishe Mordecai was not going to add to the verbal ammunition of the anti-Semites. He would rather die where he was than commit such desecration. So Moishe Mordecai stayed, and endured.

Children of Abraham

II

The spring came, and Moishe Mordecai went to his daughters in the city and obtained from them the capital for seed. Again it was the workshop which came to the rescue of the land.

On his return he sought out his plough, and after having looked at it long and earnestly, harnessed to it his one and only cow. Then he stationed Arontchik at the side and himself behind the plough. Hannah was called to the door of the farmhouse to witness the memorable event. Moishe Mordecai lifted his eyes to heaven, gave thanks to God for having vouchsafed him this happiness, and then, with the help of his son and of the cow, started the first furrow on the downward slope away from the house.

It was a day of tremendous and backbreaking effort, but Moishe Mordecai was aware of no weariness. His face flamed, the sweat poured down from his forehead, and his shirt clung to his body. He had thrown off his coat and vest. He followed the plough in a sort of dance; now it plunged down, now it lunged sideways, now it swung up. It caught him in the ribs, in the stomach, in the chest. Sometimes it stuck and refused to budge. In vain did Moishe Mordecai and Arontchik yell "Giddy-up!" to the cow, in vain did they apply the lash. The cow took everything calmly; it stood and chewed the cud, refusing to budge until father and son had pulled the plough out of the jam. But nothing mattered. Moishe Mordecai was filled with bliss; he kept on quoting verses from the Bible and the Talmud in praise of the farmer's life, the beauty of the soil, the sanctity of labor. It was as though he was trying to persuade the plough to cut smoothly because it was being guided by Jewish hands.

Neighboring farmers, gentiles, looked on with astonishment. It was a picture they had never seen before: a man ploughing with the help of his son and a cow. They shook their heads and said to each other:

"There's no bread going to come out of that ploughing."

It looked as though they were right; for day after day Moishe Mordecai and Arontchik spent most of their time standing still and yelling at the cow, while the plough was stuck fast in the ground. When their neighbors had finished ploughing their fields and had sown half of them, Moishe Mordecai and Arontchik were still sweating on the beginning of the stretch where they were planning to sow "bread."

Mr. Johnson, their nearest neighbor, came over on a hot day, and addressed them across the fence: "Listen, man, you should have done that last year, after the harvest. Do you expect to plough and sow the same year? Even a woman has to carry a child nine months." And Mr. Johnson shot a yellow stream of tobacco juice out of the corner of his mouth.

Moishe Mordecai could understand a little English, but he could not speak it. Arontchik was more familiar with the language. Moishe Mordecai felt that he was putting the whole Jewish people to shame in the presence of the gentile world. He tried to save the situation.

"Tell him," he said to his son, "that that's the way we work the soil in the old country. After we've been here a little while we'll learn to do it the American way."

Arontchik translated as well as he could. Mr. Johnson did not answer immediately. He bared two rows of enormous teeth, took a bite out of a plug of tobacco, and spat again.

"And what do you reckon to plant here on this stretch?"

"Arontchik, tell him, 'bread,'" answered Moishe Mordecai, proudly.

"What? Bread?" laughed Mr. Johnson. "You'll get figs and dates out of that land as soon as grain."

Moishe Mordecai felt that his neighbor was making fun of him, and he turned away, hurt.

"Tell your father to sow potatoes there, if he wants to have something to eat this fall. We're in New Jersey, not in Illinois, see?" And with that Mr. Johnson strode away.

Moishe Mordecai did not see. He did not understand what his neighbor was driving at. He turned back to his ploughing. Every morning he rose with the sun, harnessed the cow, took Arontchik along, and ploughed. But the days passed and he got no further.

The first green was already showing on his neighbors' fields, and he was not done yet with the ploughing. He knew that his neighbors laughed every time he came out with the boy and the cow, but he was not the man to give in. He was going to do his duty; the rest was up to God.

After a certain time had passed it became evident to the surrounding farmers that the Jew intended to stick it out; and one morning Mr. Johnson came over into the field, leading two gigantic horses. Without saying a word he unyoked the cow, yoked the two horses in its place, and handed the reins over to Arontchik. This completed, he turned to the boy.

"Tell your father that in this country we don't do our ploughing with cows, but with these," and he pointed to the horses. "I've finished my ploughing, and you can keep them till you've finished yours. But tell the old man to sow the patch with potatoes, if he wants to have something to eat next winter and doesn't want to chop wood for his living." And with that he bit off another piece of tobacco.

But neither Johnson's horses nor the planted potatoes did Moishe Mordecai any good. The summer was worse than the winter. Had it not been for the workshop in the city, they would have died of hunger. The three hundred dollar payment on the mortgage, for which the previous year's crop of potatoes should have provided the money, now fell due, and it was a question of paying or losing the farm, which meant losing their original investment and almost a year of labor on top of it. Moishe Mordecai hastened to the city. Once again the shop came to the rescue. A public credit institution advanced Moishe Mordecai the money, but it was the shop which paid back the monthly installments.

Then the winter, which Moishe Mordecai had learned to dread, came again. "This is going to be my last attempt," he kept on answering to his wife's continual objections. Hannah could not bear to see the torments which her husband and son suffered. They came back daily from the little wood, where the trees were fast disappearing, and their hands and feet were swollen with the cold.

"Moishe Mordecai," she pleaded, "Moishe Mordecai, can't you

see yourself that this is no life for you? It's work for a gentile, not for a Jew. Give it up and try something else."

"What? Just when the dawn is coming? No, no, Hannah."

"The dawn" meant the ten acres which he had ploughed with Johnson's horses, and which were ready for the spring sowing. For the time being they lay snug under a blanket of snow. But in the stable there was now, beside the cow, a young mare which Johnson had sold him on credit till the next harvest.

And Moishe Mordecai was right. The dawn was breaking over his farm. When the winter was over God came to his help. A Jewish butter merchant, who dealt in kosher butter for a pious Jewish clientele, turned up from the nearest town, and asked him to look after his cow. He also lent him the money for hay. Arontchik who, to his father's joy, was growing up a real "peasant," had obtained a number of chickens. In the winter he himself looked after them; in the summer the job was Hannah's. But the greatest help still came from the shop in the city, which sent its regular consignment of flour to the farm.

Moishe Mordecai had also begun to pay more attention to what his neighbors were doing and to understand what his nearest neighbor, Johnson, had meant with those mysterious words "We're in New Jersey, not in Illinois." The land hereabouts was mostly suitable for potatoes. "Let it be potatoes," said Moishe Mordecai. "Did my fathers and my fathers' fathers sow grain, that I should feel myself compelled to sow grain, and nothing but grain?" And for that matter, had his fathers and his fathers' fathers used a plough of wood and iron, so that he was compelled to do likewise? No, neither had they weeded the fields with their hands. He had heard and read of tractors and cultivators which did that work much better. No tradition tied him down to the old methods, and he turned to the new much more easily than his neighbors who had been working the soil generation after generation.

Once the idea of modern farm machinery had taken hold of him, it gave him no rest. He had, moreover, always had a weakness for machines. In the old days, when he had read the books of the modernizing Hebrew writers, nothing had fascinated him more

373

than Smolenskin's treatise on mathematics. Nor had his interest stopped with theory. Any kind of machine he saw set up an itching in his fingers. Whenever he had a leisure hour at home, on a Friday afternoon or a Saturday evening, he used to unhook the clock from the wall, take it apart, and put it together again, just to show that he could do it. Next to farming his ideal had been machinery. If he was not going on the soil, he was going to open a little factory of some kind. He had won such recognition as an expert on machines that whenever anything went wrong with the soda-water machine (it was the only machine in the village apart from the steam boiler in the ritual baths) he was invariably called in before they sent for the gentile mechanic. Moishe Mordecai had come pretty near to inventing a new machine of his own for the production of soda water. . . . Now, on his farm, his two ideals came to the front together and reinforced each other. "Modern farming is machinery," he said, "nothing but machinery," and he ventured on a desperate step. He went to town, drew out from the bank the dowries of his two daughters and rushed off with the money to a farm machinery factory. And thus it was Moishe Mordecai, the newcomer, who was the first to introduce mechanized farming in his locality. His neighbors, stuck fast in their inherited methods, watched him with astonishment, admiration, and uneasiness. Johnson, leaning on the fence and chewing tobacco, called out to him one morning:

"Say, you Jews sure learn fast."

"Arontchik, tell him we Jews have no time to waste. We've got to do in years what they did in generations."

III

The story flows more smoothly on paper than it did in actual life. Many days of back-breaking labor, many nights of worry, still lay ahead of Moishe Mordecai and his family. The income from the farm was uncertain, but the payments on the mortgage became due with inexorable regularity. When he managed, one way or another, to scrape together the money for these, there still remained the question of the loans from his daughters, and above all the replacement of the dowries.

This last problem, however, was mitigated by a great moral factor. When the older of the two daughters began "going out" with a young Galician Jew, the talk was not of a cash dowry, but of the family farm, and the young man was able to boast to his friends that his girl friend's father had a farm of his own. Now *that* was something: a farm in the family. A real one, too, for the dawn which Moishe Mordecai had foreseen in the darkest hour was breaking for all to see. Two years of unremitting and obstinate labor had yielded their results. Moishe Mordecai had no cash, but he had twenty acres of planted potatoes, and ten of rye. He had hay, fodder, and vegetables—the last under the care of his wife. The stable, too, was beginning to fill up. Its oldest denizen was of course their first cow, Red Malkah (every beast had been given a Jewish name, either from the Bible or, sometimes, in the case of the females, after a neighbor of Hannah's in the old home); then there was the mare acquired from neighbor Johnson; her name Mrs. Terach—in memory of the mother of Abraham, the patriarch; to these had been added a second generation, a calf out of Red Malkah and a yellow stallion out of Mrs. Terach. The stallion, the first animal born on the farm, was their special pride; they bestowed on it the name by which Ephraim is sometimes referred to in the Bible: Beloved Son—"Sonny" for short.

Actually Sonny belonged not to Moishe Mordecai but to Arontchik, for it was Arontchik who had pulled him out into the light of day and cut the umbilical cord.

Later a second colt, brown in color, was born to Mrs. Terach, and on him Moishe Mordecai bestowed the name of Jethro, the Midianite priest who was the father-in-law of Moses. Between these two colts, the sons of Mrs. Terach—or rather, between their owners, Moishe Mordecai and Arontchik, on behalf of their colts—developed a great rivalry. The young generation—it was thus that Moishe Mordecai referred always to the animals born on his farm—learned the meaning of work very early. Sonny and Jethro began to earn their keep almost as soon as they were weaned. In the summer they ploughed and pulled the hay and potatoes into the barns; in the winter they were lent out to a neighbor to pull wagonloads of wood to the city. Arontchik was specially charged with the care of the animals. He watched over them from the day of their birth, fed them, scrubbed them and kept them warm as if they were his own children. He fought with his father to prevent them from being put to work too early.

"What do you think this is?" asked Moishe Mordecai, sarcastically. "A high-class boarding house for aristocratic animals? Maybe you'd like to teach them French and take them to dances."

"A horse mustn't be broken to the yoke before it's three years old," answered Arontchik. "You'll have the neighbors laughing at us."

"On this farm everyone has to earn his keep," said Moishe Mordecai sternly.

"Don't you be afraid," retorted his son. "They'll pay their way in time."

Secretly Moishe Mordecai was delighted by the boy's thoughtfulness. Arontchik had taken naturally to the soil and all unconsciously had become part of it. In him Moishe Mordecai saw the fulfillment of his own ideals. Arontchik's love of animals was not based on calculation; he loved them because he had brought them up and because he lived with them. Similarly, Arontchik ploughed the fields not with the thought of the market, but with the thought of the house, the needs of the family and the farm. He did not even know that he was doing something he could justly be proud of, as his father did. He did not know what emotions welled up in the old man when the latter overheard one of the neighbors saying:

"Those animals are properly looked after. The Jew knows his business."

Best of all, Hannah, who had been so sceptical and rebellious in the beginning, was thoroughly reconciled to the "un-Jewish" occupation which her husband had chosen for himself. She had developed a great fondness for the chicken coops. She talked of the chickens as if they were human beings and each day had a new story to tell of their amazingly human behavior. One spring something happened which provided Hannah with food for reflection and conversation for the rest of the year. Yellow Dvoshe (most of the hens, too, were named after former neighbors in the old country) carried away some of her own eggs and hid them in a corner under a heap of feathers. There, in secret, she tried to hatch them, and she was only found out when some of the eggs were already spoiled. She was, of course, scolded and punished; the eggs were taken away from her, and she was kept without food and drink for a day. But it did no good; a week later she was up to the same trick and thereafter had to be watched closely.

"I tell you, she's just like a living soul!" exclaimed Hannah. "She wants her children! She wants to set up a home!"

She told the story to Mrs. Johnson, who taught her how to cure Yellow Dvoshe of her excessive maternal impulses. She was to set Dvoshe on a couple of eggs, tie her down, cover her with a cloth, and keep her there without food or drink for two or three days. Hannah followed Mrs. Johnson's advice, with good results. Indeed, the results were a little too good. For Dvoshe developed such an aversion to eggs that when, later on, they tried to make her hatch one, she trampled it into a yellow mess.

"Look at that!" said Hannah, aghast. "Didn't I say she's like a living soul? It's just the same with our modern young women, God help us! Their husbands don't want them to have children at first. What happens? They go wild. And afterwards, when the husbands do want children, it's the wives who refuse to have them."

The farm achieved completeness when Moishe Mordecai was at last able to buy an automobile. They had long needed one; the horse and wagon journeys to Silverton were a nuisance; Moishe Mordecai and Arontchik saw their neighbors, less advanced than they in other respects, riding to town in cars; but too much money had already gone into the modernization of the farm. They had to wait; and when they finally acquired their car, it was one of the wonders of the countryside.

It was not so much a car as a collection of spare parts from an infinite number of cars. The engine was of one make, the body of another, the cover of a third—and so on down to the fenders and mudguards, which were unidentifiable. The car had an unquenchable thirst, for when it ran it steamed not only in front, but behind, beneath, and at the sides. Or perhaps the thirst was occasioned by the wild voices which issued from every part when the car was in motion.

When Moishe Mordecai first set eyes on the incredible contraption, his face lit up. Here was something to challenge and satisfy even his appetite for machinery. He stroked the machine as though it were his favorite horse, Jethro, and said: "Now this is something like," and he bestowed upon it a phrase-name from the Bible: "Blow-the-Loud-Trumpet."

IV

Gradually the farm paid back its debts to the workshop. Summers the two daughters came out from the city for their holidays. The older daughter, Jochabed, was married, and had two children. The younger one, Sarah, was engaged, and her young man, too, was a Galician. He had a haberdashery store on Second Avenue, in New York City, and was only waiting for Moishe Mordecai's help in order to get married. But he would not have long to wait; for Moishe Mordecai had taken care of the older girl's dowry, and he was able to promise Sarah's young man that after the next harvest there would be enough cash left over to set up house for the couple. He also made it clear that all his children had a share in the farm. It was their second home. If times were bad in the city they always had this to fall back on, and even in good times they were free to use the farm whenever they felt like it.

And indeed, when summer came, the farm became half citified. On odd week-ends, too, whenever the weather was pleasant, the daughters came out, one bringing her husband and children, the other her young man, both their friends. The place took on a very different air, what with silk waists, pressed pants, city talk, and card games in the evenings.

Late one Friday afternoon Arontchik harnessed Sonny and Jethro to the farm wagon—Sound-the-Loud-Trumpet was out of

lent her his handkerchief to wipe herself. Her laughter rang
through him and mingled with the thrill of the white flesh which
he had touched.

"I'll have to think up some excuse for mother why Red Malkah
gave so little milk today," he muttered.

.   .   .

It was the Friday evening meal. From the beginning of his life
in the country Moishe Mordecai had observed the Sabbath eve with
scrupulous piety. His wife lit the Sabbath candles in the brass
candlesticks which she had inherited from her mother. The Sabbath loaves were covered with a white cloth, and near them lay
the prayer book open at the Sabbath benediction. Rose bubbled
over with enthusiasm at the beauty of it all. She hadn't seen anything like it since she left the old country as a child. She insisted
on helping Hannah lay the table. It made her feel—she hardly
knew how to put it—it made her feel a little child again. And
when the table was laid she washed, changed her waist, combed
her hair and put on her red coral beads.

At table, by the light of the lamp and the candles, Arontchik
was able to observe her at his leisure. He saw that her bright blond
hair was rather thin, and that made her look childlike and helpless.
Indeed, everything about her awakened in him a feeling of compassion. In spite of her high spirits she was frail; particularly childlike was her slender neck, rising like a flower-stem out of her waist.
Her eyes, her lips, even the pert, powdered nose, touched him to
pity. He was strong, immeasurably strong, by comparison. He kept
looking furtively at the white throat, soft, dovelike, appealing, and
set off by the blood-red coral beads. All night long he saw them
dancing on her white throat.

On the following afternoon Jochabed arrived from the city, with
husband and children, and in the evening Sarah proposed a visit
to "Pleasure Inn" or "The Fountain."

Some years after Moishe Mordecai settled near Silverton he was
delighted to learn that another Jewish farmer had bought a plot of
ground two or three miles away. He looked upon it as a good sign

—more Jews on the soil; and he was glad to have someone to talk to in his own language. This new "settler," however, turned out to be a farmer of a very different sort. He arrived one spring not with plough and horses or tractor, but with masons and carpenters. He paid no attention to his fields, but brought about a complete transformation in the old farmhouse, to which he added two stories, with a large number of blue-framed windows, which made the building look like a monstrous chicken coop. Then, when the masons, carpenters, and painters were through with their work, a truck rolled up and deposited a quantity of flimsy dressers, tables, chairs and iron cots. And "Pleasure Inn" was founded.

The new settler did not stay on the land winters; his was strictly a summer business. From early autumn to late spring house and land were abandoned to nature. With the first sign of summer the settler returned, and guests followed. They followed in such large numbers that one of them asked himself the question whether Pleasure Inn had acquired a monopoly of the summer trade, and, answering himself in the negative, proceeded to start another summer resort under the name of "The Fountain," a little distance down the road.

The Fountain differed from Pleasure Inn in one respect only; it actually had a fountain. On the lawn in front of the house there was a circular basin, and in the middle of the basin stood an iron mannikin holding aloft an umbrella from which the water ran down. The innovation was a great success and drew away a large part of the clientele of Pleasure Inn. People said they felt cooler when they heard the water dripping off the iron umbrella into the basin, and the women in particular came early in the season in order to obtain squatter's rights for their hammocks between two trees near the fountain.

Moishe Mordecai and Arontchik had no time, and very little inclination, for the delights of Pleasure Inn and The Fountain. Nor did they care much for the people who frequented these places and who seemed to think that when they paid their board at the summer resorts they acquired the right to make nuisances of themselves to the surrounding farmers. Arontchik had, as a matter of fact, accompanied his sisters two or three times to a dance at The Fountain; but he could not dance, and he had found no one he cared to talk to. The city people were too glib for him; they had their catch phrases, and poked fun at him. So Arontchik had stolen off to a movie in Silverton and left his sisters to look after themselves.

But this time he made up his mind to go along. He put on his best suit, a freshly laundered shirt, a stiff collar, and a new tie, and did his not very successful best to impart some neatness to his hair. This completed, he harnessed Sonny and Jethro to the wagon—the car was still out of commission, in spite of Moishe Mordecai's ministrations—and the five of them, Jochabed and her husband, Rose, Sarah and Arontchik, set out for The Fountain.

It was high season at the resort. The men-folk were up from the city; the women were in their week-end best, and there were children, children, children everywhere. The big dining room had been cleared of its tables and its artificial palms, the chairs had been ranged round the walls, the gramophone was going full blast, and the young people danced.

No sooner was Rose drawn into the dancing than she forgot completely about Arontchik. She found among the guests two or three acquaintances from the city, and being an excellent dancer she was soon swamped with invitations. Arontchik stood in a corner, in his best suit, his white shirt and his new tie. His eyes flamed, his hair stood up rebelliously, and he did not know what to do with his enormous hands.

He saw Rose pass from the arms of one young man to another; he saw them holding her shamelessly close as they whirled around. Her plaits flew out, the red corals danced on her throat, her bosom rose and fell under her thin waist, and the young man in the pressed white trousers held her closer and closer: silk shirt and silk waist seemed to mingle, and Arontchik felt the tips of his ears burning. His teeth were clenched, his lips parted, and he breathed heavily as the sweat started out on his forehead.

It was only on the way back, when she sat next to Arontchik behind the horses, that Rose, still hot and excited with the dancing, remembered him.

"Arontchik! Didn't you dance at all? I didn't see you anywhere. Where were you all evening?"

"I was in the dance hall," he answered, curtly.

V

Two weeks later Rose was back with Sarah, and this time she brought along a gramophone. At first it was understood that she was coming for the week-end, but she had not been there an hour before she asked if she might stay the whole week. Neither she nor Sarah had to return to the shop in a hurry; the boss had said so. They wouldn't throw her out, would they? she asked archly.

"On a farm I'm like newborn," she chattered on. "I feel myself growing stronger and healthier every day. Lots of girls don't like farm life. They just can't do without the city. But I'm different."

Moishe Mordecai was touched by these words. A poor Jewish girl who longed for the clean life of the country! Certainly she could stay, he answered; she could stay as long as she liked. What difference did one more mouth make at table? If only his own daughters were more like Miss Rose, if they were as ready as she to give up the noisy, stupid city, how happy he would be.

Hannah did not take to Miss Rose; she did not like her ways or her talk. She could not have said why. She answered her husband drily:

"Turning farmer is easier said than done. We ought to know. But of course Miss Rose is welcome to stay as long as she likes. Isn't she our daughter's friend?"

"Oh, but I'm going to earn my keep!" exclaimed Rose. "I'm not going to be idle. I'll feed the chickens, I'll churn butter."

She skipped out of the room and came back in a few moments wearing a newly-pressed waist and a neat apron.

"See! That's my dress for churning butter."

And indeed, she did not once, in the next days, ask to be taken to Pleasure Inn or The Fountain. She was through with that silly stuff, she said. But for all that, the only visible work she did was to teach Arontchik to dance. "It's much more fun to dance at home," she said. "That's what a home's for!"

The Pull of the City

Every evening Arontchik put on a fresh shirt—to his mother's unuttered distress—and took his dancing lessons to the strains of Rose's gramophone. He put his arms carefully about her, barely permitting himself to touch her body, and he followed her instructions with patient and stately clumsiness.

In the middle of the week dawned a morning of stifling closeness. The barometer indicated "Fair and sunshine," the meteorological station likewise reported over the telephone: "Today sunshine." And Hannah retorted: "Today rain; lots of it!" What did the barometer or the meteorological station know about it? She had her own barometer—the rheumatic twitch under her left arm. In vain did Moishe Mordecai and Arontchik point to the clear sky. "It's going to rain today, plenty," she repeated, and that was the end of the matter for her. Arontchik had set aside this day for bringing the hay in. "It's drying up," he said, "the cattle won't touch it." He left everything else and went out early to the fields behind the little forest, and all morning he mowed in the hot sun.

"Arontchik," said his father, when the boy came home to dinner, "this is no time for mowing. Your mother's right, it's going to rain."

"No," answered Arontchik, obstinately, "I guess the barometer and the station know better than mother's rheumatism. There isn't a speck of cloud in the sky."

After dinner he returned to the field. Two hours later he came galloping back on Sonny. There were heavy signs in the sky that Hannah's rheumatism had guessed better than the barometer and the meteorological station. Hastily Arontchik gathered up the tarpaulins to cover the hay. Moishe Mordecai was not at home. There was a meeting in Silverton, where the little Jewish community was planning to build its synagogue, and Moishe Mordecai, now that life was a little easier, had remembered that "man does not live by bread alone." There was no man about to help Arontchik, and when Rose offered her services enthusiastically he looked at her, in her neat blouse and ironed apron, and did not answer. This was no time for nonsense. Five minutes later he was back in the field, furiously raking together the cut hay, stacking it, covering it. It was a race between him and the storm. Naked to the waist, the sweat pouring down his body, he wielded the pitchfork breathlessly, with eyes for nothing but the threatened hay. The clouds gathered sullenly; here and there a ray of sunlight broke through and fell on the gleaming, rippling muscles of the frenzied worker; then the light was extinguished by a heavy curtain rolling out from behind the vast accumulation of vapor. And then suddenly, in front of him, where he could not help seeing her, was Rose, in her dainty waist and apron. She had rolled up her sleeves, and she tossed her head in a determined gesture, so that the plaits danced. Arontchik said not a word. His mind was filled with the thought of the winter. He saw Sonny and Jethro and Red Malkah standing in their stalls trying to chew the withered hay, and turning from it, their tongues hanging out. One sweep of the pitchfork gathered up half a row of bundles of hay. "Cover that!" he panted. But as he turned from the second half of the row he saw her tugging helplessly with her thin hands at the tarpaulin. He leapt over to her, gave one tug, covered the heap, and was back in the line with his pitchfork.

The first heavy drops fell. Arontchik forgot himself and shouted at Rose to run for it, to get back to the house. A terrific storm was coming on. She had nothing to cover herself with. But Rose would not hear of it. She wanted to stay and help him. And she began to tug again foolishly at another tarpaulin.

And now the rain came; a swift drumming of drops, a vast darkness, and a roaring over the fields. Arontchik threw away the pitchfork, grabbed his coat off the wagon, threw it over Rose, and covered himself with a tarpaulin.

They looked at each other silently, she smiling, he earnest. Her hair was streaming, and the dress under his coat was soaked through and through. The water ran off her dress, down her stockings and into her shoes. He took her arm and pushed her toward the wagon, pointing to the dry place underneath.

She took the hint and, laughing, crept under the wagon.

He remained standing, wrapped in the tarpaulin, and his thoughts were divided. Some were with the hay which was soaking in the rain, others were with something else, he did not quite know what. He heard her gay voice from under the wagon:

"Arontchik! Come down here! You'll be washed away!"

The fury of the rain increased; it came down in angry sheets. Rose, under the wagon, kept laughing shrilly. She wouldn't have missed this for anything in the world! She loved getting a good scare, she cried.

Arontchik does not answer. The rain whips his face, his body. The water runs down into his trousers, and the tarpaulin on his body is now like a sponge.

"Come down here, Arontchik! Don't be silly! Are you afraid of something?"

No, he is not afraid. What is there to be afraid of?

He squats to the leeward side of the wagon, and then he crawls under it. Rose snuggles up to him. She's cold. Arontchik forgets the mown hay, forgets Sonny. His ears are beginning to burn.

Then, suddenly, as he swings toward her, she throws her arms round him and presses him close, close. He is amazed by the strength in her arms. The folds of her dress hurt his naked flesh, and as his hungry arms go round her she whispers:

"No! No! Not now, Arontchik! It's daylight!"

Paralyzed between desire and fear he makes no further advances. The rain drives down harder, swifter. It turns into a cloudburst. A small lake forms round the wagon, it begins to invade the spot where they are sitting. Arontchik lifts her as if she were an infant and pulls her on top of himself, out of the wet.

Then the storm passed, as swiftly as it had come. They crept out, not looking at each other. Rose straightened her dress as well as she could, handed Arontchik back his coat, and without a word fled over the fields.

Later, when Arontchik came home, he found her in another dress, all neat and dry. She had slipped into the house unobserved, and changed; then she had told them that she had been under a tree during the storm.

All that afternoon Arontchik went about the house silently and furtively, like a man planning a theft. Now and then he went out to the stall, as though to do some work; but he only lingered there, preoccupied, and came back with nothing done.

By evening the rain had run off, the ground was dry again. A bright moon shone in a clear sky. When supper was over Arontchik left the house and hung about outside, keeping to the shadows, his eyes always glued on the door. Why, on this of all evenings, did she have to be busy with Sarah? It seemed to him that hours passed while he kept his vigil. Then, when the moon was setting and he had all but given up hope, she appeared in the doorway, her white dress glimmering. She stood there, as if waiting; then she closed the door softly behind her, and took two or three steps uncertainly into the night. Two powerful arms closed round her, lifted her, and carried her away.

VI

Some days later Arontchik, finding his parents alone in the living room, said suddenly that he was going to marry Miss Rose. Moishe Mordecai and Hannah started convulsively where they sat, and at last Hannah found her tongue.

"What is this?" she said. "Why the hurry? You don't even know who she is. Can't you wait till we have a chance to learn something about her?"

Arontchik looked away and shifted his weight from foot to foot. "I *must* marry her!" he burst out.

"Must?" asked his mother, astonished. "What do you mean?"

Arontchik was silent. Husband and wife looked at each other, and Hannah suddenly covered her face with her hands. Moishe Mordecai wrinkled his forehead, and, as his habit was when confronted with an unexpected problem, pulled his cap down over his eyes.

"What are you so puzzled about?" he said to his wife. "The lad's speaking plainly enough, isn't he? He says he must, so I suppose he knows what he's talking about."

Hannah bit her lip.

"*Must!*" she cried. "You don't always do what you must. There's always time to think it over, isn't there?"

"Hannah!" answered her husband, harshly. "What are you talking about? This is a decent girl!" He turned to his son. "What's the difference! If you must, you must. *Mazel tov!* Good luck!"

He went into the next room where Rose, it seemed, was waiting for something.

"*Mazel tov,* Miss Rose!" he said to her, abruptly. "You're going to stay with us for good! Because from now on this will be your home, won't it?"

"Of course," she cried, and tears started to her eyes. She went up to the old man and put her head on his breast. Where else would she want to live, she asked. Hadn't she been born on the land? Hadn't she passed her childhood on the land?

Moishe Mordecai led her into the living room.

"Wife! The brandy! The sponge cake!" And he stroked Rose's head tenderly.

Hannah went about the house in a daze.

. . .

Yes, of course she was going to live on the land. But she had never said that the wedding itself was going to take place on the farm. Because that was really unthinkable. It had to be a proper wedding, in the city, a wedding such as all her friends had had, in a hall, with frock coats and silk dresses, like all decent people. Not that she believed in such things, really, especially now that she was going to be a plain peasant woman, a farmer's wife. But the wedding was another matter. She had always dreamed of that as something apart, with lights, and music, and dancing.

And immediately after the wedding, when she was still in New York with her husband, she repeated: yes, it was going to be a farmer's life for her, she would keep her word, but Arontchik surely understood that farm life today wasn't what it had been in the old days. It wasn't, for instance, like farm life over there, in Poland. No; *her* home, she had always said, was going to be like a palace. She'd never consent to live in a hovel. And anyway, she'd saved up some money of her own, and she was going to use it to buy decent furniture for the two rooms Moishe Mordecai and Hannah had set apart for the young couple.

Instead of finding himself back on the farm with his wife, Arontchik found himself making the rounds of various furniture stores. The salesmen seemed to know Rose quite well; apparently she had made the same tour on previous occasions, with other young men. When she was through with the buying of the furniture—Arontchik could not understand what they needed so many things for—it transpired that her savings would not cover the cost. The fact was, she explained, that she had spent quite a bit on her wedding clothes. When they got home Arontchik asked his father for some money. Moishe Mordecai had set aside five hundred dollars from the last harvest, intending to buy six more acres of good potato land from Johnson. It had been his intention, indeed, to buy them for Arontchik; it was time for the boy to start on his own.

However, it transpired further that Rose had not been thinking at all of furnishing just the two rooms set aside for her and Arontchik. She had planned to refurnish the whole house, leaving two rooms to Moishe Mordecai and Hannah. A huge moving van appeared one day at the farm, and the truckmen carried out innumerable assorted pieces of imitation period furniture, Chippendale, Queen Anne, Colonial—settees, chairs, tables, armchairs, some of them half covered with silk. They did not quite fit in with the stoves, the less so as the cheap material soon began to warp and peel with the indoor heat.

It was still winter when the new housewife came to settle on the farm. For the first few weeks she was wholly occupied with arranging her "palace." She laid brocaded covers on the tables and sideboards. She hung up charming little curtains. She made borders of paper flowers for the mirrors. She had found, in her two rooms, quite a number of flowerpots which waited, like everything else on the farm, for the next awakening of nature. These she threw out; she had, instead, two large artificial palms which a furniture dealer had thrown in as a bonus. The rubber palms blossomed green and fresh, but the trees and fields outside were white with snow and ice.

In the dead of winter there was less work to do on the farm, and the young couple usually did not get up until noon. Hannah went about muttering at the unseemliness of it. But Moishe Mordecai defended them. "Young people . . . let them have their happiness . . ." He quoted the Bible, as was his wont. Until a year after his marriage, said the Bible, a man was exempt from military service. Moishe Mordecai was very helpful to Arontchik during those days. There was a good sleigh on the farm, there was also Sonny. So two or three times a week Arontchik harnessed the sleigh, and he and Rose went to a movie in Silverton, or some other near-by town. Hannah kept on muttering: How long was this honeymoon going to last? What was all this gadding about for? They were married now, weren't they? They had settled down, hadn't they? But Moishe Mordecai kept defending his son and daughter-in-law, and for every reproach of Hannah's had a verse from the Bible.

Since Rose had spread her "palace" through most of the house, and Hannah was left with only two rooms—one of which was the kitchen—Arontchik had become more the master than Moishe Mordecai. Exactly how and when this happened no one could have told; it just happened. Until the time of the unexpected marriage the answer to every chore had always and automatically been, "Arontchik!" If it was wood that had to be chopped, or water pumped up from the well, somebody merely shouted, "Arontchik!" But since the marriage this had changed: to be exact, not since the marriage, but since a certain little domestic scene which occurred after the marriage. Hannah, quite in the old way, had called out, "Arontchik, we need more wood for the stove."

Thereupon Rose had interjected, sharply: "Isn't there anybody around except Arontchik to chop wood? Because if there isn't, you'd better hire a man."

Moishe Mordecai got up hastily and went out to the shed. A little while later Arontchik sneaked out after him, took the axe away from his father, and finished the chore. But after that there was no more, "Arontchik, do this!" and "Arontchik, do that!" At least, not while Rose was about; and Rose was about most of the time.

The winter was drawing to a close when Rose decided that she simply had to go to New York for a visit, just for a fortnight's change. While she was gone there was less friction in the house. Moishe Mordecai and Arontchik never quarreled or got on each other's nerves. The old man had become softer toward his son since the marriage. Then, with the spring, work set in again like a flood. During the spring farmers cannot quibble about every piece of work and who is supposed to do it. The labor on the farm pulled them all in. The men were in the fields, Hannah was taken up with the chicken coops. Rose, of course, had to be spared now, because of her condition. This spring Arontchik threw himself into the work with more energy than ever before. During the potato planting Moishe Mordecai strode about the fields beaming with joy. "It's going to be a marvelous year," he said, "if only God will be good to us and send the rains on time." Arontchik went to Silverton and came back with a couple of hired men; he himself was both worker and overseer. God was good to them; it was a potato year. Arontchik worked tirelessly. He was up and in the fields before sunrise; the noise of the cultivator came back to the house out of the morning twilight. Old Moishe Mordecai was glad to see his son thinking less in terms of horses—Sonny and Jethro—and more in terms of machinery. Moreover, Arontchik was supervising the whole farm. The hay was cut and taken in at the right time; the potatoes, the rye, the other grain, were harvested in rotation. Moishe Mordecai said to Hannah: "Wife, there's nothing teaches a man as much as having a wife"—and he jerked his thumb toward the other room.

At the time when the potatoes were coming up, Rose started a queer conversation with Arontchik. She wanted to know exactly what he was in this place. Was he a partner, did he own something of his own, or was he just a hired hand? What was his status, and who was he?

"Who I am?" asked Arontchik, astounded. "Why, I'm the son."

Until that moment the question of his status had never occurred to him. He was, as he had just told Rose, the son. The farm was "our" farm. If the year was a good one, you naturally thought first of taking up some of the mortgage, and then of buying a few more acres; or else you invested in a couple of cows, or a piece of machinery. And if the year wasn't a good one, well, you were all glad to get by together. But there was no talk of "mine" and "yours." Everything was "ours."

"In America," said Rose, "there's no such thing as 'ours.' It's either 'mine' or 'yours.'"

The conversation took place in the privacy of their "salon," as Hannah sarcastically called her daughter-in-law's living room. It was a short conversation, and Rose did not revert to the subject, nor did Arontchik ever mention it to his parents. But one day Moishe Mordecai said to his wife that he "smelled" something, and the something had to do with the ownership of the farm. On a certain Saturday afternoon he went strolling with his son through the fields. That was a regular practice of Moishe Mordecai's; on the Sabbath he did not work, he rested, and he refreshed himself by walking over his farm. This time he invited Arontchik along. When they reached the potato field he stopped and said:

"Listen, son. It's time I talked to you about certain things. Maybe they've been in your mind, too. You're not a boy any more. You're a man—a married man. You've a young wife. You'll be a father soon, God willing. And I guess your wife has a right to know what's hers, or what's hers and yours. That's the way of the world. And the Bible says, too, 'Therefore shall a man leave his father's house. . . .' So listen to me, son.

"Let's go through the fields and measure off. The six acres we've added since we first bought the farm are yours. They're your work. I bought them with money you earned. But the old farm still belongs—as it always did—to me. When I pass on you'll have your share in it along with the other children. But we'll work the whole farm as we've always done, together; and whatever money comes in we'll divide between us, share and share alike."

Arontchik did not answer, but his neck, his face and his ears were as red as on that day when he had first met Rose.

When the potatoes were in, half the yield was sold at once, the other half kept for the rising market. Rose's time was now approaching, and she was therefore preparing to leave for the city.

Arontchik took the cash for his share of the potatoes, and borrowed from Moishe Mordecai on his share of the unsold half. He accompanied Rose to New York, but they found, on their arrival, that she had miscalculated, and there would be quite a wait. But she would not return to the farm, nor would she let Arontchik do so. You could never be quite sure, she said. Meanwhile, there were the Yiddish theaters, there were restaurants, there were relatives and friends of hers to be visited. Besides, she wanted to show her Arontchik how one lived in the city, not among cows and horses, but among human beings.

The plan to buy still another six acres of potato land from Johnson had of course been given up. It was a great pity to lose that good, rich black earth, which would have rounded off the patch. But there was no use talking about it now. The expenses of the confinement, and of the unexpected stay in the city, ate up not only Arontchik's share of the cash harvest for that year, but made a considerable hole in Moishe Mordecai's share, too.

Instead of six new acres added to the farm, one new member was added to the family: a boy, a tremendous fellow who nearly cost his mother her life. Rose's labor pains lasted three days and nights, and at one point the doctors almost decided that one of the two, mother or son, would have to be sacrificed.

The experience was for Arontchik not only something new, but until then something utterly unimaginable. Of course he had seen births on the farm; he had long since learned that no new life comes easily into the world. He remembered his first experience of this kind, the birth of Sonny out of Johnson's mare, when he himself had cut the umbilical cord. But a torment of three days and three nights, inflicted on a human being, and one dear to him, he had not lived through until then; and the thought of that lusty new human being tearing and thrusting its way through the narrow passage of Rose's body haunted him long after the ordeal was over.

Rose needed, of course, more than the usual obstetrical help. A specialist was called in, and the specialist's fee was the equivalent of two acres of land, or of a good cow. Well, God was good! Nothing was lost but money, and when Arontchik left the hospital after the first sight of his son, he felt like a rich man. He could not help casting up his accounts.

"Rose and the boy are mine," he said to himself. "The six acres father gave me are mine. Sonny belongs to me, so do Red Malkah and the young steer."

It was night as Arontchik walked through the streets talking to himself. A moisture-laden autumn wind blew between the houses; but all that Arontchik could see was his land, six acres of it, his own, out there near Silverton; ploughed up, open, waiting for the seed which it would nourish and turn into a rich crop.

The name for the little man who had now been added to the family was chosen by Moishe Mordecai; he called him Isaac, in memory of a great Rabbi he had known in the old country. The circumcision ceremony was held in the hospital, where Rose still lay, too weak to be moved; and Arontchik remained with her until she was something like her old self again.

But he was disappointed in his hope that now they would all go back to the farm. Rose argued that it was ridiculous to take an infant only a few weeks old to live on a farm, and in the winter at that, where you sometimes had to wait a whole day to get a doctor, and, if you were snowed in, longer than that. It was like being in a wilderness. She simply would not hear of it. Arontchik swallowed his disappointment and tried to see it reasonably. After all, Rose was a city girl; in any case, she knew much more about such matters than he. It was a blow, not only to his expectations of a normal home life, but to his financial plans. Again Arontchik had to apply to his father for money, and again Moishe Mordecai had to dig into his dwindling reserves. What else could he do?

This whole money question, and the question of what belonged to whom, ate into Arontchik. It had been working in him ever since Rose had spoken to him about "mine" and "yours" and "ours." When he came home from the city he went into the stall and divided it into parts with a bar; on one side were his animals, Sonny, the young steer, and the calf which was almost ready to become a cow; on the other side were his father's animals. There was nothing practical about this division of the stall into two parts, for the animals ate from a common stock of fodder. But Arontchik wanted to accustom himself to the idea of his separate ownership. "Let's make it clear," he said to himself, "and don't let's have any arguments about what belongs to whom." He had in mind the offspring of the calf; there was going to be no doubt as to ownership in that matter. And when he had made this division in the stall and had let the meaning of it as it were sink home, he led the calf out one morning to a near-by farm, where there was a steer of good stock, and had it covered.

Weeks passed, and Rose still remained in the city. Arontchik missed her and hankered after the child. He could not return to the old ways. He worked hard, but his mind was not on his work; it was with Rose and the little one. The days were tolerable; there was always something to keep him busy. But the evenings were a torment. He could not sit still; he could not stay in the house. He wandered about over the fields, he took the road toward Silverton and waited for the last mail, in the hope that there was a letter from Rose.

Moishe Mordecai and Hannah looked on helplessly. Hannah sighed, wept into her hands, and said: "I can't bear to see it. The boy wanders about like a ghost."

"What can you expect?" asked Moishe Mordecai. "Life is like that. Take the she-dove away from the he-dove, and he'll pine away, too."

Unable to stand the loneliness, Arontchik went up to New York twice during the winter. More than that he could not afford; he could not even afford those two visits. Rose's stay in the city was a steady drain, and his own visits also cost a few dollars. There was not only railroad fare and the food in the city; there was also Rose's demand for entertainment. She was lonesome, she said. When her husband came, she expected him to take her out, to the theater, to restaurants. Arontchik had to curtail his visits, then give them up. There was no more cash on the farm; Moishe Mordecai's reserve was all gone. There was only one way to raise money, and that was to sell some of the livestock.

With the spring, all idea of visits to the city vanished. There was too much to do on the farm. It was only then that Rose at last let herself be persuaded to come back.

It was a festive day for Arontchik when he harnessed his own Sonny to the wagon and went down to Silverton to bring home his wife and child. He felt that this was the confirmation of his independence and his manhood. He was not only a husband, he was a father; he had brought the next generation of farmers into the family heritage. He walked about more proudly and dreamed of the years ahead.

Summer came again, with its heat and its back-breaking labor. Arontchik worked harder than ever before. With a good natured smile on his face Moishe Mordecai noted how the lad (he still thought of him as "the lad") threw himself with particular fervor into the care of his own few acres, even though the profits of the farm were treated as a unit and divided equally between father and son. "You do better by your own," he said to himself. "You just can't help it." Similarly, he noticed that when Arontchik came into the stall, his first thought was for his own animals. Far from being disturbed by this partiality, Moishe Mordecai looked on it as a good sign. "You feel your own blood first," he said, approvingly.

In this general fury of labor, Rose did nothing except look after her baby. Hannah even had to take time out from her regular chores to wait on her. Rose stayed in bed every day until the early afternoon. She took breakfast and the midday meal in bed. In the evening she left the clearing up to her mother-in-law. She did not even wash the baby's things. What was more, she accepted all this service naturally, as if it were her due.

In the middle of the summer, when the heat was at its highest and the city people were streaming into the country, Rose began speaking again of the city. The country bored her. She couldn't stand it any more. She would never have married, she said, if she had known it was going to be like this. She had had a very different picture of it; but what that picture had been, she did not say, and no one could imagine.

"Look, Arontchik," she said, one day. "You don't think I'm going to pass the remainder of my life on the farm, do you? I'm too young for that."

It was the first time she had spoken up so openly and so decisively. Arontchik stood facing her, like a man dazed by a blow. His slow, peasant mind could not take it in.

"Rose," he answered, "you said you were going to live with us here on the farm, that you'd stay with us for good."

"No, no, Arontchik. I don't intend to throw away my life on cows and horses. I can't stay here."

"What do you want to do?"

"After the high holidays I'm going back to the city, and I'm taking little Isaac with me."

"We can't do it, Rose," said Arontchik in a low, timid voice. "We haven't the money for it."

"Sell one of the cows."

"What? What's that you said? Sell one of the cows?"

"All right! If you don't want to sell one of the cows, come with me to the city. You'll find a job there."

"I don't know what to do in the city. I'm lost in the city."

"Oh, don't be foolish. You'll find yourself there. Millions of people get work in the city; so will you."

"No, Rose; there's nothing for me to do there. I'm a stranger in the city. I've always worked in the fields; I know my way about here. Over there I wouldn't know where to begin."

From that day on there was nothing to be done with Rose. Neither Arontchik's patient arguments, nor Hannah's stormy denunciations, nor Moishe Mordecai's bitter silences had any effect on her. On the first cold day Rose packed her and little Isaac's things, and declared she was going back.

Sonny and the "calf." He did not understand that. If he had no
land, where was he to sow potatoes?

"Are you thinking of going back to the farm?" asked Rose.

"You mean," he said, more to himself than to her, "that I'll never
return? I'll never work the land again? I'll never drive a plough?"

It seemed to him that the floor he was standing on at the moment was melting away under his feet. His head went round.

"Rose! You actually mean I'm going to sell my farm?" he cried.

"What do you want a farm for? Millions of people live without a
farm. Why can't you?"

He shook his head heavily.

"I'll die without a farm," he said, simply. "I wouldn't be able to
live without Sonny and without the calf."

"So I mean less to you than Sonny and the calf?"

"Rose!"

"Don't be a baby," she said, contemptuously. Then, changing her
tone, she pleaded, eagerly: "You'll soon get used to it, Arontchik.
It'll be wonderful. We'll go to a theater every evening, or to
friends, or else friends will come to visit us. We'll live like civilized
people. You'll see."

"What will father say?" asked Arontchik, bewildered.

" 'Father!' " she mocked him. " 'Father!' Are you a little boy, or
a man with a wife and baby of his own?"

Arontchik breathed hard. "No," he said, heavily. "I can't do it."
His big body trembled. "Rose! Come home with me! Come back
to the farm!"

"Never!" she screamed. "Never! I've had enough of it."

There was nothing to be done with Rose. Heartsick and confused, Arontchik went back alone, and again his torments returned. During the days he stumbled about the fields, trying in
vain to keep his mind on his work. Nights he lay awake, longing
for Rose. Sometimes he would dress and go out into the lightless
fields. When he sat at table with his parents he avoided looking
at them, like a 'man who is ashamed of his thoughts.

One day Hannah, unable to endure her son's unhappiness, said,
sharply: "There's an easy way out. If you want to make the cow

go into the stall, you take away her calf. She follows. She always follows."

Moishe Mordecai pulled his cap down over his forehead and turned an angry face to his wife.

"Enough of that," he exclaimed.

For some reason which he could not fathom, Arontchik found his father's patience harder to bear than his mother's forthrightness.

"And what will you do without me?" he asked, sharply. "How will you manage?"

Stung, Moishe Mordecai answered: "A fat lot of help you've been to me since you got married. I've been managing without you anyhow. I can go on managing without you."

Arontchik stared at his father.

"I didn't know that," he said, at last.

. . . .

That spring Arontchik did not lead out a living horse or a living cow into the free and open fields. He was standing, from early morning till late at night in a stationery and candy store, selling paper cows and horses to the children of the neighborhood.

The sun shone in at the open door of his store. Arontchik could not stand still; an itch of restlessness was in his body. Whatever he turned his hand to, it seemed to him that he was wasting his time. Out there the fields were waiting for him, and here he was, fiddling around ridiculously with paper horses and paper cows.

But on the farm Moishe Mordecai, who had aged more in the last year than in all the other years he had been on the land, led out brown Jethro to the ploughing. The furrow came to an end at the old boundary, on this side of the six acres which he had sold back to Johnson. Moishe Mordecai, bent double behind the plough, did not lift his head when he reached the new fence. He was afraid that Johnson, ploughing on his side, would reach the fence at about the same time, and he did not want to face his neighbor. He was ashamed. He felt at this moment, as he had always felt, that he represented the house of Israel, while Johnson represented the gentiles of the world; and the house of Israel could no longer return, frankly and proudly, the gaze of the gentiles of the world.

But Johnson, having reached the end of his furrow, waited, leaning on the fence and chewing tobacco; and when Moishe Mordecai was opposite him, he said:

"If the young ones fly away, what's the sense in the old ones keeping up the nest, neighbor Mordecai?"

His Second Love

A YEAR or two had passed since I had seen Reb Nochum, since I had sat with him on his favorite bench opposite the little park on Washington Heights or had paused in passing to hear him conduct the discussion on world affairs among the coterie of graybeards—retired workers, peddlers and shopkeepers, pensioners of their children—who sometimes took the sun with him. I had known him a long time; or, rather, for a long time I had known next to nothing about him and a great deal about his views, which covered every subject of public interest. He had delivered himself to me, or in my presence, of sage comment and criticism on wars and revolutions, the destinies of nations, the plots of kings, the errors of mankind, the future of the planet; I had listened with interest, I had responded with counter-comment and counter-criticism. But, very oddly, he had never spoken of himself. I cannot remember whether I had ever tried to draw him out, as my way is with old people; but I am quite certain that, until he told me what I have transcribed here, he had never been for me a person with a history. And what made him so communicative on this occasion I cannot tell.

I spied him at his regular post, sitting alone. It was early evening, and the street lamps were beginning to star the settling darkness. The air was filled with the purr of automobiles, the rattle of roller skates, the yelling of children at play. Reb Nochum sat in deep meditation; he had his right hand under his beard, which he lifted up till it lay horizontally before him, like a peddler's tray, and his eyes were fixed on it broodingly.

"Reb Nochum! Reb Nochum!" I cried, joyously. "What a pleasure to see you! What's worrying you? Is it Hitler again?"

"Hitler?" he snorted, starting up. "Hitler? Pah! Is there nothing else to think about in the world? We think about him much more than we ought to. Do you know what? If the world were half as afraid of God as it is of Hitler, we shouldn't have come to this pass."

A good comment, I thought, and I had no reply. I said nothing.

"No, it wasn't of Hitler I was thinking. And not of the world. I was thinking of myself. I was remembering something—a foolish thing, if you like, and yet—" He stopped, and a smile flickered across his wrinkled eyes. It was a shy smile, one which pleaded for understanding. Still I said nothing; I only moved a little closer to him on the bench.

"I was thinking," he said, or rather blurted, "of—well, of my second love."

A faint blush crept up from under his beard. I tried hard not to show my astonishment.

"Your second love," I repeated, in a matter-of-fact voice. "Your second love. Some other woman who came into your life?"

Reb Nochum fixed two horrified eyes on me.

"Some other woman? God forbid. I'm thinking of my own Bella, may she rest in Paradise."

The blush passed away.

"What makes you stare at me, man? Don't you think anyone ever had a second love in his own wife? If a man's to fall in love in his latter years, who's half as good as his own wife? Another man's wife? Foo! I leave that to artists and actors. And when should a man fall in love with his wife, if not in his latter years? Has he got the time for it before then? No, no. All he has time for, while he's young, is the struggle. A thousand worries, a thousand problems, tear him to pieces. Here in America above all, where it's fight, fight, fight, or else you go under. Not a moment for your wife, or for your children, or for yourself, if it comes to that. Where do you spend the strength of your young years? At home? No, sir. It's subway and workshop, workshop and subway, year in, year out. And when you do come home evenings, and your wife's prepared a good meal for you, a stew, with carrots and honey for dessert, like in the old country, to comfort you for the day's labor, can you enjoy it? You fall asleep at table, your nose on your newspaper; and she has to pull the shoes off your feet and bundle you into bed.

"Could you really say that I had a wife? Did she know that I was there? Did I ever give an hour to her? I think back, and it seems to me that she and I never sat opposite each other at table for five minutes together. Because when I sat there with the children, she was in the kitchen, or serving. What sort of life was it for her? Could anyone have called her a wife? She was a kind of receptacle for all my troubles, that's all she was. She was the only one I could grumble at, complain to. When the foreman had it in for me, it was Bella who collected. That foreman! Shlomo the Shark we called him. Our boss, a pious Jew, picked out Shlomo the Shark and put him over us, because he couldn't find a meaner soul on the East Side. And what Shlomo the Shark poured out on me, I poured out evenings on poor Bella, as if it was her fault that I became a worker in a shirt factory here in America. You may not know it, my friend, but I once had other dreams and other ambitions; I didn't see myself as a shirt-maker. But those dreams and ambitions were done to death slowly by needle and scissors."

Reb Nochum looked once more at his beard, as if he was reading his past in it.

"Yes, sir, I want you to know that we were somebodies on the other side, in Bzhezhin. We were no strangers to learning, to the sacred books, to the works of the sages. And I myself, let me tell you, followed early in the footsteps of my fathers. Not Jewish lore alone, but modern knowledge, grammar, and mathematics, and Russian—though we had to study those subjects in secret, to be sure. Look at me! I was a revolutionary once upon a time, God help me. I left the Talmudical college, I was drawn into the move-

ment—those were the big years, 1904, 1905. I was a 'conspirator'
—made fiery speeches at secret meetings, liberty, humanity, progress, all the rest of it. Was caught at it, too, and got off with nothing worse than a pair of black eyes and three months in prison.
Would you believe all that of me?"

I did not answer his question.

"When I came out of jail I ran away from my native town and
went to Lodz. I hoped to become what they called a 'cutter'—
which isn't the same as a cutter in this country. Over there a 'cutter' was the man who snipped off the ends of the piece of cloth
as it came off the loom. It was a good trade. A cutter earned good
money and could always marry well. But it wasn't easy to get
yourself apprenticed to a cutter. So while I waited for my chance,
I studied Talmud, and as a Talmud student I was given 'days'
—you know the old custom: every day some other householder
would let me eat at his table. Nights I slept in the synagogue
house. And to justify my meals, I had to be seen studying every
day. Studying the Talmud, of course, not the ungodly knowledge
of the modern world. That I had to pursue in secret.

"Well, my opportunity came at last—not to become a cutter, if
you please, but to marry. One of my householders had a daughter.
I liked her, and she liked me. From the first instant we saw each
other. Yes, I can say it was love at first sight; we knew we were
meant for each other. It was my Bella, peace to her soul. Her
father was a butcher; it was rumored that he had money. I
wouldn't know of course; all I knew was that he was my best
'day'—that's where I got my best meals of the week. He was my
Wednesday, and on Wednesdays I could make up for what I
missed on the other six days. My mother-in-law, too, liked me; she
put a half chicken on the table for me, and said, heartily, 'Eat,
young man. Studying Talmud is no light labor. Fill up!' And
there my Bella stood—sweet be her lot in Paradise—under the
shining brass and copper ware on the shelves; and she shone
brighter than they. It was a beautiful, clean kitchen; my Bella's
hands were as skillful as they were industrious. The walls were
covered with embroidery pictures: Abraham bringing his son

Isaac to the sacrifice; the Wailing Wall; our father Jacob meeting
Rachel at the well; Ruth gleaning the ears in the field; that sort
of thing. All Bella's work. And then, the embroidered cushions,
the tablecloths, with proverbs worked into them, in Yiddish and
Hebrew and Russian. Beautiful!

"Well, to cut a long story short, those Wednesdays became very
precious to me. There were no other days. I would have liked the
week to consist of nothing but Wednesdays. I used to bless God
for having invented Wednesdays, because Wednesday was my
sabbath and my holy day and my festival and everything else
rolled into one. That was my first love for Bella.

"Of course my mother-in-law—God rest her soul, she's been in
the other world, the real world, many, many years now—saw what
had happened; and she was glad of it. She fancied me as a son-
in-law. At least, that's the way it looks to me now. I can't see why
else she should have stuffed me with the best in the house.

"And always Bella was standing there, under the copper ware,
her golden hair, done up in thick plaits, shining brighter than the
polished utensils. The crown on a queen's head wasn't brighter.
And do you know—it seems to me that it's only now, now after
so many years, that I understand how lovely she was. Her cheeks
were cream and cherry, and her eyes! No, I can't tell you how
beautiful she was in those days, when she became my bride. It's in
here"—and old Reb Nochum poked a finger at his heart—"the
picture's in here, but I can't bring it out.

"I shan't even try. I'll make it short. I came there Wednesday
after Wednesday, and my good mother-in-law-to-be stuffed me
like a goose—until at last a *shadchan* got on the job, a marriage
broker. Maybe you think that funny. What did we need a *shadchan* for, when everyone could see that Bella and I were destined
for each other from the beginning of time? But that's the way it
was in those days. It didn't look respectable without a *shadchan*.
The *shadchan* came to me in the study house of the synagogue.
My father-in-law—a bulky Jew with a heavy gold chain stretched
across his corporation—sent him. A celebration was arranged, the
bride's family was assembled—and we were formally engaged.

"It wasn't a long engagement, but it was a jolly one. All of a sudden the miracle had happened! Every day became a Wednesday. Nothing but Wednesdays. God send such Wednesdays to all unhappy Jews all over the world, amen!

"After the wedding my father-in-law said to me, 'Young man, what trade do you reckon to learn? I can't keep you and your wife till you become a Rabbi, or pass your examinations'—he knew I studied in secret—'because I have other children to look after, and you'll have grown-up children of your own before you become a doctor or a Rabbi.'

"What trade? I hadn't the slightest idea. We thought of this, we thought of that. And in the end my father-in-law solved the problem by buying us ship's tickets to America.

"And what was I going to do in America? We didn't know. We didn't think about it. In America everyone made a living; a living made itself, as you might say. And if worst came to worst, why, you just picked the gold off the streets. Wasn't everybody either going to America or getting the most wonderful letters from there? All sorts of ignorant and unskilled people were making money there; so was a student like myself, who had studied Talmud and Russian and grammar and mathematics, going to worry?

" 'Before you know it,' I said to my parents-in-law, 'I'll be sending you tickets to join us.' Just to show you what I thought of myself in those days.

"Well, I'll spare you the story of the journey, the dirt, the crowding, the seasickness, the herring and potato diet. It's old stuff. They say that nowadays you get on a ship and travel to Europe and back and don't even know you're on a ship. It's like one of those hotels in Florida that I hear about, only it's a floating hotel. It was very different in those days. You ate enough herring and swallowed enough salt water to become a herring yourself. But as I said, I'll spare you the story. I'll just tell you this much. I didn't know what trouble was until I set foot in America.

"It's a different world. Back in the old home you took your time. You'd wait a few months, and perhaps even a few years,

before you made up your mind what you were going to be and
what trade you were going to follow. Meanwhile you'd be living
with your father-in-law, or maybe your brother-in-law, or maybe
some other relative. And if you were up against it, why, you'd go
to an uncle, or an aunt, in another town. You'd have time to look
around, think things over. That's the way it was there. But not
here! Not in America! You weren't an hour in the country before
you came slap up against the question: 'Where's the next meal
coming from?' Mind you, I'm not complaining. They were very
decent to me. A distant relative of ours came to meet us at Castle
Garden. He took us to his home, questioned us about the folks on
the other side, and even helped us get a place to live in. But the
next day you got the hint: 'Brother, everyone looks after himself
in this country.'

"And before I knew it, the few roubles I'd brought with me
were gone. Yes, sir! The knife was on my throat—I mean I was
in it up to the neck, I was imprisoned in the workshop.

"I'll tell you how it happened. This relative of ours saw that I
hadn't the faintest notion of what was what. I was a greenhorn. I
had crazy ideas about becoming a Rabbi, or maybe a businessman;
and meanwhile I was eating up the last bit of dowry. So he took
hold of me one day, after prayers—we used to go to the same
synagogue, the Congregation Bzhezhin—and spoke very earnestly
to me: 'Here, in this country,' he said, 'we forget what we used to
be in the old country, all the snobbery, and the good family, and
the line of Rabbis and scholars and what not. Nobody wants to
know where you came from and what your ancestors were. Here
you're the same as everyone else; and if you won't be that, well,
you'll starve. Take my advice; forget that stuff about being something more than a worker. Because when the first of the month
comes, you've got your rent to pay; and if you try to pay your
rent with dreams, you'll find yourself in the gutter, with your bed
and table and chairs. See? The best thing for you to do is come
with me tomorrow morning to the workshop. You won't be a
stranger there; you'll find half of Bzhezhin waiting to greet you.'

"And don't you think he was talking sense, this distant relative of mine, Berel Kamashenshtepper? Because the next morning we were off to the workshop on Essex Street, which was owned by Reb Chaim David, also a Bzhezhin man. He'd come up in the world, Reb Chaim David. You wouldn't find him in the Essex Street workshop any more. He had other workshops, owned by him and his sons—not on the East Side but on Broadway. In those shops they had unions, and union rates. But not on Essex Street, you understand. That shop he'd reserved for the special benefit of his countrymen, immigrants from Bzhezhin. And for the special benefit of his countrymen he'd hired Shlomo the Shark as his foreman. Of course to his face we called him Reb Shlomo. This Reb Shlomo must have had Egyptian blood in him, because I don't see where he got his character if not way back from one of Pharaoh's slave-drivers.

"And so it was no God and no union in the Essex Street shop. If you asked Reb Chaim David about it, he'd tell you that he really didn't need that shop. He was keeping it open as a favor to the greenhorns from his old home town. It was a place where pious Jews could work, because it closed on Saturday. It didn't pay him, said Reb Chaim David. It was, to hear him talk, a charitable institution. And Shlomo the Shark was the superintendent. A wickeder man I never met in all my born days. And a more miserable workshop couldn't be found anywhere in the world.

"To begin with, it was a firetrap. The whole building was filled with workshops, with men and machines. Ours occupied the top floor, on the airshaft. On the opposite side of the airshaft, in the other building, you had tenements. In the summer the stink of garbage moldering at the bottom of the shaft, and of dirty linen hanging out of the windows, used to float up to the workshop. It was a sweet-sour stink, if you know what I mean. It crept not only into the nostrils but into the pores of your flesh, so that you carried it home. And above you the tin roof, almost melting under the sun, sent down waves of heat. It was like a lime-kiln. And the humidity! Most of the time we worked half-asleep. Sometimes we'd try to freshen up by starting a song, a good synagogue melody. And then Shlomo the Shark would come out of his corner.

He couldn't bear to hear us sing. He looked like a schoolmaster in the old country; all he lacked was the thongs. He wouldn't say anything, mind you. He'd just fix his cold, fishy eyes on us, and the song died away. He'd have frozen the song in the throat of a bird.

"He was not only foreman. He was a great worker. He knew how to set the pace. And he loved to do that on the hottest days, when the damp and heat and stink ate into our bones and our eyes were closing of themselves. He'd say: 'Let's see who can keep up with me!' And sometimes he'd say nothing. He'd just watch us—and that was enough.

"He had his special victims, too, people he picked on, God alone knows why. There was an elderly man who'd been working in Chaim David's workshop for years. Reb Asher, I think his name was. His hands trembled so he could hardly hold a needle. He shouldn't have been working at all; he should have been supported by his children. But there he was; so I guess he had no children, or they couldn't or wouldn't support him. And because Shlomo the Shark knew that Reb Asher had to have this job and couldn't get another, he delighted in making his life miserable.

"He'd come over to the old man, all of a sudden, and say, 'Well, Reb Asher, let's see what you've accomplished today!' He'd pick up the couple of shirts, examine them, put them down, and ask: 'Is that all? Do you expect a day's wages for that?' He wouldn't raise his voice. He'd talk softly, and smile.

"And the old man trembled with fear. 'Reb Shlomo, Reb Shlomo,' he'd say, 'that isn't all. Look, those shirts there are mine, too.' You see, we other workers used to keep an eye on Shlomo the Shark, and when we saw him coming near the old man, we'd shove some of our own finished work over, to help him out.

" 'An old man like you,' Shlomo would say, pityingly, 'oughtn't to be working here. He ought to be in an old folks' home. If your children won't look after you, you can apply to the old folks' home.' And the old man would answer stoutly—but his voice was all a-tremble: 'Don't you believe it, Reb Shlomo. I'm as good as ten of your young workers here.' And he'd try to speed up his sewing, with the result that the needle fell out of his fingers. And Shlomo the Shark would grin, and say: 'There you are! Didn't I say you ought to be in an old folks' home, Reb Asher. Or maybe you think this is one. Well, it isn't. It's a workshop. Either you'll have to get out, or take another cut.'

" 'Reb Shlomo, God bless us, what are you talking about?'—but by that time Shlomo the Shark was at another bench.

"Well, you can imagine how I felt in that shop—me, with my Talmud, and my Russian grammar, and my mathematics. 'Is this what I came to America for?' I asked myself. 'Is this going to be my future?'

"And believe it or not, bit by bit I became accustomed to that life. At first my Bella used to comfort me. She'd say: 'It's only for the time being, so we can pay the rent and have a bite to eat.' But it wasn't long before I realized that I was a lost man. I was in the grip of the workshop, and I'd never get out of it. Because, before you knew it, there was our first baby—my daughter Masha, God bless her, the one I'm living with now. And she was hardly off the breast before the second one came, my son Manny. I hadn't a chance to save a penny and look for another job. Whatever I brought home at the week end was swallowed up.

"They say America's the richest country in the world. Maybe it is. But if the country's rich, the people in it are terribly poor. In the old country it was different. If a man couldn't make a living, that wasn't the end of the world for him. He wouldn't be going around hungry, God forbid. Why, come to think of it, in our little town of Bzhezhin half the population never made a living. And yet people were born, and grew up, and married, and had children, and when their time came got themselves decently buried. Did you ever hear of anyone being put out of his house, into the gutter, because he couldn't pay the rent? Why, if a landlord tried to do that, just on account of a little thing like rent, he'd be excommunicated. Not a soul in town would talk to him. He'd be considered worse than an apostate, worse than an informer. They wouldn't bury him in the Jewish cemetery. He'd be given a donkey's burial. I'm told that things have changed now in the old country.

Maybe they have. I'm telling you how it used to be in my days.
Here, in America, you can be the most honorable citizen, with a
fifty-year record of prompt payment behind you, you can live in
the nicest house, refrigerator and radio and carpets—and if you lose
your money, or your job, and can't pay the rent, out you go, refrigerator and carpets and radio and the rest of it. I had a neighbor
once, an Irish Catholic, a good, reputable man, lived next door to
us for years, you couldn't want a finer neighbor. Salesman, he was.
Then he lost his job. And three months later I saw him rolling in
the gutter—a tramp.

"So I can tell you, I had the fear of God in me, and every time
I thought I might lose my job, I got shivering fits. I used to have
nightmares, that Shlomo the Shark had thrown me out, and I'd
wake up sopping wet with sweat. And some evenings I'd come
home a wreck; couldn't eat, couldn't sleep. What do you think it
was? Shlomo the Shark had given me one of his looks. He'd
stopped at my bench, looked through my work, and pulled a face.
That was enough to ruin the day for me. And poor Bella! She
was the one who got the worst of it.

"I had no one else to take it out on. God forgive us! We learn
the trick of taking it out on others too easily. You see how it was.
Those summer days in the workshop, when the stink and damp
came up from below, and the heat beat down from above, when
you worked half asleep, the feet pressing the treadle in a dream,
the flesh on you melting away, the bones softening inside, and
your eyes crying out for sleep! You needed all your strength just
to keep your eyelids from falling. And just when your head begins
to nod, there's an awful feeling at the back of your neck. It's
Shlomo the Shark! He's standing there! He's watching you! And
every moment you expect him to tap you on the shoulder and say,
'Mister, we won't be needing you tomorrow, or the day after, or
any other day.' So you can imagine what sort of mood I was in
when I got home. At that time we had a two-room apartment,
on Norfolk Street, a couple of blocks from the workshop. Two
little nippers rolling around on the floor, and my wife big with
the third one. I remember one evening, I came home and found

waiting for me a summer dish, pot cheese and radishes. My poor Bella! She was aging fast. Everyone aged fast in this country. Old age came stealing up on you before you had time to look around. And then, you see, she couldn't stand the climate here; the hot, damp summers. She suffered terribly. Well, on that evening, she'd taken great trouble with the meal, put a clean cloth on the table, prepared the pot cheese and radishes, with a nice plate of borscht coming first. And of course a juicy piece of salt herring. Everything clean and decent and appetizing. Because, poverty or no poverty, my Bella, God rest her, could set a table fit for a king. And what did I do? I came in with a hot, angry heart because Shlomo the Shark had frowned at me; I sat down, shoved everything to one side, and grunted, 'Don't want anything,' and buried my face in my hands.

"'Husband, what is it?' she asks. 'Is it the heat? The work? It's been terribly hot today.' Not a word about herself. And she brings a damp towel and wipes the sweat off me. 'There's a bit of vinegar on the towel,' she says, 'it's good for headaches.'

"'Don't want it!' I grunt. 'Don't want anything. I'm fired.'

"'Fired?' she gasps. 'What do you mean, fired?'

"'Fired!' I repeat. 'No more job. Finished.'

"She doesn't know what to say. She looks at me, frightened.

"'And whose fault is it, if not yours?' I go on.

"'My fault? How can it be my fault?'

"'Whose fault is it I'm in America, if not yours? It's because of you I've got to sit all day long in the workshop, with a slave-driver over me; like a little boy in school—at my age.'

"Do you think she even answered me? Not a word. She just let her head droop, as if she was the guilty party. I could see the lines deepening on her face, cutting into her; I could see all the bitterness of her life pulling at her lips. And I knew I was wrong; I knew I was behaving like a low-life. I wanted to take back what I said, put my arms round her, and wipe those lines away from her face. I didn't do it. I was too much the man, which means I wasn't man enough. And even while I was sorry for her I felt my burden lighter because I'd thrown it on her innocent shoulders.

"That's how it started, and that's the way it went on. Every insult I got in the shop, or anywhere else, I saved up to bring home and unload on her. All my weakness, my helplessness, my humiliation, I took out on my own flesh and blood. And she never answered; swallowed everything in silence. Only now and again she'd try to console me. 'Husband,' she'd say, 'this isn't the end. Better times are coming. God'll help you, and you'll go back to your books and your grammar and mathematics.'

"Because of course she knew what was eating me up, how I longed to be at my books again, and how I dreamed over the machine of taking up the study of English, so that I might become —well, I didn't know what I might become, but it would be something better than a slave in a workshop. She knew it though I never spoke a word about it—except maybe in my sleep.

"And when she spoke like that, instead of accepting her love and consolation, I answered her as if she had been my enemy. 'What do you expect me to become, with you in my shoulders?' I'd answer. 'It's going to be like this the rest of my days—the shop, the kitchen, you, you, the kitchen, the shop!'

"I've thought a lot about those days, and how different I'd have been if I'd have had the sense I have now. But you know that Polish proverb: 'The Polack's clever after the damage is done.' I had two feelings about her. I knew I was doing wrong, and yet I kept repeating to myself that she was my real enemy. *She* was the cause of my slavery. If it weren't for her . . . I know—you don't have to tell me; suppose I hadn't had her, what could I have done in America with my bit of Talmud, and Russian grammar, and half-learned high-school mathematics? I didn't know a word of English. But I had the illusion that if I didn't have to waste my years in the workshop, I'd learn everything one-two-three, and then—why, the world would be open to me, and I'd become the greatest man that ever landed on these shores.

"So I made her the scapegoat of my failure, and my disappointment, and my incompetence. I wrote on her face the record of my uselessness; and even now, when I see her face in dreams, I read in it the years of my labor, and my bitterness, and my wickedness.

His Second Love

"That's how it went on, year after year. And yet—a change did come. Yes. God didn't forsake me altogether. There must have been something in me after all. How does it say in the good Book? 'Man shall not live by bread alone.' That something in me wouldn't die. And who d'you think helped it to live, whom did God send to save me, if not my Bella, peace be with her? She did it in her own quiet way, without fuss, without drawing my attention to it, so that I might have the feeling that I was doing it all myself.

"I came home one day and found we had a lodger. An elderly Jew, a quiet, timid sort of man.

"I told you we were living in a two-room apartment. We also had a sort of half room, where the bath was supposed to be, but wasn't. There were five of us by that time, Bella and I and the three youngsters. But no bath. The landlord forgot to put it in. He'd got as far as half the plumbing and pipes, and then he'd forgotten about the rest. We used it as a store room, because my Bella, may she forgive me where she is now, was always great on order and neatness. She brought that habit with her out of her childhood; she remembered the shining pots and pans, the neat cupboards, the linens of her mother's home. She hadn't anything like that on what I was earning; but the little she did have she rubbed and washed and scrubbed and kept in apple-pie order. She'd brought over a few things—Sabbath candlesticks, embroidered pieces, a Hebrew calendar, a couple of cut-glass dishes which we used only on the Passover. I don't know how she did it on my earnings, but she managed to make our living room look like a palace. Of course it was our bedroom, too; but you wouldn't have known that by day, what with curtains, and hangings, and pictures on the walls. I say it was our living room, but we really lived in the kitchen, all five of us. That's where we cooked and ate and sat and rested; that's where I would read my newspaper, and on Sabbath afternoons that's where I studied the week's portion of the Bible. That living room, or sitting-room, was open by day only for visitors, whenever we had them. No child was ever allowed in there. It was her holy of holies.

417

Children of Abraham

"When I saw that lodger with his folding bed, I took my wife into the living room, and said to her: 'For God's sake, Bella, where are you going to put him?' 'In the kitchen,' she says. 'As soon as we've finished eating.' 'But there's no room,' I answered. 'I'll make room,' she says.

"And she did. How that woman managed I don't know. The lodger stayed with us. At first he was only supposed to sleep in the kitchen. But before you knew it, my Bella was cooking for him, too, and looking after his laundry. And I think she took in other washing—she never told me about, and I didn't ask. Yes, I'm ashamed to tell you that I didn't dare to ask. And all to make things easier for me, so that I shouldn't feel that I was a lost man, a slave for ever, sold to my workshop on Essex Street and to Shlomo the Shark.

"When the first of the month came and my wife paid the rent out of her own earnings, I could have wept—but I don't know whether it was for shame, or for relief. Because it did make a difference. It wasn't just the extra few dollars; it was the feeling that I didn't have to tremble so about my job, that even if I was fired, we wouldn't be pitched out of our home at the end of the month. It helped me to come to, gave me the courage to look around again; and I suddenly realized that the world didn't begin and end with the workshop.

"In those days the East Side was chock full of lectures and meetings and movements. In every second house you had some local or association. And every other evening they'd have a lecturer on socialism or anarchism or Zionism or God knows what other ism. Well, now that things were easier for me, and I didn't come home from the workshop half dead with fright, I began to slip into these meetings. My own inclination was toward socialism—I'd started that way in my boyhood. I don't know what it was—perhaps the years, perhaps exhaustion—but the socialists over here didn't have the same appeal for me as the socialists in the old country. Over there a speaker would get up and start lambasting 'the system.' He'd talk about 'slavery' and 'oppressors' and 'exploiters' and 'the liberation of humanity.' You knew what he wanted. But over here

418

there was no mention of such matters. All you'd hear was 'expert opinion.' Everyone was an 'expert.'

"And you soon found out that at bottom he didn't care a broken eggshell about his subject. You knew it by the way he talked—without a touch of warmth or interest. He only wanted to show you how much he knew. He'd compare this system with that system, tell you why Marxism was good or bad. But what Marxism was, or what you were supposed to do about it, you never found out. I listened, and listened, and listened, and I said to myself, 'I don't care how clever you are. Just tell me what I'm supposed to do. And if you can't deliver the goods, shut up.' I even tried to say that at one of the meetings, and nearly got myself thrown out.

"I got tired of the meetings. Maybe you think I'm all wrong. Maybe you're one of the 'experts' yourself. But that's how it was. I got tired of the expert jabber. I stopped going. I stayed home instead; and my old appetite for study came back. I had a few books that my father-in-law had given me as a wedding present, books of Hebrew scholars, commentators, a digest of the Talmud. They'd lain neglected in a corner of the 'bathroom.' If it hadn't been for my Bella, they'd have been thrown out. But she kept them, God bless her. And how happy she was when she saw this turn in my life. She didn't like my going to those socialist meetings. 'Nochum,' she used to say, 'those meetings weren't made for you. You're a scholar. You and those holy books belong together.'

"You should have seen the smile of joy, of purest joy, that settled on her face when I sat at table with one of the books of the sages before me, and how lovingly she would prepare a glass of tea for me. And when I persuaded my oldest boy to sit on my knee, and learn something, too, she was the happiest woman in the world. Except that this didn't happen very often. I guess you can figure that out for yourself. Here I am, trying to teach him something out of the good Book, and his head's full of the ball game on the street. There's a whistle—and the boy's gone! I didn't have the time to grab his coat, let alone argue with him. But that's another story.

"I'd always had a weakness for these studies, and I'd always had the knack of talking. I couldn't find myself at the socialist meetings, so I found myself where I belonged. On Saturday mornings, at the services of the Congregation Bzhezhin, I'd sometimes mount the pulpit, and try out a little sermon. At first it was only on special occasions, in connection with some appeal, say for the folks in the old country; or when there was a celebration. Or perhaps a funeral. I was pretty good at it, with a quotation from this sage and a parable from another and a verse or two of the good Book woven in. And I knew how to throw in a hint about current events, and our own affairs, about the Shlomo-the-Sharks, and the exploiters, and the brotherhood of the workers. It was my socialism coming out in me, but in a Jewish way. I didn't have to talk about world liberation—I could talk about the Exodus; I didn't have to mention the capitalists, I could talk about Pharaoh. Oh, they understood me; they were nearly all workers; they'd served their years in the sweatshops. Once I even proved that Moses was the first socialist in history. And they liked it, brother! They ate it up. Especially when I once proved from verses in the book of Exodus that the Egyptian whom Moses killed was the forefather of Shlomo the Shark. That, of course, was all by the way, a hint. Because most of my talks were straight Jewish tradition, out of the books of the moralists and the sages, of happy memory.

"And what do you think happened? The members of the Bzhezhin Congregation came to me one day and begged me to leave the shop and become their Rabbi. They knew that I was a pious Jew; they were convinced now that I had my share of learning; there was nothing on the record against me. It was a growing congregation; those were the years of big immigration, before the world war, and Bzhezhin, like many other little towns, was moving out of Russia into America. And as sure as the wheat comes to the mill, the immigrants came to the workshop, Shlomo's or another's, what difference did that make? Anyhow, the congregation was big enough to need a steady Rabbi, and why should they look for one among strangers when they could have a good one of their own?

"And so I became a Rabbi. Not one of the mighty and famous

His Second Love

—but a Rabbi. Not one of the wealthy, either. They offered me, as salary, exactly five dollars a week less than I had been earning in the workshop. But I was a liberated man. The Lord had brought me out of the land of Egypt, out of the house of bondage. My congregation promised me, too, that what with weddings, and funerals, and circumcisions, and ritual decisions I'd be called on to make, and other perquisites, I'd be rolling in wealth before I knew it. I told them that as far as the ritual decisions were concerned, I didn't feel competent to render them. No; they'd have to consult a regular Rabbi. To tell you the truth, I regarded myself as a preacher. And to make myself more useful I looked after the affairs of the Congregation Bzhezhin, collected the dues, bought the candles for Friday evenings, and that sort of thing. I was a mixture of preacher and beadle and handyman. With our congregational income we didn't have a building of our own, as you can easily guess. We just hired a hall, and there we held our services Friday evenings, Saturdays and festivals. In between, the hall was used for other purposes—mostly dances, and sometimes lodge meetings. Only on the holy days it was transformed into a synagogue. All week long the sacred Ark with the Scrolls and the movable pulpit were shoved away into a corner and covered with a curtain. Friday afternoons my Bella, God bless her memory, would go up to the hall with a pail of hot water and scrub the floor, wash the windows, purify the candlesticks, and get all the accumulation of profanity out of the place. And by the time she was through she'd sanctified that little hall; you breathed holiness when you came in. She gave the same love to that little synagogue that she gave to her home. Ah, you should have seen the candlesticks sparkling on a Friday night, the metal work of the Ark, the railing of the pulpit. There may be grander synagogues, but there wasn't a sweeter or a homier one than ours. All Bella's work—and the congregation knew it and appreciated it.

"Yes, sir, everything was just lovely at the beginning. The members liked me, and they liked my Bella. I took my job as a Rabbi, if you can call it that, very, very seriously. During the week I'd prepare my sermons, practice the melodies of the Sabbath and festival prayers, rehearse the reading of the Torah. I took an interest in the Jewish education of the children of the members. There wasn't much I could do. Sometimes I'd get hold of one of them by the ear, take him home with me, try to teach him something. But their skulls were full of baseball; no room for God's word. My members paid me something for this work, but I looked on it as part of my job. If there was a death in a family, I'd teach the youngsters at least how to say the *Kaddish*. I'd get them ready for their confirmation; show them how to wear the phylacteries. I even wove ritual fringes. And with all of this, we just had enough, my Bella and I and our little ones, to scrape through the week, and pay the rent on the first of the month. But, man, that was the least of it! We were more than contented. We were happy! You should have seen my Bella in those days. She got her youth back, her face blossomed again. No more shop! No more Shlomo the Shark! I can't tell you what it meant. Not that Bella ever said anything. She was never the one to talk. But you could read it in her eyes: 'Well, Nochum, didn't I say you weren't a lost man? Didn't I say America was the place for you?'

"That's how it was for a time—until I got into trouble with my sermons.

"It was this way. The members of our congregation began to change. I don't mean that old ones left and new ones took their places. It was the same membership, only the character of the members changed, because their circumstances changed. They became different members.

"In the beginning, when I took this job as Rabbi, or preacher, or beadle-preacher-Rabbi-teacher, or whatever you want to call it, the big majority of the members were workers, poor sinners under the lash of a Shlomo the Shark. And if it wasn't a worker in a shop, it was a little candy-store keeper, groceryman, butcher, baker, who earned his living in the sweat of his brow, and a poorer living, at that, than the workers made in the shirt factory. In a word, they were all poor, and they knew the soul of the poor, the sufferings of the workers. That was why they all liked my sermons, because I knew where the shoe pinched, and they knew it too. But as the years went by—and not many years, either—the 'stock' of my congregation began to go up. The 'brother worker' of yesterday became a little manufacturer, God save the mark. He began very small, of course, as a sub-contractor. Which meant that evenings he'd take home an extra bundle of work for his family to finish: wife, children, cousins, in-laws. And then the bundle would grow, and the sub-contractor would hire his own hands. And the hours they put in! Day and night, Sabbath and weekday! Till they worked their way up and became full-blown bosses.

"In the early stages you couldn't tell the difference between a sub-contractor and his 'hands.' The same hungry, drawn faces, the same stoop, the same weary eyes turned up at me when I mounted the pulpit to deliver my sermon. But a time came when certain members of my congregation began to take my sermons ill. How does the good Book say: 'Their faces were not as yesterday and the day before.'

"It started, I think, with a sermon on the sanctity of the Sabbath. A pretty good sermon, too. Full of quotations and verses and parables, all to prove that the Sabbath was the greatest treasure in Jewish life. I reminded them that the Sabbath was the sign of the bond between the Jewish people and God. And I also reminded them that the desecration of the Sabbath wasn't confined to the atheists and freethinkers; there were members of my own congregation who slipped into the synagogue of a Saturday morning to register with the Almighty, as it were, snatch a little prayer or two, and scuttle back to their machines to spend the rest of the sacred day in labor.

"What could I do? It was my duty to tell them. I was their Rabbi. If I didn't talk truth, who should? Well, I got more of a response than I bargained for. The deeper I ran into the sermon, the louder grew the murmuring in the synagogue. It was like the rebellious murmuring of the sons of Korah against our great lawgiver Moses. Of course there were some who were delighted by my outspokenness. They turned and *sh-sh-ed* for silence. And the others muttered. And these *sh-sh-ed*. It was a great scene—but it didn't bode any good.

423

"That day my poor Bella was brokenhearted. I knew she wanted to say something to me, didn't know what, and wouldn't have dared if she'd known what. She kept looking at me, opening her mouth, closing it again. I didn't give her a chance, though. I said, at table:

" 'I suppose you think that I oughtn't to rub my congregation the wrong way on account of the Sabbath. Well, it's no use; I'm a Jew first, and then a Rabbi. My first duty is to remind Jews of the holiness of the Sabbath.'

" 'Nochum, did I say anything?' she answered, frightened. 'Who am I to mix in these holy matters, a poor, weak, ignorant woman like me?'

" 'I'm glad you didn't say anything,' I said. 'I'm glad you're not going to say anything. Because it wouldn't do any good.'

"The next Sabbath we read that part of the Torah which contains the verse: 'And thou shalt love thy neighbor as thyself.' Now that particular verse, which the great and wise Hillel called the foundation of our faith, had always been my favorite. My hobby horse, if you like. I remember that even as a boy I studied Rashi's and everyone else's commentaries on it. I'd used it as the springboard for many a socialist speech. And even today I can deliver you at least a hundred different sermons on the same subject, and no two alike. Because those are golden words, 'Thou shalt love thy neighbor as thyself,' and you can build all the philosophy of man's life on them.

"I was in great form that Sabbath. I began by asking how did we Jews, who had given that verse to all the world, observe its content in practice among ourselves. We had forgotten its meaning. We had forgotten that we were ourselves slaves yesterday, and we became slave-drivers of our brothers, laying Egyptian bondage on them. *And not only of our brothers,* I said. Ah, they got the point! Let me explain it to you. I'd noticed that for some time now the sub-contractors among my members weren't bringing their children with them to synagogue on Saturdays. At first I thought the youngsters were too godless to be persuaded, too rebellious to be forced. But I looked into the matter and discovered

the truth: which was, that while the pious father came into synagogue on the holy Sabbath day, the sons were kept at home working on the machine. And I tell you, this was something I couldn't
stand, as a Jew and as a human being. Because I said in my heart:
'Low-life! Isn't it enough that you yourself desecrate the Sabbath
and play the hypocrite, slipping into synagogue and snatching a
prayer, then slipping out and running back to work. Must you
also make your children desecrators of the Sabbath, all for the sake
of a few cents' extra profit?' I didn't put it that way in my sermon; I was a bit more subtle. I pretended to sympathize with the
poor fathers. I said: 'It's too terrible the way the young generation
is dying out; and the children are not here in the synagogue to
say "amen" to the prayers of the fathers.' And then I went on to
speak of the love of one's neighbor and of workers who rise in the
world and become bosses, and forget what their own sufferings
were like. That was the breaking point. Because right there someone in the congregation shouts out, for everyone to hear:

" 'Hey, mister, since when did you become such a pious Jew?
Didn't we used to see you a little while ago at socialist meetings,
with priests and freethinkers and atheists?'

"And another shouted: 'That's where he got his sermons from.'

"And a third one, Leibel the loafer, was even worse. I knew him
well—only too well. I hadn't exchanged a word with him in years.
He shouted, 'Hey, mister'—you notice, I'd suddenly become 'mister'—no more Rabbi—'Hey, mister, I bet you don't even wear the
ritual fringes.' And what do you think happened? Half a dozen
of them actually swarmed up to the pulpit, opened my shirt, and
looked for the ritual fringes. Of course they found them. My poor
Bella had washed them only the day before. I don't know what
they'd have done to me if they hadn't found them. But after that
scandal, I was out. No more rabbinate.

"And do you know what my Bella said to me when we got
home? She said: 'Husband, it's a thousand times better to be an
honest worker than a dishonest Rabbi. Don't worry; everything
will be all right.' That's what she said. And with that she put the
fish on the table, and the jelly-soup, and the good, stinging horse-

radish; and the whole of that Sabbath she didn't mention the subject of the synagogue again.

"Now I ask you, if you searched the whole world through, could you find another wife like that?

"You may not think it, but it's easier for a worker to become a Rabbi than for a Rabbi to become a worker. But I did it. And who made it possible for me, if not my Bella? She showed me that even a Rabbi's wife can wash and cook for boarders! Thank God it wasn't long before I found a job. Not with Shlomo the Shark. I came across a pious Jew who had a little factory, had all his workers in the union, and yet kept closed on the Sabbath. I wouldn't have gone back to Shlomo the Shark if I'd been starving and sleeping in the gutter. And he wouldn't have had me back, either, after what I'd said about him in my sermons. And even if he had taken me back, it wouldn't have done me any good, because that shop closed soon after, and Shlomo the Shark ended up as a plain worker. But that's another story. There's only this I want to tell you, though. You modern people, you organizers of labor, made a terrible mistake in neglecting the workshops of the orthodox and observant Jews. In my days when a Jewish worker wanted to keep to his religion, observe the Sabbath, say his daily prayers, and all that, he had to pay for it in a special brand of slavery. For the privilege of going to synagogue instead of to the workshop on the Sabbath, for the privilege of five minutes out in the afternoon for the *minchah* prayer, he had to work longer hours, for lower wages, than any other worker. He paid with his life's blood for his religion. And his employer, who was also, God help us, an orthodox Jew, accounted it a great sacrifice and public service that he conducted an 'orthodox' factory. If you had the nerve to complain, you always got the answer: 'If you don't like it here, you can go to a union shop, where they don't close for the Sabbath or give you time out for *minchah*.' As if we didn't put in the Sundays in place of the Saturdays, and as if we didn't more than make up for the few minutes we took out for the afternoon prayers. What was the observant Jew to do?

"Well, I'll go on with my story. I got myself another job as a worker, and swore off the rabbinate for the rest of my life. That was the time the big change came over me. I became what the sages call, you remember, 'the happy man who rejoices in his lot.' My children were growing up, and the oldest boy began to earn a little money. Even while he was at public school he was already selling newspapers. My girl finished school, too, took a course in stenography and typewriting, and sure enough she got a job in an office. Those were the seven fat years, not long after the war. We even changed our apartment—and what a change! From Norfolk Street all the way up to Washington Heights. That wasn't easy. You get attached to streets and houses; I don't care how miserable they are, if they've been your home they're part of you. Old Norfolk Street, and the apartment without the bath—we'd lived there since the time of our arrival in America. We knew everyone in the block and every stone in the street. If it hadn't been for the children I don't think Bella and I would ever have had the heart to move.

"We were scared, Bella and I. It was like leaving America, which we'd come to love so. Because all our America was the East Side, and nothing else. We thought there wasn't a spot of Judaism, either, in those remote parts uptown. But we found out that neither America nor Judaism ended with our Norfolk and Essex Streets. The same synagogues, the same kosher restaurants and butchers and drug stores, only bigger, and better, and cleaner, and, if you please, even more Jewish. Why, the Jewishness shone out into the streets from the delicatessen stores, with their big kosher sausages and their white Sabbath bread, and from the posters of the Yiddish theater. In the evenings the radios and gramophones sent out Jewish music, synagogue melodies, through the open windows. Even the movie houses had Jewish signs.

"In our parts, I mean in Washington Heights, it isn't only the Jews who have to buy kosher. The Chinamen, too, can't get any other kind of food. Only a little while ago a Chinaman opened a *matzoth* and kosher noodle business, and he's making a pretty good living off the Jews. He got himself a Rabbi as a partner, to vouch that everything in the store is kosher, and he's competing with the 'official' *matzoth* bakeries. In our parts we all eat kosher, and we all cleanse our dishes with kosher soap. Even the laxatives, to get rid of too much kosher food, are kosher too: and we have a kosher milk of magnesia. Believe me, we've been needing that a long time.

"It was up there, in Washington Heights, that my second love began—and with my own wife, my Bella.

"You writers are always telling us of romances between married men and other men's wives, or married women and other women's husbands. Why don't you ever tell us about a romance between a man and his own wife? Believe me, it's a lot more interesting, and you can learn a lot more from it, too. And if you can't write that way, I'll tell you about it; I, an old orthodox Jew—I'll tell you of the romance I had with my own wife in her later years.

"And here's how it started.

"One Saturday evening I was sitting alone in the house with my Bella. It was winter time. The children weren't home, of course. My daughter already had a boy friend, and she was out with him. The two boys had very important matters to attend to, like baseball, or maybe football. There we were, we two old folk, my wife sitting in her corner, I in mine. In the old country, at this hour of the Sabbath, the mothers sing the Yiddish prayer, 'God of Abraham.' And it was that kind of mood in my house just then, sad, and sweet, and reminiscent of the God of Abraham. I'm in no hurry to make the *havdalah* and to end the loveliness of the Sabbath, though the beaker is standing on the table and the candles are already lit. And looking at my Bella in the candlelight, I saw, as if for the first time, that she was gray. Queer, isn't it, that I should remember noticing it only that evening. She didn't get gray all at once; but I noticed it all at once. I just hadn't bothered before. And I sat there asking myself, what's the difference if your wife's hair is gray or gold? You never bother remembering what color your own hair is. Because you are what you are, gray or black, and there's no changing it. But just the same, there was a sudden stab at my heart. My Bella was gray! And no wonder, with everything she'd gone through, the labor of those years, bringing up the children, and bringing me up, too. That's what struck me: she'd had just as much trouble with me as with them: me, and my discontents, and my ambition to be a Rabbi. Yes, a lot of that gray, perhaps most of it, was my doing. I'd woven the white wig for her. That's what I was thinking—but of course I wasn't saying anything. I only sat looking out of the corner of my eyes, and that queer feeling was inside me, the beginning of my second love.

"A few days later the youngsters took us to the movies, and I noticed that my wife was spending a long time in front of the mirror, arranging and re-arranging her hair, to hide the gray patches. So of course I have to poke my nose in where I oughtn't to—that's a good old habit of mine, you'll be thinking—and I say:

" 'Wife, for whose benefit are you hiding your gray hair? Is it Charlie Chaplin's? Take my word for it, he won't notice. You'll be looking at him, but he won't be looking at you.'

"I didn't mean it roughly, but it was a silly thing to say, wasn't it? But there it was, I'd said it. And she answers:

" 'That's a man all over! Thinks he has to know everything.' And she blushes like a young girl.

"Would you believe, I'd never noticed before whether Bella was prettying herself up, or wasn't. It just didn't seem to matter; I mean it didn't exist for me. But from this time on I did notice. I noticed every time she changed her dress or put on a different hat; and I couldn't help seeing how clever she was with those things, and what marvelous taste she had. And I couldn't help telling her about it, either. I don't know what came over me. It was as if we'd just met and we'd just become lovers. She put on an old cape of hers, which she'd made over herself, with ribbons and velvet and all those things, and she looked like a millionaire's wife.

" 'Look at that!' I said. 'Bella, where did you get that Fifth Avenue mantle of yours? It must have cost a fortune.'

" 'Fifth Avenue?' she said, looking blank. 'You mean this cape?'

" 'Sure I do,' I said. 'Why, wife, you look like a general!'

" 'God bless us,' she said, 'I've had this cape for the Lord knows how long. It was my wedding dress, Nochum, and I made it over.

Don't you remember it? It's the second time I've made it over. I've been wearing it for years whenever we went out visiting.'

" 'I never noticed it,' I said, puzzled.

" 'Husband,' she says, 'you've become a regular policeman lately —I mean the kind of policeman they use to catch spies. You notice everything, you do; how I do my hair, and what I'm wearing, and what it makes me look like. It isn't your way at all. Something must have happened to you. But what am I going to do if you don't like the way I dress? Would you like to buy me a new outfit?'

" 'Not like it?' I burst out. 'What put that idea in your head? You can't help liking it. And if I only had the money you'd do all the dressing and adorning your heart desires.'

"Well! You should have seen the way her eyes opened! She looked at me as though she was afraid I'd taken leave of my senses.

" 'Husband,' she said, 'I don't know what's happened to you.'

"I nearly said, 'No more do I.' Because, God's truth, I didn't. Because I wasn't telling her a word of a lie. I really meant that I wanted to have a lot of money just so that she could have it for dresses. Coming home evenings, I'd stop in front of a shop window and look at the women's dresses, and think which one would please her more. I hadn't done that in all the days of my life, not even when I was first in love with her. It just wasn't in me. Or I'd look at a hat and wonder how it would sit on my Bella's head. And one evening, when I had my wages in my pocket, I stopped in front of a hat store, and there was a beauty of a hat, a dream of a hat, all feathers and flowers, like they used to be in those days. I said to myself, 'I've got to buy that hat for Bella!' And then, when I had my hand on the handle of the door, I said, 'Am I crazy? What's Bella going to say if I bring her home, instead of the wages for the groceryman and the laundry man and the butcher, a hat with feathers and flowers?' But I *was* crazy! Because though I asked myself that question I walked right in to buy the hat.

"I would have done crazier things than that, if I'd only been able. What doesn't a man do when he's in love? You can answer that question better than I; you're always writing about such things in your books. And what's the difference if the woman you're in love with is your own wife or someone else's—you're just as crazy, aren't you? At that, I guess you're crazier when it's your own wife, because there's more to love and be crazy about, isn't there? You've lived with her all your life, she's borne you children, brought them up.

"Anyway, in I marched and asked for the hat. The salesgirls looked at me suspiciously, as though I was going to commit a hold-up.

" 'What's the matter?' I asked. 'I'm not buying that for a strange woman.'

" 'Well, who are you buying it for?' they ask.

" 'What do you mean, who for? For my own wife, of course.'

"And when I said that, I heard all the girls behind the counter, and all the girls working at the bench, burst out laughing and giggling. They looked up at me as if I was a freak. And I looked back at them, and thought to myself, 'What kind of mess am I getting myself into?' 'Look here,' I said, 'If you don't want to sell me that hat, you don't have to,' and I dashed out of the shop as if the devil was chasing me.

"I didn't get that particular hat for Bella. But I did get into the habit of bringing her home little presents, just like a boy courting a girl. It didn't matter what it was, or what it cost—a quarter or a nickel. But first I had to get her into the habit of noticing that I was bringing her a present.

"One evening I went out of the workshop downtown and saw a fruitstand with nice fresh red apples on it, and I remembered that my Bella had always liked fresh fruit. So I bought a bag of apples and took them home with me and put them on the table. And I'd have given a million dollars to have her notice and understand. But she didn't pay the slightest attention.

" 'Here,' I said, 'I brought you some nice fruit, wife, from downtown. I know you like nice fruit.' And she looked at the apples, turned them round, and guess what she said. She said: 'I bet you can get them cheaper here, in Washington Heights. What did you have to drag them all the way from downtown for?' I was dying to tell her it wasn't the apples, it was something else. But all I said, was: 'All right, if you don't care about apples, I'll try something else.'

"Well, the next day, coming home from work, I passed, as usual, through the Italian section, on my way to the subway. In the spring time the Italian women would sell flowers in the street. So I stopped, and bought a whole bouquet, roses and other flowers, and the woman made it up with green leaves; it cost every bit of a quarter. 'This time,' I said to myself, 'you're going to notice, and you're going to understand.' Do you think she noticed, or understood? Not a bit of it. Can you picture my embarrassment? First of all there was the subway. What d'you think I looked like, an elderly Jew hugging a bouquet of flowers in that jam. They must have thought me a lunatic. And what d'you think the flowers looked like after being squeezed for half an hour between downtown and Washington Heights? What I brought home wasn't a bouquet; it was more like a mop. Still, mop or bouquet, it was made of flowers. And I say to Bella, 'Wife, look what I've brought you.' She takes a look from the kitchen, where she's frying the onions to go with the boiled potatoes, and she says: 'What do you want to throw your money out for like that?' That's all the satisfaction she gave me. Only I got more out of it than she gave me: because I could see she was catching on to the idea.

"Ah, if she'd only lived! I could have played this game with her for a hundred years.

"But one evening I come home, and I find, as usual, the table beautifully set, with the white cloth, the piece of herring, the glass of tomato juice, everything shining with her magic. But no Bella. 'Wife, where are you?' I ask. 'Here,' she answers. 'In the bedroom. I'm lying down.' 'What is it?' I ask. 'Nothing,' she says. 'I was standing over the sink, and I felt faint all of a sudden, so I lay down.' Nothing! That's what she said. But I didn't like the looks of that nothing. Because her cheeks were white and her eyes flaming. My heart gave me warning, but I didn't betray myself. No. I pass it off with a joke. I say, 'Now, wife, is that the way to receive your husband when he comes home from work? This isn't a bit

like you.' And she smiles back at me, that sad, weak smile of hers.
And she really tries to pull herself together, as if I was being
serious. 'That's right,' she says, 'what's the matter with me? Here
you come home after a day's work, and I'm lying in bed like a
princess.' And I'm thinking to myself: 'It must be bad if my
Bella takes to her bed.' And I say aloud: 'You stay where you are,
I can manage. Did you send for Masha?' That's my daughter—
she was married by that time. 'What for?' she asks. 'You'd only
be frightening them for nothing. It's just a cold.' 'Oh God,' I think
to myself, 'I hope she's right.' And by that time I'm out of the
apartment, and half way down to the street, making for the nearest telephone.

"Why should I draw the story out. That same evening they took
my Bella away in an ambulance. 'Nothing,' she said. That nothing
was a cancer.

"The doctor asks me: 'Didn't she ever complain about stomach
cramps, or stomach ache?'

" 'No,' I answer, 'never.'

"He looks baffled. 'But that's impossible,' he says. 'It's impossible.
She's had it for years.'

" 'She never complained,' is all I can say.

"For years she'd been eaten up by the disease, and not a whimper came out of her; not a sign, until she couldn't stand on her
feet any more. And there wasn't a doctor in the hospital who could
understand it. Only one man understood—too late. If I'd only
fallen in love with her a little sooner!"

Reb Nochum sat dreaming, his eyes resting on his beard. Then
he said, not to me, and not to himself, but to someone or something invisible:

"They say that cancer comes from fret and worry and anguish
that a person suffers and suppresses. I'd like to know how much
truth there is in that. I sit and ask myself, over and over again,
'How much of a hand did I have in it?' "